★ BALLISTIC COWBOYS ★

JON & MAX

★ BALLISTIC COWBOYS ★

JON & MAX

NEW YORK TIMES BESTSELLING AUTHOR
ELLE JAMES

MILLS & BOON

Published by
Mills & Boon
An imprint of Harlequin Enterprises (Australia) Pty Limited
(ABN 47 001 180 918), a subsidiary of HarperCollins
Publishers Australia Pty Limited (ABN 36 009 913 517)
Level 19, 201 Elizabeth Street
SYDNEY NSW 2000
AUSTRALIA

MIX
Paper | Supporting
responsible forestry
FSC
www.fsc.org   FSC® C001695

Printed and bound in Australia by McPherson's Printing Group

CONTENTS

Elle James, a *New York Times* bestselling author, started writing when her sister challenged her to write a romance novel. She has managed a full-time job and raised three wonderful children, and she and her husband even tried ranching exotic birds (ostriches, emus and rheas). Ask her, and she'll tell you what it's like to go toe-to-toe with an angry 350-pound bird! Elle loves to hear from fans at ellejames@earthlink.net or ellejames.com.

Hot Combat

This book is dedicated to my three lovely writing friends who encouraged me to write like my fingers were on fire during our annual writing retreat. If not for them and the timing of the retreat, this book might not have been written! Thank you, Cynthia D'Alba, Parker Kincade and Mandy Harbin.

CAST OF CHARACTERS

Jon "Ghost" Caspar—US Navy SEAL on loan to the Department of Homeland Security for Task Force Safe Haven, a special group of military men.

Charlie McClain—Telecommuting software engineer and part-time social-media analyst for Homeland Security. Lives with her daughter in Grizzly Pass, Wyoming.

Kevin Garner—Agent with the Department of Homeland Security in charge of Task Force Safe Haven.

Max "Caveman" Decker—US Army Delta Force soldier on loan to the Department of Homeland Security for Task Force Safe Haven.

"Hawkeye" Trace Walsh—US Army airborne ranger and expert sniper on loan to the Department of Homeland Security for Task Force Safe Haven.

Rex "T-Rex" Trainor—US Marine on loan to the Department of Homeland Security for Task Force Safe Haven.

Leroy Vanders—Rancher whose cattle herd was confiscated by the Bureau of Land Management because he refused to pay his fees for grazing his cattle on government property.

Tim Cramer—Pipeline inspector who lost his job when work dried up. With his marriage on the rocks and his wife threatening to take his child and move, he has nothing more to lose.

Bryson Rausch—Formerly the wealthiest resident of Grizzly Pass, who lost everything in the stock market.

Lolly McClain—Charlie McClain's six-year-old daughter.

Chapter One

Charlie McClain pinched the bridge of her nose and rubbed her eyes. Fifteen more minutes, and she'd call it a night. The computer screen was the only light shining in her house at eleven o'clock. She'd kissed her six-year-old daughter good-night nearly three hours ago, and made it a rule not to work past midnight. She was closing in on breaking that rule and knew she would pay for it in the morning.

She looked forward to the day when her student loans were paid off and a little money was socked away in the bank. Until then, she telecommuted developing software during the day and at night she moonlighted, earning additional money surfing the internet for the Department of Homeland Security.

Fortunately, she didn't have to use her own internet provider to do the DHS surfing. She lived on the edge of town, beside Grizzly Pass's small library with free Wi-Fi service.

Since she lived so close, she was able to tap in without any great difficulty. It had been one of the reasons she'd agreed to take on the task. As long as a hacker couldn't trace her searches back to her home address, she could surf with relative anonymity. She didn't know how sophisticated her targets were, but she didn't want to take any more chances than she had to. She refused to put her daughter at risk, should some terrorist she might root out decide to come after her.

Charlie had just about reached her limit when her search sent her to a social media group with some disturbing messages. The particular site was one the DHS had her monitor on a regular basis. Comprised of antigovernment supporters with axes to grind about local and national policy, it was cluttered with chatter tonight. The group called themselves Free America.

Charlie skimmed through the messages sent back and forth between the members of the group, searching for anything the DHS would be concerned about.

She'd just about decided there wasn't anything of interest when she found a conversation thread that made her page back to read through the entire communication.

Preparations are underway for TO of gov fac.

Citizen soldiers of WY be ready. Our time draws near.

A cold chill slid down Charlie's spine. TO could mean anything, but her gut told her TO stood for *takeover*. As a citizen of the US and the great state of Wyoming, she didn't like the idea of an antigovernment revolt taking place anywhere in the United States, especially in her home state.

Granted, Wyoming stretched across hundreds of miles of prairie, rugged canyons and mountains. But there weren't that many large cities with government facilities providing prime targets. Cheyenne, the state capital, was on the other side of the state from where Charlie and her daughter lived.

Charlie backed up to earlier posts on the site. She needed to understand what their grievances were and maybe find a clue as to what government facility they were planning to take over. The more information she could provide, the more ammunition DHS would have to stop a full-scale attack. What government facility? What city? Who would be involved in the takeover? Hell, for that matter, what constituted a takeover?

Several of the members of the group complained about the government confiscating their cattle herds when they refused to pay the increase in fees for grazing rights on federal land. Others were angry that the oil pipeline work had been brought to a complete halt. They blamed the tree huggers and the politicians in Washington.

Still others posted links to gun dealer sites and local gun ranges providing training on tactical fire and maneuver techniques used by the military.

The more she dug, the less she liked what she was finding. So far, nothing indicated a specific date or location for the government facility takeover. Without hard facts, she wasn't sure she had anything to hand over to DHS. But her woman's intuition was telling her she had something here. She tried to follow the post back to its orgin, but didn't get very far.

A message popped up in Charlie's personal message box.

Who is this?

Shocked at being caught, Charlie lifted her hands off the computer keyboard.

I can see you. Come, pretty lady, tell me your name.

Charlie's breath lodged in her lungs. Could he see her? Her laptop had a built-in webcam. Had he hacked into it? She slammed the laptop shut and stared at the device as if it was a snake poised to bite. Her pulse raced and her hands shook.

Had he really seen her?

Pushing back her office chair, Charlie stood. If he had seen her, so what? She could be anyone who just stumbled onto the site. No harm, no foul. She shoved a hand through her thick hair and walked out of her office and down the hallway to the little bedroom where her six-year-old daughter lay peacefully sleeping.

The message had shaken her and left her rethinking her promise to help DHS monitor for terrorists.

Charlie tucked the blankets up around her daughter's chin and straightened. She shouldn't let the message bother her. It wasn't as if just anyone could trace her efforts at snooping back to her laptop. To track her down would require the skills of a master hacker. And they'd only get as far as the library's free Wi-Fi.

Too wound up to sleep, Charlie walked around her small cottage, checking the locks on the windows and doors, wishing she had a big bruiser of a dog to protect her if someone was to breach the locks.

Charlie grabbed a piece of masking tape, opened the laptop and covered the lens of the webcam. Feeling a little better, she took a seat at her desk and drafted an email to Kevin Garner, her handler at DHS. She'd typed This might not be anything, but check it out. Then she went back to the social media site and was in the middle of copying the site's location URL where she'd found the damning call to arms when another message popped up on her screen.

You're trespassing on a private group. Cease and desist.

Charlie closed the message and went back to pasting the URL into her email.

Another message popped up.

I know what you look like and it won't take long to trace your location. Pass on any information from this group and we'll find you.

The next thing to pop up was an image of herself, staring down at her laptop.

A horrible feeling pooled in the pit of Charlie's belly. Could he find her? Would he really come after her?

Suddenly the dead bolt locks didn't seem to be enough protection against whoever was at the other end of the computer messaging.

Charlie grabbed her phone and dialed Kevin's number. Yeah, it was after eleven o'clock, but she needed to hear the sound of someone's voice.

"I got it," Kevin's wife, Misty, answered with a groggy voice. "Hello."

"Misty, it's Charlie."

"Charlie. Good to hear from you. But what time is it? Oh, my, it's almost midnight. Is anything wrong?"

Charlie hesitated, feeling foolish, but unwilling to end the call now. She squared her shoulders. "I need to talk to Kevin."

A moment later, Kevin's voice sounded in her ear. "Charlie, what's up?"

She drew in a deep breath and let it out, willing her voice to quit shaking as she relayed the information. "I was surfing the Free America social media site and found something. I'm not sure it's anything, but it set off alarm bells in my head."

"Shoot."

She told him about the message and waited for his response.

"Doesn't sound good. Got anything else?"

"I looked, but couldn't find anything detailing a specific location or government facility."

"I don't like it, but I can't get a search warrant if I don't have a name or location."

"That's what I figured, but that isn't all."

"What else have you got for me?"

"While I was searching through the social media site, a message popped up."

"A message?" he asked.

Charlie read the messages verbatim from her laptop. "He has my picture."

"Hmm. That he was able to determine you were looking at the site and then able to take command of your laptop long enough to snap a picture has me concerned."

"You're not the only one." She scrubbed a hand down her face, tired, but too agitated to go to sleep. "I was using the library's Wi-Fi. He won't be able to trace back to my computer."

"That's good. More than likely he's near the state capital."

"Are you willing to bet your life on that?" she asked.

"My life, yes."

"What about the life of your son or daughter?" Charlie asked. She knew he had two kids, both under the age of four. "Would you be able to sleep knowing someone is threatening you? And by threatening you, they threaten your family."

"Look, can you make it through the night?" Kevin asked. "It'll be tomorrow before I can do anything."

"I'll manage."

"Do you want me to come over?"

She shook her head, then remembered she was on the phone. "No. I have a gun. I know how to use it. And I really don't think he'll trace me to my home address so quickly. We don't even know if he has that ability."

"He snapped a picture of you," Kevin reminded her. "I'd say he's internet savvy and probably pretty good at hacking."

"Great." Charlie sighed. "I'll do okay tonight with my H&K .40 caliber pistol. But tomorrow, I might want some help protecting my daughter."

"On it. I'm expecting reinforcements this week. As soon as they arrive, I'll send someone over to assess the situation."

"Thanks." Charlie gripped the phone, not in a hurry to hang up. As if by so doing, she'd sever her contact permanently with the outside world and be exposed to the potential terrorist on the other end of the computer network.

"Look, Charlie, I can be there in fifteen minutes."

"No, really. I'll be fine." And she would be, as soon as she pulled herself together. "Sorry to bother you so late."

"Call me in the morning. Or call me anytime you need to," Kevin urged.

She ended the call and continued to hold the phone so tightly her fingers hurt.

What was supposed to have been an easy way to make a little extra cash had just become a problem. Or she was overreacting.

Just to be safe, she entered her bedroom and opened her nightstand where she kept the pistol her father had purchased for her when she'd graduated college. She could call her parents, but they were on a river cruise in Europe. Why bother them if this turned out to be nothing?

She found her pistol beneath a bottle of hand lotion and a romance novel. The safety lock was in place from the last time she'd taken it to Deputy Frazier's ranch for target practice six months ago. She removed the lock, dropped the magazine full of bullets and slid back the bolt. Everything appeared to be in working order. She released the bolt, slammed the magazine into the handle and left the lock on. She'd sleep in the lounge chair in the living room so that she would be ready for anything. She settled in the chair, her gun in her hand, hoping she didn't fall asleep, have a bad dream and shoot a hole in her leg.

She positioned herself in the chair, her gaze on the front door, her ears tuned in to the slightest sound. Not that she expected anyone to find her that night, but, if they did, she'd be ready.

JON "GHOST" CASPAR woke to the sun glaring through his windshield on its early morning rise from the horizon. He'd arrived in Grizzly Pass sometime around two o'clock. The town had so little to offer in the way of amenities, he didn't bother looking for a hotel, instead parking his truck in the empty parking lot of a small grocery store.

Not ten minutes after he'd reclined his seat and closed his eyes, a sheriff's deputy had rolled up beside him and shone a flashlight through his window.

Ghost had sat up, rolled down his window and explained

to the deputy he'd arrived later than he'd expected and would find a hotel the next day. He just needed a few hours of sleep.

The deputy had nodded, warned him not to do any monkey business and left him alone. To make certain Ghost didn't perform any unsavory acts, the deputy made it his sole mission to circle the parking lot every half hour like clockwork until shift change around six in the morning.

Ghost was too tired to care. He opened his eyes briefly for every pass, but dropped back into the troubled sleep of the recently reassigned.

He resented being shuffled off to Wyoming when he'd rather be back with his SEAL team. But if he had to spend his convalescence as a loaner to the Department of Homeland Security, it might as well be in his home state of Wyoming, and the hometown he hadn't visited in a long time.

Seven years had passed since the last time he'd come back. He didn't have much reason to return. His parents had moved to a Florida retirement community after his father had served as ranch foreman for a major cattle ranch for the better part of forty years. Ranching was a young man's work, hard on a body and unforgiving when it came to accidents. The man deserved the life of leisure, soaking up the warm winter sunrays and playing golf to his heart's content.

Ghost adjusted his seat to the upright position and ran a hand through his hair. He needed a shower and a toothbrush. But a cup of coffee would have to do. He was supposed to report in to his contact, Kevin Garner, that morning to receive instructions. He hoped like hell he'd clarify just what would be entailed in the Safe Haven Task Force. To Ghost, it sounded like a quick path to boredom.

Ghost didn't do boredom well. It nearly got him kicked out of the Navy while in rehab in Bethesda, Maryland, at the Walter Reed National Military Medical Center. He was a SEAL, damn it. They had their own set of rules.

Not according to Joe, his physical therapist. He'd nearly come to blows with the man several times. Now that Ghost was back on his own feet without need of crutches, he regretted the idiot he'd been and had gone back to the therapy center to apologize.

Joe had laughed it off, saying he'd been threatened with far worse.

A smile curled Ghost's lips at the memory. Then the smile faded. He could get around without crutches or a cane, but the Navy hadn't seen fit to assign him back to his team at the Naval Special Warfare Group, or DEVGRU, in Virginia. Instead he'd been given Temporary Duty assignment in Wyoming, having been personally requested by a DHS task force leader.

What could possibly be so hot that a DHS task force leader could pull enough strings to get a highly trained Navy SEAL to play in his homeland security game? All Ghost could think was that man had some major strings to pull in DC. As soon as he met with the DHS guy, he hoped to make it clear he wanted off the assignment and back to his unit.

The sooner the better.

He'd left Grizzly Pass as a teen, fresh out of high school. Though his father loved the life of a ranch foreman, Ghost had wanted to get out of Wyoming and see the world. He'd returned several times, the last to help his parents pack up their things to move to Florida. He'd taken a month of leave to guide his parents through the biggest change in their lives and to say goodbye to his childhood home one last time.

With his parents leaving Wyoming, he had no reason to return. Having recently graduated from the Basic Underwater Demolition/SEAL training and having just completed his first deployment in his new role, Ghost was on a path to being exactly what he wanted—the best Navy SEAL he could be. A month on leave in Grizzly Pass reminded him why he couldn't live there anymore. At the same time, it reminded him of why he'd loved it so much.

He'd been home for two weeks when he'd run into a girl he'd known since grade school, one who'd been his friend through high school, whom he'd lost touch with when he'd joined the Navy. She'd been the tagalong friend he couldn't quite get rid of, who'd listened to all of his dreams and jokes. She was as quirky and lovable as her name, never asking anything of him but a chance to hang around.

With no intention of starting a lasting relationship, he'd asked her out. He'd told her up front he wasn't there to stay and he wouldn't be calling her after he left. She'd been okay with that, stating she had no intention of leaving Wyoming and she wouldn't be happy with a man who would be gone for eleven months of the year. But she wouldn't mind having someone to go out with while he was there.

No strings attached. No hearts broken.

Her words.

Looking back, Ghost realized those two weeks had been the best of his life. He'd recaptured the beauty of his home and his love of the mountains and prairies.

Charlie had taken him back to his old haunts in her Jeep, on horseback and on foot. They'd hiked, camped and explored everywhere they'd been as kids, topping it off by skinny-dipping in Bear Paw Creek.

That was when the magic multiplied exponentially. Their fun-loving romp as friends changed in an instant. Gone was the gangly girl with the braid hanging down her back. Naked, with nothing but the sun touching her pale skin, she'd walked into the water and changed his life forever.

He wondered if she still lived in Grizzly Pass. Hell, for the past seven years, he'd wanted to call her and ask her how she was doing and if she still thought about that incredible summer.

He supposed in the past seven years, she'd gone on to marry a local rancher and had two or three kids by now.

Ghost sighed. Since they'd made love in the fresh mountain air, he'd thought of her often. He still carried a picture of the two of them together. A shot his father had taken of them riding double on horseback at the ranch. He remembered that day the most. That was the day they'd gone to the creek. The day they'd first made love. The first day of the last week of his leave.

Having just graduated from college, she'd started work with a small business in town. She worked half days and spent every hour she wasn't working with Ghost. When he worried about her lack of sleep, she'd laughed and said she could sleep when he was gone. She wanted to enjoy every minute she could with him. Again, no strings attached. No hearts broken.

Now, back in the same town, Ghost glanced around the early morning streets. A couple of trucks rumbled past the grocery parking lot and stopped at the local diner, pulling in between several other weathered ranch trucks.

Apparently the food was still good there.

A Jeep zipped into the diner's parking lot and parked between two of the trucks.

As his gaze fixed on the driver's door as it opened, Ghost's heartbeat stuttered, stopped and raced on.

A man in dark jeans and a dark polo shirt climbed out and entered the diner.

His pulse slowing, Ghost let out a sigh, squared his shoulders and twisted the key in the ignition. He was there to work, not rekindle an old flame, not when he was going to meet a man about his new assignment and promptly ask to be released to go back to his unit. The diner was the designated meeting place and it was nearing seven o'clock—the hour they'd agreed on.

Feeling grungy and road-weary, Ghost promised himself he'd find a hotel for a shower, catch some real sleep and then drive back to Virginia over the next couple of days.

He drove out of the parking lot and onto Main Street. He could have walked to the diner, but he wanted to leave straight from there to find that hotel and the shower he so desperately needed. Thirty minutes max before he could leave and get some rest.

Ghost parked in an empty space in the lot, cut the engine, climbed out of his truck and nearly crumpled to the ground before he got his leg straight. Pain shot through his thigh and kneecap. The therapist said that would happen if he didn't keep it moving. After his marathon drive from Virginia to Wyoming in under two days, what did he expect? He held on to the door until the pain subsided and his leg straightened to the point it could hold his weight.

Once he was confident he wouldn't fall flat on his face, he closed the truck door and walked slowly into the diner, trying hard not to limp. Even the DHS wouldn't want a man who couldn't go the distance because of an injury. Not that he wanted to keep the job with DHS. No. He wanted to be back with his unit. The sooner the better. They'd get him in shape better than any physical therapist. The competition and camaraderie kept them going and made them better, stronger men.

Once inside the diner, he glanced around at the men seated at the tables. Most wore jeans and cowboy boots. Their faces were deeply tanned and leathery from years of riding the range in all sorts of weather.

One man stood out among the others. He was tall and broad-shouldered, certainly capable of hard work, but his jeans and cowboy boots appeared new. His face, though tanned, wasn't rugged or hardened by the elements. He sat in a corner booth, his gaze narrowing on Ghost.

Figuring the guy was the one who didn't belong, Ghost ambled toward him. "DHS?" he asked, his tone low, barely carrying to the next booth.

The man stood and held out his hand. "Kevin Garner. You must be Jon Caspar."

Ghost shook the man's hand. "Most folks call me Ghost."

"Nice to meet you, Ghost." Garner had a firm grip, belying his fresh-from-the-Western-store look. "Have a seat."

Not really wanting to stay, Ghost took the chair indicated.

The DHS man remained standing long enough to wave to a waitress. Once he got her attention, he sat opposite Ghost.

On close inspection, his contact appeared to be in his early thirties, trim and fit. "I was expecting someone older," Ghost commented.

Garner snorted. "Trust me, I get a lot of push-back for what I'm attempting. Most think I'm too young and inexperienced to lead this effort."

Ghost leaned back in his seat and crossed his arms over his chest. "And just what effort is that?"

Before the DHS representative could respond, the waitress arrived bearing a pot of coffee and an empty mug. She poured a cup and slapped a laminated menu on the table. "I'll be back."

As soon as she left, Garner leaned forward, resting his elbows on the table. "Safe Haven Task Force was my idea. If it works, great. If it fails, I'll be looking for another job. I'm just lucky they gave me a chance to experiment."

"Frankly, I'm not much on experiments, but I'll give you the benefit of a doubt. What's the experiment?"

"The team you will be part of will consist of some of the best of the best from whatever branch of service. They will be the best tacticians, the most skilled snipers and the smartest men our military has produced."

"Sorry." Ghost shook his head. "How do I fit into that team?"

Garner slid a file across the table and opened it to display a dossier on Ghost.

Ghost frowned. SEALs kept a low profile, their records available to only a very few. "How did you get that file?"

He sat back, his lips forming a hint of a smile. "I asked for it."

"Who the hell are you? Better still, what politician is in your pocket to pull me out of my unit for this boondoggle gig?" Ghost leaned toward Garner, anger simmering barely below the surface. "Look, I didn't ask for this assignment. I don't even want to be here. I have a job with the Navy. I don't need this."

Garner's eyes narrowed into slits. "Like it or not, you're on loan to me until I can prove out my theory. Call it a Temporary Duty assignment. I don't care what you call it. I just need you until I don't need you anymore."

"There are much bigger fish to fry in the world than in Grizzly Pass, Wyoming."

"Are you sure of that?" Garner's brow rose. "While you and your teammates are out fighting on foreign soil, we've had a few homegrown terrorists surface. Is fighting on foreign soil more important than defending your home turf?"

"I might fall for your line of reasoning if we were in New York, or DC." Ghost shook his head. "We're in Grizzly Pass. We're far away from politicians, presidents and wealthy billionaires. We're in the backside of the backwoods. What could possibly be of interest here?"

"You realize there's a significant amount of oil running through this state at any given time. Not to mention, it's also the state with the most active volcano."

"Not buying it." Ghost sat back again, unimpressed. "It would take a hell of an explosion to get things stirred up with the volcano at Yellowstone."

"Well, this area is a hotbed for antigovernment movements. There are enough weapons being stashed and men being trained to form a sizable army. And we're getting chatter on the social media sites indicating something's about to go down."

"Can you be more specific?"

Garner sighed. "Unfortunately, not yet."

"If you're done speculating, I have a two-day drive ahead of me to get back to my unit." Ghost started to rise, but the waitress arrived at that time, blocking his exit from the booth.

"Are you ready to order?"

"I'm not hungry."

Garner gave the waitress a tight smile. "I'd like the Cowboy Special, Marta."

Marta faced Ghost. "It's not too late to change your mind."

"The coffee will hold me." Until he could get to Cheyenne where he'd stop for food.

After Marta left, Garner leaned toward Ghost. "Give me a

week. That's all I ask. One week. If you think we're still tilting at windmills, you can go back to your unit."

"How did I get the privilege of being your star guinea pig?"

Garner's face turned a ruddy shade of red and he pressed his lips together. "I got you because you weren't cleared for active duty." He raised his hand. "Don't get me wrong. You have a remarkable record and I would have chosen you anyway, once you'd fully recovered."

That hurt. The Navy had thrown the DHS a bone by sending a Navy SEAL with a bummed-up leg. Great. So they didn't think he was ready to return to duty either. The anger surged inside him, making him mad enough to prove them wrong. "All right. I'll give you a week. If we can't prove your theory about something about to go down, I'm heading back to Virginia."

Garner let out a long breath. "That's all I can ask."

Ghost smacked his hand on the table. "So, what exactly am I supposed to do?"

"One of our operatives was threatened last night. I need you to work with her while she tries to figure out who exactly it is and why they would feel the need to harass her." He handed Ghost his business card, flipping it over to the backside where he'd written an address. "This is her home address here in Grizzly Pass."

"I know where that is." Orva Davis lived there back when he was a kid. She used to chase the kids out of her yard, waving a switch. She'd been ancient back then, she couldn't possibly be alive now. "She's expecting me this morning?"

"She'll be happy to see anyone this morning. The sooner the better."

"Who is she?"

At that exact moment Garner's cell phone buzzed. He glanced down at the caller ID, his brows pulling together. "Sorry, I have to take this. If you have any questions, you can call me at the number on the front of that card." He pushed to his feet and walked out of the building, pressing the phone to his ear.

After tossing back the last of his coffee, Ghost pulled a couple of bills from his wallet and laid them on the table. He took the card and left, passing Garner on his way to his truck.

The DHS man was deep in conversation, turned completely away from Ghost.

Ghost shrugged. He'd had enough time off that he was feeling next to useless and antsy. But he could handle one more week. He might even get in some fly-fishing.

He slid behind the wheel of his pickup and glanced down at the address. Old Orva Davis couldn't possibly still be alive, could she? If not her, who was the woman who'd felt threatened in this backwater town? Probably some nervous Nellie.

He'd find out soon enough.

And then...one week.

Chapter Two

Charlie had nodded off once or twice during the night, waking with a jerk every time. Thankfully, she hadn't pulled the trigger and blown a hole in the door, her leg or her foot.

She was up and doing laundry when Lolly padded barefoot out of her bedroom, dragging her giant teddy bear. "I'm hungry."

"Waffles or cereal?" Charlie asked, forcing a cheerful smile to her tired face.

"Waffles," Lolly said. "With blueberry syrup."

"I'll start cooking, while you get dressed." Charlie plugged in her waffle iron, mixed the batter and had a waffle cooking in no time. She cleaned off the small dinette table that looked like a throwback to the fifties, with its speckled Formica top and chrome legs. In actuality, the table did date back to the fifties. It was one of the items of furniture that had come with the house when she'd bought it. She'd been fortunate enough to find the bright red vinyl fabric to recover the seats, making them look like new.

On a tight budget, with only one income-producing person in

the family, a car payment and student loans to pay, she couldn't afford to be extravagant.

She was rinsing fresh blueberries in the sink when a dark figure suddenly appeared in the window in front of her. Charlie jumped, her heart knocking against her ribs. She laughed when she realized it was Shadow, the stray she and Lolly had fed through the winter. Charlie was far too jumpy that morning. The messages from the night before were probably all bluster, no substance, and she'd wasted a night she could have been sleeping, worrying about nothing.

The cat rubbed her fur against the window screen. When that didn't get enough attention, she stretched out her claws and sank them into the screen netting.

"Hey! Get down." Charlie tapped her knuckles against the glass and the cat jumped down from the ledge. "Lolly! Shadow's hungry and my hands are full."

Lolly entered the room dressed in jeans, a pink T-shirt and the pink cowboy boots she loved so much. The boots had been a great find on one of their rare trips to the thrift shop in Bozeman, Montana. "I'll get the bowl." She started for the back door.

I'll find you.

The message echoed in Charlie's head and she dropped the strainer of blueberries into the sink and hurried toward her daughter. "Wait, Lolly. I'll get the cat bowl. Tell you what, you grab a brush, and we'll braid your hair this morning."

Charlie waited until her daughter had left the kitchen, then she unlocked the dead bolt and glanced out at the fresh green landscape of early summer in the Rockies. The sun rose in the east and a few puffy clouds skittered across the sky. Snow still capped the higher peaks in stunning contrast to the lush greenery. How could anything be wrong on such a beautiful day?

A loud ringing made her jump and then grab for the telephone mounted on the wall beside her.

"Hello," she said, her voice cracking, her body trembling from being startled.

"Charlie, it's me, Kevin."

"Thank goodness." She laughed, the sound even shakier than her knees.

"Any more trouble last night?"

She shook her head and then remembered he couldn't see her. "No. I'm beginning to think I'm paranoid."

"Not at all. In fact, I'm sending someone over to check things out. He should be there in a few minutes."

"Oh. Okay. Thanks, Kevin."

"The guy I'm sending is one hundred percent trustworthy. I'd only send the best to you and Lolly." He broke off suddenly. "Sorry. I have an incoming call. We'll talk later."

"Thanks, Kevin." Feeling only slightly better, Charlie returned the phone to its charger and stepped out onto the porch.

Shadow rubbed against her legs and trotted to the empty bowl on the back porch steps.

"Impatient, are we?" Charlie walked out onto the porch, shaking off the feeling of being watched, calling herself all kinds of a fool for being so paranoid. She dropped to her haunches to rub the cat behind the ears.

Shadow nipped at her fingers, preferring food to fondling. Charlie smiled. "Greedy thing." She bent to grab the dish. When she rose, she caught movement in the corner of her eyes and then there were jean-clad legs standing in front of her.

She gasped and backed up so fast, she forgot she was still squatting and fell on her bottom. A scream lodged in her throat and she couldn't get a sound to emerge.

The man looming over her was huge. He stood with his back to the sun, his face in the shadows, and he had hands big enough to snap her bones like twigs. He extended one of those hands.

Charlie slapped it away and crab-walked backward toward the door. "Wh-who are you? What do you want?" she whispered, her gaze darting to the left and the right, searching for anything she could use as a weapon.

"Geez, Charlie, you'd think you'd remember me." He climbed

the steps and, for the second time, reached for her hand. Before she could jerk hers away, he yanked her to her feet. A little harder than either of them expected.

Charlie slammed against a wall of muscle, the air knocked from her chest. Or had her lungs seized at his words? She knew that voice. Her pulse pounded against her eardrums, making it difficult for her to hear. "Jon?"

He brushed a strand of her hair from her face. "Hey, Charlie, I didn't know you were my assignment." He chuckled, that low, sexy sound that made her knees melt like butter.

Her heart burst with joy. He'd come back. Then as quickly as her joy spread, anger and fear followed. She flattened her palms against his chest and pushed herself far enough way, Jon was forced to drop his hands from around her waist. "What are you doing here?" she demanded.

"I'm on assignment." He grinned. "And it appears you're it."

She shook her head. "I don't understand."

"Kevin Garner sent me. The Navy loaned me to the Department of Homeland Security for a special task force. I thought it was going to be a boondoggle, and actually asked to be released from the assignment. But it looks like it won't be nearly as bad as I'd anticipated."

Charlie straightened her shirt, her heartbeat hammering, her ears perked to the sound of little footsteps. "You were right. Get Kevin to release you. Go back to the Navy. They need you more there."

"Whoa. Wait a minute. I promised Kevin I'd give it a week." Jon gripped her arms. "Why the hurry to get rid of me? As I recall, we used to have chemistry."

She shrugged off his hand. "That was a long time ago. A lot has changed since then. Please. Just go. I can handle the situation myself."

"If you're in trouble, let me help."

"No." God, why did he have to come back now? And why was it so hard to get rid of him? He'd certainly left without a care, never looking back or contacting her. Well, he could stay gone, for all she gave a damn. "I'm pretty sure I don't need you. Ask Kevin to assign you elsewhere."

"Mommy, I found the brush." Lolly pushed through the back door, waving a purple-handled hairbrush. "You can braid my hair now." Charlie's daughter, with her clear blue eyes and fiery auburn hair tumbling down her back, stepped through the door and stopped. Her mouth dropped open and her head tilted way back as she stared up at the big man standing on her porch. "Mommy?" she whispered. "Who is the big man?"

Charlie's heart tightened in her chest. If only her daughter knew. But she couldn't tell her and she couldn't tell Jon. Not after all these years. Not when he'd be gone again as soon as he could get Kevin to release him. "This is Mr. Caspar. He was just leaving." Thankfully, her daughter looked like a miniature replica of herself, but for the eyes. No one had guessed who the father was, except for her parents, and they'd been very discreet about the knowledge, never throwing it up in her face or giving her a hard time for sleeping with him without a wedding ring.

Jon dropped to his haunches and held out his hand. "Would you like for me to brush your hair? I used to do it for your mother."

The memory of Jon brushing the hay and tangles out of her hair brought back a rush of memories Charlie would rather not have resurrected. Not now. Not when it had taken seven years to push those memories to the back of her mind. She had too much at stake.

Charlie laid a hand on her daughter's shoulder. "Mr. Caspar was leaving."

He shook his head and crossed his arms over his chest. "Sorry. I promised to stay for a week. I don't go back on my word."

No, he didn't. He'd told her he wasn't looking for a long-term relationship when he'd last been in town. He'd lived up to his word then, leaving without once looking back. "Well, you'll have to keep your promise somewhere else besides my back porch."

Her daughter tugged on the hem of her T-shirt. "Mommy, are you mad at the man?"

With a sigh, Charlie shook her head. "No, sweetie, I'm not mad at him." Well, maybe a little angry that he'd bothered to come back after seven years. Or more that he'd waited seven years to return. Hell, she didn't know what to feel. Her emotions seemed to be out of control at the moment, bouncing between happiness at seeing him again and terror that he would discover her secret.

Since Jon seemed in no hurry to leave, she'd have to get tougher. Charlie turned her little girl and gave her a nudge toward the door. "Go back inside, Lolly. We adults need to have a talk."

Lolly grabbed her hand and clung to it. "I don't want to go." She frowned at Jon. "What if the big man hurts you?"

Lord, he'd already done that by breaking her heart. How could he hurt her worse?

GHOST WATCHED AS the little girl, who looked so much like her mother that it made his chest hurt, turned and entered the house, the screen door closing behind her.

Charlie hadn't waited around for him to come back. She'd gone on with her life, had a kid and probably had a husband lurking around somewhere. "Are you married?" He glanced over her shoulder, trying to see through the screen of the back door.

"Since you're not staying, does it matter?" She walked past him and down the stairs, grabbed a bowl from the ground and nearly tripped over a dark gray cat twisting around her ankles.

When Charlie stepped over the animal and started up the steps, the feline ran ahead and stopped in front of Ghost. She touched her nose to his leg as if testing him.

Ghost grew up on a ranch with barn cats. His father made sure they had two or three at any given time, but had them spayed and neutered to keep from populating the countryside with too many feral animals with the potential for carrying disease or rabies around the family and livestock.

He bent to let the cat sniff his hand and then scratched the animal's neck. "You didn't answer my question," he said. Why would she avoid the simple yes or no question?

"I don't feel like I owe you an explanation for what I've been doing for the past seven years." Her tone was tight, her shoulders stiff.

When he'd first seen her on the deck, he hadn't immediately recognized her. Her hair was longer and loose around her shoulders. When they'd been together, all those years ago, she'd worn her hair in a perpetual braid to keep it out of her face.

Her hips and breasts were fuller, even more enticing than before. Motherhood suited her. If possible, she was more beautiful and sexier than ever.

His gut twisted. But who was the father? Lolly was small. Maybe five? Though he didn't have a claim on Charlie, he never could stomach the idea of another man touching her the way he'd touched her.

The fact was babies didn't come from storks. So Charlie wasn't the open, straightforward woman she'd been all those years ago. She probably had a reason for being more reserved. Having a child might have factored into her current stance.

He straightened. "So, tell me about the threats."

"You're not going away, are you?" Her brows drew together, the lines a little deeper than when she'd been twenty-two. She sighed. "I really wish you would just go. I have enough going on."

"Without me getting in the way?" He shook his head. "I'm only going to be here a week. Unless you have a husband who is willing to take care of you, let me help you and your family for the week." He smiled, hoping to ease the frown from her brow. "Show me a husband and I'll leave." He cocked his brows.

She stared at him for a long, and what appeared to be wary,

moment before she shook her head. "There isn't a husband to take care of us."

"Is he out of town?" He wasn't going to let it go. The thought of Charlie and her little girl being threatened didn't sit well with him. Who would do that to a lone woman and child? "I could stay until he returns."

"I told you. There isn't a husband. Never has been."

He couldn't help a little thrill at the news. But if no husband, who was the jerk who'd gotten her pregnant and left her to raise the child alone?

His heart stood still and his breath lodged in his lungs. Everything around him seemed to freeze. *No. It couldn't be.* "How old is Lolly?"

"Does it matter?" Charlie spun and walked toward the door. "If you want to see the threats, follow me."

He caught her arm and pulled her around to face him, his fingers digging into her skin. "How old is she?" he demanded, his lips tight, a thousand thoughts spinning in his head, zeroing in on one.

For a long moment, she met his gaze, refusing to back down. Finally, she tilted her chin upward a fraction and answered, "Six."

"Just six?" His gut clenched.

"Six and a few months."

Her words hit him like a punch in the gut. Ghost fought to remain upright when he wanted to double over with the impact. Instead, he dropped his hands to his sides and balled his fists. "Is she—"

"Yours?" She shrugged. "Does it matter? Will it change anything?"

"My God, Charlie!" He grabbed her arms wanting to shake her like a rag doll. But he didn't. "I have a daughter, and you never told me?"

"You were going places. You had a plan, and a family wasn't

part of it. What did you expect me to do? Get an abortion? Give her up for adoption?"

"Hell, no." He choked on the words and shoved a hand through his hair. "I can't believe it." His knees wobbled and his eyes stung.

He turned toward the back door. The little auburn-haired girl-child stood watching them, her features muted by the screen.

That little human with the beautiful red hair, curling around her face was his daughter.

Chapter Three

Charlie walked toward the house. As she reached for the door-knob, her hands shook. Now that Jon knew about his daughter, what would he do? Would he fight for custody? Would he take her away for long periods of time? Would he hate her forever for keeping Lolly from him?

Questions spiraled out of control in Charlie's mind.

Lolly stood in the doorway, watching the two adults. Had she heard what had passed between them? Did she now know the big man was her father?

Up until Lolly had started school, she hadn't asked why she didn't have a father. Her world had revolved around Charlie. She didn't know enough about having a father to miss it.

Charlie pulled open the screen door, gathered her daughter in her arms and lifted her. "Hey, sweetie. Do you still have that brush?"

Her daughter held up the brush. "Is the big man going to stay?" She shot a glare at Jon. "I don't like him."

"Oh, baby, he's a nice man. How can you say you don't like him when you don't know him yet?"

That stubborn frown that reminded Charlie so much of Jon grew deeper. "I don't want to know him."

Charlie cringed and shot a glance over her shoulder at the father of her child. Had she been wrong to keep news of his daughter from him? Would he have wanted to be a part of her life from birth?

Jon's expression was inscrutable. If he was angry, he wasn't showing it. If Lolly's words hurt…again, he wasn't letting on.

Then he smiled. Though the effort appeared forced to Charlie, it had no less of an impact on her. She remembered how he'd smiled and laughed and played with her when he'd been there seven years ago.

She still had a picture they'd taken together. He'd been laughing at something she said when she'd snapped the photo of them together.

Her heart pinched in her chest. No matter how much she might want it, they couldn't go back in time. What they had was gone. They had to move on with their lives. How Jon would fit into Lolly's world had yet to be determined, if he chose to see her again. Now that Jon knew about her, Charlie couldn't keep him from being with her. She just hoped he didn't break Lolly's heart like he'd broken Charlie's all those years ago.

"Lolly, Mr. Caspar is going to be visiting for the next week. I think you'll like him." She stared into her daughter's eyes. "Please, give him a chance."

Lolly stared over Charlie's shoulder at the man standing behind her. She didn't say anything for a few seconds and then nodded. "Okay." Then she extended the hand with the brush toward Jon. "You can brush my hair."

A burst of laughter erupted from Charlie. She clapped her hand over her mouth, realizing it sounded more hysterical than filled with humor. Trust her daughter to put the man to the test first thing.

Charlie set her daughter on her feet.

Jon nodded, his face set, his gaze connecting with Lolly's.

"I'd be honored." He took the brush from her and glanced around.

"You can have a seat in the kitchen," Charlie said. "I'll make some coffee. Have you had breakfast? I'm making blueberry waffles."

She went through the motions of being a good hostess when all she wanted to do was run out of the room screaming, lock herself in her room and cry until she had no more tears left. With a daughter watching her every move, Charlie couldn't give in to hysterics.

She'd cried more than enough tears over this man. No longer a young woman on the verge of life, she was a mother with responsibilities. Her number one priority was the well-being of her little girl.

Charlie rinsed the bowl in the sink, poured cat food into it and set it aside. Shadow jumped into the window again, startling her. "Cat, you're going to give me a heart attack," she muttered. "I'll be back."

As she left the kitchen with the cat food, she watched Jon and Lolly.

Jon had taken a seat at the kitchen table and stood Lolly with her back to him between his knees.

Charlie swallowed hard on the lump forming in her throat.

The Navy SEAL, with his broad shoulders and rugged good looks, eased the brush through Lolly's hair with a gentleness no one would expect from a man conditioned for combat.

Once outside, Charlie stood for a moment on the porch, reminding herself how to breathe. What was happening? She didn't know which was worse, being threatened by a potential domestic terrorist, or facing the man she'd fallen so deeply in love with all those years ago. Her life couldn't be more of a mess.

An insistent pressure on her ankles brought her out of her own overwhelming thoughts and back to a hungry cat, purring at her feet.

"Sorry, Shadow. I keep forgetting that I'm not the only one in this world." She set the bowl on the porch, straightened and was about to turn when she saw movement in the brush near the edge of the tree line behind her house.

Narrowing her eyes, she stared into the shadows. Sometimes deer and coyotes made their way into her backyard. An occasional black bear wandered into town, causing a little excitement among residents. Nothing emerged and nothing stirred. Yet awareness rippled across her skin, raising gooseflesh.

Charlie rubbed her hands over her arms, the chill she felt having nothing to do with the temperature of the mountain air. She retreated behind the screen door where she stood just out of view from an outside observer. A minute passed, then another.

A rabbit hopped out of the shadows and sniffed the air, then bent to nibble on the clover.

Releasing the breath she'd been holding, Charlie turned toward the kitchen. Out of the corner of her eye, she saw the rabbit dart across the yard, away from the underbrush of the tree line.

Charlie shook off that creepy feeling and told herself not to be paranoid. Just because someone threatened her on the internet didn't mean someone would follow through on his threat.

She closed the back door and twisted the dead bolt. It didn't hurt to be careful. Walking back into the kitchen, she couldn't help feeling safer with Jon there. He had Lolly's hair brushed and braided into two matching plaits.

Her daughter leaned against Jon's knee, showing him her favorite doll.

Jon glanced up, his eyes narrowing slightly.

Oh, yeah. He was angry.

Charlie didn't doubt in the least he'd have a few choice words for her when Lolly wasn't in the room. And he had every right to be mad. He'd missed the first six years of his daughter's life.

Glad she had a bit of respite from a much-deserved verbal flogging, Charlie rescued a waffle from burning, poured batter into the iron and mixed up more in order to make enough for a grown man. Flavorful scents filled the air as the waffles rose.

Milking the excuse of giving her full attention to the production of the waffles, Charlie kept her back to Lolly and Jon. Yes, she was avoiding looking at Jon, afraid he'd see in her gaze that she wasn't totally over him. Afraid he'd aim that accusing glance at her and she'd feel even worse than she already did about not telling him.

"Here. Let me." A hand curled around hers and removed the fork from her fingers. "You're burning the waffles."

Charlie couldn't move—couldn't breathe. Jon stood so close he almost touched her. If she backed even a fraction of a step, her body would press against his.

God, she could smell that all too familiar scent that belonged to Jon, and only Jon—that outdoorsy, fresh mountain scent. She closed her eyes and swayed, bumping her back into his chest.

With his empty hand, he gripped her elbow, steadying her. Then he reached around her with the fork, opened the waffle iron and lifted out a perfect waffle. "Plates?" he said.

His mouth was so close to her ear, she could feel the warmth of his breath, causing uncontrollable shivers to skitter across her body.

Plates. Oh, yeah. She reached up to her right and started to pluck two plates from a cabinet. Then she remembered there were three of them now. After setting the plates on the counter, she turned away from the stove, desperate to put distance between her and Jon. Her body was on fire, her senses on alert for even the slightest of touches.

"Come on, Lolly, let's set the table while Mr. Caspar cooks." She grabbed the plates and started around Jon.

He shifted, blocking her path. "We *will* talk."

She stared at his chest, refusing to make eye contact. "Of course."

He stepped aside, allowing her to pass.

Charlie wanted to run from the room, but she knew she

couldn't. Her daughter was a very observant child. She'd already figured out something wasn't right between her and Jon. Besides, running away would solve nothing.

Lolly gathered flatware from the drawer beside the sink.

Charlie set the plates on the table and went back to the cabinets for glasses. While she filled them with orange juice, she took the opportunity to study Jon while his back was to her.

The Navy SEALs had shaped him into even more of a man than he'd been before. His body was a finely honed weapon, his bulging muscles rippling with every movement. He'd been in great shape when he'd come home on leave seven years ago, but he was somehow more rugged, with a few new tattoos and scars on his exposed surfaces.

Charlie yearned to go to him, slip her arms around his waist and lean her cheek against his back like she had those weeks they'd been together. She longed to explore the new scars and tattoos, running her fingers across every inch of him.

He slipped waffles onto a platter and turned toward her, catching her gaze before she could look away.

Charlie froze, her eyes widening. Shoot, he'd caught her staring. Could he see the longing in her eyes?

She dragged her gaze away and darted for the stove and the pan of blueberry syrup simmering on the back burner. Her hand trembled as she poured the hot syrup into a small pitcher.

"Careful, you might get burned." Jon took the pan from her and set it on the stove.

You're telling me? She'd been burned by him before. She had no intention of falling for him again. Her life was hectic enough as a single parent trying to make a living in a small town.

She hurried away from Jon and set the syrup in front of her daughter.

Lolly pointed to the end of the table. "Mr. Caspar, you can sit there." She climbed into her chair and waited for the adults to take their seats.

Charlie felt like she and Jon were two predatory cats circling the kill. She eased into her chair, her knees bent, ready to launch if things got too intense.

Jon frowned. "Are you sure you don't want your mother to sit here?"

Lolly shook her head. "She always sits across from me so we can talk."

Jon glanced at Charlie.

Charlie gave half of a smile. "That's the way we roll."

"Before we got our house, we sat on the couch to eat," Lolly offered.

"How long have you been in your house?" Jon asked.

"We moved in on my birthday." Lolly grinned. "I had my first birthday party here."

"What a special way to celebrate." Jon reached for the syrup and poured it over his stack of waffles. "Where did you live before?"

Charlie tensed.

Lolly shrugged. "Somewhere else." Her face brightened. "Did you know mommies go to school, too?"

Jon smiled. "Is that so?"

Lolly nodded. "Mommy went to school."

His brows hiked as he glanced toward Charlie.

Heat rose up her cheeks. She didn't want to talk about herself. They didn't need to go into all the details of their lives for the past seven years.

Jon didn't need to know that the years before they'd moved into the little house in Grizzly Pass had been lean. Too many times, Charlie had skipped a meal to have enough money to feed Lolly and pay for the babysitter. Working as a waitress during the day kept a roof over their heads and school at night didn't leave much time for her to be with her daughter. But they'd made their time together special. Now that she worked from home, Charlie was making up for all the times she couldn't be home.

Her daughter shoved a bite of waffle into her mouth and sighed. "Mmm."

Charlie almost laughed at the pure satisfaction on Lolly's face. They hadn't always eaten this well, and it hadn't been that long since she'd landed a job paying enough money that she could afford to buy a small house in her hometown.

Jon took a bite of the waffle, closed his eyes and echoed Lolly's approval. "Mmm. Your mother makes good waffles."

"You helped," Lolly pointed out.

"So he did." Charlie pushed her food around on her plate, her stomach too knotted to handle anything. Not with Jon Caspar sitting at her table.

Hell, Jon Caspar, the man she'd dreamed about for years, was sitting at her table. She pushed her chair back. "If you'll excuse me, I just remembered something."

She took her plate to the sink and was about to scrape the waffles into the garbage disposal when Jon's voice spoke up. "If you aren't going to eat them, I will."

She stopped with her fork poised over the sink. Walking back to the table, she set her plate down beside Jon's and then ran from the room.

So, I'm a big fat chicken. Sue me.

In an attempt to take her mind off the man in the kitchen, Charlie entered the guest bedroom she'd converted into an office. A futon doubled as a couch and a guest bed. The small desk in the corner that she'd purchased from a resale shop was just the right size for her. She spent most of her day in her office, working for a software developer she'd interned with during the pursuit of her second degree in Information Systems.

The shiny new business degree she'd finished right before that summer with Jon had landed her nothing in the way of a decent job. She'd stayed in Grizzly Pass with her parents through Lolly's birth, making plans and taking online courses.

She'd moved to Bozeman to return to school for a degree in Information Systems, looking for skills that wouldn't require her to move to a big city to make a living. She'd chosen that degree because of the opportunities available to telecommute. It had been a terrific choice, giving her the flexibility she needed to raise Lolly where she wanted and provide the family support her daughter needed. She had no regrets over her decision and now had the time to dedicate to her work and her small family of two.

She booted up her laptop and waited for the screen to come to life. As she waited, she glanced around the small room, wondering if Jon could fit his six-foot-three-inch frame on the futon. Ha! Fat chance. But he wasn't going to sleep in her room. Seven years apart changed everything.

Everything but the way her body reacted to his nearness.

Hell, he'd probably had a dozen other women.

Her heart stopped for a moment as another thought occurred. An image of Jon standing beside a woman wearing a wedding dress popped into her head and a led weight settled in her belly. He might have a wife somewhere. He'd said he was there for only a week. He might have someone waiting for him back home.

And kids.

Charlie pressed her hand to her mouth, her heart aching for Lolly. How would she feel about sharing her father with other children? Would she get along with a stepmother?

Her eyes stung and her throat tightened. Lolly's life had just gotten a lot more complicated.

The screen on her laptop blinked to life. No sooner had she opened her browser than a message popped up on her screen.

You told.
Beware retribution.

"Damn." She shut the laptop and laid her head on top of it. If only wishing could fix everything, she'd wish her problems away.

"Are you okay?" A large hand descended on her shoulder.

For a moment Charlie let the warmth chase away the chill inside her. Jon had always had a knack for making everything all right. He would help her figure out this problem. In one week, they'd solve the mystery of who was threatening her and possibly a government facility in the state of Wyoming. Just one week. And then she could get back to life as usual.

Who was she kidding? Jon wouldn't leave for good. He'd be back. For Lolly.

Charlie shrugged Jon's hand off her shoulder and sat straight, opening her laptop again. "I've had another message." When the screen lit, she leaned back, allowing Jon to read the message.

"Do you think it's some kid yanking your chain?" Jon asked.

"I wish it was." Charlie pushed her hair back from her forehead. She clicked the keyboard until she found the URL she'd bookmarked and brought it up. Scrolling through the messages, she searched for the one that had started it all. She backed up through the messages from around the date and time the call to arms had been made. It was gone.

"What the hell?" Charlie scrolled farther back. "It was here last night."

"Whoever posted it could have come back in and erased the message."

Charlie snorted. "That's fine. I saved a screenshot, just in case." She pulled up the picture and sat back, giving Jon a moment to read and digest the words. "Do you think I was overreacting by reporting it to DHS?"

Jon shook his head. "With everything happening in the country and around the world, you can't be too cautious." He reached around her and brought up the social media site and scrolled through the messages again.

"Yesterday, there were a lot more messages expressing dissatisfaction with the way the government was handling the grazing rights and pipeline work."

"Apparently, someone scrubbed the messages. These all appear to be regular chatter."

Charlie sighed. "I'm beginning to think I imagined it."

"You did the right thing by alerting DHS." He straightened and crossed his arms over his chest. "Let them handle it. They have access to people who can trace sites like this back to the IP address."

The phone on her desk rang, making Charlie jump. She grabbed the receiver and hit the talk button. "Hello."

"Charlie, Kevin here. I take it you've met Ghost?"

"Ghost?" She glanced up at Jon.

He nodded and whispered, "My call sign."

Heat rose in her chest and up into her cheeks. "Yes, I've met him." She'd met him a long time ago, but she didn't want to go into the details with her DHS handler. Kevin wasn't from Grizzly Pass, and there were certain things he didn't need to know.

"Is he there now?" Kevin asked.

"Yes."

"Let me talk to him."

Charlie handed the phone to Jon. "It's Kevin."

Jon took the phone.

When their fingers touched, that same electric shock she'd experienced the first time he'd touched her shot up her arm and into her chest. She couldn't do this. Being close to him brought up all the same physical reactions she'd felt when she was a young and impressionable twenty-two-year-old.

She pushed back in her chair and rose, putting distance between them. It wasn't enough. Being in the same room as Jon, aka Ghost, made her ultra aware of him. She wasn't sure how long she could handle being this close and not touching him.

"GHOST HERE." HE HELD the receiver to his ear, unused to using landlines. But then cell phones were practically useless in the remote towns of Wyoming.

"The rest of the team has arrived. I'd like you to meet them and talk through a game plan for the security of the area."

"I thought you wanted me to stay with Ms. McClain."

"I wanted you to assess the situation and give me feedback.

I think she'll be okay in broad daylight. For now, you need to come to my digs above the Blue Moose Tavern and meet the rest of the men."

Ghost glanced at Charlie.

She paced the length of the small office, chewing on her fingernail.

"I'll bring her and the child with me." His gaze locked on her.

Charlie's head shot up and she met his glance with a frown. "Wherever you're going, you'll have to go by yourself. I had plans to take Lolly with me to the grocery store and the library. You don't need to come with me. We can take care of ourselves."

"Is that Charlie talking?" Kevin asked.

Ghost nodded. "It is."

"Tell her I only need you for about an hour. Then she can have you back."

Ghost covered the mouthpiece with his hand. "Garner said he only needs me for an hour. Are you sure you and Lolly will be okay for that time?"

She nodded. "Nobody will attack us in broad daylight."

Ghost snorted. Too many people assumed that same sentiment and were dead because of it. "Stay out of the open and report in every time you come and go from a location."

"I really think we might be paranoid, but okay." She raised her hands. "I'll stay out of the open, and I'll report my comings and goings." Charlie crossed her arms over her chest and tilted her head back. "Happy?"

"Not really," he said, his lips pressing together. "I'd rather drop you where you want to go and pick you up later."

Her lips pressed into a thin line.

Ghost decided it was better not to argue while Garner waited on the phone.

"Everything set?" Garner asked.

Ghost stared at Charlie, not sure he was happy with the arrangement, but Charlie wasn't budging. "Yes. I'll see you in twenty minutes. That will give me time to take a shower."

"Will do." Garner ended the call.

"I have to meet with DHS and the team Garner is assimilating. Are you sure you'll be okay?"

She gave a firm nod. "Positive."

How she could be so certain was unfathomable to Ghost. He wasn't sure *he* was okay. Being near Charlie brought back too many memories and a resurgence of the passion he'd felt for the woman seven years ago.

When he met with Garner, he'd have to tell him that he might not be the right man for the job. They had a huge conflict of interest. He and Charlie had slept together. Hell, they had a child together.

Tired and grungy, he couldn't think straight. "I need a shower."

"What do you want me to do about it?" She stood with her arms crossed, a semibelligerent frown on her face.

The corners of his lips twitched. Ghost stepped up to her and tipped her chin with his finger. "There was a time when you would have offered to shower with me."

"I was young and stupid."

He chuckled. "And you don't want to get stupid together? There's a lot to be said for being stupid. Especially when you do this—" Before he could talk sense into his own head, he bent and touched his lips to her forehead. "And this." He moved from her forehead to the tip of her nose.

She closed her eyes and her chest rose on a deep, indrawn breath. She unwound her arms and laid her hands on his chest.

At first he thought she would push away, but her fingers curled into his shirt, giving him just enough encouragement.

"And this." Ghost pressed his lips to hers, tasting what he'd missed for all those years, drinking in her sweetness. Sweet ecstasy, he couldn't get enough. He slid his hands to her lower back and pressed her closer. Why had he stayed away so long?

He skimmed the seam of her lips with his tongue. When she opened her mouth on a gasp, he dived in, caressing her tongue with his in a long, slick slide, reestablishing his claim on her mouth.

She felt different, her curves fuller, her arms stronger, her hair longer, but she was the same inside. This woman was the only one who'd stayed with him over the years, her image tucked in the recesses of his mind as he prepared for combat. She was the reason he'd dedicated his life to serving his country. To protect her and all the other people who depended on him to secure their freedom. He risked his life so that others could live free and safe.

For a long moment, he pushed every reason he'd had for leaving her out of his mind and reveled in the warm wetness of her kiss, the sweet taste of blueberry syrup on her lips and the heat of her body pressed to his. His groin tightened, the fly of his jeans pressing into her belly.

"Mommy?"

Ghost leaped back as if he'd been splashed with ice water.

"What do you need, Lolly?" Charlie pressed one hand to her swollen lips and the other smoothed her hair before she turned to face her daughter standing in the doorway.

"Why were you kissing Mr. Caspar?"

Ghost half turned away from the child, his lips twitching. He'd leave that answer for Charlie. Although, he'd like to know the answer to that question, too.

Chapter Four

"Sweetheart, let's get your shoes on. We're going to get groceries. After that, we're going to the library. So gather your books." Charlie didn't answer her daughter's question, choosing to hustle her daughter out of her office and away from the man who'd just kissed her socks off. She called over her shoulder, "Help yourself to the shower. There are towels in the linen closet and plenty of soap and shampoo."

Her lips tingled, and she could still taste the sweetness of his mouth. Dear, sweet heaven, how was she going to keep her hands off the man if he was around all the time?

She needed air. She needed space. What she wanted was another kiss just like that one. With her knees wobbling, Charlie left Lolly in her room and hurried into the master bedroom where the bed was still neatly made. She jammed her feet into her cowboy boots and yanked a brush through her hair, securing it at the nape of her neck in a ponytail. After checking that the safety switch was set on her handgun, she slid it into her purse, hooked the strap over her shoulder, braced herself and stepped into the hallway.

Thankfully, Jon wasn't anywhere in sight.

Charlie released the breath she'd held.

Lolly emerged from her room carrying a stack of children's books.

"Let's put those in a bag." She gathered the books and carried them back into Lolly's room where she found her book backpack and slid them inside.

Lolly slipped the backpack over her shoulders and led the way from the room.

She ran ahead to the living room.

Charlie shook her purse, listening for the jingle of keys. When she didn't hear it, she returned to her bedroom and grabbed them from the nightstand.

Hurrying into the hallway, with her head down, tucking the keys into her purse, she ran into a wall of muscles.

Big, coarse hands gripped her arms, steadying her.

"Are you all right?"

Hell no, she wasn't. Her pulse raced and she was out of breath before she'd even begun her day. "I'm fine," she said, studying her hands resting on his chest.

And boy, was he fine, too. Charlie couldn't help but stare at the expanse of skin peeking through his unbuttoned shirt. She remembered the smattering of hair on his chest and how she used to run her fingers through the curls. Her fingers curled into his skin, wanting to slide upward to test the springiness of those hairs.

"Are you ready?"

More than you'll ever know. Charlie shook herself and pushed way. "I'm taking my car since I have to stock up on groceries."

"I'll follow you there."

"No need. It's only a block from Kevin's office. If I run into any trouble, you won't be far away." She shook her head. "We'll be fine."

He stared at her for a long moment.

Charlie met his gaze and held it, refusing to back down. He'd

been gone seven years. He couldn't just walk back into her life
and take over.

"Okay." He started buttoning his shirt. "Let's go."

Charlie's glance dropped to where his fingers worked the
buttons through the holes. Seven years ago, she would have
helped him button up, and then undo them one at a time, kissing a path down his chest.

Ghost's fingers paused halfway up. "I remember, too," he
said, his voice low and gravelly.

Shivers rippled through her body and Charlie swayed toward him. Then she stopped, mentally pulled herself together
and said, "I don't know what you're talking about. And I don't
care. Let's go."

She pushed past him, her arm bumping into his, the jolt of
electricity generated in that slight touch turning her knees to
jelly.

The sooner she got away from him, the sooner she'd get her
mind back. What was it about the man that scrambled her brain
and left her defenseless against his magnetism?

Lolly stood by the door, her thumbs hooked through the
straps of her backpack.

Charlie grabbed her hand and stepped out. She waited for
Ghost to exit as well before she turned to lock the door. Her
hand shook as she tried to slide the key into the dead bolt lock.
She fumbled and dropped them to the porch.

Ghost scooped them up, locked the door and dropped the
keys into her open palm. "You sure you don't want me to come
with you?"

Lolly looked up, a happy smile on her face. "Could he,
Mommy?"

"Sweetheart, Mr. Caspar has to go to a meeting."

Ghost touched his daughter's chin and gave her a brief smile.
"I'll see you in about an hour."

"Mommy, can we get ice cream at the Blue Moose?"

"Why don't we get ice cream at the grocery store and bring it home to eat?"

"Okay." Lolly skipped down the steps toward the Jeep.

Charlie followed, not wanting to prolong her time or conversation with Ghost. The more she was with him, the more she wanted to be with him, and the harder it would be when he left again.

The drive to the grocery store took less than three minutes. She could have walked the five blocks, but she didn't want Lolly to be exposed to the nutcase who was threatening her. And carrying enough groceries for them for the week would be difficult, especially since she planned to purchase enough for Ghost, if he stayed for the full week. A man that big had to have an appetite to match. If it was anything like it had been when he'd gotten back from BUD/S training, he could put away some groceries.

He'd looked thin and a little gaunt after his SEAL training. She'd read about BUD/S to understand a little more of what he'd gone through. They'd put him through hell. And those who stuck it out came out tougher and ready to take on anything.

He'd been tired but exhilarated at making it through.

Now, he appeared more battle weary than anything. And he limped. Had he been injured? Charlie pressed a hand to her belly. The thought of Ghost going into battle, being shot at and explosions going off around him, made her stomach twist. When he'd left her, she'd done her best to push him as far to the back of her mind as she could. But she couldn't turn off the television when she'd seen reports of Navy SEALs dying in a helicopter crash or risking their lives to save hostages in Africa or some other place halfway around the world.

Now that he was back and larger than life, all those fears would be even harder to suppress.

DESPITE HER ASSURANCE they'd be all right, Ghost followed Charlie all the way to the grocery store in his truck. He waited in the parking lot until they were safely inside the store. Then he drove the additional block to the Blue Moose Tavern. As he pulled into a parking space on Main Street, a disturbance in front of the feed store two blocks down caught his attention.

He climbed out of his truck and studied the gathering crowd.

"Ghost, glad you could make it." Kevin Garner stepped out of the tavern, followed by three other men. He stuck out his hand.

Ghost shook it. "Charlie and Lolly are getting groceries. What's going on at the feed store?"

"Some of the local ranchers are gathering to protest the Bureau of Land Management's increase in fees for grazing livestock on government land."

He'd read about the issues the ranchers were having and how BLM had confiscated entire herds of cattle from ranchers who refused to pay the fees in protest.

As the crowd got louder, a van rolled into town with antennas attached to the top. A cameraman and reporter leaped out and positioned themselves with a view of the angry ranchers behind them.

"Is this part of the problem we're here to help with?" one of the men standing near Kevin asked. He stuck out his hand to Ghost. "Name's Max Decker. My Delta team calls me Caveman."

Ghost gripped the man's hand. "Jon Caspar. Navy SEAL. Call me Ghost."

The next man stepped up and gripped Ghost's hand. "Trace Walsh. Marine. Expert marksman, earned the nickname Hawkeye."

A tall man with a crooked nose stepped up. "Rex Trainor. Army Airborne Ranger. They call me T-Rex."

Kevin turned back to the group. "Now that you've all met, let's take it to the loft." He led the way up the stairs on the side of the tavern and entered a combination office-apartment.

Ghost followed and entered a large room with a fold-up table stretched across the center. A bank of computers stretched across one wall, the screens lit. A wiry young man sat in front of a keyboard, his gaze shifting between three monitors.

"That's Clive Jameson. We call him Hack. He's the brains behind the computer we're using to track movement and data."

"Movement of what?" Caveman asked.

"What data?" T-Rex stepped up behind Hack.

"Grab a seat, I'll explain." Garner waved his hand at the metal folding chairs leaning against the wall. "It's not the ideal location and can get pretty noisy on Friday and Saturday nights, but it gives me the space I need to run the operation."

"What operation?" Hawkeye asked.

Kevin pointed to a large monitor hung on the wall. "Hack, could you bring up the map?"

The computer guy behind them clicked several keys and a digital map came up on the monitor.

"This is the tristate area of Wyoming, Montana and Idaho. There's been a lot of rumbling going on for various reasons in the area. Between the pipeline layoffs and the cattle-grazing rights, things are getting pretty hot. We're afraid sleeper cells of terrorists are embedding in the groups and stirring them up even more and providing them with the funding and weaponry to create havoc."

"This is a hot area, anyway. Haven't there been rumblings from the Yellowstone Caldera?" T-Rex asked.

Garner nodded. "That's another reason why you four were brought into this effort. The scientists at the Yellowstone Volcano Observatory have been tracking specific trembles. They think there might be an eruption in the near future. They don't think it will be a catastrophic event, but it has generated a lot of interest and tourists are pouring into Yellowstone National Park."

"So, what specifically makes you think something big is about to happen?" Ghost asked.

"Last week, we had two men go missing from the BLM. They had been out riding four-wheelers in grizzly country near some of the park's active hot springs." Garner stared at each of the men, one at a time, then said, "They didn't come back.

"Because they were armed with GPS capability we were able to find their ATVs hidden in the brush near a particularly deadly spring. There was no sign of a bear attack, which was the rescue team's first inclination. But they did find a shoe near the spring and skid marks as if someone was either dragging or pushing a body toward the toxic water. If the BLM men found their way into that pool, either on their own, or by other more forceful means, there would be absolutely nothing left for a family member to claim. Their tissue and bones would have dissolved."

"The perfect place to hide the bodies," T-Rex said, his tone low, his eyes narrowed.

"Why bring in the military?" Ghost asked.

"DHS is spread thin, monitoring our boarders and the entrance and exit points of airports and ports. We don't have the manpower to provide assistance to a potentially volatile situation here. And frankly, I don't think we have sufficient combat training as afforded to active duty military." Kevin lifted his chin, his chest swelling. "I do know what our country is capable of, and what the best of the best could do to help the situation. You see, I'm prior military. Eight years as a Black Hawk helicopter pilot. I ferried troops in and out of combat as a member of the 160th Night Stalkers."

Ghost sat back in his chair. "So you've seen as much battle as any one of us."

"Not as intensely as you four have. But I've seen what you can do when the time comes. You're smart and you act instinctively when you need to."

Hawkeye tapped his fingers on the table. "We've been fighting in a war environment. That's not what this is."

"No? You saw that mob out there. It could escalate into a shooting match in seconds."

"Still, it's not up to us to police civilians," Caveman said. "That's why we have law enforcement."

"The law enforcement is either tapped out or worse." Garner shook his head. "We think some might be working with the people stirring things up."

Ghost leaned forward. "What exactly are you asking us to do here?"

"I need you to do several things. We have hot spots in the tristate area." Garner pointed to the map. "One is a survivalist group on the edge of Yellowstone National Park. With all the tourists flooding the park, I'm afraid they'll use it as an excuse to stage something big. I need someone to get inside the group, spy and report back."

"I'll take that one." T-Rex raised his hand. "I can infiltrate the survivalists' group."

"All I'm looking for now is information. If they do anything, you are not to engage." One by one, Garner looked each man in the eye. "Repeat, you are not to engage."

Caveman scratched the back of his head, his brows twisting. "We're combat veterans. Why involve us if we're not to engage?"

"We want to reserve engagement until it's the last resort." The DHS task force leader placed both hands on the table and leaned toward the men. "Think of it as a reconnaissance mission. You infiltrate wherever I need you to go, assess the situation and report back."

Ghost studied Kevin, his gut telling him the man wasn't giving it to them straight. "What else are you not telling us?"

Kevin straightened, his eyes narrowing, his lips thinning into a thin line. "One of the folks we employ who monitors the internet for anything that could be construed as a potential attack, ran across a message last night. More or less, it was a call to arms to take over a government facility."

The Marine, Army Ranger and Delta Force man leaned forward.

Because he'd already heard this story, Ghost sat back in his chair and waited for the rest of whatever Kevin had to say.

"Where?" T-Rex asked.

"When?" Hawkeye wanted to know.

"We don't have that information. I need you all to keep an ear to the ground. If you hear anything, no matter how inconsequential it might sound, relay it to me."

Ghost shook his head. "The disappearing BLM men and a poorly worded message can't be all that has you calling in the cavalry. What else?"

Kevin met Ghost's gaze. "We've also been concerned about message traffic from some of the people we've been monitoring for the past six months. Men who are connected with ISIS. We intercepted a message we decoded indicating a weapons movement to this area. Enough guns and ammunition to stage a significant takeover of a state capital. Enough ammunition for a standoff. Or the murder of a great number of people."

Ghost's gut clenched. His daughter was in the area in question. If something went down, she could be caught in the cross fire. He'd just found his daughter. He'd be damned if he lost her so soon.

He couldn't wait to get out of the meeting and back to his family.

His family. Ha! If Charlie had her way, he wouldn't be anywhere near them. He'd just have to convince her she'd be better off with him sticking around.

Chapter Five

Once inside the grocery store, Charlie whirled the cart around the narrow aisles, hurrying through the tiny store, gathering only what she needed for the week. The shelves appeared barer than usual. When she got to the counter, Mrs. Penders, one of the owners of the mom-and-pop store checked her items.

"Why are the shelves so empty, Mrs. P?" Charlie asked, setting her items on the counter, one at a time. "Are you expecting a delivery today?"

She snorted and rang up a loaf of bread, the last one on the shelf. "I got a shipment this morning. We had a run on the store earlier. Did you see the crowd gathering in front of the feed store?"

She hadn't. Charlie had been more concerned about Ghost following her that she hadn't glanced farther down the street. "I'm sorry. I didn't see the crowd. What's going on?"

"A group of ranchers are taking a stand against the Bureau of Land Management over what they did."

"What did they do?"

"They confiscated half of LeRoy Vanders's herd. He refused

to pay his fees for grazing rights on federal land in protest of the increase."

"Confiscated a herd of cattle?" Charlie set the jug of milk on the counter. "Can they do that?"

Mrs. Penders nodded. "Can and did. Got all the local ranchers up in arms. Sheriff's talking to them now out front of the feed store.

"I hear Jon Caspar is back in town." Mrs. Penders rang up the milk and slid it into a bag, before she raised her gaze to capture Charlie's. "You two were a thing way back in the day, weren't you?"

Charlie shrugged. "We dated."

"If he needs a place to stay, I have a room over my garage," the store owner offered.

"Mr. Caspar is staying with us." Lolly tugged on her mother's shirt. "Isn't he, Mommy?"

Heat filled Charlie's cheeks. "Just for the week while he's in town. Then he'll have to go back to his job with the Navy."

"Can't he stay forever?" Lolly asked. "I like the way he brushes my hair."

"We'll discuss this later," Charlie said, hurriedly placing the last items on the counter.

Mrs. Penders was one of the worst gossips in town. By the time Charlie reached home, the older woman would have word spread across the county that Charlie and Ghost were shacking up. She wouldn't be surprised if she got a call from her parents all the way in Europe asking about the man sleeping in her little house.

Mrs. Penders gave her a total, Charlie paid and pushed the cart out into the parking lot. Lolly helped her load the items into the back of her Jeep.

As she pulled out of the parking lot of the store, she glanced down the street toward the feed store. Just as Mrs. Penders had said, a crowd gathered, some of the men raised their hands, shaking fists in the air.

"This can't be good," Charlie muttered, turning the opposite direction, heading for her little house on the edge of town. She passed the library.

"Aren't we going to the library?" Lolly asked.

"After we unload and put the groceries away. It won't take long, and we can walk next door."

"Okay." Lolly helped her unload the groceries, carrying in the lighter bags.

Charlie put away the items, grabbed her own bag of books and Lolly's backpack. "Let's go see Ms. Florence. She might have some new books for you today."

Grizzly Pass was a very small town, but the residents were proud of the little library they'd helped to fund. Rebecca Florence was the preacher's daughter, with a fresh degree in library science. A quiet soul, she'd returned to her hometown, glad to escape the hustle and bustle of Denver, where she'd attended her father's alma mater.

Happy to take over duties of town librarian from her aging mother, she slipped into the role with ease. Though shy and quiet, she managed to bring the library up to twenty-first century standards, writing for grant money to have computers installed and providing Wi-Fi internet for those who couldn't afford their own satellite internet.

Charlie enjoyed talking with Rebecca about the latest books. The woman was a wealth of knowledge and read extensively in fiction and nonfiction.

Before Charlie left the house, she placed a call to Kevin. His computer guy, Hack, answered the call. "He stepped out front. Is this an emergency? Do you want me to run out and catch him?"

"No. Just have him relay to Mr. Caspar that Charlie made it home and is now taking Lolly to the library. Thank you." She ended the call, grabbed Lolly's hand and left the house.

Less than twenty steps brought them to the front of the old colonial house that had been converted into the library. The wide front porch had several rocking chairs for patrons to use when they just wanted to sit outside and read a book.

Charlie and Lolly had spent a few beautiful summer days reading on that front porch. Now, they pushed through the front door with the open sign hanging in the window.

"Ms. Florence?" Charlie called out.

When she got no answer, she didn't worry. Rebecca sometimes was in the back kitchen making tea.

Charlie and Lolly laid their books on the return counter and went in search of some they hadn't read.

After a few minutes, Charlie went in search of Rebecca. She hoped the librarian could help her find more information on grazing rights and what it meant to the ranchers in the area.

She understood many of the ranchers had grazed their cattle on government land for years. Some families had been grazing cattle on government land for several generations. Paying a grazing fee wasn't the only expense they incurred. They were responsible for maintaining the fences on the land where they grazed their cattle and providing for the water, if it wasn't readily available.

"Rebecca?" Charlie pushed through a swinging door leading into the back of the house where the kitchen was. As soon as she passed through the door, she heard a soft moan, coming from the other side of an island.

Her heart slammed hard against her ribs and she ran forward.

Rebecca lay on the floor, her strawberry blond hair tangled and matted with blood. A gash on her forehead dripped blood into her eyes and onto the floor.

"Rebecca?" Charlie leaned down and grabbed the woman's hand. "What happened to you?"

"Charlie?" she said, though her voice sounded muffled. She tried to open her eyes, but couldn't seem to. Instead she gripped Charlie's hand. "Get out."

"What?" Charlie shook her head. "I'm not leaving until I get you some help."

"Go," she said. "Not safe." She coughed and spit up blood.

"Is the man who attacked you still here?"

She lay still for a moment before answering. "I don't think so." Her words ended on a moan.

Anger burned in Charlie's gut. How could anyone do this to as gentle a soul as Rebecca?

Charlie smoothed a lock of her reddish-blond hair from her face. "I'm calling the sheriff and an ambulance." She started to rise, but Rebecca tightened her hold on her hand.

"Angry. Said I told."

"Who was it?"

"Don't know." She coughed, her body tensing. "Wore a mask. Said I…was ruining…everything…" Her grip loosened and her hand dropped to the floor.

Her throat constricting, Charlie pressed her fingers to the base of Rebecca's throat, hoping to find a pulse and nearly crying when she felt the reassuring thump against her fingertips. She stood and feverishly searched the kitchen for a telephone. Thankfully, there was one on the wall near the back door.

Charlie grabbed the phone and dialed 911. After passing the information to the dispatcher, she hung up and dialed Kevin's number.

Kevin answered the phone on the first ring. "Garner speaking."

"Kevin. Thank God. It's Charlie."

"What's wrong?"

"Rebecca Florence was attacked here in the library. I've notified 911. But she was more worried about me than herself. She said the guy who attacked her was angry. She said he was mad because she told. Is Ghost with you?"

"He just left to go to your house. He should be there about now."

Charlie dropped the phone as the sound of a siren wailed toward the little house. She pushed through the swinging door, suddenly afraid for her daughter she'd left in the children's section of the library.

"Lolly!" she shouted.

Lolly emerged from the front room, carrying a colorful book, her brow pressed into a frown. "What's wrong?"

Charlie gathered her into her arms and hugged her close.

Ghost slammed through the front entrance, his eyes wide and his face tense until he spotted Charlie and Lolly. "Are you two okay?"

Charlie nodded and then tipped her head toward the kitchen door. "But Rebecca isn't. Could you take Lolly while I help her?"

"You stay with Lolly. I've had training in first aid." He stepped past her and entered the kitchen.

A few minutes later, a young sheriff's deputy entered the library, his gun drawn.

"I don't think you'll need that," Charlie said. They didn't need some rookie deputy shooting a man who was only attempting to render aid. "Jon Caspar is in the kitchen with Ms. Florence. He's one of the good guys."

The deputy didn't lower his weapon, instead, he entered the kitchen. Voices sounded through the wood paneling of the door.

Moments later the fire department paramedics entered. Charlie directed them to the kitchen and then pulled Lolly into the front parlor of the old house that Rebecca had designated as the children's room.

While she waited for Ghost to emerge from the kitchen, she read a story to Lolly.

"Mommy, you're not doing a very good job," Lolly said.

"Then *you* read it to *me*," she said, too tired to argue with her daughter.

Lolly read the story, slowing over some words, but far advanced for her age.

Charlie only half listened, her chest tight, her stomach knotted. When she saw the paramedic wheel Rebecca through the house on a stretcher, she stood.

Ghost followed, stopping in the doorway.

Charlie ran into his arms and hugged him around the middle. "Is she going to be all right?"

Ghost smoothed the hair on the back of her head. "I believe so. She took a pretty hard hit to the forehead. They'll keep her in the hospital to observe for concussion. Before she passed out, did she say who did it?"

"She didn't know. Apparently he wore a mask." Charlie wrung her hands. "I think she was attacked because of me." She stared up into Ghost's eyes, her own filling with tears. "I couldn't live with myself if something happened to her because of me."

"Why because of you?"

Her stomach roiled. "She said he attacked her because she told."

"Why would he attack *her*, if he was looking for *you*?"

"He might have thought she was me. I was tapped into the library Wi-Fi when I was looking at the social media site. I have auburn hair, Rebecca has strawberry blond. The picture he sent was not absolutely clear, he could have mistaken her for me."

"That's it. I'm staying with you and Lolly."

"Okay."

He went off as if she'd never spoken. "Until we know what's going on, you and I need to stick together. No argument."

Her lips twitched as she touched a hand to his chest. "I said okay."

Ghost stopped talking and stared down into her eyes. "About time we agreed on something." He bent to capture her lips in a soul-defining, earth-shattering kiss that left her boneless. She leaned against him, completely dependent on his strength to hold her up.

He glanced down at Lolly staring up at them. "Yes, Lolly, I kissed your mother."

GHOST KEPT IT together all the way back to Charlie's house. He couldn't tell her that hearing her crying out Lolly's name with a touch of panic in her voice had made his heart practically explode out of his chest. Then seeing what had happened to Rebecca and knowing it could have been Charlie made him nearly crumple to his knees.

He'd been back only a day and already he was as deeply in love with Charlie as he'd been seven years ago. The connection they'd shared had never quite gone away, instead it was there and stronger than before. The things he knew, the places he'd been and the experiences he'd survived made him even more aware of how fleeting life could be. One day a man could be on the earth, alive and healthy. The next, he could be six feet under or in the case of the two BLM men, they could have fallen into a toxic pit, leaving nothing left to identify.

He'd had friends die in his arms. He carried the pain with him every day of his life, never quite able to erase the images of them. They seemed to line up at night and dare him to sleep.

Knowing that could have been Charlie on the floor of the library left him feeling more panicked and uncertain than ever. He hadn't come back to find her, but fate placed her directly in his path and revealed to him the fact he had a child. How could he not stay and protect the two women who meant the most to him?

"You two stay here." Before he could allow them to go much farther than the front entryway, Ghost thoroughly searched the entire house. As soon as the guy who had attacked Rebecca discovered she wasn't the one he was after, he'd come back.

Ghost had to be ready.

When he returned, he found Charlie holding Lolly in her arms. The little girl was sobbing on her mother's shoulder.

Ghost's heart broke at the sound of the child's sobs. "Hey, what's all this?" he said softly.

"Ms. Florence is hurt." She sniffed and leaned back to look

at Ghost. Her eyes were red-rimmed and puffy and tears stained her cheeks.

"Come here." He held out his arms. When Lolly went to him, his chest swelled two times bigger. She trusted him enough to come to him when she was distressed. That meant a lot.

Charlie stood with her hand on her daughter's back, her own eyes suspiciously glassy.

Holding Lolly in one arm, he opened the other.

Charlie stepped in and wrapped her arms around him and Lolly. For a long moment, the three of them remained in the tight hug.

Ghost had no desire to break it off anytime soon. The scent of Lolly's hair filled his nostrils. Baby shampoo and fresh air. He inhaled deeply and kissed the top of her head. Then he dropped a kiss on Charlie's temple, wishing he hadn't been such an idiot when he'd been there last. If he hadn't told her he wasn't interested in a long-term relationship, she might have let him in on the secret of his child. He wouldn't have missed all of her firsts. The first tooth, the first time she giggled. Her first step.

As he stood with his arms full of the two women he loved, he came to the conclusion he had to give up something. His career as a Navy SEAL or the family he'd just discovered.

He didn't want to give up either, but he had no right to ask Charlie and Lolly to wait around for him when he went out on missions. So many SEALs were divorced or never married. The waiting killed relationships. Most women wanted their man at home at night. Every night. And the worry of whether or not he'd come home alive, not in a body bag, was real and destructive to a spouse's peace of mind.

When his leg started aching and he couldn't stand still another minute longer, he asked, "Who wants hot cocoa?"

Lolly lifted her head from his shoulder. "Me."

"Me," Charlie agreed. "I'll fix it."

"No. Let me. Just point me in the right direction." He handed Lolly to her mother. "I can make a great cup of cocoa."

"We can all help." Charlie set Lolly on her feet and took her hand.

Lolly slipped her free hand in Ghost's and they entered the kitchen together. In a few short minutes, Ghost had the hot cocoa ready and Charlie made hot dogs for lunch.

"I know I bought ketchup," she said, sorting through the bottles of condiments in the refrigerator. When she didn't find it there, she went to the pantry. After a moment, she came back to the table with mustard. "I'm sorry. I must have forgotten it at the store."

"I put it in the refrigerator," Lolly said. She jumped up and went to the appliance and yanked open the door. "I put it right here." She pointed to an empty spot in the door.

"Well, it's not there," Charlie said. "You'll have to have mustard or eat your hot dog plain."

Lolly's bottom lip stuck out and she frowned. "I guess I'll eat mine plain." She sat at the table, and nibbled at the naked hot dog and drank the hot cocoa, gaining a white melted-marshmallow mustache on her upper lip.

Charlie slathered mustard on her hot dog and ate.

Ghost filled his bun with mustard and sweet relish and savored every bite. "That was delicious."

"Sweetheart," Charlie said softly to Lolly. "If you're done with your lunch, you can take your plate to the sink and go play in your room."

"Okay." She slid out of her chair and carried the plate to the sink.

As the child left the room, Charlie grimaced. "She usually won't eat a hot dog without the requisite ketchup."

Ghost smiled. "A girl who knows what she likes. We'll have to ease her into mustard and relish. It's an acquired taste. But so good."

Charlie stared at him for a moment, her brows pinched lightly.

Ghost tried to think of what he'd said that would make her stare at him with that look of concern.

"Now that you know about Lolly, what are you going to do?"

He glanced in the direction Lolly had gone, not wanting to discuss the future of their daughter in front of her. "If you're finished with your meal, let's take this discussion out on the back porch."

He gathered her plate and his and carried them to the sink.

"Leave them. I'll take care of them later." She led the way to the back door and waited for him to follow before she opened it wide, stopped dead in her tracks and gasped.

Ghost nearly bumped into her, she stopped so fast.

There on the porch was the bottle of ketchup and written in bright red tomato sauce were the words *I KNOW WHERE YOU LIVE.*

Chapter Six

Charlie staggered backward into Ghost's arms. He pulled her away from the door and closed it between them and the damning writing on the porch.

"How did he get in?" Charlie turned and buried her face in Ghost's chest. "I'm positive I locked the doors."

"I double-checked the windows, as well as the doors." He smoothed his hand over the back of her head, his voice low and steady. "He must have picked the lock."

"He knows who I am, and he knows now where I live. He must have figured out Rebecca wasn't the one who tapped into his messages. We're not safe. I should pack up, take Lolly and leave."

"Then he wins."

"Good God, Ghost!" She slapped her palms on his chest. "This isn't a game."

"To him, it might be." He held her arms and stared down into her face. "He might follow you wherever you go."

"Or not. He might be trying to scare me away from Grizzly Pass until he and his following do whatever dastardly deed they have planned." She shook her head and stared at the closest button on his shirt. "I can't risk Lolly's life on a game some psycho is playing with me."

"You forget something."

"What?" She stared up at him, her eyes a little wild, scared.

"You forget that you have me."

"I could have been in the library when he attacked Rebecca," she said, a shiver slithering down the back of her neck. "You weren't there."

"I will be from now on. And you can't go anywhere without me until we catch the bastard."

"Then he wins by making me a prisoner in my own home." Charlie spun out of Ghost's grip and walked across the kitchen and back. "Look, you can stay until we figure this out. But you have to sleep on the couch. We're not picking up where we left off seven years ago. I'm a different person than the naive girl I was back then."

He nodded. "Agreed." He grinned. "About the couch and about being different. You're a much more beautiful woman, you're more independent and an incredible mother."

"And…" Her chin lifted and she captured his gaze with a cool steady one of her own. "I don't need anyone else in my life to make me happy," she insisted, if not to convince him, to convince herself.

"And you don't need anyone else in your life to make you happy," he repeated. "I get that. But when you're ready to talk, I want to discuss who Lolly needs in *her* life."

Charlie pinched the bridge of her nose and shook her head. "Can we postpone that one for another day? I have ketchup bleeding in my mind. And I'm not ready to start a custody battle."

He stepped toward her, his hand outstretched. "It doesn't have to be a battle."

She backed up. "No? I can't see anything but a battle in our future." When he opened his mouth, she held up both hands. "Please. For now, let's not go there. I can't deal with everything and a terrorist out to kill me." She looked at the floor, seeing Rebecca's limp body lying in her own blood. "I can't believe he attacked Rebecca. She wouldn't hurt a fly." She glanced up. "And it's my fault. If I hadn't been snooping on the internet for a few measly dollars extra, none of this would have happened."

"Darlin', you can't blame yourself. You didn't hurt Rebecca. *He* did. We'll deal with this together."

Though her heart warmed when he referred to her as darlin', she couldn't ignore the most important part of the equation. "What about Lolly? I don't want her to be collateral damage. She's just a child." God, what had she done? This was supposed to be an easy gig. She was supposed to be anonymous. No one would know she was the one surfing, searching for terrorist activities.

"Tell you what," Ghost said. "I'll have Garner bring new locks and keys. I can install them today."

She shook her head. "What good will that do? He'll just pick those, too."

Ghost shrugged. "It'll make *me* feel better."

She flipped her hand. "Fine. And I can get online and see if I can find the IP address of the social media group. Maybe we can chase down the leader through it."

"Garner will have Hack working on that, as well."

She nodded. "I did give him the URL. I would think Hack could find it before I can, but two heads are better than one."

Ghost clapped his hands together. "Good. You have a plan. I have a plan. Let's get to it."

Charlie went back to work in her office, searching through the internet, looking for the IP address that the Free America group occupied.

She could hear Ghost placing a call to Kevin, explaining what had happened with the ketchup. Half an hour later, a man she didn't know arrived at her door.

Apparently, Ghost did, calling him by an unusual nickname. "Hey, Caveman. Thanks for bringing these."

"I'm staying to help install them," Caveman said.

"That'll get it done faster," Ghost agreed. "Thanks."

They didn't ask her opinion or assistance, which was perfectly okay with her. Charlie didn't leave her office, except to check on Lolly. She spent the afternoon trying everything she knew, and searching the internet for techniques she didn't know that could help her find the man who'd threatened her online.

About the time Caveman left, Charlie could hear the two men talking softly near the front door, their voices carrying down the hallway, but not clearly enough to make out their words.

Charlie didn't care. She trusted Ghost to keep her and Lolly safe. She had to get to the bottom of who was threatening her, or she'd have no peace.

Ghost appeared in the doorway a few minutes later, carrying a cup of hot tea. "Any luck?"

"I wish I could say yes, but I'm no computer forensics expert. That's not what I studied in my Information Systems degree."

"So you've been in school again?"

She nodded.

"You had just completed a degree when we met seven years ago."

"In business. It was pretty general. When I realized I was pregnant, I knew I had to get something with more of a skill I could work with at home. So I went into Information Systems and learned about databases, data management, design and programming."

"I'm impressed."

She shrugged. "My goal was to work from home so that I could live wherever I wanted." And she'd wanted to come home to Grizzly Pass to raise Lolly. It was a more laid-back and safe environment. Until now.

"I'm impressed. You've been busy."

"What about you?" She'd been dying to ask, but hadn't wanted to know more about him that would make her fall more deeply in love with the man. Still she couldn't resist knowing what he'd gone through in the past seven years. "Are you still based out of California?"

"I'm out of Virginia, now. I completed some training in riverine ops with SEAL Boat Team 22 out of Stennis Space Center in Mississippi. I've had over forty deployments since last we saw each other. But I've also managed to complete my online degree in financial management. Since I'm rarely in town, I don't have time to spend the money I make. I invest it."

She smiled up at him. "You've been busy, too."

He nodded. "Anything I can do to help?"

Her lips twisted and she shook her head. "Not unless you're an experienced hacker, along with being a trained SEAL."

He disappeared, leaving her to her work.

Charlie's senses were tuned into his movements. She could tell when he'd gone into Lolly's bedroom. Their voices drifted to her, making her want to give up on her search and join them. Normally, she would break from her work for the Bozeman software company to spend time with her daughter. But what she was doing was more important. She couldn't let the man threatening her get away with it. And since he'd attacked Rebecca, apparently he would follow through on his threat.

Charlie shivered and dug deeper, following leads on the computer, searching through videos on how to find an IP address. Everything she tried ran her into a brick wall.

The smell of cooking onions drifted into her office and brought her out of her focused concentration.

Ghost was in the kitchen and, by the sound of it, Lolly was helping. Charlie smiled. At least her daughter had a chance to get to know the man who was her father.

Ghost was a good man. Charlie shouldn't have kept the news of his daughter from him. He'd missed so much of her life already and it wouldn't be fair of her to keep him from seeing her in the future. They'd have to come up with a plan to trade off on weekends and holidays.

The thought saddened her. Charlie had grown up with parents who had been married for more than thirty years. They were still as in love with each other as the day they'd met. Their marriage was the standard by which Charlie measured all other relationships.

Perhaps theirs was the exception, not the rule. Wasn't having a part-time father who loved her better than no father at all? She had a lot of thinking to do, and perhaps this wasn't the time to do it. Her problems were more immediate than setting up a visitation schedule.

Lolly appeared in the doorway with a hand-folded paper hat on her head and a towel over her shoulder. She stood straight, her lips twitching. "Your dinner is served," she said in her most formal tone. She spoiled the effect by giggling. "Come on, Mommy. Mr. Caspar and I set the table. We made a lasagna for dinner."

"Lasagna?" Charlie's stomach rumbled. "It smells wonderful."

"It is wonderful." The child grabbed her hand and pulled Charlie to her feet. "Hurry. I'm hungry."

Charlie chuckled and let her daughter practically drag her down the hallway to the kitchen.

Ghost stood at the sink, an apron looped around his neck and tied around his narrow waist. He glanced over his shoulders. "Have a seat. Dinner is just about done."

"Can I do anything?" Charlie asked.

"You can sit down and look beautiful with Lolly." He winked at the little girl. "She even brushed her own hair and changed into that dress."

Lolly nodded. "All by myself."

Charlie stood back, studying her daughter's clothes and hair. "Good job." She gave her a high five and pulled out a chair for her daughter to slide into.

Dinner was perfect. The lasagna tasted so good, Charlie accepted a second helping and ate until she was so full, she couldn't form a coherent thought. "What did you put into that pasta? I suspect it was some kind of sleeping potion." A yawn slipped out and she covered her mouth. "I think I'll get a shower and go to bed." She glanced at Lolly. "Are you about done?"

"Don't worry about Lolly. She and I have a date with her favorite book tonight. I'll help her through bath time and pajamas. Go. Get your shower and sleep."

Charlie didn't argue. The stress of the day and not being able to sleep the night before had left her exhausted. She trudged her way to the bathroom, stripped down and stepped beneath the spray. If she wasn't so tired, she'd be tempted to invite Ghost to join her.

Her eyes widened. What was she thinking? Invite Ghost in the shower with her? She wasn't a twenty-two-year-old anymore. Ghost wasn't going to be around forever, and she refused to put herself and Lolly through the heartbreak of a man entering and leaving her life with no commitment to return.

He might be okay with that lifestyle, but she couldn't take that yo-yo effect. Lord forbid if he should bring back a wife on one of his visits to Lolly.

Her hands clenched and heat burned through her body. She twisted the knob on the faucet to cold and stood beneath the showerhead, letting the water chill her until she shivered.

Then she remembered she hadn't grabbed a towel from the hall linen closet. She stepped out of the shower onto the bath mat, dripping wet and chilled to the bone. Grabbing her shirt, she held it up to her chest and opened the door a crack. No one was in the hallway. She could hear voices in the kitchen. With the coast clear, she darted across the hall to the closet, flung open the door and snatched a towel. She had just turned to dash back into the bathroom when the wood floor squeaked at the other end of the hallway and she heard Ghost say, "I'm going to check to see if your mother is finished in the shower. I'll be right back."

She didn't make it across the hall. Her feet froze to the floor.

Holding the towel in front of her, she couldn't think, couldn't move and only stared at Ghost.

His gaze slipped over her, traveling slowly downward from her face to her breasts, where she'd pressed the towel to the swells. Lower still, his gaze moved to the flare of her hips, clearly visible with the towel draped down only the middle of her torso.

His eyes flared and his body stiffened.

Heat rose from Charlie's core and spread throughout her body. The moisture from that short, cold shower steamed off her body as passion flared and burned a path outward, making her ache for him in every part of her existence.

"Charlie." The word came out in a low, sexy tone. He stepped toward her, his hand reaching out.

Charlie was caught in the spell, the temptation to run into his arms so strong, her arm relaxed, the towel inching downward.

"Mr. Caspar?" Lolly called out from the kitchen.

And snap. Just like that, the spell was broken.

Charlie flung herself into the bathroom, closed the door and leaned her back against it, breathing hard as if she'd run a marathon instead of three feet across the hallway.

From sleepy to wide-awake in two seconds flat. She scrubbed her body with the towel, hoping the added abrasion would push Ghost out of her mind. It had the opposite effect. Her skin tingled from the heated gaze he'd spread over her body. Her nipples were tight, puckered for his touch.

She moaned, threw the towel onto the floor and stomped it. "No. No. No. I will not make love to that man."

"Everything all right in there?" Ghost's voice sounded through the door. Was that a chuckle she heard?

Charlie channeled her desire into something just as heated. Anger. Shoving her head into her nightgown, she pulled it down over her body and slipped her arms into the matching robe. Then she frowned, fearing the garment was a little too revealing. Since she didn't have anything else with her in the bathroom, she sighed. It would have to do. She reached for her panties, but the counter was bare.

Damn. Had she forgotten them? She opened the door and peered out.

Ghost stood in the hallway, dangling a pair of soft blue bikini panties from his index finger. "Missing something?"

Her eyes widened and she reached for the panties.

He pulled them back at the last minute.

Charlie's forward momentum carried her toward him and she slammed into his chest.

Ghost clamped an arm around her waist and held her tight against him. "You felt it, too, didn't you?"

"I don't know what you're talking about." She reached for the panties again, her breasts rubbing against his chest through the thin fabric of her nightgown. "Let me have those."

He raised his eyebrows. "Say *please*."

She gritted her teeth, her core tightening, the ache building the longer she stood with her nearly naked body pressed to his. Instead of arguing over underwear, she wanted to wrap her legs around his waist. Hell, she wanted him inside her, filling that space that had been empty for so long. God, she'd missed him. And she'd miss him when he was gone.

Charlie slumped in his arms. "Fine. You can keep them. But let me go. There really can't be anything between us."

His arm tightened around her. "Why?"

"You have your responsibilities. I have mine. I gave you my heart once. I'm not willing to do it again."

For a long moment, he held her in his arms, his gaze locked on hers.

She refused to look away first. Losing him the first time had been so hard. Carrying his baby, knowing he wouldn't be a part of their lives had nearly killed her. She couldn't let him back into her life, only to have him leave again and break not only her heart, but Lolly's, too.

FINALLY, GHOST LOOSENED his hold. He could see the hurt in Charlie's eyes and he wanted to take it all away. He'd caused that. He'd been the one to break her heart. If he wanted her back, he'd have to earn her trust.

He released her, but he didn't hand back her panties. Instead, he wadded them up and shoved them into his pocket. Yeah, it might be juvenile, but he wanted something that belonged to her, should she end up kicking him out of her life. "Lolly's ready for her bath and bedtime story."

"I can take care of her."

"Get her through her bath. I'll take it from there."

"You don't need to. I'm awake now."

"I don't care if you're awake. I want to read to my daughter—to get to know her." His mouth formed a thin line, his brows dipping low. "At least give me that."

She nodded. "Fair enough." Charlie stepped away from him, spun on her heels and walked into her bedroom.

Knowing she wasn't wearing panties nearly made Ghost come undone. The sway of her hips and the way she flung her damp hair over her shoulder was so enticing, he almost went after her. The way her nipples puckered, making little tents in her silky nightgown, was proof she wasn't immune to him.

Yeah, he had a long way to go to convince her he was worth a second chance.

You broke my heart once...

Was he selfish to want her back? He adjusted his jeans to accommodate his natural reaction to her bare-bottom state. Hell, yeah, it was selfish. What he needed to consider was if he was the man for her. Charlie was special. She deserved someone who could be there for her always.

As a Navy SEAL, he couldn't be in Wyoming except when he took leave. If she and Lolly wanted to be with him, they'd have to leave Wyoming and join him at Little Creek, Virginia. Even then, they'd only see him when he wasn't deployed. The advantage to living on or near a Navy base was the support network of the military and other military spouses.

God, she deserved so much more.

After his last deployment and being injured, Ghost had worried he wouldn't get the medical clearance to return to his unit. Now he wondered if it wasn't time for him to step down. Take a medical retirement, find a less dangerous job that allowed him to be home more often.

He walked back into the kitchen to find Lolly drying the last plate.

"I couldn't reach the cabinet." She pointed upward.

Ghost opened the cabinet and set the cleaned and dried plates inside. Then he dropped his hand to the top of Lolly's soft, red hair. He wanted the chance to be with his daughter. To get to know her, and for her to get to know him. Dragging them around the nation was selfish. But, damn it. He wanted to be a part of Lolly's life, even if Charlie didn't want anything else to do with him.

"Come on, it's time for your bath and a bedtime story." He held out his hand.

Lolly laid hers in his, so trusting. Would she be better off with a stepdad who could be there for her? Would he be kind to her and treat her like she was his own daughter?

Ghost couldn't imagine Lolly with any other father, any more than he could imagine Charlie with another man.

"You get your pjs while I run the water."

"Roger," she said and grinned up at him. "I said that right, didn't I?"

He'd been teaching her how SEALs talked to each other. The child picked up quickly. Smart as a whip. Just like her mother.

"Roger." He gave her a nudge toward her bedroom. "Go. Get those pjs." Ghost entered the bathroom. It still smelled like Charlie's shampoo, making him want to skip Lolly's bath and go straight into her mother's bedroom, climb into her bed and make crazy, passionate love to her.

Instead, he sat on the side of the bathtub, turned the handles on the faucet and adjusted the temperature to just right for a six-year-old.

Lolly entered carrying her colorful pjs, tossed them on the counter and stuck her hand in the water. "Just right."

"Need any help here? If not, I'll go find the perfect book for us to read together."

"I can take my own bath. Mommy thinks I need help, but I don't." She puffed out her chest and lifted her chin, just like Charlie did when she was standing up for herself or someone else. Lolly was so much like her mother, it made Ghost's chest hurt just looking at her.

"Okay, then." He dropped a kiss on top of her head and left her to do her thing, propping the bathroom door open so he could listen for her.

He walked back to the living room, found the phone and dialed the number for Garner.

"Charlie, how's it going?"

"It's Ghost," he said. "So far we're okay. What's the status on the librarian?"

"She's holding her own. Minor swelling on the brain. They're watching her closely and keeping her sedated. By all indications, she'll live."

"I also wanted to know if Hack found anything in those messages that would lead us to whoever has targeted Charlie."

"Nothing so far. He's close to finding the IP address. As soon as he does, I'll send one of the guys out to recon."

"I'd like to be the one to corner that man."

"You and me both. He's a slick bastard. But I find it hard to believe a rancher or pipeliner is crafty enough to pull off a takeover without some help from outside."

Ghost's fists clenched. "You think the ranchers and pipeliners are too dumb to pull this off?"

"No, no. Don't get me wrong. I think they're plenty smart. I just don't know that they could pull it off without some tacti-

cal training and influence from outside the ranching and pipeline community."

"So far, all I've seen in the way of an uprising was the ranchers protesting the confiscation of a herd of cattle. Was anyone
arrested?"

"No. As long as there was no harm to anyone and no property damage, they were free to protest."

"Did you or one of the others get some names of the primary instigators?"

"Hawkeye spoke with one rancher who had twenty-eight
hundred head of cattle confiscated, LeRoy Vanders," Garner
said. "He was hopping mad and ready to rip into the BLM."

"And?"

"The sheriff managed to calm him. The crowd has since dis-
sipated, but there are a lot of angry ranchers. Hack's checking
online records for some of the names Hawkeye came up with
from the protesters. T-Rex will be positioning himself at the
County Line Bar tonight to make some new friends among the
survivalist groups."

"What about Hawkeye?"

"He'll be downstairs in the Tavern striking up conversations
with the ranchers and unemployed pipeline workers who come
in each night to get a drink and commiserate."

"Mr. Caspar?" Lolly called out from down the hall.

Ghost lowered his voice. "I have to go. Let us know anything you might find out about the man stalking Ms. McClain.
As *soon* as you find out. Even if it's in the middle of the night."

"Roger," Garner said. "I'll have Caveman swing by a couple
of times during the night."

"Thanks," Ghost said. "Out here." He ended the call and hurried down the hall to the bathroom.

Lolly was out of the tub, wearing her panties, her nightgown
pulled over her head, but stuck halfway down.

Ghost untangled the gown and dragged the hem downward
to her knees.

She smiled up at him. "Thank you." Then she skipped past him to her bedroom and selected a book from her shelf. "Read this," she demanded.

Ghost took the book from her. "Did you brush your teeth?"

She clapped a hand to her mouth and darted for the door. "I'll be right back."

He grinned and waited for her, thumbing through the book she'd chosen about a little girl pretending to be a beauty shop lady. He chuckled at some of the descriptions. Then he turned down the comforter on Lolly's bed and sat on the edge.

Lolly was back in two minutes, smiling wide. "Clean. See?"

He frowned down at her. "You sure you brushed long enough?"

She nodded. "I sang 'Happy Birthday' all the way through twice."

"Okay. Let's find out what's going on in this book." Ghost opened the book and started reading, getting as caught up in the character's plight as Lolly by the end of the story.

"Now, this one," Lolly insisted, opening another book and handing it to him.

After reading two more books, Ghost told Lolly it was time to close her eyes and go to sleep.

Lolly pouted for a brief moment and then flopped down on her back and burrowed into the sheets and comforter, until all Ghost could make out was Lolly's cute little head poking out of the big bed. "Aren't you going to stay?" She patted the bed beside her.

Ghost sat on the edge of the bed and bent to kiss her good-night. She captured his head between her palms and kissed him soundly on the cheek.

He laughed and kissed the top of her head. "Good night, princess."

"Good night, Mr. Caspar." She yawned, stretched and closed her eyes. "I love you."

Ghost's heart squeezed hard in his chest. Those three little words practically brought him to his knees. The child hardly knew him, but she trusted him to take care of her and to be there when she woke up.

He wanted to gather her in his arms and hold her tight. Forever. His little girl.

In less than five minutes she was asleep, her breathing slow and steady. But Ghost remained perched on the side of her bed, watching her angelic face as she slept, and his heart grew fuller by the minute.

If anyone tried to hurt her… His fists clenched. He'd rip the attacker apart, one limb at a time. No one messed with his family.

"No one," he whispered.

Chapter Seven

Charlie woke with a start and stared into the darkness. She'd had a dream about someone chasing her through the rooms of the library next door. He'd almost captured her, when she'd forced herself to wake.

Her heart thundered against her ribs and perspiration beaded on her forehead. A glance at the clock indicated she'd been asleep for four hours. She hadn't even heard when Lolly went to bed. That was a first in the six years she'd been a mother. Going to sleep before her daughter wasn't something she ever did. It was a testament to the trust she had in Ghost.

Which reminded her. Though she trusted him to keep her and her daughter safe through the night, she shouldn't trust him with her heart. She wasn't sure she would survive a second time around of a broken heart.

Shoving aside the covers she got out of bed and padded barefoot down the hallway to Lolly's bedroom.

Her daughter lay curled on her side, an arm wrapped around her favorite teddy bear and sleeping peacefully with a smile curling her lips. A few books lay on the nightstand beside her bed.

Charlie smiled, imagining Ghost reading them to her daughter. She'd have him reading more than that if he let her talk him into it.

Tucking the blanket around Lolly's chin, she bent to kiss her daughter's cheek.

Lolly rolled over and whispered, "I love you, Mr. Caspar."

Charlie's breath caught at the constriction in her throat. Her daughter was already falling in love with the man who'd broken Charlie's heart seven years ago. Would Lolly's little heart be broken as well when Ghost left to return to his SEAL team?

On silent feet, she tiptoed down the hallway where she peered into the living room.

Ghost lay in the lounge chair, shirtless, wearing boxer shorts and nothing else. He leaned back, his arms crossed over his chest, his eyes closed and his breathing deep and regular. Asleep.

Charlie took the opportunity to drink her fill of him, studying his face, chest, arms and thick, muscular thighs. How she wished she could go to him, straddle his waist and press her hot center to him. She had yet to find another pair of panties. She wondered what he'd done with the ones he'd taken.

That he wanted to keep them must mean something. But what? That he wanted to make love to her? She had no doubt about that. When he'd held her close, the ridge beneath his jeans had been firm and insistent, pressing against her belly.

Warmth spread through her body, igniting the flames at her center. She burned uncontrollably, wanting the man more than she'd wanted anyone or anything in her life. If she gave in to her carnal lust, he wouldn't resist. Hell, he'd welcome her with the same level of passion. Their sex life had never been the problem between them.

Yeah, Charlie had told Ghost she didn't care if a relationship with him was only temporary. But that had been before she'd discovered she was in love with him. When he'd left, she'd held it together until that night when she'd been alone in her bed.

Then she'd cried. And cried some more. Two weeks later, she was crying even harder when she discovered she'd missed her period and the early pregnancy test proved positive.

Seven years ago, she'd given her heart to this man. And based on the way she felt at that moment, she still loved him. If not as much, then even more.

Her eyes stinging, Charlie backed away from the living room and escaped into the kitchen. She peered through the curtain over the window on the back door. Moonlight shone onto the porch, bathing everything in a dark blue glow.

The ketchup had been cleaned off the wooden planks. She'd have to thank Ghost in the morning. It was one fewer thing she had to face on her own. Though the message was gone, it remained seared into her mind.

Unable to face going back to her lonely bed, Charlie tiptoed into her office, half closing the door. She booted her computer and went to work, trying to find the man responsible for the attack on Rebecca and the ketchup message on her back porch. The threats had to stop. Both to herself and to whatever government facility he had in mind by his call to arms.

She returned to the site with the entries from people who had legitimate gripes with the way they'd been treated by local and national authorities. One by one, she followed each posting, tracking them back to their own social media pages. Each had pictures of their families posted. These were real people with loved ones. All they wanted was to be treated fairly. They were all upset about the confiscation of LeRoy Vanders's herd, wanting the authorities to return the man's animals as they were his livelihood. If he couldn't get them back, he wouldn't have the means to provide for his family. He'd posted, You might as well shoot me now. I'm worth more to my family dead than alive.

She followed LeRoy to his page. There he had posted messages from Bible scripture, praying for a peaceful resolution to the current crisis. It didn't sound like a man crazy enough to threaten someone for spying on his messages.

But then Charlie didn't know what set a man like that off. If desperate enough, he might go off the deep end and come out fighting.

She tried scanning the internet for other terrorist threats that could be tied to the state of Wyoming. At one point she found a message from a man claiming to be a member of ISIS. His threat was to all American infidels. He was coming. Be prepared to convert or die.

A shiver rippled across her as she stared into the eyes of a man who looked like he could kill without it impacting him in the least. His brown eyes had that intense crazy look that burned into her, even from a computer screen.

Charlie pushed her chair away from the monitor and keyboard. She stood, stretched and walked to the window overlooking the street in front of her house. Moonlight streamed through the window, bathing her in its pale, blue glow.

Why did something so beautiful three nights ago seem so sinister now? She'd always loved nighttime in Wyoming. She'd loved staring up at the stars with her father, identifying constellations and planets.

The night she'd spent in the back of Ghost's pickup, they'd had fun naming different stars as if they were the scientists who'd discovered them. They laughed and rolled into each other's arms. A kiss led to a caress. The caress moved from outside their clothes to bare skin. Soon, they were naked, bathed in starlight, making love.

Charlie wrapped her arms around her middle and sighed. Why couldn't things have remained the same? That had been their last night together. The next day, he'd driven to his new assignment in California and she'd stayed in Wyoming, nursing a broken heart.

She raised her hand to push her hair back from her forehead.

Seven years later, he was in her living room, wearing nothing but boxer shorts, sexier than ever, and she was staring out at the night sky wishing for something that would only bring her more heartache.

"Hey." Ghost's voice echoed in her head, like a memory she couldn't forget. Why had she never been able to forget him? Why couldn't she ignore him now?

"Charlie, darlin'." That voice again, made the ache in her belly grow.

Big hands descended on her arms, turning her to face the man she'd never stopped loving.

GHOST HAD REMAINED in the doorway to Charlie's office for a long time before he'd made a sound.

She'd stood by the window, her body swathed in a pale glow turning her into an ethereal blue image of lush, unaffected beauty.

She was sexy, but appeared sad, staring out into the darkness. He wanted to tell her to step away from the window in case someone decided to take a shot at her. As still as she was, she'd make an easy target.

When she raised her arm to push her hair back the moonlight shone through the thin fabric of her nightgown, exposing the silhouette of her naked body beneath.

His breath lodged in his lungs, or he would have moaned aloud. Every cell in his body burned for her. His pulse sped through his veins carrying red-hot blood angling south to his groin. He had to have her, to hold her in his arms. To feel her skin against his.

"Hey," he managed to say.

When she didn't turn to face him, he eased into the room. Perhaps she'd been sleepwalking and wasn't hearing him through her dream.

"Charlie, darlin'," he whispered. Gripping her arms, he turned her toward him.

She glanced up at him, recognition in her gaze and something else. Longing. Pure, unrestricted passion.

Charlie pressed her hands to his chest and slid them up to lock around the back of his neck. Then she stood on her toes, pulling his head down to hers. "Call me all kinds of a fool, for making the same mistake twice, but I want you."

"If wanting you is a mistake, I don't care what you call me. Just let me have you for a moment," he said, drawing her into his arms. He wrapped his hands around her waist and pressed her hips against his. His erection swelled, pressing into her belly, when he'd rather be pressing it into her.

He claimed her mouth in a long, hard kiss. When he traced the seam of her lips, she opened to him, meeting his tongue with hers in a twisting tangle of urgency.

She drew her arms down his chest and around to his backside, sliding her fingers beneath the elastic of his boxers. Slim, warm hands cupped his buttocks and squeezed gently.

He broke the kiss, dragging in a deep breath, barely able to hold back, when wave after wave of lust washed over him, urging him to take her now. In the office, on the desk, against the wall. Anywhere he could get inside her. Now.

He bunched her nightgown in his hands, pulling it up over her bottom and groaned.

She hadn't found another pair of panties. Her sex was bared to him, there for the taking.

Ghost slid his hands down the backs of her thighs and lifted her, wrapping her legs around his waist.

She locked her ankles behind him and captured his face between her palms. "This is for now. Nothing has changed between us. Don't expect anything from me tomorrow."

His heart tightened in his chest. He understood why she said these things. She didn't trust him. Didn't expect him to stay and she had to guard her heart and Lolly's from the hurt she expected him to inflict when he left.

He knew all of this as the truth, but he couldn't stop. He had to have her. He'd work on the trust later. When he wasn't consumed by his need to feel her against him. The need to lose himself inside her.

He carried her down the hallway to her bedroom, careful not to make enough noise that would wake the little one. Once inside, he pushed the door half-closed with his foot and carried Charlie to the bed. "Protection?"

"I'm on birth control and I'm clean."

"I'm clean, too."

She kissed his lips and whispered against his mouth, "Then what are you waiting for?"

He sat her on the edge of the bed, grabbed the hem of her nightgown and pulled it slowly over her head.

She raised her arms to accommodate the removal of her only garment. Charlie leaned back on her elbow in the glow of a night-light and spread her knees wide. She ran one hand down her belly to the triangle of curls covering her sex and threaded her fingers through them. She tipped her head toward his boxers. "Are you going to wear those all night?"

"Oh, hell no." Ghost shucked the shorts and stood before her, his shaft jutting out, his body on fire for her. His first inclination was to take her, hard and fast, to thrust deep inside her glistening entrance. But he didn't want to scare her away. He wanted her to know the depth of need and passion he was experiencing. Hell, he wanted to bring her to the very edge and make her beg for him to take her.

Ghost dropped to his knees in front of her and draped her legs over his shoulders.

Her eyes widened and her breathing became more labored. She threaded her fingers through the fluff of hair over her sex to the folds beneath.

Ghost stroked her hand and her fingers and brushed them aside to take over. He parted her folds, exposing the narrow strip of flesh between. Leaning in, he flicked her with the tip of his tongue.

She moved her hands, weaving them into his hair, while digging her heels into his back, urging him to continue.

He tongued her again, this time swirling around, laving until she pulled on his hair, a moan rising from her throat.

Ghost remembered how she had given herself to him so completely when they were younger, yelling out his name in the throes of their shared passion. He wanted to capture that same sense of abandon.

While his tongue took control of her nubbin, he thrust one of his fingers into her slick channel, reveling in how wet she already was, knowing it would ease him inside her soon. He added a second finger in with the first and stretched her, feeling her muscles contract, gripping his fingers.

Teasing and tasting, he licked, swirled and flicked that amazing bundle of nerves that made her crazy with desire.

And she responded by raising her hips, pumping them upward, pulling on his hair to keep him focused on her pleasure.

He didn't need the encouragement. Making her come apart was his goal. If he read her right, she was nearing her climax.

Charlie's body tensed, her heels dug into his back and she thrust her hips upward.

Ghost didn't relent, continuing his frenzied assault until he stormed past her resistance.

Charlie's fingers curled into his scalp and she cried out softly, "Ghost!" as she gave in with abandon, her body shaking with her release.

Ghost continued to stroke her with his fingers and tongue, slowing the movement as she relaxed and sank back to the mattress.

"Oh, my," she said, her head tossing from side to side. "I didn't know it could be even better than before."

Ghost chuckled and scooted her up farther on the bed. He lay beside her, his hand cupping her sex, his shaft throbbing with his need. He wanted her to be sure.

She finally looked into his eyes, her own narrowing. "Why did you stop?"

"I want you to be sure."

"Sweet heaven. I've never been more sure." She dragged him over her, parted her legs and let him slide between them. "Please. Don't make me wait another minute."

Releasing a long breath, he eased up to her entrance, dipping in slowly. "Tell me to stop and I will."

"Don't you dare." She raised her legs, clamped them around his waist and dug her heels into his buttocks, urging him to take her. "I want you. All of you. Inside me. Now."

Unable to hold back another second, he drove into her, thrusting all the way until he was completely encased in her slick, tight wetness.

He bent to kiss her, taking her tongue with his as he moved out and back into her. Slowly at first, then faster and faster until he pumped in and out of her like a piston in an engine.

The faster he went, the harder he got, the tension building, pushing him to the edge. One. Last. Thrust. And he shot into the stratosphere, spiraling to the stars, his body exploding with electric shocks that spread through him from his shaft to the very tips of his fingers. He dropped down on her, still buried deep inside and held steady until his shaft stopped throbbing and he could breathe normally again.

At long last, he rolled to his side and pulled her with him, curling her up against his body.

Charlie laid her cheek against his chest and chuckled. "Your heart is racing."

"You do that to me."

She sighed and circled her fingers around his hard, brown nipple. "I'd say I could get used to this, but I can't."

"Can't, or won't?"

"Does it matter?" she whispered. "You're here today. But you'll be gone soon."

"What if I come back?"

"In another seven years?" She snorted and shook her head.

"How about in a couple of months?"

"Would it be fair to Lolly?"

He thought about it. "I want to know my daughter. I want to watch her grow."

"You can't do that if you aren't here."

He knew what she said was true. But lots of SEALs had families willing to be there when they got home.

"Charlie, I want you—"

She pressed a finger to his lips. "Shh. I just want to hold you for tonight. We don't have to talk. In fact, I'd rather not ruin what we shared with words we might regret."

Ghost clamped his teeth down on his tongue, wanting to say more, wanting to force her into some kind of commitment, but he didn't want her to kick him out of her bed. For that night, he would shut up and hold her. Tomorrow, they'd have to make time to talk. They had too much at stake to remain silent for long.

Chapter Eight

Charlie lay in the warmth of Ghost's arms, listening to the beat of his heart. This was where she'd always wanted to be. She didn't want the night to end. For a long time, she lay awake, until her eyes closed and she drifted into sleep.

A sharp ringing sound jerked her out of a lovely dream, jarring her awake. She sat up, thinking it was the smoke alarm. When it stopped and then rang again, she realized it was the phone on the other side of the bed.

Ghost grabbed the phone from the cradle and handed it to her.

She took it, almost afraid to answer. "Hello," Charlie said, her voice hoarse with sleep.

"Ms. McClain, Hack here. You wanted me to call when we got a hit on the IP address."

Charlie sat up straighter, pushing the fog of sleep out of her head. "Whose is it?"

"We traced it back to a man who died several months ago, but I have one of our guys headed out to the physical address. Apparently it's local. I thought you'd want to know."

"I do. Is that all?"

"So far. I'm still tracking some of the people in that chat room. When I have more, I'll let you know."

"Thank you." She handed the phone to Ghost and he set it back on the charger.

"They're sending someone out to the physical address associated with the IP address," she said, draping her arm over her eyes.

Ghost rose up on his elbow and stared down at her. "Whose was it?"

She moved her arm and stared up into his eyes, her own narrowing. "That's the strange part. Hack said it was registered to a dead man."

"A what?" He brushed a strand of her hair from her face, tucking it behind her ear.

She leaned into his hand and kissed his palm. "Someone who'd died several months ago."

Ghost bent to kiss her forehead. "I would like to know if he died of natural causes, or if he was murdered." Then he kissed her nose.

Charlie closed her eyes, loving the feel of his lips on her skin, while blocking the thought of someone who might have been murdered for his connection to an IP address. She opened her eyes. "What time is it?"

Ghost leaned back to glance at the clock on the nightstand. "Nearly seven o'clock."

Her heart leaped. "Lolly will be up any minute." She shoved against his chest. "You have to get out of here."

"Why?"

"She's super curious and asks a lot of questions. Frankly, I'm not prepared to answer any about you."

"Like, 'Mommy, why are you in bed with Mr. Caspar? And why are you naked?'" He lowered the sheet and tweaked the tip of her nipple.

Her core responded with an answering ache. But she couldn't allow herself to go for round two with the chance of Lolly run-

ning in and jumping into the bed, like she did so often. As much
as she would have liked to see his tweak and raise it to a much
more satisfying conclusion, she didn't feel like facing a lot of
questions from her daughter.

"Out." She rolled away and shot out of the bed.

Ghost got up and stretched, his body naked in the light peeking around the edges of the curtains. God, he was gorgeous.

A sound from the room down the hallway made her race to
her closet, grab the first pair of jeans she could find and jam
her legs into them. "For the love of Mike, cover yourself," she
hissed. "Lolly's awake."

Ghost grabbed his boxers from the floor and slipped them
up his thighs.

Charlie pulled a sweatshirt over her head and ran for the door.
"I'll distract her while you find more clothes."

His laughter followed her out the door and down the hallway to Lolly's room.

Her chest swelled with an unbidden joy at the sound. The
joy faded when she thought about the end of the week and his
ultimate departure. She wasn't certain her heart could take the
pain again. Refusing to think that far ahead, she entered Lolly's
room and found her standing by the bed, pushing her bright auburn hair out of her face. "I'm hungry," she said.

"Let's get you dressed and then you can help me fix breakfast." Charlie spun her daughter away from the door and walked
her over to her dresser.

As Charlie helped Lolly choose an outfit, out of the corner
of her eye, she saw Ghost pass by in the hallway, with a big
grin and a little wave.

When Lolly was dressed in a hot pink shirt, jeans and her
pink cowboy boots, she was hard to hold back.

Charlie stepped out of her way, hoping Ghost was completely
dressed and presentable. Apparently he was, because she heard
Lolly in the kitchen talking to him.

With a few minutes to herself, Charlie washed her face,

brushed her hair and her teeth and dressed in something more attractive than jeans and a bulky sweatshirt. Feeling a little more put together in dark jeans, a white blouse and her cowboy boots, her curly hair secured behind her head in a barrette, she entered the kitchen to find Ghost and Lolly waiting for her, the stove cold, the kitchen table empty.

"We're going to have breakfast at the tavern," Lolly said, grinning.

"We are?" Charlie's gaze met Ghost's, her brows rising.

"We are. My treat," he said. "Shall we go?" He took Lolly's hand in his and cupped Charlie's elbow.

"Actually, it sounds good." She hadn't treated herself or Lolly to a breakfast out in a very long time. Eating at a fast-food restaurant in Bozeman on her way to drop Lolly at the daycare didn't count.

Ghost insisted on taking his truck, moving Lolly's booster seat into the back center seat of the crew cab. Lolly liked being high above the ground, claiming she could see everything.

Charlie climbed into the passenger seat and waited for Ghost to slip into the driver's side and start the engine. "Anything else from Kevin?"

He shook his head. "No."

"We could stop by there on the way home, if you like."

With a nod, he reversed, turned around and headed down the road to the tavern.

Since it was early on a regular workday, the tavern parking lot was full, with vehicles lining the street, as well.

Charlie suspected they might not get a table as full as it was. But once inside, they waited for only ten minutes before they were seated in a booth near the door.

"Hi, Charlie." Lisa Lambert, a young, bleach-blonde waitress, set a cup in front of Ghost, one in front of Charlie and poured coffee into both. She winked at Lolly. "Juice or chocolate milk?" she asked.

Lolly rocked in her seat. "Chocolate milk!"

After Lisa left, Charlie tried to focus on the menu, when she'd rather stare at the man she'd made love to the night before. When the waitress returned with Lolly's chocolate milk, Charlie still didn't know what she wanted to eat.

"We don't see you in here for breakfast often, Charlie. Who's your fella?"

Charlie's face heated. "He's not—"

Ghost stuck out his hand and smiled at Lisa. "Jon Caspar. Nice to meet you." He leaned close to read her nametag. "Lisa, is it?"

She shook his hand, blushing. "That's right. You must be new in town. I know I'd remember you, if I'd seen you around."

"I'm not actually. But I'm so much older than you, you wouldn't remember me. I'm back in town for a visit." He reached across the table and laid his hand over Charlie's. "Charlie was good enough to put me up for the week."

"Are you thinking of moving back?" Lisa asked, taking a pad and pen out of her apron pocket.

Charlie's breath caught in her throat and she leaned forward, wanting to hear his answer, even though she knew he was putting on a show for Lisa.

He gave Lisa a friendly smile. "I don't know yet. It depends on the job."

"We're ready to order," Charlie interrupted.

"Oh, right." Lisa pressed her pen to the tablet. "What would you like?"

They placed their orders and Lisa left, her cheeks flushed with color from the smile Ghost gave her before she turned away.

Charlie wanted to smack the grin right off his face. She'd slept with him the night before. How could he flirt with the waitress in front of her?

"Nice one, that Lisa," he said, with a smile playing around his lips. "Why don't I know her?"

Charlie's lips thinned. "Because she was practically in diapers when you were in high school."

He cocked his brows. "Jealous?"

"Not in the least. She's barely out of high school. What use would you have with her? She's not much older than Lolly."

Lolly glanced up from her chocolate milk, her gaze curious.

Ghost's smile faded. "Okay, I'll behave myself, if you'll stop being so serious. Deal?" He held out his hand.

Charlie took his, knowing as soon as they touched, she'd feel that electric shock running through her body. And there it was, searing a path straight to her heart. "Deal."

GHOST DIDN'T KNOW why he'd flirted with the young waitress. He supposed he wanted to get a reaction out of Charlie when she was holding him at arm's length that morning.

He didn't let go of her hand immediately, staring across the table at her. "Just to set the record straight, you're the only woman who interests me."

"For now," Charlie added, trying to pull her hand from his.

He held tight, refusing to release her yet. "For always."

"Please." She finally freed her hand and placed it in her lap, out of his reach. "I find that hard to believe when you haven't been back for seven years."

She was right. He'd tried to forget her in those seven years, but he'd been unsuccessful. The intensity of his training and deployments had made the time seem to fly. But always in the back of his mind, she was what kept him sane and focused.

The tavern door opened behind Charlie.

Ghost glanced up, his gaze taking in the newcomers entering.

Charlie turned in her seat.

A man in a law enforcement uniform and a woman who appeared to be his wife stepped through the door. They waved at the man behind the counter and were shown to a seat at a table beside Charlie and Ghost's.

Charlie smiled at the man. "Good morning, Sheriff and Mrs. Scott."

The woman smiled. "Good morning, Charlie, Lolly. It's always a pleasure to see you two." She turned to include Ghost in her smile and greeting. "And you are?"

The sheriff nodded, his gaze narrowing on Ghost. "Aren't you Tom Caspar's son?"

Ghost nodded and reached across to shake the sheriff's hand. "Tom is my father."

"Used to be the foreman out at the Dry Gulch Ranch, wasn't he?" the sheriff asked.

"That was him," Ghost said.

"How's he doing down in Florida?"

Ghost grinned. "They love that they haven't had to shovel one scoop of snow since they moved."

The sheriff smiled, nodding. "That's good. Thinking about taking Fran down there for a vacation to see if it's something we'd like for our retirement."

"You should visit my folks," Ghost said. "I'm sure they'd love to see you."

"Might do that." The sheriff turned his attention to the menu.

Lisa returned with three plates of food, setting them in front of Charlie, Ghost and Lolly. "Enjoy," she said and walked away.

The door behind Charlie swung open again with a bang that shook the booth they were sitting in.

Ghost frowned, his gaze following the man who'd entered. He thought he recognized him. His father had met with him on more than one occasion to discuss trading bulls. He'd called him Vanders.

"Sheriff Scott, what are you going to do about the cattle thieves who stole my herd?" the man shouted.

Charlie spun in her seat. "LeRoy?"

He ignored her, his attention on the sheriff. LeRoy Vanders stomped toward the section where the sheriff and his wife sat. He planted his fist on the table and glared at the man.

"LeRoy, we've been over this. You signed on to graze your herd on government property. You read the contract. So, they raised the rates. The contract you signed gives them the right. And it's still cheaper than leasing private property." Sheriff Scott tilted his chin up and narrowed his eyes. "Pay your fees and I'll bet they'll give back your herd."

"My family has been grazing our cattle on that land for over a century. As far as I'm concerned, the government stole that land and is extorting money from me." He pounded his fist on the table.

"What do you expect me to do, LeRoy? You have to take it up with the Bureau of Land Management."

"I expect you to arrest the rustlers who stole my cattle." LeRoy's voice rose. "I was due to take them to the sale. That's the money I use to feed my family and heat my house through the winter. How am I supposed to make do until spring without that money?"

"I can't help you. You have to pay your fees." The sheriff started to rise.

LeRoy pushed him back into his seat and pulled a gun from beneath his jacket.

Mrs. Scott screamed.

Charlie gasped and used her body to block any stray bullets from hitting Lolly.

LeRoy pointed the gun in the air. "I'm tired of being pushed around on my own land. I'm tired of the government taking what belongs to me. I'm tired of the law protecting the criminals and not me and my family."

Ghost eased out of his seat, keeping low, staying out of LeRoy's peripheral vision. He didn't want to startle the man into pulling the trigger. At the angle he was currently holding the gun, LeRoy would put a sizable hole in Ghost if he fired the weapon.

"LeRoy, put down the gun and discuss this like a reasonable man."

"I'll show you reasonable," LeRoy said. Before LeRoy could pull the trigger, Ghost grabbed the man's hand, jerked it into the air and yanked the gun from his grip. Then he twisted the rancher's arm up behind his back.

"Let go of me, damn you!" LeRoy shouted. "Mind your own business. This discussion is between me and the sheriff."

Ghost leaned close to LeRoy's ear. "This discussion stopped being just your business when you pulled the gun." Ghost nodded toward the sheriff. "You want to take him away, or should I?"

A young sheriff's deputy burst through the door. "Got a call from dispatch. Where's the perpetrator?"

The sheriff shook his head. "Over here, Matthews."

Matthews hurried to where Ghost held Mr. Vanders immobile. He snapped the cuffs on the man's wrists and led him toward the exit.

Vanders twisted out of Matthews's grip. "This isn't over by a long shot, Sheriff. I'm not the only one angry about what's going on. You just wait. This isn't the last you'll be hearing from us." He glared at Ghost and Charlie. "And we don't take kindly to interference."

Matthews hooked LeRoy's arm and dragged him out of the door.

Ghost waited until the man was out of the building before he relaxed.

Sheriff Scott held out his hand. "I'll take that. It's evidence."

Ghost gladly handed over the gun.

"Thank you for taking charge," the sheriff said. "I never would have thought Vanders would pull a gun on me. He used to be a reasonable man." He touched his hand to his wife's shoulder. "Are you okay?"

She nodded.

The sheriff sighed. "I'm thinking Florida is looking pretty good about now. How about you, dear?"

Fran pressed a hand to her chest, her face pale, her eyes worried. "People are getting crazy around here. I've never seen them so mad about so much."

A man rose from the table behind the sheriff and shook Sheriff Scott's hand. "You handled that well, Sheriff."

The sheriff frowned. "Should I know you?"

The man smiled. "Randall Gaither. I work with the Apex Pipeline Authority. It's good to see local law enforcement enforcing the laws."

The sheriff's brows twisted. "Just doing my job. Now, if you'll excuse me, I'd like to have breakfast with my wife."

The man nodded. "Of course. Of course." He resumed his seat at the table on the other side of the sheriff and lifted his coffee cup.

Ghost took his seat and stared down at his plate for a moment before he raised his chin and met Charlie's gaze.

Charlie stared at him across the table. "You're as cool as a cucumber." She lifted her glass and her hand shook so much orange juice spilled onto the table. "And I'm shaking like a leaf. You were amazing."

He shrugged. "I was hungry. I figured I wouldn't get to eat my eggs while they were hot, if someone didn't shut him up." He winked at Lolly. "How are your Belgian waffles?"

And just like that, they continued their breakfast as if a man hadn't just pulled a gun in a public place. The less he made of the incident, the better they all were. For Lolly's sake, he didn't let on that he'd been almost as shaken as Charlie. A man had entered the tavern with a gun. He could have started shooting and hurt Charlie or Lolly.

Ghost couldn't let that happen. Wouldn't let it. Hopefully, their problem was solved by the arrest of LeRoy Vanders. Maybe now, they could relax and enjoy the rest of the week.

He shook his head. Nothing ever was that easy. Hadn't Vanders said he wasn't the only one unhappy about the current state of government in Wyoming? If he was right, he might have been only the tip of the iceberg.

The week ahead didn't look like it was going to be a picnic.

Chapter Nine

"Is today Mother's Day Out?" Lolly asked as they left the tavern.

Charlie had barely been able to choke down her food. After all of the excitement, the patrons of the tavern had either gotten up to leave or stayed to gossip about LeRoy's tirade and Ghost's handling of the situation.

Lisa had been all over Ghost. Forney, the tavern owner, had offered to give them their meal for free.

Ghost had insisted they could pay and did so. He didn't look comfortable with the notoriety. As soon as Lolly finished her meal, he hurried them out the door.

Charlie nodded. "As a matter of fact, today is Mother's Day Out. Would you like to go play at the center?"

"Yes, please. Can I go?" Lolly danced around Charlie, her eyes wide, her hands pressed together. "Please?"

Charlie glanced over her head at Ghost. "Think it would be okay?"

"Are they inside much of the day?"

"They have arts and crafts and play games in the center."

"It should be okay. We can give the teacher a heads-up to be watchful."

Charlie stared down at her daughter and sighed. The threats had been against her, not her daughter. With LeRoy detained, perhaps the problem had been solved. "Okay," she said to Lolly. "You can go for a couple of hours." It would give her time to meet with Kevin and his computer guy to see if they had anything more to tell them. She was anxious to hear what they found at the address Caveman was supposed to check out that morning.

"Do you remember where the community center is?"

Ghost nodded. "I think so."

"That's where they have the Mother's Day Out. Lolly goes three times a week to play with her friends during the summer." She started to help Lolly up into the truck, but Ghost nudged her aside.

He lifted Lolly, settled her into the booster seat and buckled the seat belt around her.

When he rounded the truck to hold the door for Charlie, he whispered in her ear. "Are you sure it's a good idea to leave her at the daycare?"

"The threats were against me," Charlie said. "Not Lolly. And she so looks forward to going. I hate to disappoint her." Though she'd had the same misgivings. "How about we let her stay long enough for us to do some digging here in town? We won't be far, if anything happens."

He nodded. "Okay." Ghost helped her up into the truck and climbed into the driver's seat.

The community center was on the edge of town, with a wide, open field used for baseball, soccer and football practice. The center was a converted US Army Armory. The inside was a gymnasium with basketball hoops on either end of the open room. Back when the US Army National Guard occupied the building, they had used the gym for formations on bad weather days and for hip-pocket training in buddy care and field stripping their weapons.

Now the gym was used by locals for the occasional game of basketball and for the Mother's Day Out program, offering the community children a place to play with others their age.

As they drove up to the center, Ghost commented, "Looks better than when I used to come here."

Charlie smiled. "We recently had a Fix It Day. Everyone turned out to paint and do much-needed roof repairs."

"What's with the signs?" He pointed to a grouping of signs outside the center, indicating other businesses besides the community center.

"The city overhauled the old armory offices. The mayor and the county treasurer occupy two of them and the others were rented out to a real estate agent and an insurance salesman. They have access to the outside without going through the gymnasium where the kids play."

Charlie remembered spending a lot of time in the community center as she was growing up. From the annual Halloween parties and Christmas craft shows, to the Fall Festival dances. The community center had been a hub of social gatherings in the Grizzly Pass area.

Ghost parked and helped Lolly out of her seat.

The little girl ran toward the entrance, her face alight with excitement. She had to wait for Charlie to enter the pass code to open the outer door. But once inside, she ran through the front lobby straight into the gym.

Ghost and Charlie followed at a more sedate pace.

Inside, a dozen children were playing four square on the wooden floor of the gymnasium, their shouts echoing off the walls.

Charlie found the woman who ran the Mother's Day Out, her friend from high school, Brenda Larson.

Brenda pushed a stray strand of hair out of her face and smiled as she weaved through a couple of smaller children to where Charlie and Ghost stood. "Charlie, I'm so glad Lolly was able to come today. Ashley and Chelsea missed her yesterday."

After hugging Charlie, Brenda stood back, her gaze raking over Ghost. She tipped her head, her eyes narrowing. "You look familiar..." Then her face lit. "Jon? Jon Caspar?" She flung her arms around him and hugged his as tightly as she'd hugged Charlie. "You look so much larger than life. You were all buff when you came through several years ago, but look at you." She stood back and ran her gaze over him again. "I barely recognized you. When did you get back in town?"

"Yesterday," he said. "It's good to see you, Brenda."

"What a wonderful surprise." She glanced from Charlie to Ghost and back. "Any special reason you're here?" She paused.

Heat rose up Charlie's neck into her cheeks. "No. Not really. He's here on leave."

Brenda's brows rose again. "Your parents moved south several years ago. I would think you would vacation in Florida with them."

Ghost shrugged. "I haven't been back here in a while. It's nice to be here and explore all of my old stomping grounds."

"I'm sure." Brenda's lips curled up on the corners. "Where are you staying?"

Charlie wasn't up for answering her friend's questions with Ghost standing beside her. "I'm only leaving Lolly for a couple of hours while I run some errands."

Brenda crossed her arms over her chest and nodded. "I see how it is. Ignore the questions and maybe she'll stop asking." She winked at Ghost. "Have it your way." She turned toward the kids. "We're making sock puppets today. I think Lolly will enjoy that. Don't forget we're going on a field trip tomorrow to the Yellowstone Nature Center. You won't want Lolly to miss that. We were able to get an educational grant from the state to fund the bus and the snacks for the trip. If you want to come and help supervise, I'd gladly take all the help I can get."

Charlie frowned. "I'd forgotten that was tomorrow. Lolly's been looking forward to the trip all summer."

"Have her here a few minutes early." Brenda touched her arm. "And don't worry if you can't come along. I know you work from home and it's hard to get away sometimes."

Charlie took Brenda's hand. "About Lolly. Could you keep an extra special close eye on her?"

Brenda glanced toward the happy child, bouncing a ball with three other little girls. "Is she not feeling well?"

Charlie explained the situation with the threats. "I don't know if she'll become a target because of my meddling."

"Wow." Brenda squeezed her hand. "I'm sorry to hear this is happening to you. I'll be sure to keep her close. We don't plan on leaving the building until after lunch."

"I'll be sure to get her before then."

Brenda's lips twisted as she stared at the little girls. "She'll be disappointed that she won't get to go out on the play set with her pals." Charlie's friend turned back to the adults. "But I understand completely. I'd be leery, as well."

"Thank you, Brenda." Charlie touched her friend's arm.

"We should get together for a girl's night out in Bozeman sometime soon."

"I could use a break," Charlie agreed. "When this mess clears, you're on."

Brenda smiled. "You sure tall, dark and hunky won't mind?"

Charlie glanced up at Ghost. He wouldn't be around when that time came around.

"Whatever makes Charlie happy," Ghost said. His gaze met hers and held it for a long time.

A flash of hope filled Charlie's chest. If Ghost really believed that sentiment, he'd stay in Grizzly Pass with her and Lolly and give up his life with the Navy SEALs. But as much as he loved the path he'd chosen, the likelihood of him leaving it behind was slim to nada.

"Come on, we have some things to check on. And I really do

have a job I need to work on. My boss is patient, but he likes it when I meet my project deadlines."

After one last glance in Lolly's direction, Charlie turned toward the door.

Ghost hooked her elbow and walked with her.

The familiarity of his grip on her arm gave her comfort at the same time as it fanned the smoldering embers burning inside. If they didn't have bigger problems to solve, she'd have him take her back to her house to make love to her until it was time to pick up Lolly.

And if wishes were horses...

He handed her up into his truck and closed the door. Then he rounded to the driver's side and climbed in behind the steering wheel. "Where to?"

The first word on the tip of her tongue was *Home.* But she tamped down the urge and answered, "Kevin's. I want to know what they've come up with."

GHOST DROVE BACK to the Blue Moose Tavern and parked in back of the building. Because it was broad daylight, he sent Charlie up first and followed, shortly after.

Garner answered on the first knock. "Come in. I'm glad you stopped by. And, by the way, thank you for disarming LeRoy before he shot through the ceiling and hit one of us or the computers."

Caveman rose from a chair beside Hack's and held out his hand.

Ghost shook it and nodded toward the computer screens. "Find anything at the physical address for the IP address?"

The D-Force man stretched and shook his head. "Nobody there, only a server and a satellite internet setup. What I gather from the neighbor a half a mile away is that Old Man Huddleston died in his sleep and no one found him until he'd stopped picking up his mail for two weeks."

Garner continued the story. "The mailman notified the sheriff who checked on him and found him in his lounge chair, dead. No one turned off the electricity or gas to the place and someone has been mailing in the payments with cashier's checks."

"The satellite internet is a hack job. Someone with a little know-how is tapped into several satellites. No subscription or paid service."

"Seems like a lot of trouble to keep a social media site up and running."

"And anonymous," Hack said.

"After the demonstration yesterday, I ran into Vanders's wife at the grocery store. She was stocking up on pantry staples, as if she was getting ready for a big snowstorm. I asked her if she'd seen the internet reports about the demonstration. She laughed and said she rarely looked at their computer and didn't know how to use it, anyway."

"That rules out Vanders's wife, but not Vanders himself as the one who'd been leaving threats with Charlie."

"You would think he would have singled me out more at the tavern, if he was angry with me," Charlie pointed out.

"We're still researching Don Sweeney. There's not much on him."

Caveman nodded. "He was the other name I came out of the demonstration with. He's younger and likes to hear himself get loud. He might be in his late twenties. I imagine he knows a little about the internet. Most kids under thirty have been exposed to computers and the internet. Hell, most of them can run circles around me."

Hack turned to face the others. "I found his name on a list of recent layoffs from the Apex Pipeline Authority. I traced him through state birth records. He's the son of a local cattle rancher, Raymond Sweeney, who fell on hard times and had to sell several hundred acres to pay for his wife's cancer treatments. Apparently Don wanted to work on the ranch but had to take a job with the pipeline as soon as he left high school.

His mother died last year. Don was laid off this year when the oil prices plummeted."

Ghost narrowed his eyes. "Has he had any run-ins with the law?"

"He had a DUI when he was nineteen, right after his brother died in a farming accident," Hack said, "But other than that, nothing else showed up on his record."

"No tie-in between him and the server setup at the Huddleston place?" Charlie asked.

Caveman rubbed his fist into his opposite palm. "Want me to have a talk with the man?"

"Supposedly, he's up in Montana looking for work in Bozeman."

"Can you verify that?" Charlie asked.

"Already did. His credit card purchases are around the Bozeman area as late as this morning."

Charlie shook her head and drew in a deep breath. "I feel a need for more groceries."

"What?" Ghost shot a glance at her, wondering why the sudden urge to buy more food when she'd been to the store the day before.

A smile tilted Charlie's lips. "Mrs. Penders, one of the owners, is a notorious gossip. If anyone knows anything, she does."

"What are we waiting for?" Ghost turned toward the door.

"*I'm* going. Alone." She gave him a stern look. "She might clam up with both of us hitting her with questions."

Ghost frowned. "I don't like it when you're out by yourself."

"I've been managing on my own for years," she said.

Taking that punch to the gut, Ghost nodded. "Maybe so, but not with someone threatening your life."

"It's walking distance." She pressed her lips together for a moment before adding, "If you want to walk with me, you can." She held up her finger. "But you're *not* going in."

Caveman, Hack and Garner watched their interchange, their lips twisting.

Heat flooded Ghost's cheeks. He didn't like being told what to do. Still, Charlie didn't belong to him. He had no right to order her around. Even if he and Charlie were a thing, he wouldn't be able to control her. She had a mind of her own.

"She'll be okay," Garner reassured. "And you'll be right outside the store."

"Fine." He turned toward the door. "Let's go."

As they descended the stairs to the ground, Ghost worried. "I don't like leaving you unprotected."

"I'll be fine. I have my gun in my purse."

"You carry?"

"I have since before Lolly was born."

He stared at her. He'd taught her how to shoot a 9 millimeter pistol when he'd been back in town seven years ago. She'd been pretty good, even after only one lesson. "Do you practice?"

"Every chance I get. At the very least, I make it a point to go quarterly. I figure it's no use having a weapon if you don't know how to use it."

Ghost chuckled. "Okay. I feel a little better knowing you can defend yourself."

"And Lolly," she reminded him.

"And Lolly," he agreed. "But it doesn't hurt to have someone covering your six."

"Your six?"

"Navy speak for your six o'clock position," he said with a grin.

"Oh, you mean my back." She smiled. "I like it when you go all military on me. As long as you explain it to me. I don't know much about what you do."

His smile faded. "It's probably just as well. Most of it isn't pretty or something you write home about."

She touched his arm. "I hope someday you'll tell me about why you limp."

"That's easy." He shrugged. "Took shrapnel in my thigh."

She shivered. "You say that like it's no big deal."

"It happens in wartime situations."

"It must be hard to go into battle knowing you or some of your friends might not come out alive."

"Not as hard as thinking about the ones we leave behind. Most SEALs aren't worried about themselves."

"They're worried about their families," she said, finishing his thought. "Is that why you pushed me away when you were setting off for your first assignment as a SEAL?"

They walked along the sidewalk in front of the hardware store, their pace slowing as they neared Penders Grocery.

"I knew what I was getting into would be difficult. I couldn't ask you to wait for me. I'd already heard too many stories about SEALs' wives and girlfriends leaving them when they were on deployment. Some came back to an empty house. Others came back to find other men had taken up residence in their beds."

She stopped short, her hands going to her hips. "And you thought I would do that?"

"No. But other women cracked under the pressure of waiting, not knowing if their men were coming back alive or in a body bag."

"So you decided to spare me the pain?"

He nodded.

"Without giving me the choice." She stared at him a moment longer.

Ghost had left her, convinced he was doing the right thing by letting her live her life without the worry of losing him. Looking at the color in her cheeks, the anger blazing from her eyes, he decided he might have been wrong.

They'd arrived in front of the grocery store.

"Are you sure you don't want me to go in with you? I can keep my distance while you're talking to Mrs. Penders."

She dropped her hands from her hips, inhaled and exhaled before she responded. "I'm quite capable of taking care of myself, and making my own decisions. And have you ever considered that you might need someone back home to cover your six? To be there when you get back and to take care of you when you were wounded?"

He stiffened. "What if I'd lost my leg or an arm? Or hell—what if I came back a paraplegic?"

"You'd still be you where it counts." She touched his chest. "And Lolly would have had a father."

"Lolly has a father. And I want to be a part of her life."

Charlie nodded. "I was wrong to keep her from you, but now isn't the right time to break that to her. We have to figure out who the hell is stirring up trouble. When the dust settles, we'll figure out how to make sure you get to see her." She lifted her chin and stuck her hand out. "Deal?"

He took her hand in his and yanked hard enough to pull her off balance.

Charlie fell into his chest, her hand trapped between them.

"Deal." He pressed a kiss to her lips, taking her mouth with a searing-hot passion he hadn't felt since the last time they'd been together. Whatever happened with the stalker, Ghost refused to walk away from this woman ever again. It had taken him seven years to figure out what was wrong with him, why he felt like he was walking through life with a hole in his chest. He'd been missing a part of himself. The part that was Charlie.

He broke off the kiss, wanting to say so much to her, but the timing wasn't right. Somehow, it never felt right. "Go. Before I say to hell with it and take you back to your house and make crazy love to you."

She stared up at him, her tongue sweeping across her bottom lip. "And that's a bad idea?"

"When someone's after you and we don't know who it is?" He nodded. "Probably not a good idea. See if Mrs. Penders has anything to go on. Find out who has been having trouble besides Vanders."

She cupped his face with her palm. "After all of this, we need to talk."

"Damn right we do," he said. Then he turned her and gave her a gentle nudge toward the store entrance.

Chapter Ten

"Charlie!" Mrs. Penders exclaimed.

Still reeling from Ghost's kiss, Charlie had barely entered the store when the older woman swept her into her arms and hugged her.

"I heard about what happened in the tavern with LeRoy." She stood back and stared at Charlie, running her gaze over her as if searching for injuries or blood. "You're not hurt, are you?"

"No, I'm fine. No bullets were fired. No blood was shed."

"I heard LeRoy went crazy with the sheriff and threatened to shoot him."

Charlie nodded, encouraging the woman to go on about the earlier tussle with the angry Mr. Vanders. "I can't get over how LeRoy behaved toward the sheriff."

"He's just the first rancher in the county to stand up to the law. The man has to be feeling pretty desperate. With his cattle confiscated, he has no way to support his family."

"He said there were others who felt the same. What did he mean by that?" Charlie asked. "Are there more people in the county struggling to make ends meet?"

"Oh, sweetie, there are so many."

"How could I not know this?"

"Most of them keep their troubles to themselves." Mrs. Penders leaned close. "But I hear things as they check out here at the grocery store."

Charlie almost felt guilty for prying into her neighbors' affairs. But it if helped to find Rebecca's attacker and her own stalker, then so be it. "What do you hear?"

"The Parkers are selling their prized, registered quarter horses to pay the mortgage on their place. Because of the increased fees per head of cattle, they aren't making enough off the sale of their steers to keep feeding all of their horses and pay the bills."

"Circle C quarter horses?" Charlie's stomach fell. "They've raised quarter horses for a century."

Mrs. Penders nodded. "I imagine Ryan's grandfather is turning over in his grave. And then there's Bryson Rausch."

"The richest man in the county? I remember his daughter driving a Cadillac convertible to high school. He's having trouble?"

Mrs. Penders nodded, glanced around at the store to make sure no one else was listening. "He bet on the wrong stock in the market and lost everything."

Mr. Rausch had always been very nice to Charlie when she'd run into him in town or at the county fair. Though she'd been envious of his daughter Sierra, she'd always liked Mr. and Mrs. Rausch and hated to know they were in financial trouble.

"Then there's Timothy Cramer," Mrs. Penders went on.

Charlie frowned. "Timothy?"

"Goes by Tim. You might have known his wife, Linnea."

"Oh, yes. Linnea." Her frown deepened. "Her second child died of SIDS not long ago."

Mrs. Penders nodded. "So tragic. It broke Linnea's heart and busted up their marriage."

"That's awful."

"Tim went on a drinking binge and disgraced himself with

some floozy in Bozeman. Linnea tried to forgive him, but she couldn't. Not when he didn't even show up for the baby's funeral. She filed for divorce and took half of everything he owned. He's having to sell his grandmother's farm north of town because he can't afford to buy her out. And to add to his misery, he worked as an inspector for the pipeline and lost his job when he was caught falsifying reports.

"The Vanderses and the Parkers aren't the only ones hurting from the increase in range grazing fees. The Mathis family, the Herringtons, Saul Rutherford and the Greenways are all angry with the changes made by the Bureau of Land Management. They can't afford to pay the fees and they can't afford to lease private land. They'll end up selling their cattle at a loss and not having a way to support their families and pay their mortgages next year."

"I'm so sorry to hear that. It makes me sick to know so many are hurting."

"And some are more vocal than others. I wasn't surprised when I heard LeRoy was hauled off to jail. He was a powder keg set to go off. Thankfully someone stopped him from taking others down with him."

"Are there any others as angry and vocal as Mr. Vanders?" Charlie asked.

A customer walked into the store and waved at Mrs. Penders. She waved back and lowered her voice. "Oh, sure. Ernie Martin is angry because the government cut subsidies to his production of angora wool. He's been raising those goats for the past couple of years, making a killing and spending it as fast as he made it. But the money comes from the subsidies, not from the goats or the wool. Now that he's been cut off, he needs it more than ever to make payments on the second mortgage he took out to purchase all of those goats. Ernie's been madder than a hornet about losing the subsidies. He was forced to take a job with the pipeline company, but was laid off when the gas prices dropped. The poor man has had nothing but bad luck."

"Anyone else?" Charlie pushed, knowing she was running out of time with Mrs. Penders. As soon as her customer came to the counter, she'd be interrupted and remember she had a store to run and clean.

"Just about any of those folks who were tagged with bigger grazing right fees. None of them are happy. And they don't know where they'll get the money to pay the fees. Some of them have said they'll stand and defend their herds of cattle from being confiscated by the BLM. Some are willing to die." Mrs. Penders clucked her tongue. "I've never seen people so hot or determined."

"Mrs. Penders. Charlie, what are you ladies doing?" Linnea Cramer stepped up to the counter, carrying a quart of orange juice and carton of eggs. "You two look entirely too intense. What's going on?" Then her eyes widened. "Oh, wait. You have to be talking about the near-shooting at the tavern this morning. Is that it?" Linnea leaned closer. "I heard that you were there when Vanders tried to shoot the sheriff. Someone said Jon Caspar was there and subdued the man. You weren't hurt, were you?"

Charlie smiled and shook her head. "I'm fine. I feel sorry for Mr. Vanders. He was not happy about his cattle being taken."

"We're all struggling a little from the economy tanking and the oil prices falling. People in this area don't have a lot of choices for jobs. That's why we lose so many young people to the bigger cities."

Mrs. Penders squeezed Charlie's hand. "I was so glad to see you come home to Grizzly Pass."

Charlie's eyes misted as she hugged the older woman. "Mrs. Penders, you're so sweet to say that." She moved away to allow Linnea to reach the counter with her purchases.

"I wish I could say I was happy to be in Grizzly Pass, but I'm not. As soon as my ex-husband sells his property, I'm free to go wherever I choose."

"And where will that be?" Mrs. Penders asked, adding Linnea's grocery items as they spoke.

"I think I'll move to Seattle. At least there I can go to the theater, visit a museum and see the ocean whenever I want."

"I thought you liked it here in Grizzly Pass," Mrs. Penders said.

Linnea's lips thinned. "I did. But things change." She shoved the items across the counter toward Mrs. Penders.

"Is this all?" the store owner asked.

"All I can afford for now," Linnea said.

Mrs. Penders placed the items into bags and counted out Linnea's change. "I hope things work out for you."

Charlie touched Linnea's arm. "I hope you find the happiness you're searching for."

"Me, too. And the same to you, Charlie. At least, in our daughters, we have someone to love, who loves us unconditionally. Count your blessings. I know I would." She gathered her bags and left the store in a hurry, her eyes suspiciously shiny.

"Poor woman. To lose her second baby and her husband all in less than six months. Thankfully, her first child keeps her grounded." Mrs. Penders transferred her gaze to Charlie. "Here I've been talking all this time. What did you come into the store to get?"

Charlie glanced at the clock on the wall. She'd been there the better part of half an hour. Already it was getting close to lunch and time to collect Lolly. She thought about everything happening in her community, the families falling apart, losing their homes and loved ones. All she wanted to do was gather hers closer. She couldn't wait until her parents were back from their river cruise in Europe. For now, she wanted to spend time with Lolly and Ghost. "I was wondering if you had something I could take out on a picnic. I'm feeling the need to spend time with my family."

Mrs. Penders smile spread across her face. "All of the gloom and doom talk getting to you? You're a smart woman to put your family first." She grabbed Charlie's hand and walked her to the bakery section of the store where she and her husband stocked the glass cases with fresh bread and pastries. "Let me make up some sandwiches and a tub of potato salad and baked beans for you to take with you."

While she waited, Charlie thought about all of the people she knew who had reason to be mad at the world, who might want to take it out on the government. Their list of suspects had grown from one or two to what felt like an entire town. Her heart ached for all of them. But it made it abundantly clear that she, as a mother, needed to focus on what was most important. Her family.

GHOST HAD FOUND a bench in front of the hardware store and settled back to keep an eye on Penders Grocery. In the meantime, he watched as people passed in cars, trucks or on foot. Some stopped to say hello and renew acquaintances with Ghost, taking him for a short stroll down memory lane before they moved on to conduct their business or duck into the tavern for an early lunch.

He'd been there for five minutes when a man around his own age, stopped by and sat next to him. "Heard you were back in town." He held out his hand. "Tim Cramer. You might not remember me. I was a couple years ahead of you in school."

"I remember. You were our star quarterback. You helped the Grizzlies win state that year for the first time in nobody could remember how long."

Tim's lips turned upward on the corners. "That was a long time ago. Back when nothing could stop us." He stared out at Main Street. "What about you? What brings you back to this hellhole?"

"Felt like visiting the place I grew up," Ghost said.

Tim's lip lifted in a half smile bordering on a sneer. "Not someone in particular?"

Ghost shrugged. "Not really." Not at first, anyway. Now that he was there, he wanted to spend all of his time with Charlie and Lolly.

"Didn't you join the Navy?" Tim asked.

Ghost nodded.

Tim glanced his way. "What happened with that?"

"Injury sidelined me."

"Sorry to hear that." He leaned back again. "I hope you're not looking for a job. You'll have to get in line. Half the men in the county are unemployed or barely making it by."

"That's what I'm hearing," Ghost said. "They don't have to worry about me taking their jobs. I won't be here more than a week."

"Yeah, well, enjoy your vacation and tell Charlie hello. See ya around." Tim rose from the bench and walked away, his hands in his pockets.

Ghost remembered Tim as being a lot bigger. Or was it that Ghost had been a lot smaller, being three years behind him in high school? The man had been cordial and friendly, but something about him struck Ghost wrong. He tried to pinpoint it, but he couldn't. Soon Charlie emerged from the store with a sack full of food.

"What did you find out?" he asked.

"Let's go to Garner's loft before we talk." She crossed the street and stopped at Ghost's truck. He unlocked it and helped her load the bags into the back seat.

She led the way up the stairs to where they found Hack and Garner bent over a computer screen.

"Anything?" Charlie asked.

"We did some digging into LeRoy Vanders's family. Seems his sons have been in trouble with the law on more than one occasion. Some of their arrests include driving under the influence." Hack read through a report he had up on one of the monitors. "Both Vernon and Dalton have a couple of DUIs each. Vernon has been arrested on multiple occasions for hunting out of season and poaching on federal land. Dalton has been in several fistfights and has a restraining order against him. LeRoy's oldest son did some time in federal penitentiary, for shooting at a law enforcement officer."

Garner nodded toward Charlie. "What did you learn from Mrs. Penders?"

She listed a number of names and circumstances that made the men potential suspects. One jumped out at Ghost.

"Tim Cramer?"

Charlie nodded. "Divorce. He's losing his daughter and half of everything he owns, including the land and house his grandmother left him."

"I spoke with him while waiting for you to come out of the store."

Charlie's eyes narrowed. "What did he say?"

Ghost shrugged. "Nothing incriminating. He asked if I was looking for work and told me I'd have to get in line since half the men in the county were unemployed. He also told me to say hello to you." He captured Charlie's gaze. "I couldn't read anything into what he said."

"I ran into his ex-wife in the store. Was he watching for her to come out, do you think?"

"Was that the woman who came out before you did?"

"Yes."

"No, he was gone before she emerged."

"We'll look into his background and see if we can come up with anything." Garner half sat on the edge of a table, his leg dangling over. "I feel like we're searching for the needle in the haystack."

"I checked the Vanderses' utility bills," Hack said. "They have a phone line and internet. They are all on the same plan. They might be involved in whatever takeover they're planning, but we don't know if it's one of them, or all of them. And we don't know if they are computer savvy enough to tap into Charlie's webcam. That takes more sophistication and technical knowledge."

"Check Cramer, Rausch and Parker," Charlie said. "Any one of them would have to be computer savvy to do their business. Raising prized horses would require a website and email in these times. A man who makes and loses his wealth in the stock market is heavily involved with technology. And a man working for the pipeline as an inspector has to have the ability to communicate using modern technology."

"On it," Hack said.

"In the meantime, we're heading out to lunch," Charlie said.

Ghost shot a glance her way. "We are?"

She nodded. "After we pick up Lolly."

As they descended the stairs, he asked, "Where are we going for lunch?"

She responded, "Out."

Ghost wasn't sure he liked the vague answer, but he went with it. "Just promise me we're not going into the lion's den."

She shot a sideways glance at him. "Huh?"

"You know. We're not taking Lolly into a potentially dangerous location where crazy men wield guns."

Her lips twitched and a smile spread across her face.

Ghost swallowed hard on the constriction in his throat. This was the Charlie he remembered from seven years ago. Happy, carefree and in love with life.

"Uh, Ghost, we've already done that today. You remember. The tavern?"

He would have laughed at her teasing, but the thought of LeRoy Vanders shooting that gun inside the restaurant where Lolly and Charlie were close enough to be killed with a single bullet made his chest hurt. "Yeah."

She was right, but it wasn't funny.

Lolly was in the middle of playing hopscotch with her girlfriends when they arrived. She dragged her feet, her bottom lip sticking out just a little. "Can I stay longer?"

"No, sweetheart," Charlie said, taking her daughter's hand. "But I have a special surprise I think you'll like."

Lolly's face perked and she hopped up and down. "What is it?"

"My question, exactly," Ghost muttered.

"Now, it wouldn't be a surprise if I told you, would it?" Charlie winked at Lolly and lifted her chin when she glanced toward Ghost.

He liked this teasing, fun Charlie. She didn't seem as weighted by responsibility. She appeared to be making an effort to include them in the fun.

Ghost went along with her. "Come on, sugar bear." He swung Lolly up in his arms and carried her toward the truck. "The sooner we get going, the sooner we discover what this big surprise is."

Minutes later they were on the road heading toward Charlie's house.

As Ghost neared the turn, Charlie put her hand on his arm. "Keep going."

"Where to?" he asked.

"I think you'll know when you get there." She sat back in her seat. "Follow the highway heading south out of town."

He increased his speed as he left the town limits and hit the open road. Before long, his instincts knew where they were going without Charlie telling him. "We're going to the Dry Gulch Ranch, aren't we?"

She smiled.

His chest tightened, his mind filling with memories of growing up on the Dry Gulch Ranch. Five generations of Whitakers had owned the ranch. Ghost's father had worked for the fourth of the five. Ghost had grown up with Trace Whitaker, riding horses, swimming in the creek, hunting and fishing on the Dry Gulch. They'd been best friends even though his father had worked for Trace's father.

"Has Trace returned from his stint in the Army?" Ghost asked.

"Not yet. But the foreman is aware we're coming out and

Trace left word with him that you're welcome to have run of the ranch anytime you're home on leave."

"I haven't been back since my parents moved away."

"It hasn't changed a whole lot. I came out once to help the foreman's wife set up her new computer."

Ghost focused his attention on maneuvering through the huge gate with the cattle guard over the road. Then he drank in the view leading up to the first place he'd ever called home. The winding drive through pastures with the mountains as a backdrop was forever seared into his memory.

He rolled down the window to smell the scent of the pinion pines as he neared the ranch housing compound. The drive wove through a stand of trees. At the last curve, the trees seemed to part and the big rock-and-cedar house with the wide porches and huge expanses of windows appeared.

To Ghost, it felt like coming home. He turned before he reached the house and drove around to the back where the foreman's quarters sat near the huge old barn.

Charlie had been right. Nothing much had changed, except one major item. His parents wouldn't be there to welcome him and he wasn't home. This was another foreman's lodgings now.

Still, the surprise was one he could enjoy anyway.

Jonesy, the wiry cowboy with salt-and-pepper hair who'd taken over from Ghost's father, met them in front of the barn with a friendly smile.

Charlie helped Lolly out of the truck while Ghost went to greet the older man.

"Jon Caspar, you're a sight for sore eyes." Jonesy had been one of the ranch hands Ghost's father had trained to take over his position as foreman. He'd been there as Ghost was growing up on the ranch.

Ghost engulfed the man in a hug. "How are you and Mrs. Jones?"

"The missus is doing fine. She would have been here, but she's in Bozeman picking up some ranch supplies and some fabric for her quilting bee or some such nonsense." He stepped back and looked at Ghost. "You look great. The Navy must be treating you right." His smile slipped. "Heard you were injured." He tilted his head from side to side, his gaze skimming over Ghost. "Nothing permanent, I hope."

Ghost laid a hand on his leg. "Took a bit of shrapnel to the thigh. I'll be okay." He didn't go into the detail of how long the doctors spent in the operating room removing all of the shards of metal and reattaching major veins. Or the physical therapy it took to get him back to where he was, standing on his own two feet, with only a limp.

He knew he still had a long way to go before they would allow him to return to his unit. Hell, he still had to face the Medical Review Board. They might decide to medically retire him. He refused to think of that now. Not when the sun was shining and he could smell the hay in the barn and the earthy scent of horse manure.

"I saddled a couple of horses and a pony for your ride. I think you'll like the ones I picked." Jonesy's brows drew down. "I didn't think about it, but can you ride with your injury?"

Ghost wasn't sure. "I'll let you know after I've given it a try."

"I gave you a gentle gelding, and Charlie has one of our sweetest-tempered mares."

"What about me?" Lolly asked, her eyes wide, excited.

Jonesy bent to Lolly's level. "You get to ride Annabelle, a rescue pony Mr. Whitaker insisted on giving a home. She's just the right size for a little girl like you." He straightened and gave Charlie a direct look. "Annabelle is very well trained and will behave herself with the little one."

Charlie smiled. "I know you wouldn't give Lolly anything she couldn't handle. She's been taking riding lessons at the Red Wagon Stables on the other side of town, so she knows a little bit about sitting in the saddle and handling the reins."

"That's great. You can't start them too young. If you ever want to come ride, you can come out here. Mr. Whitaker would like knowing his horses are getting some exercise besides what me and the missus are giving them."

Charlie shifted the bag she carried into one arm and hugged the man with the other. "Thank you, Jonesy. It's good to see you. I don't get out here nearly enough." She glanced down at what she was carrying. "I brought the food for a picnic. I don't suppose you have an old blanket and some saddlebags?"

"A picnic?" Lolly clapped her hands. "We're going on a picnic."

"When you called to tell me what you wanted to do, I got things ready for you. The saddlebags are on Jon's horse and the blanket is tied to the back of yours."

"Thank you." Charlie kissed the older man's cheek.

A moment later, Jonesy brought out the horses and the pony and tied them to a hitching post.

Ghost helped Charlie put the food in the saddlebags and then he stood at the ready while Lolly mounted the chocolate brown pony with the cream-colored mane and tail. Annabelle stood patiently while Lolly settled into the saddle.

Jonesy adjusted the stirrups to fit her legs and handed her the reins. "If you tap her gently with your heels, she'll walk. Pull back on the reins when you want her to stop."

"I learned this at my lesson," Lolly said. She tapped her heels and the pony moved forward.

Lolly's grin filled Ghost's heart with joy. He'd never thought about children of his own, but deep down, he'd wanted them, and he'd wanted his children to ride horses and have a love of the outdoors.

Ghost held the mare's head while Charlie mounted. Then he approached the gelding, praying he could hoist himself into the saddle. Thankfully, it was his right leg that had been damaged the most. He set his boot in the stirrup and swung his leg over. So far, so good. He had trouble setting his right foot in the stirrup, but eventually managed. "Where to?"

Charlie shook her head. "You know the ranch better than I do. Lead the way."

Jonesy opened the pasture gate for them and waited as Charlie and Lolly passed through. When Ghost rode abreast of him, he leaned toward him. "Take them to the pool in the creek where you and Trace used to swim. That's about the prettiest place on all of the ranch."

Ghost nodded. "You're right. I will."

Jonesy glanced up at the clear blue sky. "The weatherman calls for rain this afternoon."

"We'll be back before then," Ghost said.

"If you get caught up on the mountain—"

"I know of a place we can hole up until we can get down."

Jonesy smiled and nodded. "You should. You spent most of your youth in those hills." His smile faded. "Keep an eye out for bears. I've seen bear scat and claw marks on trees out that direction. They're around."

"Will do," Ghost promised.

Jonesy closed the gate behind them and headed back to the barn.

Ghost nudged the gelding into an easy trot to catch up with the others. When they came abreast, he was glad when the horse settled into a steady walk. The constant jolt of a trot was too hard on his recovering leg.

The three of them ambled across the pasture, their pace set by the pony.

Ghost pointed to wildflowers and trees, naming them for Lolly. She asked questions, curious about the birds and the ground squirrels they saw along the way. They spied antelope in the distance and admired a bald eagle flying overhead.

By the time they arrived at the creek pool it was well past lunchtime. As soon as they tied the horses to the bushes, they worked to spread the blanket over the grass and set out the food Mrs. Penders had prepared for their picnic.

Ghost ate in silence, enjoying the sounds of the birds and the rustle of leaves as a gentle breeze rippled through the branches. When they finished, they packed the leftover food in the saddlebag and set it aside.

Charlie stretched out on the blanket, her arms crossed behind her head, a smile lifting the corners of her lips.

Lolly played nearby, skipping stones in the pool.

Ghost leaned up on one elbow, his gaze on Charlie, Lolly in his peripheral vision. "I understand why my parents moved to Florida, but I can't help thinking that this is as close to heaven as you can get."

She closed her eyes, her smile widening. "I thought you might like to get away from town for a little while."

"What made you think of coming here?"

Her smile slipped as she looked up at him. "After listening to Mrs. Penders talking about all the troubles people were having, I needed a pick-me-up, and I figured you could use one, too. Life's too short to go around looking for what's wrong with it. If you just open your eyes, you can see the beauty all around you."

Ghost nodded, soaking in the beauty that was Charlie. "I agree."

"Seriously, look around us. Have you seen anything more beautiful?"

"Never."

She turned toward him. "You're not looking at the trees and the sky."

"No. I'm not." He touched her cheek with the back of his knuckles. Her skin was as soft and smooth as it had been seven years ago. And her lips... He bent to taste them.

She didn't resist. Instead, she opened to him and met his tongue with her own in a long, languid caress that stirred his blood and made his heart beat faster.

Eventually, he lifted his head to stare down at her.

"Remember the last time we were here?" she asked, cupping his cheek with her palm.

He nodded. "We skinny-dipped in the pool."

She smiled. "Uh-huh. I think this is where Lolly was conceived."

He shook his head, his heart full to bursting. He glanced across at Lolly, the beautiful little girl with hair as fiery as her mother's.

A movement behind the child made Ghost refocus his attention on the dark brown woolly mass on the other side of the pool, rearing up on its hind legs.

Grizzly!

Chapter Eleven

Ghost lurched to his feet. "Lolly," he said, his voice low and urgent. "Lolly," he said a little louder.

She was bending over picking flowers.

Charlie rolled to her feet and stared in the direction Ghost was looking. Her gasp indicated she'd seen what he was looking at. She started forward, but Ghost put out a hand to stop her. "Get to the horses and be ready to mount with Lolly. I'm going to distract the bear while you two get away."

"You can't run on that leg. I should distract her while you and Lolly get away."

"Just do it," he said, his voice low, his tone unbending.

Charlie left the blanket and the saddlebag and eased toward the horses, quickly untying them from the bushes.

Lolly had yet to see the grizzly. She glanced up and looked in Ghost's direction. "Aren't these pretty?" she called out.

Ghost froze, his gaze on the grizzly across the pool from Lolly. Then he saw movement in the brush behind the big bear. Two cubs emerged.

Holy hell. It was a mama grizzly and her two cubs. Lolly was in mortal danger.

"Lolly, look at me," Ghost said. He bent to gather the saddlebag and blanket. "Sweetheart, go to the horses." In a commanding tone, he said, "Now."

She frowned, looked down at the flowers and back up at him, "But—"

"Now," he repeated swinging wide, away from Lolly toward the narrower end of the pool. If the grizzly charged, it would be slowed by the deeper water. In which case, Lolly would have time to run to the horses. Hopefully, Charlie would get her in the saddle and the hell out of there before the grizzly cleared the pool.

If the bear was smart enough to go around to the shallow end, she'd focus her ire on Ghost and he'd use the saddlebag and the blanket as distractors to give himself time to get away.

That was the plan and the backup plan. It was up to the bear to make the first move.

Lolly frowned and started toward the horses.

The grizzly mama roared and ran into the water.

Lolly spun toward the sound, saw the grizzly and screamed.

"Run!" Ghost yelled.

"Run, Lolly!" Charlie said. She had the horses' reins in her hands. They'd spotted the grizzly and were dancing backward, pulling her away from Lolly.

The girl seemed to be frozen for a moment. Then she dropped the flowers, turned and ran as fast as her little feet could carry her, straight for her mother.

The grizzly started into the water. When it got too deep, she changed direction toward the shallow, narrow end where Ghost was waiting. He waved the blanket, catching her attention.

The bear roared again and ran toward him.

Ghost took off, pain shooting through his bum leg. Too late, he remembered he wasn't as agile as he used to be. He sure as hell couldn't outrun a grizzly. His only hope was to fool her into attacking the blanket while he climbed a tree. He wasn't fool enough to believe she wouldn't climb up after him, so he'd have to make the blanket convincing enough to keep her occupied while he made good his escape.

The mama bear roared again and charged out of the deeper water toward him.

Ghost ran for the brush. As he passed a big bush, he lifted the blanket letting it catch the wind enough to spread it out, then he laid it down over a tall bush and ran behind it.

Moving from bush to bush, he ran as fast as he could, careful not to let the grizzly see him. When he reached a tree he thought he could climb, he popped his head above the bushes enough to locate the grizzly.

She was mad, slapping at the blanket and the bushes with her murderous claws. Once she'd ripped the blanket to shreds, she reared up on her hind legs again and gave another terrifying roar.

Ghost eased himself up into the tree, reaching only for the branches on the far side of the thick trunk. Several times he leaned around the side to spy the grizzly sniffing through the bushes, trying to find him.

He kept climbing, higher and higher. The narrower the branches, the less likely the grizzly could reach him. Despite common misconception, he knew grizzlies could climb trees. It was harder for them than for the black bears, because of their giant claws, but they could climb. His best bet was not to draw attention to himself.

When he'd gone as high as he could, he stopped and remained absolutely still.

The bear kept coming, her nose to the ground, sniffing for him. When she reached the base of the big tree, she circled it several times, sniffing and looking up into the branches.

Ghost held his breath, praying she didn't see him and hoping Charlie and Lolly had gotten far enough away that the grizzly couldn't easily catch up to them.

Several minutes crept by. The bear reared on her back legs

and hugged the base of the tree. For a heart-stopping moment, Ghost thought she would climb.

Then the sound of a cub calling out in the woods came to him and the grizzly at the same time.

For a moment, she continued to stare up into the branches of the tree. With one last roar, she dropped to all fours and hurried toward the sounds of her cubs.

Ghost watched her until he couldn't see her anymore. Then he gave it another two or three minutes before he eased his way down through the branches. As he got close to the ground, he paused, took a moment to scan the area. When he was absolutely positive the bear had gone, he slipped to the ground and crept through the woods, making his way toward the pool. The grizzly and her cubs had moved on.

Ghost walked back along the trail they had arrived on earlier, hoping to catch up to Charlie and Lolly. His leg ached and the clouds had settled in over the hills.

Soon fat drops splattered on the ground and in his face. Part of him hoped Charlie and Lolly had gone back to the barn. Another part hoped they were just ahead of him on the trail.

The drops turned to a deluge of cold rain soaking through his clothes, chilling him to the bone.

He was wiping his eyes for the tenth time when he glanced up to see dark masses blocking the trail ahead. For a moment his heart skipped several beats. His first thoughts were of the bear and her cubs. Then he could make out the shapes of two horses and a pony, a woman leading them and a little girl huddled close to her mother's legs.

Limping faster, Ghost hurried toward them. "Charlie! Lolly!"

They turned as one and ran toward him, flinging their arms around him.

"We were so scared," Lolly said, her words coming out on a sob.

"Are you all right?" Charlie asked, rain streaming down her

face. She leaned back and studied him, her gaze going over him from head to foot.

"I'm fine. I don't think I've climbed a tree that fast since I was a kid." He grinned and lifted Lolly into his arms. "Come on, I know of a hunting cabin close by. We can take shelter until the storm passes."

He settled Lolly on the pony, helped Charlie into her saddle and pulled himself up onto his horse.

Within a few minutes, he'd found the cabin they'd used during the fall hunting season, years ago. The door opened easily and the inside was dry, even if it wasn't warm. Fortunately, someone had stacked dry cordwood next to the potbellied stove. Matches and tinder were right where they had always been. Soon Ghost had a fire going and the interior of the cabin grew cozy warm.

The one-room structure had two twin beds, the thin mattresses folded over to keep the dust from settling on the surface.

Charlie stood at the window, staring out at the rain coming down. "It doesn't look like it will let up soon and it'll be getting dark soon."

Ghost removed his soaked shirt and hung it on a nail on the wall, close to the stove. "We might as well get comfortable. Looks like we'll be spending the night."

Lolly sat on one of the two chairs, her eyes wide. "Will the bear find us here?"

"No, sweetheart," Charlie reassured her.

"If she does, will she break down the door?" Lolly shivered.

"You'll be okay here in the cabin," Charlie said. "She only chased us because she was protecting her babies."

"I'm scared," Lolly whispered, a violent shiver shaking her body.

Charlie smoothed a hand over her daughter's damp head. "You know what I do when I'm scared?"

Lolly shook her head.

"I get busy." She drew Lolly to her feet. "Let's get these beds ready to sleep in."

Ghost pitched in to help them shake the dust from the mattresses. They found sleeping bags rolled up in an airtight plastic container in one of the corners. On one of the shelves they found cans of beans and corned beef and hash. Another shelf contained a pot and an old, manual can opener. Soon, they had dinner of beans and corned beef and hash.

Charlie stripped Lolly out of her damp clothing and tucked her into a sleeping bag. She hung the items near the stove to dry.

With the warmth of the fire, a full belly and the people he loved surrounding him, Ghost couldn't think of a place he'd rather be.

Could he have a different life than that of a SEAL? Was he ready to leave it to the younger, more agile men coming out of BUD/S training?

He looked around at the small cabin, tucked away from the world and realized this was his world. These were the people he cared most about. He wasn't sure of what he'd do career-wise, but he would take into account the need to be with his daughter. If Charlie gave him a second chance, he'd spend the rest of his life making up to her for the past seven years.

CHARLIE ARRANGED THE sleeping bags over the thin mattresses and settled Lolly into one of the small beds.

Lolly reached out for her mother's hand. "Will you sleep with me?"

"You bet." Charlie had already decided the beds were too small for her to sleep with Ghost. With Lolly in the same room, she didn't think it right for her to be in bed with a man who was more or less a stranger to her daughter.

She lay down beside Lolly, pulled her close and sang the soft ballad she'd sung to her daughter since she was a tiny baby.

Ghost settled in the bed beside them and turned on his side, his gaze on her and his daughter.

Soon, Lolly's breathing grew deeper and her body went limp. With her hand tucked beneath her cheek, she slept.

Charlie stared past her to the man who'd risked his life to save them from being mauled by a grizzly. With an injured leg, he'd run through the woods, providing a sufficient distraction for them to get away.

Her heart squeezed hard in her chest like it had when she'd ridden away with Lolly, not knowing if he would escape the bear. For all Charlie knew, Ghost might have been killed or wounded so badly, he could have been lying on the ground bleeding to death.

She and Lolly had ridden hard, putting half a mile distance between them and the pool where the grizzly had appeared.

About that time, the clouds lowered on them. It began to drizzle and Charlie couldn't go any farther without knowing. She'd turned back the way they'd come, determined to find Ghost. Lolly had been just as worried about him, insisting they go back.

The sky had opened up, dumping rain on them. They couldn't see ahead and the horses slipped on the trail. She'd gotten down from the saddle and set Lolly down beside her. If Ghost was to be found, she had to be close enough to the ground to see him.

When he'd emerged from the deluge, walking toward them, Charlie's heart had nearly exploded with the joy she'd felt.

She and Lolly had run to him, hugging him close. At that moment, Charlie knew she was still hopelessly and irreversibly in love with the man.

And she'd been terribly wrong to keep news of his daughter from him.

"I'm sorry," she whispered, capturing his gaze in the soft glow coming from the potbellied stove.

His brows dipped. "For what?"

She smoothed a hand over her daughter's drying hair. "For keeping Lolly from you."

"I didn't make it easy for you to come out and tell me," he

said. "I'm sorry I was so selfish when I left, that I didn't consider what I was leaving behind."

"You were just starting your career. You didn't need to be saddled with the worry of a family."

"And you shouldn't have had to go it alone with a child to care for."

"We made mistakes," Charlie said.

"The question is, do we continue to make the same mistakes, or do we make things right?"

His words were softly spoken, but they were heavy, weighing on Charlie's mind. "You still have a career with the military. I can make sure you see Lolly on holidays."

"I want to be with her more than that."

Charlie's gut clenched and her breath caught in her throat. Was he going to sue for custody? God knew he had a right to.

"Being back…being with you…makes me want more." He swung his legs over the side of the little cot and winced. "Being a SEAL used to be everything to me. The training I went through made me want to prove something to my team and to myself. But after the first year or two, I realized there will always be another battle and another enemy to fight. I didn't think it would be right to bring someone else into my personal life, when my life wasn't guaranteed."

"Nobody's life is guaranteed," Charlie argued. "I could be hit by a bus tomorrow. Or worse, we could be targeted by homegrown terrorists. You can't live thinking about what *could* happen. You have to muddle through with what you know and what you have."

"I know that, but a SEAL's life expectancy is a hell of a lot lower than most people's. It wouldn't be fair to subject a loved one to the constant worry."

Charlie stiffened, the heat of anger rising in her chest. "So you make that determination unilaterally? Have you ever thought it isn't fair to exclude a loved one from the decision?"

His lips twisted. "I thought it was the right decision."

"Well, you might be the only one who thought it. If you bothered to include all involved in the decision-making process, you might have come to an alternate conclusion."

Charlie flipped over onto her other side. Her eyes stung and she swallowed hard. She wouldn't cry another tear for Ghost. The man could be so thickheaded. The way he was thinking would doom them to the same mistake they'd made seven years ago. When would he ever learn?

With a child to care for and protect, she couldn't spend her days mooning over a man who couldn't commit.

"Charlie, I've never stopped loving you," he said.

"Yeah, yeah," she muttered, without turning over. "You have a funny way of showing it." The last of her words came out garbled as she choked back a sob.

"Please don't turn away from me," he said.

"I have a job, Lolly has plans for tomorrow and I need sleep. I have two lives to think of. Figure out your own life."

"But—"

"Please," she whispered. "Just leave me alone. I'm too tired to think or argue."

"We're not through with this conversation," he said, his tone firm.

She lay silent, tears slipping down her cheeks. She refused to sniffle. He couldn't know that he was breaking her heart all over again.

Charlie lay awake, pretending to be asleep long after Ghost settled back in his bed.

She hurt so much it was a physical pain she couldn't ignore. Before the sun rose, she was up, looking out the window at the gray light of predawn.

"How long have you been awake?" Ghost whispered.

"Not very." She didn't face him. She couldn't. Her heart weighed heavily in her chest and one little word from the man she loved and she might burst into tears.

"I'm hungry," Lolly said. She stretched in the bed and rubbed her knuckles against her eyelids. "Are we going home?"

"As soon as you get your clothes and boots on, we can start back," Charlie said.

Lolly rolled out of bed and dressed in her dry clothing and then pulled on her pink cowboy boots. "My boots are still wet."

"We'll get you into some dry clothes and shoes when we get back home."

"And breakfast?" Lolly asked.

"And breakfast." Charlie forced a smile to her lips and turned in Lolly's direction. "Ready?"

Ghost had his boots on and had tucked his shirt into his waistband. Without saying a word, he left the little cabin, gathered the horses and waited for Charlie and Lolly to mount before he swung up onto his horse.

They rode down the mountain as the sun edged over the horizon.

Charlie's gaze scanned the hillside and the brush for grizzlies, not wanting a repeat of their encounter from the day before. The ride remained blissfully uneventful.

Jonesy greeted them at the barn, leading a saddled horse, his brows furrowed. "I was just about to ride out to find you three."

"We had a grizzly sighting and got caught in the rain," Ghost informed the man.

Jonesy shook his head. "I'd noticed bear scat in that area, but I'd hoped you wouldn't run into one."

"It was a mama and her two cubs," Lolly said. "She didn't like it that we were around."

"Glad you got away without injury. Some aren't as fortunate." Jonesy grinned. "Did you stay in the hunting cabin?"

Ghost nodded. "I'll bring some canned goods and firewood to replenish what we used."

"No, don't do that. I was going to run some up this week anyway. Glad you found dry wood and something to eat."

"We are, too," Charlie said. "Otherwise it would have been

a much more uncomfortable night." She slid out of her saddle and started to lead the horse into the barn.

"I'll take care of the horses. You three look like you could stand some breakfast. The missus has extra scrambled eggs if you're hungry."

"I'm hungry," Lolly exclaimed.

"Are you sure it's not a bother?" Charlie asked.

"She'd be happy to have someone to fuss over," Jonesy reassured her.

"We can't stay long," Charlie glanced down at Lolly. "Today is the day for the field trip to Yellowstone National Park. We have to be there early."

"I'll hurry," Lolly promised.

They made their way to the foreman's little cottage where Mrs. Jones had breakfast waiting on the table.

"How did you know we were coming?" Lolly asked.

Mrs. Jones blushed. "I was watching through the window."

"We don't want to burden you," Ghost said.

She waved her hands. "It was no trouble at all. We get so few visitors, it's a pleasure to cook for someone else."

Ghost, Charlie and Lolly took seats at the table and dug into the scrambled eggs and thick slices of ham Mrs. Jones served.

Charlie hadn't felt much like eating, but the ham and eggs hit the spot and helped lift her flagging spirits. By the time she left the Dry Gulch Ranch, she was resigned to whatever happened.

Lolly's chatter filled the silence on the drive home.

While Lolly took a quick shower, Charlie changed into dry clothes and shoes, washed her face and brushed her hair back into a ponytail. She'd considered wearing makeup, but decided it was too late to impress a man who wasn't going to stick around. Resigned to going without makeup, she ducked into her office and powered up her computer. Once the monitor flashed to life, she clicked on the URL of the Free America group and scrolled through the messages. She'd just about reached the bottom when Lolly called out.

"I'm ready." Her daughter entered her office wearing jeans and her community center T-shirt and sneakers.

"You were fast," Charlie remarked. She glanced at the computer one last time and frowned.

A message popped up on the group that caught her attention.

Let it begin with a meeting of the mines

A chill slithered down Charlie's spine as she turned toward Lolly. The message wasn't directed at her, this time. It was directed toward the Free America group. So much for assuming LeRoy Vanders was the leader. He was safely in jail with no access to the internet.

Though Charlie wasn't sure what the message meant, one thing was certain, something was about to start. What, she didn't know.

"Come on, Mommy. We're going to be late and miss the trip." Lolly spun on her heels and ran down the hallway.

Charlie rose and met Ghost by the front door where he held Lolly's hand.

What did it mean? Had they meant to spell mines or had it been a misspelling intended to be minds? The hills were dotted with abandoned mines from the gold rush era. "Ready?" Charlie asked, her mind on the message, her stomach churning.

"Yes!" Lolly jumped up and down. "We're going to Yellowstone today. We get to ride on a bus."

Her excitement brought a small smile to Charlie's lips. As she gathered her keys and purse from the hallway table, the phone next to them rang.

Charlie froze, almost afraid to answer. Would it be another harbinger of potential doom? She lifted the phone from the charger. "Hello."

"Charlie, Kevin here."

"Hey, Kevin," she said. "What's up?"

"We have some satellite images that might interest you and Ghost."

Her gaze met Ghost's and a tremor of awareness rippled through her. "We're on our way to town. I have to drop off my daughter at the community center, then we'll be there."

"See you in a few, then." Garner ended the call.

Ghost met her gaze with a question in his eyes.

"He has some satellite images he wants us to look at." She looped her purse over her shoulder and followed Ghost and Lolly outside.

"We can take my Jeep. I feel like driving." She might as well get used to being that single parent again. It wouldn't be long before Ghost left.

Ghost didn't argue, but moved the booster seat from his truck into the backseat of her Jeep and buckled Lolly in.

Once again, Lolly jabbered away. If the adults weren't responding, the little girl was too excited about riding in the bus to notice.

As they neared town, Charlie pulled up in front of the tavern first. "Why don't you get started reviewing the images? I'll be back in less than five minutes."

"I can wait," he said, not budging from the passenger seat.

"Please," she said, staring straight out the front window without looking into his eyes. "I need just a few minutes alone."

He hesitated.

In her peripheral vision she could see his jaw harden and his lips press into a thin line. Then he leaned into the backseat and chucked Lolly beneath her chin. "Have a great time at Yellowstone. Don't pet any bison while you're there."

"Don't be silly. Bison are wild animals," she said.

He climbed out of the Jeep and stood on the sidewalk watching as they drove away.

Charlie felt as if she was leaving him for good, knowing perfectly well she'd be back to study satellite images. But she couldn't help looking at him in the rearview mirror. He looked so sad, and that made her heart hurt even more.

What were they going to do? How could they fix a relationship that wasn't meant to be?

More immediately, she worried about the message.

Let it begin with a meeting of the mines.

Chapter Twelve

Ghost wanted to kick himself. Hard. Last night he could have made things right with Charlie. He could have told her he loved her and wanted to be with her more than he wanted to breathe. Instead, he'd fumbled the pitch and struck out.

She'd dropped him off like she wanted nothing to do with him. If he didn't know better, he'd bet she didn't come back to view the images Garner's team had come up with.

And then there were the threats against Charlie that had him worried. She ran around town without him as if no one would attempt to harm her. And maybe no one would, but that didn't make Ghost any more confident. He had half a mind to jog down to the community center and make sure she was all right. It was only a few blocks. But wait. He wasn't quite up to jogging. Not without a whole lot of pain.

He didn't believe LeRoy Vanders was the one posting the threats. Frankly, the man didn't seem technologically advanced enough to track her back to her webcam. But if not Vanders, then who?

Yeah, he was being foolish. Instead of following her, he climbed the stairs to Garner's office and knocked.

Caveman opened the door. "Good, you're here. You'll want to see this." He stepped aside.

Garner, Caveman and Hawkeye stood at the large monitor mounted on the wall, staring at a satellite image.

Garner glanced over his shoulder. "Ghost, glad you made it. Where's Charlie?"

"She went on to the community center. She'll be here in five minutes."

"Do you want us to wait until she gets here to go over what we found?"

"No, she said to get started without her." Ghost stepped up beside Garner. "What's this a picture of?"

"The mountain between Grizzly Pass and the highway turn-off that leads to Yellowstone National Park. The image is from a week ago." Most of the mountain was dark and dense with lodgepole pine trees. Garner pointed to a place that appeared to be a gash in the landscape. "See this?"

"Looks like an old mining camp," Ghost noted.

"It is. We looked it up. It's the abandoned Lucky Lou's Gold Mine. It played out about forty years ago and has been closed since." Garner glanced back at Hack. "Show two nights ago."

Hack clicked his mouse and the screen in front of the others flickered. For a moment, it appeared unchanged. Until Ghost leaned closer and noticed a change in the mine area.

"Are those vehicles?"

Garner nodded. "We counted half a dozen. And if you look here at that bright dot, we think that's a campfire, and next to it are people. Show the infrared shot," he called out.

Hack clicked and another image appeared with green spots of color. Where the campfire had been was brighter, almost white.

Garner pointed to several smaller dots of green lined up from the back of one vehicle to the side of a hill. "Why would they be lined up at the back of one of the vehicles and all the way to the mine entrance?"

"Are they unloading something?" Ghost asked.

Garner nodded. "That's the only thing we could think of. Caveman, Hawkeye and I are headed out this morning to check on it."

"I want to go," Ghost said.

"Do you think Charlie will be okay without you to keep an eye on her?"

Ghost wrestled with his desire to go with her and his desire to find out what someone was storing in an old mine in the middle of the night. "I'd better stay."

The phone rang in Kevin's office.

Hack lifted it. "Yeah." A moment later, he held it up. "It's for you, Kevin."

The DHS team leader grabbed the phone. "Kevin, here." He listened for a moment and nodded. "Are you sure you'll be all right?" He paused. "Okay. I'll tell him." The man handed the phone back to Hack and turned to Ghost. "That was Charlie. The woman who was scheduled to go with the field trip got sick and couldn't make it. Charlie offered to go with them."

Ghost stiffened. "When are they leaving?"

Garner looked at him. "Now. Do you want to try to catch up to them?"

Ghost hesitated. He didn't have transportation to follow the bus and if he risked running to the community center, he might miss them. Apparently Charlie wanted a little more time to herself without him. "No."

"She should be all right. No one was expecting her to be on that field trip."

"I guess it will have to be all right."

"You could take my SUV if you want to follow and make sure they're safe," Garner offered.

"No." Ghost shook his head. Charlie hadn't wanted him along. "Let's go see what's in that mine."

Garner grabbed his keys. "We can go in my vehicle." He stopped at a large safe near the door and twisted the combination back and forth until it clicked and he opened it. Inside was an arsenal of weapons. He reached in and pulled out an AR-15 military-grade rifle and handed it to Ghost. "We don't know what we're in for at the mine. If they have stashed something illegal or deadly, they might have guards positioned there." He reached in again and handed Caveman another AR-15. To Hawkeye, he handed a specially equipped sniper rifle with a high-powered scope.

Then he moved to a footlocker beside the safe and unlocked the padlock with a key and threw it open. Inside were rifle magazines and boxes of ammunition.

"Most of the magazines are already loaded. Grab what you think you might need. You can load everything into these duffel bags. We don't want to alarm the natives as we carry them out to the SUV."

Ghost wasn't sure what they'd run into at the mine. Being armed to the teeth was better than being outgunned.

Once they had everything they could possibly need for a prolonged standoff with a small army, they headed out the door and down the steps.

Caveman carried the duffel bag with the rifles, Ghost and Garner carried gym bags filled with ammo. Hawkeye carried the case with the sniper rifle. One by one, they loaded them into the back of Garner's SUV.

With the smell of weapons oil in his nostrils and the hard shell of armored plating strapped around his chest beneath his shirt, Ghost closed the hatch.

He'd started around the side of the SUV when an explosion rocked the street.

Ghost automatically dropped to the ground and rolled beneath the SUV. His pulse pounded and flashbacks threatened to overwhelm him with memories he preferred to forget.

For a moment, he was back in that Afghan village, being fired on by a Soviet-made rocket-propelled grenade launcher manned by a Taliban fighter positioned on top of one of the stick-and-mud buildings. He lay pressed to the ground, trying to breathe past the panic paralyzing his lungs.

Chapter Thirteen

Charlie sat beside Brenda Larson in the front seat of the bus headed north toward Yellowstone National Park, wondering what Kevin had found that they'd needed to see. Though she knew Ghost had their best interests at heart, she would have liked to have been there to gauge for herself the importance of the new information.

They were ten miles out of town and the children had settled back in their seats when Brenda hit her with, "So what's up between you and Jon Caspar?"

"What do you mean?" Charlie stalled, not really wanting to talk about Ghost or what was or wasn't happening between them.

"He's back. You're in love." Brenda sat back, her brows raised, her gaze direct, unflinching. "When can we expect an announcement?"

"There won't be an announcement." Charlie stared out the window, her chest tight, her eyes stinging. A tear slipped free and trailed down her cheek. Damn. And she'd promised herself she wouldn't cry that day. The field trip was all about the kids, not her pathetic excuse for a love life. She swiped at the tear and grit her teeth to keep others from falling, hoping Brenda wouldn't see them. Then she glanced at her reflection in the window and Brenda's beside it. Too late, Brenda could see everything in her reflection.

Her friend laid a hand on her arm. "What's wrong, Charlie?"

What was the use holding back now? And she really needed a shoulder to lean on. "He's going to leave again and I love him."

Brenda's face brightened. "Maybe he'll take you with him? Not that I want you to leave Grizzly Pass. Friends our age are hard to come by around here."

"He doesn't think his life is conducive to having a family." Charlie sniffed and wished her voice hadn't sounded so wobbly.

Brenda tilted her head to the side and touched her finger to her chin. "He might have a point. They move around a lot."

Charlie frowned. "You're not helping. Besides, I already knew that."

"He's a Navy SEAL. They are in a high-risk job. He might get killed on a deployment." Brenda smiled. "Perhaps he doesn't want you to be just another military widow."

"He won't give me that choice."

"Would you be okay with him staying in the military?"

"Of course."

"Would you move to be with him when he's not deployed?"

Charlie nodded.

Brenda raised her hands, palms up. "Then what's the problem?"

"He hasn't asked." Another tear slipped down her cheek.

"Have you given him a chance?" Brenda chuckled. "I've seen you when you get all stubborn and hardheaded. It's pretty intimidating."

Charlie thought about how she'd shut Ghost down the night before and how she hadn't encouraged a frank conversation since. "Maybe not."

"Then wipe your tears, have fun with the kids today and when you get home, hit him up with how you feel. If he feels the same, he'll ask you to go with him. If he doesn't, at least you will know and you can stop crying over him."

"You're right." Charlie wiped her tears and straightened, forcing a smile to her face.

She squeezed her friend's hand. "Thank you. I needed someone to talk to."

"Glad to help. Anytime."

The bus lurched, flinging her forward.

Kids screamed and the brakes smoked.

"What the—" Charlie glanced up in time to see a big, army-style dump truck straddling the highway in the middle of a curve.

The bus driver had jammed his foot on the brake and now stood on it in an attempt to stop the bus before it slammed into the truck.

"Hold on!" Charlie yelled and braced for impact.

Brakes smoked and the bus skidded across the pavement toward the truck. With a bluff on one side and a drop-off on the other, they didn't have a choice.

As if in slow motion, the bus went from fast to slow, the truck rising up before them, filling the windshield. Charlie braced herself, but couldn't close her eyes as the bus slowed, slowed, slowed but not fast enough for her. Just when she thought they would crash into the truck, the bus stopped, its front bumper scraping the side of the truck.

When the smoke from the brakes cleared, Charlie sat up and glanced back at the children, her gaze darting to the seat Lolly had occupied with Ashley Cramer and Chelsea Smith. At first she didn't see them. Then, one by one, their heads popped up over the top of the back of the seat in front of them and they looked around.

The rest of the children crawled up off the floor and into their seats, some crying, others looking frightened and disoriented.

Brenda stood and walked toward the back. "Hey, guys. Everyone okay?"

Most children nodded. One little boy shook his head, his nose bleeding, tears streaming down his cheeks.

"Come here, Elijah." Brenda gathered him up into her arms. "For now, stay in your seats until we figure out what's going on. Everything will be all right."

Charlie leaned over the back of the seat and touched the bus driver, Mr. Green's, shoulder. "Are you all right?"

He nodded. "Didn't see that coming." The old man wiped the sweat from his brow and peered through the windshield. "That could have been really bad."

Charlie looked to either side of the truck for a driver to find out why the truck was parked in the middle of a dangerous curve. Movement around the rear of the truck captured her attention and she watched as a man emerged, wearing camouflage pants, camouflage jacket and a black ski mask. He carried a military-grade rifle with a black grip and stock and he was headed straight for the door of the bus.

Charlie's heart fluttered and a cold chill shivered down her spine. "This doesn't look good. I think the truck is the least of our worries."

Another man dressed from head to toe in camouflage followed the first, also wearing a ski mask and carrying a rifle with a curved magazine loaded in it.

They stopped at the bus door.

"Open the door," the guy in front ordered.

The bus driver shook his head, shoved the shift in Reverse and pressed the accelerator.

"Go. Go. Go!" Charlie said.

He popped the clutch in his hurry and the bus engine stalled.

The men holding the rifles pointed them at the door and opened fire.

Charlie staggered backward, the seat hit her in the backs of her knees and she sat hard.

Mr. Green grunted and slumped forward over the steering wheel.

One of the men kicked what was left of the door open and entered the bus. "Stay down and don't move!" he yelled and waved his rifle at the occupants of the bus.

Charlie wanted to go to Mr. Green, but was afraid if she moved, the attackers would open fire in her direction and hit one of the children. So she stayed down, praying Lolly would remain seated.

The second man entered the bus, pulled the driver out of his seat and dragged him to the side. Then he slipped into the driver's seat and started the engine.

The dump truck engine roared to life. The big vehicle turned away from them and lumbered north along the highway until they reached a dirt road on the left. The truck turned onto the road and disappeared between the trees.

Charlie held her breath, as the bus turned as well and followed the dirt road the truck had taken. She wanted to go to Lolly and hold her in her arms, but she didn't want to draw any attention to herself or the children.

The kids sat in silence or softly sobbing, holding on to the seatbacks in front of them as they bounced along the rutted road.

Where were they going? What was going to happen to the children?

Charlie wished Ghost was with them. He'd know what to do. With only two men wielding guns, surely he would have been able to subdue them before they shot Mr. Green. She glanced down at the old bus driver, her stomach knotting.

The man's face was even paler than before and his chest didn't appear to be moving. Dear God, he was dead.

Charlie closed her eyes briefly and prayed for a miracle. Then she opened them and focused on the road ahead. She had to keep her wits about her to ensure the safety of the children.

The bus slowed around a curve in the dirt road and came to an open clearing, facing a giant hill that had been carved away at the base. It appeared to be an old mine.

The hills and mountains of Wyoming were dotted with the

remnants of old gold mines from the gold rush era of the 1860s. This was just one of many that had been abandoned when the gold played out.

The man driving the bus slowed, as he headed toward the entrance to the mine.

Charlie leaned forward, her heart leaping into her throat. "What are you doing?"

"Shut up!" the man wielding the rifle backhanded her, knocking her across the seat.

She picked herself up and watched in horror as he drove right up to the mine, parking the bus so that the door opened into the mine entrance.

The driver parked the bus and clicked on a flashlight.

"Everyone out!" he yelled. He grabbed Mr. Green and dragged him down the steps and into the mine.

Charlie pressed a hand to her bruised cheek. "What are you going to do with us?"

"You have two choices—shut up and get out, or die." He pointed his rifle at her chest.

She raised her hands. "I'm getting out." Charlie eased to the edge of her seat. The rifleman backed up, giving her enough room to pass.

For a moment, she thought of all the self-defense classes she'd taken. None of them had prepared her for the possibility of children being used as target practice or shields. Her instinct was to jam her elbow into the man's gut and shove the heel of her palm into his nose. But she couldn't. If he jerked his finger on the trigger, he could shoot a kid.

Charlie could never live with herself if her actions were the cause of one of these babies being killed. She glanced back at Lolly as she stepped down off the bus.

The man with the flashlight waved Charlie to the side. "Do something stupid and one of these kids will get hurt."

She raised her hands. "Please don't hurt the children. Just tell me what you want me to do. I'll do it."

"Stand over there and keep quiet." He shone the flashlight toward a stack of crates.

Charlie followed the beam and stopped when the light swung back toward the bus.

Three children dropped down from the bus, huddling together, sniffling in the dark. The flashlight swung her way.

Charlie opened her arms and the kids ran into them.

She counted them as they emerged, one by one. When Lolly reached the ground, she looked for her mother.

Charlie nearly cried. Again the flashlight swung her way and Lolly ran to her. Charlie held her in her arms, smoothing her hand over her hair. "It's going to be all right," she whispered. "I promise." Somehow they'd get out of this in one piece. She refused to break her promise to her daughter.

Brenda brought up the rear with Lolly's friends Chelsea and Ashley.

Another man joined the two in camouflage. This one was dressed all in black with a matching black ski mask. He stood beside the other two as Brenda walked by with the two little girls.

He grabbed Ashley and swung her up into his arms. "I'll take this one."

Brenda leaped forward. "Don't you hurt her!"

The man with the flashlight swung it, clipping Brenda in the side of the head.

Brenda crumpled to the ground and lay still.

Chelsea dropped down beside her, crying hysterically.

"Take the brat before I hit her, too," Flashlight Guy shouted.

Charlie rushed forward and dragged Chelsea back to where the rest of the children huddled. She told them to stay where they were and then she eased forward to where Brenda lay with her face down, her eyes closed.

"Get back!" the man with the gun yelled.

Charlie inched back to stand with the cluster of kids and

waited for the men to leave or at least back up enough to let her get to Brenda and the bus driver.

The bus moved away from the opening of the mine and a triangle of sunlight shone in.

Charlie studied everything around her, looking for an escape route, counting the number of men involved, evaluating her options and coming up with no plan that would save twenty children.

Yet another man wearing camouflage stepped into the cave entrance where the original captors stood. He was bigger than first two, and he carried a 9 millimeter pistol. "Where's Cramer?"

"Hell if I know. He drove the truck," Flashlight man said.

"He was here a minute ago," the rifleman said. "Took one of the kids and walked out."

The man muttered a curse. "Dalton, find him. Vern, help me move the plate in place."

"What about them?" Vern said.

"If one of them moves, we'll shoot them," the big man said.

Based on the names they were calling each other, Charlie knew who they were. The Vanders brothers. And it appeared Tim Cramer had come along for the ride in order to steal his daughter away. Charlie would bet Cramer had already escaped the compound with his girl. Dalton wouldn't find them.

For the next few minutes, the two men worked to move a huge metal plate into position over the entrance of the mine.

Charlie took the opportunity to study the boxes lining the walls. She reached into an open one. Inside were sticks of dynamite and dozens of empty cartridge boxes. She searched for a weapon among the boxes, only to find more empty boxes. Another crate contained empty cases of what appeared to have at one time contained new AR-15s. More than the number carried by the men holding them hostage. A lot more. In one crate alone, she counted over twenty empty AR-15 boxes. And there were a lot of crates lining the walls of the mine. What were they planning? A total takeover of the state?

Once the metal door was in place, most of the light was blocked. A little at the top and sides gave just enough for Charlie to make it over to Brenda and Mr. Green. She felt for a pulse on the bus driver. His skin was cold, he lay very still and no matter how long Charlie pressed her fingers to the base of his throat, she couldn't find a pulse. The man was dead.

Her heart hurt for his wife. They were a childless couple who loved each other and their menagerie of dogs.

Moving to Brenda she touched the caregiver's shoulder. "Brenda."

Brenda moaned.

"Sweetie, please. Wake up and tell me you're all right."

She moaned again and rolled onto her back. "Why is it so dark?" she croaked.

"We're in a mine."

"Oh, God." She tried to lift her head but dropped it back to the ground. "The kids?"

"All here and okay, except Ashley Cramer."

"Where's she?" She rolled to her side and tried to push to a sitting position. "Linnea will be frantic."

"I think Tim took her."

"That bastard." Brenda pressed her hand to her lips. "Sorry."

Charlie wanted to say a whole string of curses, but it wouldn't get them out of the mess they were in. "Tim was in on this."

"What is *this*, anyway?" Brenda asked, blinking her eyes before staring around at the walls of the mine.

"The Vanders brothers have taken us hostage. We're in some mine shaft."

"Those idiots?" She tried to get up, but couldn't quite make it on her own. "What do they hope to accomplish?"

"I don't know." Charlie helped Brenda to her feet and she staggered over to the children where she collapsed to a sitting position.

The children gathered around her, all wanting to be held and comforted, every one of them frightened out of their minds.

Charlie knelt beside Lolly. "Are you doing okay?"

She nodded. "Are those bad men going to let us out of this cave?"

"I don't know if they will, but someone will find us and let us out." She hoped it was true. As far as she knew, nobody would know where to look for them.

"Mr. Caspar will find us. He's a real hero."

Charlie hugged her close. "Yes, Lolly, he is." That's what he did. He fought for his country. For her and Lolly and everyone else. He was the real hero.

"Miss Brenda told me." Lolly snuggled against Charlie. "I'm cold."

Charlie rubbed her arms and pulled her closer.

"I hope my daddy comes soon."

Charlie swallowed the lump in her throat to say, "Your daddy?" Had she overheard them talking about her? Had she put the pieces together and guessed?

"Mr. Caspar. He's nice and he's a hero. I want him to be my daddy."

"Oh, baby." Charlie held her tight and fought the tears. She wanted Ghost to be Lolly's daddy, too. And Charlie wanted him to be her husband. If she had another chance, she'd get right to the point and ask him if he would marry them. If he said no, she'd figure out how to live without him. But on the slim chance he said yes, she'd be the happiest woman alive and follow him to the ends of the earth, if that's what it took.

"WHAT THE HELL was that?" Caveman called out from behind a parked pickup.

The sound of the Delta Force soldier's voice penetrated the fog of memories and yanked Ghost back to the present and Grizzly Pass, Wyoming.

Caveman and Hawkeye had sought cover behind vehicles

while Garner knelt near the corner of a brick building. Ghost waited a moment, trying to determine where the sound had come from. When no other explosions shook the ground, he rolled from beneath the SUV and stood.

"Sounded like it came from the south end of town," Garner said.

A siren wailed from the north, heading toward the tavern.

Ghost hurried toward the front of the building in time to see a sheriff's vehicle racing south along Main Street.

"Come on," Garner said. "Let's go check it out."

All four men climbed into the SUV and took off after the sheriff.

At the other end of town people were coming out of their homes and businesses, standing in clumps, talking to each other, holding their small children close. The sheriff's car was positioned at the end of Main Street, blocking traffic from entering or leaving town.

Garner parked a block away. The men piled out and hurried toward one of the abandoned buildings on the edge of town. The front wall had been blown out, the bricks scattered across the street.

Behind them, another siren sounded and the volunteer fire department engine truck rolled down the street, passing them to stop next to the sheriff's vehicle. Firefighters jumped to the ground and started unrolling a long hose.

The sheriff emerged from the building, covered in dust, shaking his head. "You won't need that. Looks like someone set off a stick of dynamite. No fire, no smoke, just a big mess."

Ghost inhaled and let out a long, slow breath and asked, "Why?" He turned to Garner and the others. "Why would someone want to blow up an old building in a little town?"

"Kids bored in the middle of summer?" Caveman offered.

No. Ghost wasn't buying it. Someone had deliberately set that dynamite to blow in that particular building at that particular time.

"It didn't do much damage." Hawkeye studied the scene. "It was an old building not worth anything. Whoever did it, did the town a favor, getting the demolition started."

"Why would they pick this building on the south end of town?" Ghost asked, his mind wrapping around the possibilities and coming up with one. "Unless they were creating a diversion to draw all of the attention away from something."

The radio clipped to Sheriff Scott's shoulder chirped with static. "Sheriff, we have a problem," came the tinny voice.

Sheriff Scott touched the mic. "Give it to me."

Ghost's attention zeroed in on that radio and what was being said, his gut clenching.

"Someone's demanding LeRoy Vanders's release."

"Demanding?" The sheriff snorted. "On what grounds?"

"They want to negotiate his release in exchange for a bus-load of our kids."

The words hit Ghost like a punch in the gut.

The sheriff's face paled and everyone standing in hearing range of the sheriff's radio froze.

"What is he asking for?" Sheriff Scott asked.

"He wants you to bring LeRoy Vanders to Lucky Lou's Gold Mine in one hour, in a helicopter. If you aren't there in exactly one hour, they will blow up the entrance to the old mine with dynamite. With the children inside."

Ghost grabbed Garner's arm. "That's my woman and my kid on that bus."

"We have to work with the sheriff to get those kids to safety," Garner said. He stepped toward Sheriff Scott. "Sir."

"Don't bother me now. I have a crisis to avert." The sheriff hit his mic. "Who the hell can we call with a helicopter?"

Garner got in front of the sheriff. "I can get one in under an hour."

The sheriff looked at Garner and nodded. Then he keyed the mic. "Get Vanders ready. I'll let you know when the helicopter lands." He stared at Garner. "If you're wrong, you might cost us the lives of those kids."

"I can get one from Bozeman in thirty minutes." He gave the sheriff instructions on how to contact his resource at the Bozeman airport. A helicopter would be dispatched in less than ten minutes.

Ghost paced the pavement, desperate to do something. "We can't wait for them to make the trade. What if they decide to bury those kids in the mine anyway? They could have that whole place rigged with explosives."

"We'll make the exchange," the sheriff said. "We can't risk the lives of the children."

"Sheriff." Ghost planted himself in front of the sheriff. "You have four of the most highly skilled military men at your disposal. Let us get in there, recon the situation and report what we see."

"I don't know." The sheriff shook his head. "If they see you, they might detonate the explosives."

"We know how to get in without being seen. We can get a count on the number of combatants. You'd be better off knowing numbers in case they start shooting at the men delivering Vanders."

"He has a point," Garner added. "Let us be your eyes and ears while you're putting the exchange in place."

The sheriff stared at Garner. "How do I know you won't do something stupid?"

Ghost grabbed the man's arm. "The woman I love and my little girl were on that bus. I wouldn't do anything that would cause them harm. Please. Let us do this."

The sheriff stared into Ghost's face. "I've known you for a long time. I knew your father. He was proud that you made it through SEAL training. From what they say, only the best of the best can be a SEAL." He stared at the others. "I trust Jon Caspar. If he trusts you, I guess I have to, as well. Go."

Ghost turned to run.

The sheriff snagged his arm. "We have to bring those kids back alive. One of them is my grandson."

Ghost nodded and took off for the DHS agent's SUV. Hawkeye, Garner and Cavemen beat him to it, climbing in. Ghost settled in the seat and leaned forward, staring through the front windshield as they blew through town and north toward Lucky Lou's Gold Mine. He prayed they could get in without being seen and that none of the passengers on the bus had been hurt in the hostage takeover.

Chapter Fourteen

Lolly fell asleep, leaning against Charlie.

Unable to sit still without coming up with a plan, she eased Lolly to the floor and stood, stretching the kinks out of her muscles. She wondered how long it had been since they'd been captured. Thirty minutes? An hour? More?

Some children were still sniffling, huddled up to Brenda, seeking comfort from each other.

Charlie crossed to the metal plate covering the opening of the mine and strained to hear what was happening outside.

"They'll be here on time if they want to see those kids again," a voice said.

Charlie recognized it as the man who'd been carrying the flashlight, Dalton Vanders.

"What if they bring in the feds?" The slower, deeper voice of Vernon Vanders said. "We aren't equipped for a standoff."

"We have the detonators." The third voice could only be the man in charge. The oldest of the Vanders brothers, GW. "The mine entrance is rigged to blow. If they don't give us what we want, we blow the entrance."

Charlie gasped. If they blew the entrance, everyone inside could be buried alive. Should, by some miracle, they live through the blast, they might suffocate before anyone could dig them out.

"They better hope they bring Dad in that helicopter," Dalton said.

"Ten minutes. If they don't show by then, we blow and go," GW said, his voice moving away from the mine entrance.

Ten minutes. Charlie looked around in the limited lighting. They had ten minutes to figure out how to get out of the mine.

Going deeper without lights was suicide. They could fall down open vertical shafts in the floor, or die due to poisonous gases. She went back to the boxes and searched for something, anything she could use to move the door enough they could slip out.

The only thing she could find was a broken slat from one of the crates. If she could use it as leverage, she might be able to move the heavy metal plate that had taken two men to slide in place.

Charlie jammed the slat into the sunlit gap at the base of the metal barrier. Holding on to the end, she leaned back as hard as she could, putting all of her weight into it. The plate budged, but only half an inch. She pulled the slat out and lay down on the floor.

She could see a little bit of daylight and movement. A couple of yards from the entrance, stood someone wearing camouflage pants and black work boots.

She didn't know where the others were, but she couldn't wait for them to appear. She had to get a wide enough gap to slip the children out and away from the men before they got really stupid and detonated the charges that would seal twenty children and the adults in the mine.

Fitting the slat back in the gap, she pulled again, the gap widening until a four-inch opening stretched from the top to the bottom of the entrance.

On her third attempt, the slat cracked and broke. Charlie fell on her butt with a bone-jarring thud and groaned. The additional space she'd gained was less than another inch. Five inches wide might get a small child out, but not Brenda and Charlie. And the children would need to be guided into the nearby trees and underbrush to hide. Without the leverage of the slat, she'd have to work with her bare hands. As heavy as the metal plate was, she doubted she'd get far, but she had to try.

The sky darkened, as if clouds had blocked the sun.

Charlie crawled to the widened gap and peered out. She spotted all three Vanders brothers. They stood near the dump truck. Two of them held the AR-15s. The one she figured was GW had the 9 millimeter in a holster on his hip and his hand wrapped around a small gadget Charlie assumed was the detonator.

Her teeth ground together. Any man who could contemplate blowing up the entrance to a mine with children trapped inside was no man at all. He was an animal.

She looked to her right and her left. If she remembered correctly from their drive in, the mine entrance had several bushes growing next to it and a young tree sprouting near the base of the hill. If they could get the kids to the bushes they might make it to the forest before their escape was discovered. The men outside must have felt pretty confident in the ability of the rusty metal plate holding their hostages inside. Either that or they were too busy watching for whatever they'd demanded to arrive to keep a close eye on a bunch of kids and two women.

Charlie leaped to her feet. Time was running out. She had to get the children to safety before the crazy brothers sealed their fates inside a mine shaft tomb.

Brenda disentangled herself from the children and rose to assist. "Let me help," she said.

With her heart pumping adrenaline through her veins, Charlie grabbed the metal plate.

Brenda curled her fingers around the rusty steel.

Together they leaned back, straining to move the heavy sheet of metal. By God, they'd move that barrier if it was the last thing they did.

Charlie prayed it wasn't.

ARMED WITH A headset radio and an AR-15 rifle, Ghost lived up to his nickname and eased up to the edge of the mine compound, clinging to the brush. "Three targets, two carrying rifles and one with the prize."

"I got one vehicle leaving by road." Caveman was working his way toward the mine by paralleling the road in and out. "Notifying 911. They have the state highway patrol on standby. They should pick him up on the highway."

"I'm in position in the bird's nest," Hawkeye said from his position on a ridge high above the mine clearing.

"Ready when you are," Garner added.

The big guy in the middle had his fist closed around a small box of some sort. If it was a detonator, they'd have to get him to let go of it before they took out the other two men. It would do no good to kill any of them, if the guy holding the key to the show pressed that button.

He studied the layout. An older model dump truck was parked a couple of yards away from the mine entrance. One of the men stood near the rear of the truck, watching the road in. Another used the other end of the truck as cover, also monitoring the only road in.

The man with his hand on the detonator pulled what appeared to be a satellite phone off the web harness he wore and hit several buttons.

"Where's Vanders and our bird?" he demanded. "My thumb is a hair's breadth away from the ignition button." He listened for a moment. "I don't care if it takes time to get a helicopter here. Five minutes. That's all that's left between you and those kids. Five." He jabbed the phone, ending the call. "Get ready. Either they'll show up with him and the bird, or we set off some fireworks and get the hell out of here."

"I think I hear something coming," one of the men shouted.

"'Bout time," the guy at the other end of the truck said. "I need a beer."

The sound of rotor blades beating the air came over the top of the hill.

"Got my sights on the prize holder," Hawkeye reported.

"Do not engage," Garner reiterated the sheriff's instructions. He was positioned to the right of Ghost and twenty yards to his rear. He was to transfer data to the sheriff as the others took their positions.

"Holding steady," Hawkeye reassured.

Ghost scanned the area for other bad guys but was surprised there were only three. It didn't take an army to take a school bus full of children and unarmed adults. And with the lives of those children held in the balance, these men could demand the world and get it.

The helicopter crested the hill and hovered over the mine.

"What are they waiting for?" one of the men shouted.

"I don't know," the man holding the detonator yelled back over the roar of the helicopter.

"There's someone with a gun in there!" One of the men with a rifle pointed his weapon at the helicopter.

"Don't shoot!" detonator man yelled.

"They've got a gun!" He raised his weapon to his shoulder and fired.

Ghost shook his head. Just what they needed, a trigger-happy bad guy firing at the helicopter carrying their bargaining chip. "The situation has escalated, request permission to move in and take out the targets," Ghost said.

"Sheriff said do not engage," Garner reminded him.

"The sheriff didn't get the word to the bad guys. Things are about to get really bad." Ghost bunched his muscles, ready to charge into the gray.

"I've got the shooter in my sights," Hawkeye reminded them.

"I'm in position and have the other dude with the gun in mine," Caveman said.

Ghost couldn't wait for the men to freak out and blow up the mine entrance. "I'm going in for the man with the prize. Boss, either you're with me or you're not."

"I got your six, coming up on your left," Garner said. "Sheriff gave the go-ahead. They're lifting off."

As the helicopter climbed higher into the sky, the team moved in.

Hawkeye took out the man firing at the bird. Caveman fired at the other, nicked his leg and sent him to the ground. Unfortunately, he still had his gun in hand and was firing back in the direction of Caveman.

Ghost was almost across the open ground when the man with the detonator turned toward the mine entrance and raised his hand.

Making a flying tackle, Ghost hit the man in his midsection, sending him staggering backward. He stumbled and hit the ground flat on his back. The detonator flew from his grasp and skittered across the dry ground, landing in front of the man firing at Caveman.

He flung his rifle to the ground and low-crawled toward the detonator.

Ghost punched the man he'd tackled in the nose and scrambled to his feet, flinging himself at the man as he reached for the detonator.

Before he could get to him, the man's hand slammed down on the red button.

The world erupted behind Ghost, sending him flying forward and slamming him to the ground. He laid for a moment, stunned, his ears ringing. The man who'd hit the button lifted his head and stared at him, then reached for his rifle.

Ghost lurched to his feet and kicked the rifle out of the other man's grip.

A shot rang out behind him and the big guy he'd tackled

stood facing him, his eyes wide, blood spreading across his camouflage shirt. He took one step and fell forward like a tree toppled by lumberjacks.

Garner lay on the ground nearby, his rifle up to his shoulder. "Told you I had your six."

Ghost scanned the area. Caveman came out of the woods, the helicopter dropped lower and landed on the other side of the dump truck and people rushed toward the mine entrance.

"Charlie. Lolly." Ghost's head still rang and his leg ached, but none of that mattered. The woman he loved and his only child were trapped behind the rocks and rubble blocking the entrance to the old mine.

He ran toward the jumble of boulders and rocks. Dust swirled in a cloud making it hard to see clearly. Or were those tears clouding his vision?

"Charlie! Lolly!" Oh, dear God, how was he going to get them out of there? He lifted a boulder and tossed it to the side. He lifted another and threw it to the side, too.

"Ghost!" Hawkeye said his name several times before he heard the sound through his headset.

"They're in there," Ghost said, his heart ripped to shreds, his mind numb. "They're in there, and I can't get to them."

"Ghost, listen to me," Hawkeye said. "I have them in my sights."

"What?" Ghost straightened from the pile of rocks. "How?"

"They're in the woods to the south of the mine. I count more than a dozen kids and two adults."

From desperation to hope, Ghost left the rocks and ran toward the south side of the mine. He crashed through brush, tripped over logs and fell several times before he spotted something pink through the dense foliage.

When he broke through the underbrush, he stumbled and fell to his knees in front of all the children and two women. "Charlie! Lolly!" He coughed, choking with the dust he'd inhaled and the emotion he couldn't hold back.

"Ghost?" Charlie ran forward and knelt beside him. "Is that you?" She rubbed her hands across his face, her fingers getting coated with a fine layer of dust. "Oh, thank God." She flung her arms around him and kissed him, dirt and all.

He held her close for a long time. His leg hurt like hell and his ears still rang, but Charlie, Lolly and the rest of the kids were okay.

"Mr. Caspar?" Lolly inched forward, her brows knit, her cheeks streaked with dried tears.

"Lolly, baby, come here." He held out an arm, making room for her in his embrace.

She ran to him and wrapped her arms around his neck. "I was so scared."

He laughed. "So was I." He kissed her cheek with a loud smack. "But we're okay now."

She leaned back and stared at his face. "You're dirty."

He laughed out loud, his heart filled with so much joy, he was afraid it might explode. "Yes, I am. And I'm so happy you and your mama are all right."

Her eyes filled with tears. "Mr. Green didn't come out with us."

Charlie smoothed a hand over her hair. "No, sweetie, he didn't. But the sheriff will make sure they get him out of there. You'll see."

Ghost's gaze connected with Charlie's.

"The bus driver," she whispered and shook her head, her eyes filling.

He nodded. With Charlie's help, Ghost lurched to his feet and straightened his leg, the pain shooting up into his hip. He ignored it, looking at the children huddled around another young woman. He shook his head, thankful they were all alive. "How did you get them out of the mine?"

Charlie held up her hands, stained with rust and marked with cuts and scrapes. "Brenda and I moved the metal plate they'd used to block the entrance. They thought it could keep a couple of women with a bunch of children contained." She snorted. "They didn't count on the adrenaline rush we'd get at the mention of blowing the entrance." Charlie lifted her chin and smiled at the other woman. "The important thing is, we got it open enough to get all of the children out while the Vanders brothers were shooting at the helicopter. It was close, but we were able to get all of the children out of the mine before the explosion."

Ghost shook his head, a grin spreading across his face. "You are amazing."

"And you should have seen Lolly, herding the kids into single file like the little soldier she is." Charlie smiled down at their daughter. "She's so much like you it hurts sometimes."

Lolly stared up at Ghost. "Mr. Caspar, will you be my daddy?"

Her words hit Ghost in the gut and he sucked in a breath before responding. "I don't know." He turned to Charlie. "What does your mother think about the idea?"

Charlie's eyes filled again, tears spilled over the edges and her bottom lip trembled. "I was going to wait until I was wearing a pretty dress and my hair was fixed." She stared down at her wrecked hands. "And after a manicure." She laughed, the sound coming out as more of a sob. "But I don't want to wait another minute to know." She dropped to one knee and took Ghost's hand.

"What are you doing?" he asked. He tried to lift her back to her feet, but she resisted.

"Jon Caspar, you big, sexy SEAL, with a heart as big as the Wyoming sky, will you make an honest woman of me and marry me?" She stared up at him, tears running down her dirty face, her hair a riot of uncontrollable curls, her clothes torn and smeared with rust. She was the most beautiful woman in the world.

Ghost's heart swelled in his chest to the point he thought it could no longer be contained.

Lolly clapped her hands together, her eyes alight with excitement. "Please say yes!"

Ghost laughed and drew Charlie up into his arms. "I would have liked a shower before I proposed to you. But since we're here, the sun is shining and I'm holding the most beautiful woman in the world, I can't think of a better answer than yes." He drew in a deep breath and bent to kiss the tip of her nose. "Yes, I'll marry you. Yes, I'd love to have Lolly as my very own daughter. And yes, we'll work things out, somehow, because that's what people do who love each other as much as we do. I love you, Charlie, from the tips of my toes to my very last breath."

"Jon, I've always loved you," Charlie said. "From our first date, I knew you were the one for me. I just had to wait until *you* knew I was the one for you."

He brushed a strand of her hair out of her face and tucked it behind her ear. "I've always loved you, but I didn't want to hurt you by dragging you through the life of a SEAL's wife."

Charlie laughed. "So you hurt me by leaving me behind?" She shook her head. "That's man thinking." She cupped his face and leaned up on her toes to kiss him. "I'd follow you to the ends of the earth, and I'd always be there for you when you came back from deployment."

"Me, too." Lolly hugged him around his knees. "I love you, too. I'm going to have a daddy of my own." She looked up at him with his blue eyes and her mother's red hair and grinned. "We're going to be a family."

"You bet, we are." Ghost lifted her up on his arm and wrapped the other around Charlie. Together, they led the others out of the woods and back to the clearing in front of the mine.

CHARLIE FELT AS if she'd gone from one movie set to the other and wondered if she had been dreaming through all that had happened. She had a hard time wrapping her mind around all of it from having the bus hijacked to being trapped in a mine, to the fairy-tale proposal in the woods and back to the cacophony of every kind of motor vehicle and dozens of uniformed personnel filling her vision.

A fire truck had arrived, along with rescue vehicles from across the county. Every sheriff's deputy on duty was there along with the Wyoming Highway Patrol. The sheriff was in the middle of all of it speaking with the DHS representative, Kevin Garner.

When Charlie emerged from the woods with Ghost, Brenda and all of the children, a round of applause erupted from the rescue personnel.

Paramedics rushed forward to check out the children, Brenda and Charlie.

She suffered through the delay of having her hands cleaned and bandaged, while Ghost carried Lolly over to where the sheriff directed the remaining efforts.

Charlie hurried over as soon as she could break away.

Tim Cramer was tucked into the backseat of one of the Wyoming Highway Patrol cars, his face angry, his hands cuffed behind him.

A deputy escorted a pale and shaky Linnea Cramer into the fray where she was reunited with her daughter, Ashley, in a tearful reunion.

"Thank God, they got Ashley back," Charlie said as she joined the group gathered around the sheriff.

"We had a roadblock set up on the highway headed toward Montana. We figured he'd make a run for Canada with the child," the sheriff said. "Wyoming Highway Patrol picked him up. If he thought he had problems before, he's in a heap more trouble now. Rebecca Florence came to this morning and said it was Tim Cramer who'd attacked her in the library. He'd worn the ski mask he was found with today, but she knew it was him when he told her it was her fault he was losing his wife."

Charlie frowned. "What do you mean it was her fault? I didn't think she and Linnea were even friends."

The sheriff's mouth twisted. "Apparently, Ms. Florence was in Bozeman for a library conference staying at the same hotel where Cramer was entertaining a young lady who wasn't his wife in a room on the same floor as Rebecca's."

"And she told Linnea." Charlie nodded. "So he beat her up for squealing on him."

The sheriff nodded.

"What about the Vanders brothers?" Charlie asked, looking around as paramedics loaded a sheet-draped body into the back of one of the waiting ambulances.

"Dalton is dead, Vernon and GW will live to face time in the state prison," the sheriff said.

Charlie couldn't feel sorry for any of them. How long would it be before the children got over the terror they'd faced on the bus and in the dark mine? "I hope they get what they deserve."

Ghost slipped an arm around her.

She leaned into his strength, glad he was there.

"If not for Garner's team, it could have been a whole lot worse," Sheriff Scott said. "The chopper took hits from Dalton's gun. The pilot is being treated for a gunshot wound to his leg and Dalton shot his own father." The sheriff shook his head. "LeRoy Vanders took a bullet to the chest. They're working on him now and loading him into the helicopter his son tried to shoot down. I doubt he'll make it all the way to the hospital in Bozeman."

"What about Mr. Green?" Charlie asked. Her heart ached for the old man who'd done nothing to deserve being killed for driving a busload of kids. "He's still inside the mine." She shook her head. "He didn't make it. Vernon took him out on the bus."

The sheriff's lips thinned and released a long sigh. "His wife will be devastated." He pinched the bridge of his nose before continuing. "I ordered excavation equipment in case we had to dig you and the kids out. It's on its way. We'll get him out."

Charlie nodded.

Sheriff Scott shot a glance at the crumbled mine entrance.

"What I don't understand is where they got all the explosives and detonators."

Ghost's jaw tightened. "From what I saw of the detonator, it was military grade. I knew the Vanderses had an arsenal of guns from all the hunting they do. But the explosives are an entirely different game."

Charlie touched the sheriff's arm. "I found at least a dozen wooden crates in the mine. They were filled with empty boxes from what appeared to be a large number of rifles, boxes of ammo and the curved magazines I've seen used with the semi-automatic weapons the military use. What would the Vanders brothers need with that many weapons?"

"Unless they aren't the only ones stockpiling weapons," Kevin Garner said. "We have infrared satellite photos of a group of people unloading items from a truck into the mine. It was from only a few days ago."

"Those crates were empty except for the boxes the weapons came in."

"Where did all of those guns and ammo go?" the sheriff asked. "And who shipped all of them? There has to be a paper or money trail."

Garner nodded. "I have my tech guy working on that. In the meantime, getting into that mine and going through those crates might help us trace the weapons back to the buyer."

The sheriff's face grew grim. "Sounds like someone is trying to build an army."

"Then we better find out who before they succeed," Garner said.

Charlie shivered in the warm country air. Her peaceful hometown of Grizzly Pass, Wyoming, had darker secrets than she'd ever expected. She began to wonder if bringing her daughter there to raise had been a good idea after all.

Ghost tightened his hold around her waist, reminding her that if she hadn't come back, she wouldn't have found Ghost again.

Everything happened for a reason. And she couldn't be happier that she now had her family back together. Whatever the future held, wherever they went, it would be as a family. Anything else, they could deal with, as long as they were together.

An hour later, Kevin Garner loaded his team of specialists into his SUV along with Charlie and Lolly and took them back to town.

He dropped Charlie, Lolly and Ghost at the community center where Charlie had left her Jeep.

Charlie handed over her keys. "If you don't mind, my hands are shaking too much to drive."

He took the keys in exchange for a kiss and helped her and Lolly into the vehicle.

Once they were all inside, he glanced over at Charlie and took her hand. "Just so you know, I plan on staying until the situation is resolved here in Grizzly Pass. After that, I hope you'll be patient and flexible with where we go next."

Charlie squeezed his fingers. "I'm one hundred percent okay with that plan. As long as you're here with us. I don't think we've found the people at the crux of what's been going on around here."

"Me either," he said. "But I know one thing."

"What's that?"

"I'm not leaving until we do. And when I do leave, you and Lolly are coming with me." He lifted her hand and pressed a kiss to the backs of her knuckles.

"Good," Charlie said. "Because I'm not letting go this time."

"How do you feel about being a Navy wife?"

"I couldn't be prouder, as long as my Navy husband is you."

"Good, because once we've completed this assignment, I want to rejoin my unit in Virginia."

"I've always wanted to go to Virginia," she said, a happy smile spreading across her face.

"And if the medical board invites me to leave the military?"

She turned her head toward him. "We could come back to Wyoming."

"I'm glad you feel that way. Being back reminded me how much I love this state. More than that, it reminded me of how much I love you."

* * * * *

Hot Target

This book is dedicated to my mother and father,
who taught me that the sky was the limit, and all I needed
was to apply the hard work to reach for my dreams.
I love you both to the moon and back.

CAST OF CHARACTERS

Max "Caveman" Decker—US Army DELTA Force soldier on loan to the Department of Homeland Security for Task Force Safe Haven.

Grace Saunders—Biologist working on the Wolf Project with Yellowstone National Park. Witnessed a murder, thus becoming a target of the killer.

Kevin Garner—Agent with the Department of Homeland Security in charge of Task Force Safe Haven.

Jon "Ghost" Caspar—US Navy SEAL on loan to Department of Homeland Security for Task Force Safe Haven, a special group of military men assigned to Homeland Security.

Tarce "Hawkeye" Walsh—US Army Airborne Ranger and expert sniper, on loan to the Department of Homeland Security for Task Force Safe Haven.

Rex "T-Rex" Trainor—US Marine on loan to the Department of Homeland Security for Task Force Safe Haven.

Ernie Martin—Rancher angry about cessation of government subsidies on his Angora goat ranching business.

Quincy Kemp—Local meat processor and taxidermist.

Bryson Rausch—Formerly the wealthiest resident of Grizzly Pass, who lost everything in the stock market.

RJ Khalig—Pipeline inspector who replaced previous one who had been giving false reports.

Chapter One

Max "Caveman" Decker clung to the shadows of the mud-and-brick structures, the first SEAL into enemy territory. Reaching a forward position giving him sufficient range of fire, he dropped to one knee, scanned the street and buildings ahead through his night-vision goggles, searching for the telltale green heat signatures of warm enemy bodies. When he didn't detect any, he said softly into his mic, "Ready."

"Going in," Whiskey said. Armed with their M4A1 carbine rifles with the Special Forces Modification kit, he and Tank eased around the corner of a building in a small village in the troubled Helmand Province of Afghanistan.

Army Intelligence operatives had indicated the Pakistan-based Haqqani followers had set up a remote base of operations in the village located in the rugged hills north of Kandahar.

Caveman's job was to provide cover to his teammates as they moved ahead of him. Then they would cover for him until he reached a relatively secure location, thus leapfrogging through the village to their target, the biggest building at the center, where intel reported the Haqqani rebels had set up shop.

Caveman hunkered low, scanning the path ahead and the

rooftops of the buildings for gun-toting enemy combatants. So far, so good. Through his night-vision goggles, he tracked the progress of the seven members of his squad working their way slowly toward the target.

An eighth green blip appeared ahead of his team and his arm swung wide.

"We've got incoming!" Caveman aimed his weapon at the eighth green heat signature and pulled the trigger. It was too late. A bright flash blinded him through the goggles, followed by the ear-rupturing concussion of a grenade. He jerked his goggles up over his helmet, cursing. When he blinked his eyes to regain his night vision, he stared at the scene in front of him.

All seven members of his squad lay on the ground, some moving, others not.

No! His job was to provide cover. They couldn't be dead. They had to be alive. He leaped to his feet.

Then, as if someone opened the door to a hive of bees, enemy combatants swarmed from around the corners into the street, carrying AK-47s.

With the majority of his squad down, maybe dead, maybe alive, Caveman didn't have any other choice.

He set his weapon on automatic, pulled his 9-millimeter pistol from the holster on his hip and stepped out of the cover of the building.

"What the hell are you doing?" Whiskey had shouted.

"Showing no mercy," he shouted through gritted teeth. He charged forward like John Wayne on the warpath, shooting from both hips, taking out one enemy rebel after the other.

Something hit him square in his armor-plated chest, knocking him backward a step. It hurt like hell and made his breath lodge in his lungs, but it didn't stop him. He forged his way toward the enemy, firing until he ran out of ammo. Dropping to the ground, he slammed magazines into the rifle and the pistol and rolled to a prone position, aimed and fired, taking down as many of the enemy as he could. He'd be damned if even one of them survived.

When there were only two combatants left in the street, Caveman lurched to his feet and went after them. He wouldn't rest until the last one died.

He hadn't slowed as he rounded the corner. A bullet had hit him in the leg. Caveman grunted. He would have gone down, but the adrenaline in his veins surged, pushing him to his destination. He aimed his pistol at the shooter who'd plugged his leg and caught him between the eyes. Another bogey shot at him from above.

Caveman dove to the ground and rolled behind a stack of crates. Pain stabbed him in the shoulder and the leg, and warm wetness dripped down both. He leaned around the crates, pulled his night-vision goggles in place, located the shooter on the rooftop and took him out.

With the streets clear, he had a straight path to the original target. Holstering his handgun, he pulled a grenade out of his vest, pushed to his feet and staggered a few steps, pain slicing through him. He could barely feel his leg and really didn't give a damn.

Two steps, three... One after the other took him to the biggest structure in the neighborhood. As he rounded the corner, one of the two guards protecting the doorway fired at him.

The man's bullet hit the stucco beside him.

Caveman jerked back behind the corner, stuck his M4A1 around the corner and fired off a burst. Then he leaped out, threw himself to the ground, rolled and came up firing. Within moments, the two guards were dead.

The door was locked or barred from the inside. Pulling the pin on the grenade, Caveman dropped it in front of the barrier and then stepped back around the corner, covering his ears.

The blast shook the building and spewed dust and wooden splinters. Back at the front entrance, Caveman kicked the door the rest of the way in and entered the building.

Going from room to room, he fired his weapon, taking out every male occupant in his path. When he reached the last door, he kicked it open and stood back.

The expected gunfire riddled the wall opposite the door.

After the gunfire ceased, Caveman spun around and opened fire on the occupants of the room until no one stood or attempted escape.

His task complete, he radioed the platoon leader. "Eight down. Come get us." Only after each one of his enemies was dead did he allow himself to crumple to the ground. As if every bone in his body suddenly melted into goo, Caveman had no way left to hold himself up. Still armed with his M4A1, he sat in the big room and stared down at his leg. Blood flowed far too quickly. In the back of his mind, he knew he had to do something or he'd pass out and die. But every movement now took a monumental amount of effort, and gray fog gathered at the edges of his vision. He couldn't pass out now, his buddies needed him. They could be dead or dying. No matter how hard he tried, he couldn't straighten, couldn't rise to his feet. The abyss claimed him, dragging him to the depths of despair.

"CAVEMAN," A VOICE SAID.

He dragged himself back from the edge of a very dark, extremely deep pool that was his past—a different time…a terrible place. He shook his head to clear the memories and glanced across the room at his new boss for the duration of this temporary assignment. "I'm sorry, sir. You were saying?"

The leader of Homeland Security's Special Task Force Safe Haven, Kevin Garner, narrowed his eyes. "How long did you say it's been since you were cleared for duty?"

"Two weeks," Caveman responded.

Kevin's frown deepened. "And when was the last time you met with a shrink?"

"All through the twelve weeks of physical therapy. She cleared me two weeks ago." His jaw tightened. "I'm fully capable of performing whatever assignment is given to me as a Delta Force soldier. I don't know why I've been assigned to this backcountry boondoggle."

Kevin's shrewd gaze studied Caveman so hard he could have been staring at him under a microscope. "Any TBI with your injury?"

"I was shot in the leg, not the head. No traumatic brain injury." Anger spiked with the need to get outside and breathe fresh air. Not that the air in the loft over the Blue Moose Tavern in Grizzly Pass, Wyoming, was stale. It was just that whenever Caveman was inside for extended periods, he got really twitchy. Claustrophobia, the therapist had called it. Probably brought on by PTSD.

A bunch of hooey, if you asked Caveman. Something the therapist could use against him to delay his return to the front. And by God, he'd get back to the front soon, if he had to stow away on a C-130 bound for Afghanistan. The enemy had to pay for the deaths of his friends; the members of his squad deserved retribution. Only one other man had survived, Whiskey, and he'd lost an eye in the firefight.

The slapping sound of a file folder hitting a tabletop made Caveman jump.

"That's your assignment," Kevin said. "RJ Khalig, pipeline inspector. He's had a few threats lately. I want you to touch bases with him and provide protection until we can figure out who's threatening him."

Caveman glared at the file. "I'm no bodyguard. I shoot people for a living."

"You know the stakes from our meeting a couple days ago in this same room, and you've seen what some of the people in this area are capable of. As I said then, we think terrorist cells are stirring up already volatile locals. Since we found evidence that someone is supplying semiautomatic weapons to what we suspect is a local group called Free America, we're afraid more violence is imminent."

"Just because you found some empty crates in that old mine doesn't mean whoever got the weapons plans to use them to start a war," Caveman argued.

"No, but we're concerned they might target individuals who could potentially stand in the way of their movements."

"Why not let local law enforcement handle it?" Caveman leaned forward, reluctant to open the file and commit to the assignment. He didn't want to be in Wyoming. "If this group picks off individuals, would that not be local jurisdiction?"

Kevin nodded. "As long as they aren't connected with terrorists. However, the activity on social media indicates something bigger is being planned and will take place soon."

"How soon?"

Kevin shook his head. "We don't know."

"Sounds pretty vague to me." Caveman stood and stretched.

"I set up this task force to stop a terrible thing from happening. If I had all of the answers, likely I wouldn't need you, Ghost, Hawkeye or T-Rex. I'm determined to stop something bad from happening, before it gets too big and a lot more lives are lost."

"I don't know if you have the right guy for this job. I'm no investigator, nor am I a bodyguard."

"I understand your concern, but we need trained combatants, familiar with tactics and subversive operations. As you've seen for yourself and know from experience, it's pretty rough country out here and the people can be stubborn and willing to take the law into their own hands. I'm afraid what happened at the mine two days ago could happen again."

Caveman snorted. "That was a bunch of disgruntled ranchers, mad about the confiscation of their herd."

"Agreed," Kevin said. "Granted, the Vanders family took it too far by kidnapping a busload of kids. But they knew about the weapons stored in that mine."

"Are any of them talking?"

"Not yet. We're waiting for one of them to throw the rest under the bus."

"You might be waiting a long time." Caveman crossed his arms over his chest. "People out here tend to be very stubborn."

"You're from this area," Kevin said. "You should know."

"I'm from a little farther north, in the Crazy Mountains of Montana. But we're all a tough bunch of cowboys who don't like it when the government interferes with our lives."

"Hold on to that stubbornness. You might need it around here. For today, you'll be an investigator and bodyguard. Mr. Khalig needs your help. He has an important job, inspecting the oil and gas pipelines running through this state. Contact his boss for his location, find him and get the skinny on what's going on. You might have to run him down in the backwoods."

Until he was cleared to return to his unit, Caveman would do the best he could for his temporary boss and the pipeline inspector. What choice did he have? As much as he hated to admit it, they needed help out in the hills and mountains of Wyoming. The three days he'd been there had proven that.

Caveman had met with Kevin's four-man special operations team members. One Navy SEAL, one Delta Force soldier, an Army ranger and a highly skilled Marine. Ghost, one of the Delta Force men, had been assigned to protect a woman who had been surfing the web for terrorist activity. Her daughter had been one of the children who had been kidnapped on the bus.

Caveman, Kevin and the other three members of the task force had mobilized to save the children and the three adults on board the bus. The bus driver didn't make it, but the children and the two women survived.

Kevin stood and held out his hand. "Thanks for helping out. We have such limited resources in this neck of the woods, and I feel there's a lot more to what's going on here than meets the eyes."

"I'll do what I can." Caveman shook Kevin's hand and left the loft, descending the stairs to the street below. When he'd entered the upstairs apartment, the sky had been clear and blue. In the twenty minutes he'd been inside, clouds had gathered. The superstitious would call it an omen, a sign or a portent of things to come. Caveman called them rain clouds. If he was going to get out to where Khalig was, he'd have to get moving.

GRACE SAUNDERS PULLED her horse to a halt and dismounted near the top of a ridge overlooking the mountain meadow where Molly's wolf pack had been spotted most recently. Based on the droppings she'd seen along the trail and the leftover bones of an elk carcass, they were still active in the area.

She tied her horse to a nearby tree and stretched her back and legs. Having been on horseback since early that morning, she was ready for a break. Moving to the highest point, she stared out at the brilliant view of the Wyoming Beartooth Mountain Range, with the snowcapped peaks and the tall lodgepole pines. The sky above had been blue when she'd started her trek that morning. Clouds had built to the west, a harbinger of rain to come soon. She'd have to head down soon or risk a cold drenching.

From where she stood, Grace could see clear across the small valley to the hilltop on the other side. She frowned, squinted her eyes and focused on something that didn't belong.

A four-wheeler stood at the top of the hill, halfway tucked into the shade of a lodgepole pine tree. She wondered what someone else was doing out in the woods. Most people stuck to the roads in and out of the national forest.

It wasn't unusual for the more adventurous souls to ride the trails surrounding Yellowstone National Park, since ATVs in the park itself were prohibited. Scanning the hilltop for the person belonging to the four-wheeler, Grace had to search hard. For a moment she worried the rider might be hurt. Then she spotted him, lying on his belly on the ground.

Grace's heartbeats ratcheted up several notches. The guy appeared to have a rifle of some sort with a scope. Since it was summer, the man with the gun had no reason to be aiming a rifle. It wasn't hunting season.

Grace followed the direction the barrel of the weapon was pointed, to the far side of the valley. She couldn't see any elk, white-tailed deer or moose. Was he aiming for wolves? Grace raised her binoculars to her eyes and looked closer.

A movement caught her attention. She almost missed it. But then she focused on the spot where she'd seen the movement and gasped.

A man squatted near the ground with a device in his hand. He stared at the device as he slowly stood.

Grace shifted the lenses of her binoculars to the man on the ridge. He tensed, his eye lining up with the scope. Surely he wasn't aiming at the man on the ground.

Her pulse hammering, Grace lowered her binoculars and shouted to the man below. "Get down!"

At the same time as she shouted, the sound of rifle fire reached her.

The man on the floor of the valley jerked, pressed a hand to his chest and looked down at blood spreading across his shirt. He dropped to his knees and then fell forward.

Grace pressed a hand to her chest, her heart hammering against her ribs. What had just happened? In her heart she knew. She'd just witnessed a murder. Raising her binoculars to the man on the hilltop, she stared at him, trying to get a good look at him so that she could pick him out in a lineup of criminals.

He had brown hair. And that was all she could get before she noticed the gun he'd used to kill the man on the valley floor was pointing in her direction, and he was aiming at her.

Instinctively, Grace dropped to the ground and rolled to the side. Dust kicked up at the point she'd been standing a moment before. The rifle's report sounded half a second later.

Grace rolled again until she was below the top of the ridge. Afraid to stand and risk being shot, she crawled on all fours down to where she'd left her horse tied to a tree.

An engine revved on the other side of the ridge, the sound echoing off the rocky bluffs.

Her pulse slamming through her body, Grace staggered to her feet, her knees shaking. She ran toward the horse. The animal backed away, sensing her distress, pulling the knot tighter on the tree branch.

Her hands trembling, Grace struggled to untie the knot.

Tears stung her eyes. She wanted to go back to the man on the ground and see if he was still alive, but the shooter would take her out before she could get there. Her best bet was to get back down the mountain and notify the sheriff. If she rode hard, she could be down in thirty minutes.

Finally jerking the reins free of the branch, Grace swung up onto the horse.

The gelding leaped forward as soon as her butt hit the saddle, galloping down the trail they'd climbed moments before.

Grace slowed as she approached a point at which the trail narrowed and dropped off on one side. With the gelding straining at the bit to speed up, Grace held him in check as they eased down the trail. She glanced back at the ridge where she'd been. A four-wheeler stood on top, the rider holding a rifle to his shoulder.

Something hit the bluff beside her. Dust and rocks splintered off, blinding her briefly. Throwing caution to the wind, she gave the horse his head and held on, praying they didn't fall off the side of the trail. She didn't have a choice. If she didn't get around the corner soon, she'd be shot.

Her gelding pushed forward, more sure of his footing than Grace. She ducked low in the saddle and held on, praying they made it soon. The bluff jutted out of the hillside and would provide sufficient cover for a few minutes. Long enough for her to make it to the trees. The shooter could still catch up, but the trail twisting through the thick trunks of the evergreens would give her more cover and concealment than being in the open. If she made it down to the paved road, she could wave someone down.

Riding like her hair was on fire, Grace erupted from the

trees at the base of the mountain trail. A truck with a trailer on the back was parked on the dirt road. She slowed to read the sign on the door, indicating Rocky Mountain Pipeline Inc. No sooner had she stopped than a shot rang out, plinking into the side of the truck.

Grace leaned low over her horse and yelled, "Go, go, go!" The horse took off across a field, galloping hard.

Then, as if he tripped, he stumbled and pitched forward.

Grace sailed through the air, every move appearing in slow motion. She made a complete somersault before she landed on her feet. Momentum carried her forward and she landed hard on her belly in the tall grass, her forehead bumping the ground hard. For a moment, she couldn't breathe and her vision blurred. She knew she couldn't stay there. The guy on the four-wheeler would catch up to her and finish the job.

An engine roared somewhere nearby.

Grace low-crawled through the grass, blinking hard to clear the darkness slowing her down. When she could go no farther, she collapsed in the grass, no longer able to fight against the fog closing in around her. She closed her eyes.

It wouldn't take the gunman long to find her and end it.

Then she felt a hand on her shoulder and heard a man calling to her as if from the far end of a long tunnel.

"Hey, are you all right?" a deep, resonant voice called out.

Grace gave the last bit of her strength to pushing herself over onto her back. She made it halfway and groaned.

The hand on her shoulder eased her the rest of the way, until she lay facing her attacker. "Are you going to kill me?"

"What?" he said. "Why would I want to kill you?"

"You killed the man in the valley. And you tried to kill me," she said, her voice fading into a whisper.

"I'm not here to kill anyone."

"If you do. Just make it quick." She tried to blink her eyes open, but they wouldn't move. "Just shoot me. But don't hurt my horse." And she passed out.

Chapter Two

Caveman shook his head as he stared down at the strange woman. "Shoot you? I don't even know you," he muttered. He glanced around, searching for others in the area. She had to have a reason to think he was there to kill her.

He ran his gaze over her body, searching for wounds. Other than the bump on her forehead, she appeared to be okay, despite being tossed by her horse.

The animal had recovered his footing and taken off toward the highway.

Caveman would have the sheriff come out and retrieve the horse. For now, the woman needed to be taken to the hospital. He ran back to his truck for his cell phone, knowing the chances it would work out there were slim to none. But he had to try. He checked. No service.

How the heck was he supposed to call for an airlift? Then he remembered where he was. The foothills of the Beartooth Mountains. He didn't have the radio communications he was used to, or the helicopter support to bring injured teammates out of a bad situation.

With no other choice, he threw open the truck's rear door,

returned to the woman, scooped her up in his arms and carried her to his truck. Carefully laying her on the backseat, he buckled a seat belt around her hips and stared down at her. Just to make certain she was still alive, he checked for a pulse.

Still beating. *Good.*

She had straight, sandy-blond hair, clear, makeup-free skin and appeared to be somewhere between twenty-five and thirty years old. The spill she'd taken from her horse could have caused a head, neck or back injury. If they weren't in the mountains, where bears, wolves and other animals could find her, he would have left her lying still until a medic could bring a backboard, to avoid further injury. But out in the open, with wolves and grizzlies a real threat, Caveman couldn't leave the woman.

He shut the door and climbed into the driver's seat. The man he was supposed to meet out there would have to wait. This woman needed immediate medical attention.

As soon as he got closer to the little town of Grizzly Pass, he checked his phone for service. He had enough to get a call through to Kevin Garner. "Caveman here. I have an injured woman in the backseat of my truck. I'm taking her to the local clinic. You'll have to send someone else out to meet with Mr. Khalig. I don't know when I'll get back out there."

"Who've you got?" Kevin asked.

"I don't know. She was thrown from the horse she was riding. She hasn't been conscious long enough to tell me her life history, much less her name."

"Grace," a gravelly voice said from the backseat.

Caveman glanced over his shoulder.

"My name's Grace Saunders." The woman he'd settled on the backseat pushed to a sitting position and pressed a hand to the back of her head. "Who are you? Where am I?"

"I take it she's awake?" Kevin said into Caveman's ear.

"Roger." He shot a glance at the rearview mirror, into the soft gray eyes of the woman he'd rescued. "Gotta go, Kevin. Will update you as soon as I know anything."

"I'll see if I can find someone I can send out to check on Mr. Khalig," Kevin said.

His gaze moving from the road ahead to the reflection of the woman behind him, Caveman focused on Kevin's words. "I found a truck and trailer where his office staff said it would be, but the man himself wasn't anywhere nearby."

"I suspect that truck and trailer either belong to the dead man or the man who was doing the shooting," the woman in the backseat said.

"Dead man?" Caveman removed his foot from the accelerator. "What dead man? What shooting?"

"I'll tell you when we get to town. Right now my head hurts." She touched the lump on her forehead and winced. "Where are we going?"

He didn't demand to know what she was talking about, knowing the woman needed medical attention after her fall. "To the clinic in Grizzly Pass." He'd get the full story once she had been checked out.

"I don't need to go to the clinic." She leaned over the back of the seat and touched his shoulder. "Take me to the sheriff's office."

Caveman frowned. "Lady, you need to see a doctor. You were out cold."

"My name is Grace, and I know what I need. And that's to see the sheriff. *Now*."

He glanced at her face in the mirror. "Okay, but if you pass out, I'm taking you to the clinic. No argument."

"Deal." She nodded toward the road ahead. "You'd better slow down or you'll miss the turn."

Caveman slammed on his brakes in time to pull into the parking lot.

Grace braced her hands on the backs of the seats and swayed with the vehicle as it made the sharp turn. "I was okay, until you nearly gave me whiplash." She didn't wait for him to come to a complete stop before she pushed open her door and dropped down from the truck, crumpling to the ground.

Out of the truck and around the front, Caveman bent to help, sliding his hands beneath her thighs. "We're going to the clinic."

She pushed him away. "I don't need to be carried. I can stand on my own."

"As you have so clearly demonstrated." He drew in a breath and let it out slowly. "Fine. At least let me help you stand upright." He slipped an arm around her waist and lifted her to her feet.

When she was standing on her own, she nodded. "I've got it now."

"Uh-huh. Prove it." He let go of her for a brief moment.

Grace swayed and would have fallen if he'd let her. But he didn't. Instead he wrapped his arm around her waist again and led her into the sheriff's office.

With his help, she made it inside to the front desk.

The deputy on the other side glanced up with a slight frown, his gaze on Caveman. "May I help you?" His frown deepened as he looked toward the woman leaning on Caveman. "Grace?" He popped up from his desk. "Are you all right?"

"I'm fine, Johnny. Is Sheriff Scott in? I need to talk to him ASAP."

"Yeah. I'll get him." He glanced from her to Caveman and back. "As long as you're okay."

Anger simmered beneath the surface. Caveman glanced at the man's name tag. "Deputy Pierce, just get the damn sheriff. I'm not going to hurt her. If I was, I would have left her lying where her horse threw her."

The deputy's lips twitched. "Going." He spun on his heels and hurried through a door and down a hallway. A moment later, he returned with an older man, dressed in a similar tan shirt and brown slacks. "Grace, Johnny said you were thrown by your horse." He held out his hand. "Shouldn't you be at the clinic?"

Grace took the proffered hand and shook her head. "I don't

need to see a doctor. I need you and your men to follow me back out to the trail I was on. Now."

"Why? What's wrong?" Sheriff Scott squeezed her hand between both of his. "The wolves in trouble?"

"It's not the wolves I'm worried about right now." She drew in a deep breath. "There was a man. Actually there were two men." She stiffened in the curve of Caveman's arm. "Hell, Sheriff, I witnessed a murder." She let her hand drop to her side as she sagged against Caveman. "I saw it all happen…and I was too far away…to do anything to stop it." She sniffed. "You have to get out there. Just in case he isn't dead. It'll get dark soon. The wolves will find him."

"Is that why you were riding your horse like you were?" Caveman asked.

She nodded. "That, and someone was shooting at me. That's why Bear threw me." Her head came up and she stared at the sheriff. "I need to find Bear. He's running around out there, probably scared out of his mind."

Sheriff Scott touched her arm. "I'll send someone out to look for him and bring him back to your place." He glanced at Caveman. "And you are?"

"Max Decker. But my friends call me Caveman."

The sheriff's eyes narrowed. "And what do you have to do with all of this?"

Grace leaned back and stared up at the man she'd been leaning on. "Yeah, why were you out in the middle of nowhere?"

"I was sent to check on a Mr. Khalig, a pipeline inspector for Rocky Mountain Pipeline Inc. I was told he'd been receiving threats."

"RJ Khalig?" the sheriff asked.

Caveman nodded. "That's the one."

"He's been a regular at the Blue Moose Tavern since he arrived in town a couple weeks ago. He's staying at Mama Jo's Bed-and-Breakfast," Sheriff Scott added.

Grace shook her head. "I'll bet he's the man I saw get shot.

He appeared to be checking some device in a valley when the shooter took him down."

"What exactly did you see?" Sheriff Scott asked.

"Yeah," Caveman said. "I'd like to know, as well."

GRACE'S INSIDES CLENCHED and her pulse sped up. "I was searching for one of the wolves we'd collared last spring. His transponder still works, but hasn't moved in the past two days. Either he's lost his collar, or he's dead. I needed to know." Grace took a breath and let it out, the horror of the scene she'd witnessed threatening to overwhelm her.

"I was coming up to the top of a hill, hoping to see the wolf pack in the valley below, so I tied my horse to a tree short of the crown of the ridge. When I climbed to the crest, I saw a vehicle on a hilltop on the other side of the valley. It was an all-terrain vehicle, a four-wheeler. I thought maybe the rider had fallen off or was hurt, so I looked for him and spotted him in the shade of a tree, lying in the prone position on the ground, and he was aiming a rifle at something in the valley." She twisted her fingers. "My first thought was of the wolves. But when I glanced down into the valley, the wolf pack wasn't there. A man was squatting near the ground, looking at a handheld device.

"When I realized what was about to happen, I yelled. But not soon enough. The shooter fired his shot at the same time. The man in the valley didn't have a chance." She met the sheriff's gaze. "I couldn't even go check on him because the shooter must have heard my shout. The next thing I knew, he was aiming his rifle at me." She shivered. "I got on my horse and raced to the bottom of the mountain."

"And he followed?"

She nodded. "He shot at me a couple of times. I thought I might have outrun him, but he caught up about the time I reached the truck and trailer Mr. Decker mentioned. He shot at me, hit the truck, my horse threw me and I woke up in the backseat of Mr. Decker's truck." She inhaled deeply and let it all out. "We have to go back to that valley. If there's even a chance Mr. Khalig is alive, he won't be by morning."

"I'll take my men and check it out."

Grace touched his arm. "I'm going with you. It'll take less time for you to find him if I show you the exact location."

"You need to see a doctor," the sheriff said. "As you said, I don't have time to wait for that." He glanced at Caveman. "Do you want me to have one of my deputies take you to the clinic?"

Grace's lips firmed into a straight line. "I'm not going to a clinic. I'm going back to check on that man. I won't rest until I know what happened to him. If you won't take me, I'll get on my own four-wheeler and go up there. You're going to need all-terrain vehicles, anyway. Your truck won't make it up those trails."

The sheriff nodded toward his deputy. "Load up the trailer with the two four-wheelers. We're going into the mountains." He faced Grace. "And we're taking her with us."

"I'll meet you out at Khalig's truck in fifteen minutes. It'll take me that long to get to my place, grab my four-wheeler and get back to the location." She faced Caveman. "Do you mind dropping me off at my house? It's at the end of Main Street."

"I'm going with you," Caveman said.

"You're under no obligation to," she pointed out.

"No, but when you find an unconscious woman in the wilderness, you tend to invest in her well-being." His eyes narrowed. He could be as stubborn as she was. "I'm going."

"Do you have a four-wheeler?"

"No, but I know someone who probably does." Given the mission of Task Force Safe Haven, Kevin Garner had to have the equipment he needed to navigate the rocky hills and trails. If not horses, he had to have four-wheelers.

"I'm not waiting for you," Grace warned.

"You're not leaving without me," he countered.

"Is that a command?" She raised her brows. "I'll have you know, I'll do whatever the hell I please."

Caveman sighed. "It's a suggestion. Face it, if your shooter is still out there, you'll need protection."

"The sheriff and deputy will provide any protection I might need."

"They will be busy processing a crime scene."

"Then, I can take care of myself," Grace said. "I've been going out in these mountains alone for nearly a decade. I don't need a man to follow me, or protect me."

The sheriff laid a hand on her arm. "Grace, he's right. We'll be busy processing a crime scene. Once you get us there, we won't have time to keep an eye on you."

"I can keep an eye on myself," she said. "I'm the one person most interested in my own well-being."

Caveman pressed a finger to her lips. "You're an independent woman. I get that. But before now, you probably have never had someone shooting at you. I have." He took her hand. "Even in the worst battlefield scenarios, I rely on my battle buddies to have my back. Let me get your back."

For a moment, she stared at his hand holding hers. Then she glanced up into his gaze. "Fine. But if you can't keep up, I'll leave you behind."

He nodded. "Deal."

SHE GAVE THE truck and trailer's location to the sheriff and the deputy. Because she didn't want to slow them down from getting out to the site, she was forced to accept a ride from the man who'd picked her up off the ground and carried her around like she was little more than a child.

A shiver slipped through her at the thought of Caveman touching her body in places that hadn't been touched by a man in too long. And he'd found her unconscious. Had she been in the city, anything could have happened to her. In the mountains, with a shooter after her, she hated to think what would have happened had Caveman not come along when he had.

If the killer hadn't finished her off, the wolves, a bear, a mountain lion could have done it for him. Much as she hated to admit it, she was glad the stranger had come along and tucked her into the backseat of his truck.

"We'll meet you in fifteen minutes," Grace said to the sheriff.

He tipped his cowboy hat. "Roger." Then he was all business back on the telephone before Grace made it to the door.

Once outside, Grace strode toward Caveman's truck, now fully in control of the muscles in her legs. She didn't need to lean on anyone. Nor did she need help getting up into the truck.

Caveman beat her to the truck and opened the passenger door.

She frowned at the gesture, seeing it as a challenge to her ability to take care of herself.

"Just so you don't think I'm being chauvinistic, I always open doors for women. My mother drilled that into my head at a very young age. It's a hard habit to break, and I have no intention of doing that now. It's just being polite."

Grace slid into the seat and gave a low-key grunt. "You don't have to make a big deal out of it," she said through clenched teeth.

Caveman rounded the front of the truck, his broad shoulders and trim waist evidence of a man who took pride in fitness. She'd bet there wasn't an ounce of fat on his body, yet he didn't strut to show off his physique. The man had purpose in his stride, and it wasn't the purpose of looking good, though he'd accomplished that in spades. And he was polite, which made Grace feel churlish and unappreciative of all he'd done for her.

When he slid into the driver's seat beside her, she stared straight ahead, her lips twisting into a wry smile. "Thank you for helping me when I was unconscious. And thank you for giving me a ride to my house." She glanced across at him. "And thank you for opening my door for me. It's nice to know chivalry isn't dead."

His lips twitched. "You're welcome." Twisting the key in the ignition, he shot a glance toward her. "Where to?"

She gave him the directions to her little cottage sitting on an acre of land on the edge of town. She hoped Bear had found his way home after his earlier scare. The town of Grizzly Pass was situated in a valley between hills that led up into the mountains. Grace had ridden out that morning from the little barn behind her house.

As she neared the white clapboard cottage with the wide front porch and antique blue shutters, she leaned forward, trying to see around the house to the barn. Was that a tail swishing near the back gate?

Caveman pulled into the driveway.

Before he could shift into Park, she was out of the truck and hurrying around to the back of the house.

Her protector switched off the engine and hurried after her. "Hey, wait up," he called out.

Grace ignored him, bent and slipped through the fence rails and ran toward the back gate next to the barn, her heart soaring.

Bear stood at the gate, tossing his head and dancing back on his hooves.

She opened the gate and held it wide.

Bear slipped through and turned to nuzzle her hand.

Grace reached into her jeans pocket and pulled out the piece of carrot she'd planned on giving Bear as a treat at the end of the day. She held it out in the palm of her hand.

Bear's big, velvety lips took the carrot and he crunched it between his teeth, nodding his head in approval.

Wrapping her arms around his neck, Grace hugged the horse, relieved he wasn't hurt by the bullet or by wandering around the countryside and crossing highways. "Hey, big boy. Glad you made it home without me." She held on to his bridle and leaned her forehead against his. "I bet you're hungry and thirsty."

Bear tossed his head and whinnied.

With a laugh, Grace straightened and walked toward the barn. Bear followed.

Inside, she opened the stall door. Bear trotted in.

She removed Bear's bridle and was surprised to find Caveman beside her loosening the leather strap holding the girth around the horse's middle. "I can take care of that," she assured him.

"I know my way around horses," he said, and pulled the saddle from Bear's back. "Tack room?"

"At the back of the barn. I can handle the rest. I just want to get him situated before we leave."

"No problem." He took the saddle and carried it to the tack room. Caveman reappeared outside the stall. "I'll be right back."

"I'm leaving as soon as I'm done here."

"Understood." He took off at a jog out of the barn.

With her self-appointed protector gone, Grace suddenly had a feeling of being exposed. Shrugging off the insecurity, she went to work, giving the horse food and water, and then closed the stall.

From another stall, she rolled her four-wheeler out into the open. She hadn't ridden it in a month and the last time she had, it had been slow to start. She'd had to charge the battery and probably needed to buy a new one, but she didn't have time now. She'd promised to meet the sheriff in fifteen minutes. Already five had passed.

The next five minutes, she did everything she knew to start the vehicle and it refused.

Just when she was about to give up and call the sheriff, a small engine's roar sounded outside the barn.

She walked out and shook her head.

Caveman sat on a newer-model ATV. "Ready?"

"Where did you get that?"

"My boss dropped it off." He checked the instruments, revved the throttle and looked up. "I thought you'd be gone by now."

"I can't get mine to start, and we're supposed to be there in five minutes."

"Let me take a look." He killed the engine and entered the barn.

Okay, so she wasn't that knowledgeable about mechanics.

She knew Wally, who had a small-engine repair shop in his barn. He fixed anything she had issues with. That didn't mean she couldn't take care of herself.

"Your battery is dead." Caveman glanced around. "You got another handy?"

She shook her head. "No. Fresh out."

"Got a helmet?"

She nodded. "Yeah, but I won't need it if I can't get my ATV started."

He spun and headed for the barn door. "You can ride on the back of mine," he called out over his shoulder.

Grace's heart fluttered at the thought riding behind Caveman, holding him around the waist to keep from falling off. "No, thanks. Those trails are dangerous." She suspected the danger was more in how her pulse quickened around the man than the possibility of plunging over the edge of a drop-off.

"I grew up riding horses and four-wheelers on rugged mountain trails. I won't let you fall off a cliff." He held up a hand. "Promise."

She frowned. But she knew she only had a few minutes to get to the meeting location and relented, sighing. "Okay. I guess I'll put my life in your hands." She followed him out of the barn and closed the door behind her. "Although I don't know why I should trust you. I don't even know you."

Chapter Three

Caveman settled on the seat of the ATV and tipped his head toward the rear. "Hop on."

Grace fitted her helmet on her head and buckled the strap beneath her chin. "Wouldn't it make more sense for me to drive, since I know the way?"

"Actually, it does." He grinned, scooted to the back of the seat and glanced toward her, raising his brows in challenge.

Still, Grace hesitated for a moment, gnawing on her bottom lip.

God, when she did that, Caveman's groin clenched and he fought the urge to kiss that worried lip and suck it into his mouth. The woman probably had no clue how crazy she could make a man. And he was no exception.

Finally, she slid onto the seat in front of Caveman. "Hold on." She thumbed the throttle and the four-wheeler leaped forward.

Caveman wrapped his arms around her waist and pressed his chest to her back. Oh, yeah, this was much better than driving.

Grace aimed for the back gate to the pasture, blew through and followed a dirt road up into the hills, zigzagging through fields and gullies until she crossed a highway and ended up on the road leading to Khalig's truck and trailer. Another truck and trailer stood beside the original, this one marked with the county sheriff logo. Sheriff Scott and Deputy Pierce were mounted on four-wheelers.

Grace nodded as she passed them, leading the way up the side of a mountain, the trail narrowing significantly. There was no way a full-size truck or even an SUV could navigate the trajectories. Barely wide enough for the four-wheeler, the path clung to the side of a bluff. The downhill side was so steep it might as well be considered a drop-off. Anyone who fell over the edge wouldn't stop until they hit the bottom a hundred or more feet below.

Now not so sure he'd chosen the right position, Caveman wished he had control of steering the ATV. He tightened his arms around Grace's slim waist, wondering if she had the strength to keep them both on the vehicle if they hit a really big bump.

Caveman vowed to be the driver on the way back down the mountain. In the meantime, he concentrated on leaning into the curves and staying on the ATV.

As they neared the top of a steep hill, Grace slowed and rolled to a stop. "This is where I tied off my horse."

The sheriff and deputy pulled up beside them. Everyone dismounted.

Fighting the urge to drop to a prone position on the ground and kiss the earth, Caveman stood and pretended the ride up the treacherous trail hadn't been a big deal at all. "You rode your horse down that trail?"

She nodded. "Normally, I take it slowly. But I had a gunman taking shots at me. I let Bear have his head. I have to admit, I wanted to close my eyes several times on the way down."

The sheriff nodded toward the ridgeline. "Was that your vantage point?"

She nodded, but didn't move toward the top. "The shooter was on the ridge to the north."

Sheriff Scott and the deputy drew their weapons and climbed. As they neared the top, they dropped to their bellies and low-crawled the rest of the way. The sheriff lifted binoculars to his eyes.

Caveman stayed with Grace in case the shooter was watching for her.

A couple minutes later, Sheriff Scott waved. "All clear. Grace, I need you to show me what you were talking about."

Grace frowned, scrambled up to the top and squatted beside the sheriff.

Caveman followed, his gaze taking in the valley below and the ridge to the north. Nothing moved and nothing stood out as not belonging.

Grace pointed to the opposite hilltop. "The shooter was over there." Then she glanced down at the valley, her frown deepening. "The man he shot was in the valley just to the right of that pine."

The sheriff raised his binoculars to his eyes again. "He's not there."

"What?" She held out her hand. "Let me see."

Sheriff Scott handed her the binoculars. Grace adjusted them and stared down at the valley below. "I don't understand. He was in that valley. Hell, his truck and trailer are still parked back at the road. Where could he have gone?" She handed the binoculars back to the sheriff. "Do you think he was only wounded and crawled beneath a bush or something?" She was on her feet and headed back to the ATV. "We need to get down there. If that man is still alive, he could be in a bad way."

The sheriff hurried to catch up to her. "Grace, I want you to stay up here with Mr. Decker."

She'd reached the ATV and had thrown her leg over the seat before she turned to stare at the sheriff. "Are you kidding? I left him once, when I could have saved him."

The sheriff shook his head. "You don't know that. You could have ended up a second victim, and nobody would have known where to find either one of you." He touched her arm. "You did the right thing by coming straight to my office."

When the lawman turned away, Grace captured his hand. "Sheriff, I need to know. I feel like I could have done something to stop that man from shooting the other guy. I know it's irrational, but somehow I feel responsible."

The way she stared at the sheriff with her soft gray eyes made Caveman want the sheriff to let her accompany him to the valley floor.

"You promise to stay back enough not to disturb what could potentially be a crime scene?" Sheriff Scott asked.

She held up her hand like she was swearing in front of a judge. "I promise."

The sheriff shot a glance at Caveman. "Mr. Decker, will you keep an eye on her to make sure she's safe?"

"I will," Caveman said. He wanted to know what was in that valley as well, but if it meant leaving Grace alone on the ridge, he would have stayed with her.

"Fine. Come along, but stay back." Sheriff Scott and the deputy climbed onto their four-wheelers and eased their way down a narrow path to the valley floor.

Caveman let Grace drive again, knowing she was better protected with his body wrapped around her than if she'd ridden on the back.

At the bottom of the hill, Grace parked the four-wheeler twenty yards from the pine tree she'd indicated. "We'll see a lot more on foot than on an ATV."

"True." Caveman studied the surrounding area, careful to stay out of the way of the sheriff and his deputy.

"Grace," the sheriff called out.

She and Caveman hurried over to where the sheriff squatted on his haunches, staring at the dirt. He pointed. "Is this the spot where he fell?"

Grace glanced around at the nearby tree and nodded. "I think so."

The sheriff's lips pressed together and he pointed at the ground. "This looks like dried blood."

Caveman stared at the dark blotches, his belly tightening. He'd seen similar dark stains in the dust of an Afghanistan village where his brothers in arms had bled out.

"Got tire tracks here." Deputy Pierce stared at the ground a few yards away.

The sheriff straightened and walked slowly toward the deputy. "And there's a trail of blood leading toward the tracks."

Caveman circled wide, studying the ground until he saw what he thought he might find. "More tracks over here." The tracks led toward a hill. Without waiting for permission, Caveman climbed the hill, parallel to the tracks. As the ground grew rockier, the tracks became harder to follow. At that point, Caveman looked for disturbed pebbles, scraped rocks and anything that would indicate a heavy four-wheeler had passed that direction.

At the top of the hill, the slope leveled off briefly and then fell in a sheer two-hundred-foot drop-off to a boulder-strewn creek bed below. Caveman's stomach tightened as he spotted what appeared to be the wreckage of an ATV. "I found the ATV." He squinted. What was that next to the big boulder shaped like an anvil? He leaned over the edge a little farther and noticed what appeared to be a shoe…attached to a foot. "I'm sorry to say, but I think I found Mr. Khalig."

Grace scrambled to the top of the hill and nearly pitched over the edge.

Caveman shot out his hand, stopping her short of following the pipeline inspector to a horrible death. "Oh, dear Lord."

Wrapping his arm around her shoulders, Caveman pulled her against him.

She burrowed her face into his chest. "I should have stayed."

"You couldn't," Caveman said. "You would have been shot."

"I could have circled back," she said, her voice quivering.

"On that trail?" Caveman shook his head. "No way. You did the right thing."

Sheriff Scott appeared beside Caveman. "Mr. Decker's right. You wouldn't be alive if you'd stopped to help a man who could have been dead before he went over the edge."

Grace lifted her head and stared at the sheriff through watery eyes. "What do you mean?"

"We noticed footprints and drag marks in the dirt back there," Deputy Pierce said.

The sheriff nodded. "I suspect the killer came back, dragged the body onto the ATV and rode it up to the hill. Then he pushed it over the edge with Mr. Khalig still on it." He glanced over at the deputy. "We'll get the state rescue team in to recover the body. The coroner will conduct an autopsy. He'll know whether the bullet killed him or the fall."

"Is there anything we can do to help?" Grace asked.

Sheriff Scott nodded. "I'd like you to come in and sign a statement detailing what you saw and at what time."

"Anything you need. I'll be there." Grace shivered. "I wish I'd seen the killer's face."

"I do, too." The sheriff stared down at the creek bed. "Murder cases are seldom solved so easily." He glanced across at Grace. "You might want to watch your back. If he thinks you could pick him out in a lineup, he might come after you."

Grace shivered again. "We live in a small town." Her gaze captured the sheriff's. "There's a good chance I might know him."

"If the law isn't knocking on his door within twenty-four hours," Caveman said, "he might figure out that you didn't see enough of him to turn him in."

"In which case, he'd be smart to keep a low profile and leave you alone," the sheriff added.

"Or not." Grace sighed. "I can't stay holed up in my house. I have work to do. I still haven't found my wolf."

"It might not be safe for you to be roaming the woods right now," the sheriff said. "By yourself, you present an easy target with no witnesses."

Grace's shoulders squared. "I won't let fear run my life. I ran today, and Mr. Khalig is dead because I did."

Caveman shook his head. "No, Mr. Khalig is dead because someone shot him. Not because you didn't stop that someone from shooting him. You are not responsible for that man's death. You didn't pull the trigger." The words were an echo from his psychologist's arsenal of phrases she'd used to help him through survivor's guilt. Using them now with Grace helped him see the truth of them.

He hadn't detonated the bomb that had killed his teammates, nor had he pulled the trigger on the AK-47s that had taken out more of his battle buddies. He couldn't have done anything differently other than die in his teammates' place by being the forward element at that exact moment. He couldn't have known. It didn't make it easier. Only time would help him accept the truth.

"THERE IS SOMETHING you could do for me," the sheriff said.

Grace perked up. "Anything." After all that had happened, she refused to be a victim. She wanted to help.

"Go back down, get in my service vehicle and let dispatch know to call in the mountain rescue crew. Johnny and I will stay and make sure the wolves don't clean up before they get here."

"Will do," Grace said. "Do you need me to come back?"

"No. We can handle it from here. You should head home. And please consider lying low for a while until we're sure the killer isn't still gunning for you."

"Okay," Grace said. Though she had work to do, she now knew she wasn't keen on being the target of a gunman. She'd give it at least a day for the man to realize she hadn't seen him and couldn't identify his face. "You'll let me know what they find out about the man down there?"

"You bet," Sherriff Scott said. "Thank you, Grace, for letting us know as soon as possible."

But not soon enough to help Mr. Khalig. She turned and started back down the hill. Her feet slipped in the gravel and she would have fallen, but Caveman was right beside her and helped her get steady on her feet. He hooked her elbow and assisted her the rest of the way down the steep incline.

At the bottom, he turned her to face him. "Are you okay?"

She nodded. "I'm fine, just a little shaken. It's not every day I witness a murder."

His lips twisted. "How many murders have you witnessed?"

"Counting today?" She snorted. "One." With a nod toward the ATV, she said, "You can drive. I'm not sure I can hold it steady." She held up a hand, demonstrating how much it trembled.

"Thanks. I would rather navigate the downhill trail. Coming up was bad enough." He climbed onto the ATV and scooted forward, allowing room for her to mount behind him.

At this point, Grace didn't care that he was a stranger. The man had found her unconscious, sought help for her and then gone with her to show the sheriff where a murder had taken place. If he'd been the shooter, he'd have killed her by now and avoided the sheriff altogether.

She slipped onto the seat and held on to the metal rack bolted to the back of the machine, thinking it would be enough to keep her seated.

"You need to hold on around my waist," Caveman advised. "It's a lot different being on the back than holding on to the handlebars."

"I'll be okay," she assured him.

Caveman shrugged, started the engine and eased his thumb onto the throttle.

The ATV leapt forward, nearly leaving Grace behind.

She swallowed a yelp, wrapped her arms around his waist and didn't argue anymore as they traversed the downhill trail to the bottom.

When she'd been the target of the shooter, she hadn't had time to worry about falling off her sure-footed horse. Now that she wasn't in control of the ATV and was completely reliant on

Caveman, she felt every bump and worried the next would be the one that would throw her over the edge. She tightened her hold around his middle, slightly reassured by the solid muscles beneath his shirt.

For a moment, she closed her eyes and inhaled the scent of pure male—a mix of aftershave and raw, outdoor sensuality. It calmed her.

Although she'd always valued her independence, she could appreciate having someone to lean on in this new and dangerous world she lived in. Before, she'd only had to worry about bears and wolves killing her. Now she had to worry about a man diabolical enough to hunt another man down like an animal.

By the time they finally reached the bottom and made their way back to the parked trucks, Grace's body had adjusted to Caveman's movements, making them seem like one person—riding the trails, absorbing every bump and leaning into every turn.

When the vehicles came into view, she pulled herself back to the task at hand.

Caveman stopped next to the sheriff's truck and switched off the ATV's engine.

Grace climbed off the back, the cool mountain air hitting her front where the heat generated by Caveman still clung to her. Shaking off the feeling of loss, she opened the passenger door of the sheriff's vehicle, slid onto the front seat, grabbed the radio mic and pressed the button. "Hello."

"This is dispatch, who am I talking to?"

"Grace Saunders. Sheriff Scott wanted me to relay a request for a mountain rescue team to be deployed to his location as soon as possible."

"Could you provide a little detail to pass on to the team?" the dispatcher asked.

Grace inhaled and let out a long slow breath before responding. "There's a man at the bottom of a deep drop-off."

"Is he unconscious?"

The hollow feeling in her chest intensified. "We believe he's dead. He's not moving and he could be the victim of a gunshot wound."

"Got it. I'll relay the GPS coordinate and have the team sent out as soon as they can mobilize."

"Thank you." Grace hung the mic on the radio and climbed out of the sheriff's SUV.

"Now what?" Caveman asked. He'd dismounted from the four-wheeler and stepped up beside the sheriff's vehicle while she'd been talking on the radio.

She shrugged. "If you could take me back to my place, I have work to do."

Caveman frowned. "When we get there, will you let me take you to the clinic to see a doctor?"

"I don't need one." Her head hurt and she was a little nauseated, but she wouldn't admit it to him. "I'd rather stay home."

"I'll make a deal with you. I'll take you home if you promise to let me take you from there to see a doctor."

She sighed. "You're not going to let it go, are you?"

He crossed his arms over his chest and shook his head. "Nope."

"And if I don't agree, either I walk home—which I don't mind, but I'm not in the mood—or I wait until the sheriff is done retrieving Mr. Khalig's body."

His lips twitched. "That about sums it up. See a doctor, walk home alone or wait for a very long time." He raised his hands, palms up. "It's a no-brainer to me."

Her eyes narrowed. "I'll walk." She brushed past him and lengthened her stride, knowing she was too emotionally exhausted to make the long trek all the way back to her house, but too stubborn to let Caveman win the argument.

The ATV roared to life behind her and the crunch of gravel heralded its approach.

"You might also consider that by walking home, you put yourself up as an easy target for a man who has proven he can take a man down from a significant distance. Are you willing to be his next target?"

His words socked her in the gut. She stopped in her tracks and her lips pressed together in a hard line.

Damn. The man had a good point. "Fine." She spun and slipped her leg over the back of the four-wheeler. "You can take me to my house. From there, I'll take myself to the clinic."

Caveman shook his head, refusing to engage the engine and send the ATV toward Grace's house. "That's not the deal. I take you home. Then I will take you to the clinic. When the doctor clears you to drive, you can take yourself anywhere you want to go."

"Okay. We'll do it your way." She wrapped her arms loosely around his waist, unwilling to be caught up in the pheromones the man put off. "Can we go, already?"

"Now we can go." He goosed the throttle. The ATV jumped, nearly unseating Grace.

She tightened her hold around Caveman's waist and pressed her body against his as they bumped along the dirt road with more potholes than she remembered on the way out. Perhaps because she noticed them more this time because she wasn't the one in control of the steering. Either way, she held on, her thighs tightly clamped around his hips and the seat.

By the time they arrived at her cottage, she could barely breathe—the fact having nothing to do with the actual ride so much as it did with the feel of the man's body pressed against hers. She was almost disappointed when he brought the vehicle to a standstill next to her gate.

Grace climbed off and opened the gate. The distance between them helped her to get her head on straight and for her pulse to slow down to normal.

He followed her to her house. "We'll take my truck. Grab your purse and whatever else you'll need."

When she opened her mouth to protest, he held up his hand.

"You promised." He frowned and crossed his arms over his chest again. "Where I come from, a promise is sacred."

Her brows met in the middle. "Where *do* you come from?"

His frown disappeared and he grinned. "Montana."

Caveman started toward the house, Grace fell in step beside him. "Is that where you were before you arrived in Grizzly Pass?"

His grin slipped. "No."

She shot a glance his direction. A shadow had descended on his face and he appeared to be ten years older.

"Where *did* you come from?"

He stared out at the mountains. "Bethesda, Maryland."

There was so much she didn't know about this man. "That's a long way from Montana."

"Yes, it is." He stopped short of her porch. "I'll be in my truck when you're ready." Before she could say more, he turned and strode toward the corner of her house.

For a moment, Grace allowed herself the pleasure of watching the way his butt twitched in his blue jeans. The man was pure male and so ruggedly handsome he took her breath away. What was he doing hanging around her? Since she was being forced to ride with him to the clinic, she'd drill him with questions until she was satisfied with the answers. For starters, why did he call himself Caveman? And what was the importance of Bethesda, Maryland, that had made him go from being relaxed and helpful to stiff and unapproachable?

Caveman disappeared around the corner.

Grace faced her house, fished her key from her pocket and climbed the stairs. She opened the screen door and held out the key, ready to fit it into the lock when she noticed something hanging on the handle. It rocked back and forth and then fell at her feet.

She jumped back, emitting a short, sharp scream, her heart thundering against her ribs. With her hand pressed to her chest, she squatted and stared at the item, a lead weight settling in the pit of her belly as she recognized the circular band with the rectangular plastic box affixed to it.

It was the radio collar for the wolf she'd been looking for earlier that day, and it was covered in blood.

Chapter Four

Caveman had been about to climb into his truck when he heard Grace's scream. All thoughts of Bethesda, physical therapy and war wounds disappeared in a split second. He pulled his pistol from beneath the seat and raced back around the house to find Grace sitting on the porch, her back leaning against the screen door, her hand pressed to her chest.

"What's wrong?" His heart thundered against his ribs and his breathing was erratic as he stared around the back porch, searching for the threat.

"This." She pointed toward something on the porch in front of her. It appeared to be some kind of collar. Her gaze rose to his, her eyes wide, filling with tears. "This is the collar for the wolf I was looking for when I ran across the murder scene."

"What the hell's it doing here?"

"It was hanging on the handle of the door. Someone put it there."

"Do you have any coworkers who would have brought it to you?" Caveman reached out a hand to her.

She laid her slim fingers into his palm and allowed him to

pull her to her feet and into his arms. "It has blood on it and it's been cut."

"Why would someone put it on your doorknob?" he asked.

She drew in a deep breath and let it out. "I was out in the mountains where I was because I was following the signal for this collar. It had stopped moving as of two days ago. The only other people aware of the wolf's movement, or lack thereof, were my coworkers on the Wolf Project out of Yellowstone National Park. This collar belonged to Loki, a black male wolf out of Molly's pack. I rescued him as a cub when his mother had been killed by a local rancher." Her jaw tightened, she drew herself up and gave him a level stare through moist eyes. "We suspected he was dead, but had hoped of natural causes. That someone brought me the collar without a note of why it was covered in blood leaves me to think all kinds of bad things."

"You think the shooter who killed Khalig might have killed the wolf?"

"If he didn't kill the wolf, I think he wants me to believe he did."

"And he left the collar as a warning or a trophy?"

Grace stared down at the offensive object and nodded. "What else am I supposed to think? Unless someone else owns up to leaving the collar on my back porch doorknob, I can only imagine why it was left." She bent, reaching for the collar.

Caveman grabbed her arm to keep her from retrieving it. "Leave it there for the sheriff. They might be able to pull fingerprints from the plastic box."

Grace straightened. "Why do people have to be so destructive and heartless with nature?"

"I don't know, but let's get you inside, just in case the shooter is lurking nearby."

Grace shot a glance over her shoulder. "Do you think he might be out there watching?" A shiver shook her body.

"He could be." Caveman held out his hand. "Let me have your key."

She pointed at the porch near the collar, "I dropped it."

Caveman retrieved it from the porch and straightened. "Let's go through the front door." Slipping his arm around her, he shielded her body with his as much as possible as he led her around the house to the front door. There he opened the screen door. Before he fit the key into the lock, he tried the knob. It was locked. He fit the key in the knob, twisted and pushed the door open. "Let me go first."

She nodded and allowed him to enter first, following right behind him.

Closing the door behind her, he stared down into her eyes. "I want to check the house. Stay here."

Again, she nodded.

Caveman moved from room to room, holding his 9-millimeter pistol in front of him, checking around the corners of each wall before moving into a room. When he reached the back door, he checked the handle. The door was locked. As far as he could tell, the house hadn't been entered. "All clear," he called out.

"The sheriff will be busy up in the hills until they retrieve the body," Grace said, walking into the kitchen, her arms wrapped around her body. "I don't like the idea of leaving the collar on the porch."

"Do you have a paper bag we can use and maybe some rubber gloves?"

"I do." She hurried into a pantry off the kitchen and emerged with a box of rubber gloves and what appeared to be a paper lunch bag. Setting the box of gloves on the counter, she pulled on a pair. "These won't fit your big hands. I'll take care of the collar."

He opened the back door and looked before stepping over the collar and standing on the porch. He used his body as a shield to protect Grace in case the shooter had her in his sights. Given the killer had good aim with a rifle and scope, he could be hiding in the nearby woods, his sights trained on her back door.

Grace scooped up the collar by the nylon band and dropped it into the paper bag, touching as little as possible.

Once she had the collar in the bag, she nodded. "I'll grab my purse. We can drop this off at the sheriff's office."

"On the way to the clinic," Caveman added.

Her lush lips pulled into a twisted frown. "On the way to the clinic." The frown turned up on the corners. "You are a stubborn man, aren't you?"

He grinned and followed her back into the house, locking the door behind him. "I prefer to call it being persistent."

She walked back through the house. "If you give me just a minute, I'd like to wash my hands and face."

"Take your time. I'll wait by the front door."

Grace turned down the hallway and ducked into the bathroom, closing the door behind her.

Caveman waited in the front entrance, staring at the pictures hanging on the walls. Many were of wolves. Some were of people. One had a group of men and women standing in front of a cabin, all grinning, wearing outdoor clothing. Another photo was of Grace, maybe a few years younger, with a man. They were kissing with the sun setting over snowcapped peaks in the background. She looked young, happy and in love.

Something tugged at Caveman's chest. He'd assumed Grace was single.

The door opened to the bathroom and Grace appeared, her face freshly scrubbed, still makeup-free. She'd brushed her hair and left it falling around her shoulders the way it was in the picture.

"You have some interesting pictures on your wall." Caveman nodded toward the wolves.

She nodded. "I'm living my dream job as a biologist working on the Wolf Project, among others. The pictures are of some of the wolves I've been tracking for the past five years."

Caveman pointed toward the group picture.

Grace smiled. "Those are the crew of biologists working in

Yellowstone National Park. We keep in touch by phone, internet and through in-person meetings once a month."

"Do you live alone?" Caveman asked, his gaze on the picture of her kissing the man. "Should I be concerned about a jealous husband walking through the door at any moment?"

The smile left Grace's eyes. "Yes, I live alone. No, you don't have to worry." She grabbed a brown leather purse from a hallway table and opened the front door. "I'm ready."

"I take it I hit a sore spot," he said, passing her to exit the house first.

"I'm not married, anymore."

But she was once. Caveman vowed not to pry. Apparently, she wasn't over her ex-husband. Not if she still had his picture hanging in her front entrance.

Grace paused to lock the front door and then turned to follow him toward the truck. "For the record, I'm a widow. My husband died in a parasailing accident six years ago."

GRACE CLIMBED INTO the passenger seat of Caveman's truck. "You really don't have to take me to the clinic. I've been getting around fine for the past couple of hours without blacking out. I could drive myself there, for that matter."

"Humor me. I feel—"

"Responsible," she finished for him. "Well, you're not. You've done more than you had to. You could have dropped me off at the sheriff's office earlier today and been done with me."

"That's not the kind of guy I am."

She tilted her head and stared across the console at him. "No, I got that impression." She settled back in her seat, closed her eyes and let him take control, something she wasn't quite used to. "Well, thank you for coming to my rescue. If you hadn't been there…" She shivered. What would have happened? Would the shooter have caught up to her and finished her off like he'd done Mr. Khalig?

A hand touched hers.

She opened her eyes, her gaze going to where his hand held hers and warmth spread from that point throughout her body. She hadn't had that kind of reaction to a man's touch since Jack had died, and she wasn't sure she wanted it.

"I'm glad I was there." Caveman squeezed her fingers gently, briefly and let go. "I'm sorry about your husband."

"Yeah. Me, too. We were supposed to be doing this together." She shrugged and let go of the breath she hadn't known she was holding the whole time Caveman's hand had been on hers. "But that was six years ago. Life goes on. Turn left at the next street. The clinic is three blocks on the right."

They arrived in front of the Grizzly Pass Clinic a few minutes before it was due to close. "I doubt they can get me in."

"If they can't, where's the nearest emergency room?" Caveman shifted into Park and stepped down from the truck. Rounding the front of the vehicle, he arrived in time to help her down.

"The nearest would be in Bozeman, an hour and a half away."

"Guess we better get inside quickly." He cupped her elbow and guided her through the door.

Fortunately, the doctor had enough time left to check her over while her self-appointed bodyguard waited in the lobby.

"You appear to be all right. If you get any dizzy spells or feel nauseated, you might want to call the EMTs and have them transport you to the nearest hospital for further evaluation. But so far, I don't see anything that makes me too concerned." He offered her a prescription for painkillers, which she refused. "Then take some over-the-counter pain relievers if you get a headache."

She smiled. "Thank you for seeing me on such short notice."

"I'm glad I was here for you." He walked her to the door. "Have you considered wearing a helmet when you go horseback riding?"

"I have considered it. And I might resort to it, if I continue to fall off my horse." She might also consider a bulletproof vest and making the helmet a bulletproof one if she continued to be the target of a sniper. She didn't say it out loud, nor had she told the doctor why she'd fallen off her horse. The medical professional had been ready to go home before she'd shown up and he wasn't the one being shot at.

When she stepped out of the examination room into the lobby, she found Caveman laughing at something the cute receptionist had said. The smile on his face transformed him from the serious, rugged cowboy to someone more lighthearted and approachable. The sparkle in his eyes made him even more handsome than before.

A territorial feeling washed over Grace. Suddenly she had a better understanding of the urge the alpha wolf had to guard his mate and keep her to himself. Not that Caveman was Grace's mate. Hell, they'd just met!

But that didn't stop her fingers from curling into her palms or her gut from clenching when the receptionist smiled up at the man.

"Are you ready to take me home?" Grace asked, her voice a little sharper than usual.

Caveman straightened and turned his smile toward her, brightening the entire room with its full force. Then it faded and his brows pulled together. "What did the doctor say?"

"I'm fine. Can we go now?" She started for the door, ready to leave the office and the cute, young receptionist as soon as possible.

Grace was outside on the sidewalk by the time Caveman caught up with her and gripped her arm. "Slow down. It might not be safe for you to be out in the open. Care to elaborate on the doctor's prognosis?"

"He said I'm fine and can carry on, business as usual." She shook off his hand.

"No concussion?"

"No concussion. Which means you can drop me off at my house, and your responsibility toward me is complete."

He nodded and opened the truck door for her. "If you don't

mind, I'd like to stop by my boss's office for a few minutes. I need to brief him on what happened. He might want to hear what you have to say."

"Now that we're not being shot at, and I'm not dying of a concussion, maybe you can answer a few questions for me."

"Shoot." He winced. "Sorry. I didn't mean the pun."

She inhaled and thought of all the questions she had for this man. "Okay. Who's your boss?"

"The US Army, but I'm on temporary loan to a special task force with the Department of Homeland Security. I'm reporting to a man named Kevin Garner."

"I've seen Kevin around. I didn't know he was heading a special task force."

"It's new. I'm new. I got in a couple days ago, and I'm still trying to figure out what it is I'm supposed to be doing."

"Army?" That would explain the short hair, the military bearing and the scars. "For how long?"

"Eleven years."

"Deployed?"

He nodded, his gaze on the road ahead. "What is this? An interrogation?"

"I've been all over the mountains with you and I don't know who you are."

"I told you, I'm Max Decker, but my friends call me—"

"Caveman." She crossed her arms over her chest. "Why?"

"Why what?"

"Why do they call you Caveman?"

"I don't know. I guess because I look like a caveman? I got tagged with it in Delta Force training, and it's stuck ever since."

"Army Delta Force?" She looked at him anew. "Isn't that like the elite of the elite?"

He shrugged. "I like to think of it as highly skilled. I'm not an elitist."

"And you're assigned to the Department of Homeland Security?" She shook her head. "Who'd you make mad?"

His fingers tightened on the steering wheel until his knuckles turned white. "I'd like to know that myself."

"Wait." Her eyes narrowed. "You said you came from Bethesda. Isn't that where Walter Reed Army Hospital is located?"

A muscle ticked in his jaw. "Yeah. I was injured in battle. I just completed physical therapy and was waiting for orders to return to my unit."

"And you got pulled to help out here." It was a statement, not a question. "Any you carried me to your truck." She raked his body with her gaze. "I don't see you limping or anything."

"I told you. I finished my physical therapy. I've been working out since. I'm back to normal. Well, almost."

"What did you injure?"

He dropped his left hand to his thigh. "My leg."

"Gunshot?"

"Yeah."

"I'm sorry." She dragged her gaze away from him. "I didn't mean to get too personal."

"It's okay. When you're in the hospital, everyone gets pretty damned personal. I'm used to it by now."

"It had to be hard."

"What?"

"The hospital."

His replaced his hand on the steering wheel, as he pulled into the parking lot of the Blue Moose Tavern. "At least I made it to the hospital," he muttered.

Grace heard his words but didn't dig deeper to learn their meaning. She could guess. He'd made it to the hospital. Apparently, some of his teammates hadn't.

Sometimes recovering from an injury was easier than recovering from a loss. She knew. Having lost her husband in a parasailing accident, she understood what it felt like to lose someone you loved.

From what she knew about the Delta Force soldiers, they

were a tightly knit organization. A brotherhood. Those guys fought for their country and for each other.

Grace realized she and Caveman had more in common than she'd originally thought.

Chapter Five

Caveman got out of the truck in front of the Blue Moose Tavern, his thoughts on the men who'd lost their lives in that last battle. For a moment, he forgot where he was. He looked up at the sign on the front of the tavern and shook his head.

Like Grace had said, life moves on. He couldn't live in the past. Squaring his shoulders, he focused on the present and the woman who'd witnessed a murder. Kevin would want to hear what she had to say. Since the man who'd been shot was most likely RJ Khalig, it had to have something to do with the threats the man had reported, the reason Garner had sent Caveman out to find the pipeline inspector.

A pang of guilt tugged at his insides. If he hadn't delayed his departure, arguing over his assigned duties, would he have found Khalig before the sniper?

He shook his head. When he'd arrived at the base of the trail, he wouldn't have been able to find the man without GPS tracking and an all-terrain vehicle. *No.* He couldn't have gotten to Khalig before the shooter.

Grace was out of the truck before Caveman could reach her

door. She sniffed the air. "I didn't realize how hungry I was until now."

Caveman inhaled the scent of grilled hamburgers and his mouth watered. "Let's make it quick with Garner. If you're like me, you haven't eaten since breakfast this morning."

"And that was a granola bar." She glanced toward the tavern door. "They make good burgers here."

"Then we'll eat as soon as we're done upstairs." Caveman waved a hand toward the outside staircase leading up to the apartment above the tavern.

Grace rested her hand on the railing and climbed to the top.

Caveman followed closely, once again shielding Grace's body from a sniper's sights.

Before they reached the top landing, the door swung open. Kevin Garner greeted them. "Caveman, I'm glad you stopped by." He stepped back, allowing them to enter the upstairs apartment. Once they were inside, he closed the door, turned to Grace and held out his hand. "I've seen you in passing, but let me introduce myself. Kevin Garner, Department of Homeland Security."

"Grace Saunders. I'm a biologist assigned to the Wolf Project, working remotely with the National Park Service out of Yellowstone."

"Interesting work." Garner shook her hand. "I'm glad you stopped by. I wanted to hear what happened today. The last thing I knew, you were recovering from being thrown by your horse, and Caveman needed a four-wheeler to go back into the mountains. Care to fill me in on what's happened since you got up this morning?"

Grace spent the next five minutes detailing what she'd seen on that ridge in the mountains and what had followed, taking him all the way to her back porch and the present she'd received.

She held out the paper bag with the dog collar inside. "Can I assume you have some of the same capabilities or access to the same support facilities as the sheriff's office?"

Garner took the bag, opened it and stared inside, his brows furrowing. "What do you have here?"

"The collar for number 755. Loki, the wolf I was tracking when I went up in the mountains this morning."

"I don't understand." His glance shot from Grace to Caveman and back to Grace. "Where's the wolf?"

Her lips firmed into a tight line. "Most likely dead. But I haven't seen the body to confirm." Grace nodded toward the bag. "That was left on my back porch as a gift."

"We suspect that whoever killed Khalig might have killed the wolf and decided to leave this on Grace's back porch," Caveman said.

Kevin's brows twisted. "Why?"

His jaw tightening, Caveman glanced toward Grace. "Possibly as a warning to keep her mouth shut about the murder she witnessed."

Kevin stared at the collar. "Or he might be a sadistic bastard, trying to scare her. Otherwise, why would he kill the wolf?"

"Target practice?" Grace suggested, her face pale, her jaw tight.

"Could he be one of the local ranchers who has lost livestock because of the reintroduction of wolves to the Yellowstone ecosystem?" Garner asked.

Grace nodded. "He could be."

"Or he could be a game hunter wanting a trophy for his collection," Caveman said. "Why else would he remove the collar?"

Grace frowned. "You think he killed the wolf before he took out Mr. Khalig?"

Caveman caught Grace's gaze and held it. "You said, yourself, the collar had been stalled in the same location for two days. He had to have killed the wolf two days ago."

"And he retraced his steps to where he'd killed him just to retrieve the collar?" Grace shook her head. "Doesn't make sense. I saw him kill Mr. Khalig. You'd think he'd get the hell off the mountain and come up with an alibi for where he was when I witnessed the murder."

"Unless he's cocky and wants to play games with you," Caveman said.

Grace shivered and wrapped her arms around her middle. "That's a lot of assumption."

"Still, if this guy thinks he can get away with the murder, and he's flaunting that fact by gifting you with this collar, you need to be careful," Garner said. "If he thinks you can identify him, he might take it a step further."

Grace turned and paced away from Garner and Caveman. Then she spun and marched back. "I don't have time to play games with a killer. I have work to do."

Caveman closed the distance between them and gripped her arms. "And who will do that work if you're dead?"

She stared up at him, her gray eyes widening. "You really think he'll come after me?"

"He already has once, right after the murder. If he left that collar, that makes two times."

"Three's a charm," Grace muttered, raising her hands to rest on Caveman's chest. Instead of pushing him away, she curled her fingers into his shirt. "What am I supposed to do?"

Garner tapped an ink pen on a tabletop where he had a map of the area spread out. "Khalig had received threats. I hadn't been able to pinpoint from whom. I have to assume whoever was threatening him had to have a gripe with the pipeline industry."

"What kind of threats?" Caveman asked.

"Someone painted 'Go Home' on his company truck's windshield two days ago. Yesterday, he had all four tires slashed. I tried to talk him out of going out into the field until we got to the bottom of it, but he insisted he had work to do."

Caveman raised his brows and stared down at the woman in his arms. "Sound familiar?"

"Okay." Grace rolled her eyes. "I get the point." She stepped back, out of Caveman's grip. "I don't know anything about the pipeline. Except that it goes through this area. Supposedly it's buried deep and not in an active volcanic location."

"There's been quite a bit of controversy about the pipelines and whether or not we should even have them. Activists love a cause," Garner said. "With oil prices going down, a lot of pipeline employees are out of work. That makes for some unhappy people who depended on the pipeline companies for their jobs. Then there are the ranchers who are angry at the pipeline companies having free access to cross their lands."

"And there are the ranchers who are mad at the government interfering with grazing rights on government property," Caveman added. "Like Old Man Vanders, whose herd was confiscated because he refused to pay the required fees for grazing on federally owned land."

Garner nodded. "That's what stirred up a lot of folks around here. There's a local group calling itself Free America. We found empty crates in the Lucky Lou Mine with indication they'd once been full of AR-15 rifles. We think the Free America folks have them and might be preparing to stage an attack on a government facility." Garner raised a hand. "I know. It's a lot to take in. Thus the need for me to borrow some of the best from the military."

Grace shook her head. "I had no idea things were getting so bad around here." She snorted. "With all that, don't forget the ranchers angry with the government for reintroducing wolves to the area. I know I get a lot of nastiness from cattlemen when they find one of their prize heifers downed by a wolf pack."

Caveman crossed his arms over his chest. "Since Khalig is a pipeline inspector, is it safe to assume the shooter targeted him because of something to do with the pipeline?"

"That would be my bet. But that doesn't negate the possibility that Khalig might have stumbled across something secret the Free America militia were plotting."

"He was checking some kind of instrument," Grace reiterated. "From what I could tell, he didn't appear to be afraid or nervous about anything. He straightened, still glancing down at his equipment, when the shooter took him down."

"For whatever reason he was murdered," Garner said, "we don't want anything to happen to you, just because you witnessed it."

Grace stiffened. "Don't worry about me. I can take care of myself."

"Do you own a gun?" Kevin asked.

Her chin tilted upward. "I do. A .40-caliber pistol."

"Do you know how to use it?" Caveman asked.

Her gaze shifted to the wall behind him. "Enough to protect myself."

"Are you sure about that?"

"I know how to load it, to turn off the safety and point it at the target."

"When was the last time you fired the weapon?" Caveman asked.

Her cheeks reddened. "Last year I took it to the range and familiarized with it."

Caveman's eyes widened. "A year?" He drew in a deep breath and let it out slowly. "Lady, you're no expert."

Her lips firmed and she pushed back her shoulders. "I didn't say I was. I said I knew how to use my gun."

"It's not enough," Garner said.

Grace turned her frown toward the DHS man. "What do you mean?"

Garner's gaze connected with Caveman's.

Caveman's gut tightened. He knew where Garner was going with what he'd just stated, and he knew he was getting the task.

"You need protection," Garner turned toward Grace.

She flung her hands in the air. "Why won't anyone believe me when I say I don't need someone following me around?" Those same hands fisted and planted on her hips. "I can take care of myself. I don't need some stranger intruding in my life."

"I wasn't going to suggest a stranger," Kevin said.

"Well, the sheriff's department has their hands full policing this area and finding a murderer," Grace shook her head. "I wouldn't ask them to babysit me, when I have my own gun."

"You need someone to watch your back." Garner held up a hand to stop Grace's next flow of words. "I wasn't going to suggest a stranger." He shifted his glance toward Caveman.

His lips twitching on the corners, Caveman couldn't help the grin pulling at his mouth when he stared at the horrified expression on Grace's face. Suddenly, being in Wyoming on temporary duty didn't seem so bad. Not if he could get under the skin of a beautiful biologist. As long as when it was all said and done, he could return to his unit and the career he'd committed his life to.

"You want *HIM* to follow me around?" Grace waved her hand toward Caveman. "He doesn't even want to be in Wyoming." She narrowed her eyes as she glared at Garner. "And you said you wouldn't suggest a stranger. I didn't know this man until sometime around noon today when I found myself loaded in the backseat of his truck like a kidnap victim." She shook her head. "No offense, but no thanks."

Garner's brows dipped. "Am I missing something? I thought you two were getting along fine."

Oh, they had gotten along fine, but she couldn't ignore the sensual pull the man had on her. "You are missing something," Grace said. "You're missing the point. I don't need a babysitter. I'm a grown woman, perfectly capable of taking care of myself." Perhaps the more she reiterated the argument, the more she would begin to believe it. Today had shaken her more than she cared to admit.

"Agreed," Garner said. "In most cases. But based on the evidence you've presented, you have a sniper after you. Who better than another sniper to protect you? Caveman is one of the most highly trained soldiers you'll ever have the privilege to meet. He understands how a sniper works, having been one himself."

Grace glanced at Caveman. Was it true? Was he a sniper as well as a trained Delta Force soldier?

He nodded without responding in words.

Her belly tightening, Grace continued to stare at this man who was basically a war hero stuck in Grizzly Pass, Wyoming.

"He's the most qualified person around to make sure you're not the next victim," the Homeland Security man said.

"But I—" Grace started.

"Let me finish." Garner laced his fingers together. "I'll speak with the sheriff's department and ask them if they have someone who could provide twenty-four/seven protection for you."

Grace shook her head. "They don't have the manpower."

"Then I'll query the state police," Garner countered.

"They're stretched thin." Grace wasn't helping herself by shooting down every contingency plan Garner had.

"Look, Grace." Garner lifted her hand. "Let Caveman protect you until I can come up with an alternative." He squeezed her hand. "What's it going to hurt? So you have to put him up for a few nights. You have enough room in your house."

Caveman chuckled. "I promise to clean up after myself. And I can cook—if you like steaks on the grill or carryout."

She chewed on her bottom lip, worry chiseling away at her resistance. "You really think I'm at risk?"

Garner held up the paper bag and nodded. "Yes."

"And you can't always be looking over your shoulder," Caveman added. "I respect your independence, but even the most independent of us need help sometimes. I'll do my best not to disturb your work and stay out of your way as much as I can. The fact is, a killer has taken one life and he's left his calling card on your door. If I was you, I'd want a second pair of eyes watching out for me."

"What do you say?" Garner pressed.

Grace's lips twisted and her eyes narrowed as she stared at Caveman. She didn't want to be around him that much. He stirred up physical responses she hadn't felt since her husband died. It confused her and made her feel off balance. But they were right. She couldn't keep looking over her shoulder. She needed help. "I still want to get out and check on the other wolves."

"We'll talk about it," Caveman said.

"We'll do it," she insisted. "And I won't be confined to my house."

"We'll talk about going out in the woods. And I promise not to confine you to your house." He waved his hand out to the side. "We're having dinner at the tavern today. See? I can be flexible."

Another moment passed and Grace finally conceded. "Okay, but only for the short term. I'm used to living by myself. Having another person in my house will only irritate me."

"Fair enough." Garner grinned. "I'll see what I can do to resolve the situation so that you don't need to have a bodyguard."

"Thank you." Grace's stomach rumbled loudly, her cheeks heated and she gave a weak smile. "As for eating, *clearly* you know that I'm ready."

Again, Caveman chuckled. "Let's feed the beast. We can talk about where to go from here, over a greasy burger and fries."

Her belly growled again at the mention of food. "Now you're talking."

Garner walked them to the door and held it open. "Be careful and stick close to Caveman. He'll protect you."

"What about the collar?" Grace asked.

"I'll get it to the state crime lab. If they can lift prints, they'll be able to run them through the nationwide AFIS database to see if they have a match. I'll let you know as soon as I hear anything."

"Thanks, Kevin." Grace held out her hand.

He took it, his lips lifting on one corner. "You're welcome. I'm glad you'll be with Caveman."

Caveman was first out the door of the upstairs loft apartment, his gaze scanning the area, searching for anything, or anyone, out of the ordinary or carrying a rifle with a scope.

Apparently satisfied the coast was clear, he held out his hand to Grace. "Stay behind me."

"Why behind you?" she asked.

"The best probability of getting a good shot comes from the west." He pointed toward the building on the south. "The buildings provide cover from the north to the south. And I'm your shield from the west. The staircase blocks the shooter's ability to get off a clear shot."

His explanation made sense. "But I don't want you to be a shield. That means if the killer takes a shot, he'll hit you first."

"That's the idea. If that happens, duck as soon as you hear the shot fired. If I'm hit and go down, he'll continue to fire rounds until he gets you."

"Seriously. You can't be that dense." She touched his shoulder, a blast of electricity shooting through her fingers, up her arms and into her chest. "I don't want you to take a bullet for me."

"Most likely the shooter won't be aiming for me. If I'm in the way, he'll wait for me to move out of the way so that he can get to you."

"That makes me feel *so* much better," she said, her voice strained. "We don't know that he'll come gunning for me, anyway."

"No, we don't. But are you willing to take the risk?"

Grace sighed. "No." What use was it to argue? The longer they were out in the open, the longer Caveman was exposed to Grace's shooter. "Hurry up then, before I pass out from hunger."

A chuckle drifted up to her. "Bossy much?"

"I get cranky when my blood sugar drops."

"I'll try to remember that and bring along snacks to keep that from happening." Caveman paused at the bottom of the stairs, hooked her arm with one of his hands and slipped the other around her shoulders.

Her pulse rocketed and she frowned up at him. "Is that necessary?"

"Absolutely. My arm around you makes it hard for anyone to distinguish one body from the other. Especially at a distance." His lips quirked on the edges. "I'll consider your reaction more of the low blood sugar crankiness."

Again, shut up by a valid argument, Grace suffered in silence. Although suffer was a harsh word when in fact she was far from suffering, unless she considered unfulfilled lust as something to struggle with.

Caveman opened the door to the tavern and waved her inside.

"Grace, it's been a while since you were in." A young woman with bright blond hair and blue eyes greeted them. "Would you like a table or to sit at the bar?"

"Hi, Melissa. We'd like a table," Grace responded.

"Hold on, just a minute. Let me see if there's one available." She disappeared into the crowded room.

"Is it always this busy?" Caveman stared around the room, his brows rising.

"As one of two restaurants in town, yes. The other one doesn't serve alcohol."

"I understand." He glanced around the room. "Do you know most of the people here?"

"Most," she said. "Not all. It's a small town, but we have people drift in who work on the pipeline or cowboys who come in town looking for work."

Caveman nodded. "It was like that in Montana, where I'm from. Everyone knew everyone else."

Melissa appeared in front of them. "I have a seat ready, if you'll follow me. Is this a date?" she asked, her gaze shooting to Grace.

"No," Grace replied quickly. She wasn't interested in Caveman as anything other than a bodyguard to keep her safe until they caught the killer.

"Oh? Business?" She turned her smile on Caveman.

"You could say that," Grace said.

"Yes, strictly business," Caveman agreed.

"That's nice." Melissa's eyelids dropped low. "In town for long?"

"I don't know," Caveman said.

Grace wasn't sure she liked the smile Melissa gave to Caveman, or that she was openly flirting with him when Grace was on the other side of the man. She wanted to call the girl out on her rude behavior, but was afraid she'd look like a jealous shrew. So she kept her mouth shut and seethed inwardly.

Not that she cared. Caveman could date any woman he wanted. Grace had no hold on him and would never have one. She'd sworn off men years ago, afraid to date one or form a bond. The men she'd been attracted to in the past had all died of one cause or another. The common denominator was their relationship with her.

Though she was a biologist and didn't believe in ghosts or fairy tales, she couldn't refute the evidence. Men who professed an affection for her died. What did that say about her? That she was a jinx.

The first had been her high school sweetheart, Billy Mays, who'd died in a head-on collision with a drunk man. The second had been when her husband, Jack, who'd died in a freak parasailing accident on their honeymoon in the US Virgin Islands. The third had been Patrick Jones, a man she'd only dated a few times. He'd died when he'd fallen off the big combine he'd been driving, and had been chopped into a hundred pieces before anyone could stop the combine.

Since then, she'd steered clear of relationships, hoping to spare any more deaths in the male population of Grizzly Pass, Wyoming. Which meant staying away from any entanglements with Caveman, the handsome Delta Force soldier who was only there on a temporary duty assignment. When he'd completed his assignment, he'd head back to his unit. Wherever that was. Even if she wasn't cursed, a connection with Caveman wasn't possible.

This meant she had no right to be jealous of Melissa's flirting with Caveman. The waitress was welcome to him.

Yeah, maybe not. The woman could have the decency to wait until Grace wasn't around.

In the meantime, Grace would have his full attention. She might as well find out more about the man, to better understand the person who would be providing her personal protection until a murderer was caught and incarcerated.

She hoped that was sooner rather than later. It was hard to take a seat across the table from the soldier who made her pulse thunder. It reminded her of everything she'd been missing since she'd given up on men.

Chapter Six

Caveman leaned across the table and captured Grace's hand in his. He'd been watching her glancing right and left as if searching for an escape route from the booth. "Hey. I really don't bite."

She gave him a poor attempt at a smile. "Sorry. I guess I've been alone so much lately that being in a crowded room makes me antsy."

"Concentrate on the menu." He picked up one and opened it. "What are you going to have?"

"A bacon cheeseburger," she said without even looking. "They make the best."

"Sounds good." He closed the menu without having looked. "I'll have the same."

A harried waitress arrived and plunked two cups of ice water on the table. "What can I get you to drink?"

"A draft beer for me."

"Me, too," Grace said. "And we're ready to order."

The waitress took their order and left, returning a few minutes later with two mugs filled with beer.

Caveman lifted his. "To finding a killer."

"Hear, hear." Grace touched her mug to his and drank a long swallow.

"I don't know too many women who like beer," Caveman said.

"And you say you're from Montana?" Grace snorted. "Lots of women drink beer around here."

He nodded. "It has been a while since I've been back in this area of the country. Hell, the world."

Grace set her mug on the table, leaned back and stared around the tavern. "Is it hard coming back?"

He nodded. "I feel like I have so much more to accomplish before I retire from the military."

"More battles to be fought and won?" Grace asked.

"Something like that." More like retribution for his brothers who'd lost their lives. He wanted to take out the enemy who'd lured them into an ambush and then slaughtered his teammates. Caveman shook his head and focused on Grace. "What about you? Are you from this area?"

She nodded. "Born and raised."

"Why don't you go live with your folks while the police search for the murderer?"

She laughed. "My work is here. My parents left Wyoming behind when my father retired from ranching. They live in a retirement community in Florida. They're even taking lessons on golfing."

"Are you an only child?"

A shadow crossed her face. "I am now."

"Sorry. I didn't mean to bring up bad memories."

"That's okay. It's been a long time. My little brother died of cancer when he was three. Leukemia."

"I'm so sorry."

"We all were. William was a ray of sunshine up to the very end. I believe he was stronger than all of us."

The waitress reappeared carrying two heaping plates. She

set them on the table in front of them, along with a caddy of condiments. "If you need a refill, just wave me down. Enjoy."

She was off again, leaving Caveman and Grace to their meals.

Caveman gave himself over to the enjoyment of the best burger he'd ever tasted. "You weren't kidding," he said as he polished off the last bite. "I've never had a burger taste that good. What's their secret?"

"They grill them out back on a real charcoal grill. Even in the dead of winter, they have the grill going." Grace finished her burger and wiped the mustard off her fingers.

Caveman waved for the waitress and ordered two more draft beers and sat back to digest. "Do you mind my asking what happened to your husband?"

A shadow crossed her face and she pushed her fries around on her plate. "I told you, he died in a parasailing accident."

"You couldn't have been barely out of college six years ago."

"That's where we met. We were both studying biology. He went to work with Game and Fish, I landed a job with Yellowstone National Park. A match made in heaven," she whispered, her gaze going to the far corner of the room.

"That must have been hard. Was it on a lake around here?"

Her lips stretched in a sad kind of smile. "No, it was on our honeymoon in the Virgin Islands," she said, her voice matter-of-fact and emotionless.

Her words hit him square in the gut. "Wow. What a horrible ending to a new beginning." He covered her hand with his. "I'm sorry for your loss."

She stared at the top of his hand. "Like I said. It was a long time ago."

"You never remarried?"

She shook her head. "No."

"Didn't you say life goes on?"

"Yes, but that doesn't mean I had to go out and find another man to share my life. I'm content being alone."

Caveman wasn't dense. He could hear the finality of her

statement. She wasn't looking for love from him or any other man. Which was a shame. She was beautiful in a natural, girl-next-door way. Not only was she pretty, she was intelligent and passionate about her work. A woman who was passionate about what she did had to be passionate in bed. At least that was Caveman's theory.

He found himself wondering just how passionate she could be beneath the sheets. His groin tightened and his pulse leaped at the thought. "You sound pretty adamant about staying alone. Don't you want to fall in love again?"

"No." She said that one word with emphasis. "Could we talk about something else?"

"Sure." He lifted his mug. "How about a toast to the next few days of togetherness."

"Okay. Let me." She raised her mug and tapped it against his, her gaze meeting his in an intense stare. "To keeping our relationship professional."

Caveman frowned. He didn't share her toast and didn't drink after she'd said the words. Though he knew he'd only be there until he got orders to return to his unit, he didn't discount the possibility of getting to know Grace better. And the more he was with her, the more he focused on the lushness of her lips and the gentle swell of her hips. This was a woman he could see himself in bed with, bringing out the same intensity of passion she displayed for her wolves.

Hell, he could see her as a challenge, one he'd meet head-on. Maybe she only *thought* she liked being alone. After a week with him, she might change her mind.

The thought of staying with her for the night evoked a myriad of images, none of which were professional or platonic. He had to remind himself that he was there to work, not to get too close to the woman he was tasked with protecting. She obviously had loved her husband. Six years after the man's death, she had yet to get over him.

He could swear he'd felt something when he touched her. An

electric surge charging his blood, sending it pulsing through his body on a path south to pool low in his belly. Riding behind her on the ATV, his arms wrapped around her slim waist, he'd leaned in to sniff the fresh scent of her hair, the mountain-clean aroma reminding him of his home in Montana.

He'd take her to her house, make sure she got inside all right and then he'd sleep on the porch or on the couch. The woman was hands-off. He didn't need the complication a woman could become. Especially one with sandy-blond hair and eyes the gray of a stormy Montana sky.

They didn't talk much through the remainder of their dinner. Before long, they were on their way to her house, silence stretching between them. The thought of being with this desirable woman had Caveman tied in knots.

His fingers wrapped tightly around the steering wheel all the way to her house. When he pulled up in her drive, he wondered if he should just drop her off and leave. She had temptation written all over her, and he was a man who'd gone a long time without a woman. Grace was not the woman with whom to break that dry spell.

Chapter Seven

Caveman pulled up the driveway in front of Grace's house, shoved the gear into Park and climbed down from the truck.

Grace pushed her door open and was halfway out when he made it around the front of the truck to help her down. With his hand on her arm, he eased her to the ground. "How are you feeling?"

The color was high in her cheeks, but she answered, "Fine. Really. No dizziness or nausea. I don't see any reason for you to stay the night here. I'll lock the doors and sleep with my gun under my pillow."

He shook his head, the decision already made. "No use shooting your ear off. I'm staying."

She frowned, pulled the keys from her pocket and opened the door. "I can take—"

"I know. I know. You can take care of yourself." Hell, she'd given him the out he needed. Why was he arguing?

She unlocked the door and entered.

Caveman stopped her before she got too far ahead of him. "Do you mind if I have a look around before you get comfortable?" he asked.

"Are you going to do this every time we enter my house?" she asked.

He nodded. "Until the killer is caught."

"Be my guest." She stepped into the hallway and made room for him to pass.

He slipped by, pulled his gun from beneath his jacket and made a sweep of the house, checking all the rooms. By the time he'd returned from the back bedrooms, Grace had left the front hallway.

He followed sounds of cabinet doors opening and closing in the kitchen where he found Grace, nuking a couple of mugs in the microwave.

"I hope you like instant coffee or hot tea."

"Coffee. Instant is fine."

The microwave beeped and she pulled the mugs out, set them on the counter and plunked a tea bag in one of them. "I'd drink coffee, but I don't want to be up all night. How do you do it?"

"Do what?"

"Sleep after drinking coffee?" she asked.

"You learn to sleep through almost anything when you're tired enough. Including a shot of caffeine."

She scooped a couple of spoonfuls of instant coffee into the hot water, dropped the spoon into the mug and set it on the kitchen table. Then she fished in the cupboard pulling out a bag of store-bought cookies. Carrying the cookies and her tea, she took the seat across from Caveman.

"So what's your story?" Grace dropped a teabag into her mug of hot water and dipped it several times.

The aroma of coffee and Earl Grey tea filled Caveman's nostrils and it calmed him without him actually having taken a sip. He inhaled deeply, took that sip and thought about her question.

Sitting in the comfort of her kitchen, the warm glow of the overhead light made the setting intimate somehow. Her gray-eyed gaze was soft and inviting, making him want to tell her everything there was to know about Max Decker. But he wouldn't be around long enough to make it worth the effort. She was part of the job. He was going back to his unit soon. No use wasting time getting to know each other. "I don't have a story."

"We've already established that you're from Montana." She raised her tea to her lips and blew a stream of air at the liquid's surface.

The motion drew his attention to the sexiest part of her face—her lips. Or was it her eyes?

"It's not a secret." He lifted his mug and sipped on the scalding hot coffee, more for something to do. He really hadn't wanted the drink.

She tipped her head to the side. "What did you do before the military?"

Grace wasn't going to let him get away with short answers. He might as well get the interview over with. "Worked odd jobs after high school. But I left for the military as soon as I graduated college."

Her gaze dropped to the tea in her cup. "Married?"

Cavemen felt his lips tug upward at the corners. "No."

"Ever?" Grace met his gaze.

"Never."

"Never have?" Her eyes narrowed. "Or never will?"

"Both."

Grace lifted her mug to her lips and took a tentative sip of the piping hot liquid and winced. "How long have you been away from your unit?" she continued with the inquisition.

Caveman sighed. "Fourteen weeks, five days and thirteen hours."

"But who's counting?" Grace smiled, the gesture lighting her eyes and her face.

Wow. He hadn't realized just how pretty she was until that moment. Her understated beauty was that of an outdoorsy woman with confidence and intelligence.

"Some say you either love the military or hate it? Which side of the fence are you on?" she asked.

His chest swelled. "Yeah, there have been some really bad times, but being a part of the military has been like being a part of a really big family. It's a part of me."

"I'll take that as a 'Love it.'"

Turnabout was fair play. She didn't have the corner on the questions market. Caveman told himself, he wanted to learn more about her because the information might help him keep her safe. But that wouldn't be totally true. He really was interested in her answers. He leaned back in his seat. "What about you?"

GRACE STIFFENED. "NOPE. This interrogation is all about you. If I'm to trust you, I need to know more about you."

Caveman's lips quirked upward on the corners. "That's an unfair advantage."

"I never said I was fair. I am, however, nosy." She grinned and eased her mug onto the table to let the tea cool a little before she attempted another sip. "How are you with horses?"

He frowned. "Why?"

She pushed to her feet. "I need to feed and water my gelding. He's probably a little skittish after being shot at today." Grace started for the back door.

Caveman reached it before her. "You know, you put yourself in danger every time you step out into the open."

"I know, but I put my livestock in danger by not feeding or watering them. I'm going out to take care of my horse. You can come or finish your coffee. Your choice."

"Coming." He opened the door and stepped out on the porch. After a cursory glance in both directions, he waved her out onto the porch and slipped his arm around her. "Just stay close to me. Don't give a shooter an easy target."

As much as she hated to admit it, she liked the feel of Caveman's arm around her. Though she knew a shooter could kill them both, if he really wanted to, she felt safer with the man's body next to hers.

Inside the barn, Bear whinnied and pawed the stall door.

"I'm coming," Grace said. She scooped a bucket of grain from the feed bin, opened the stall door and stepped inside.

Caveman grabbed a brush and entered with her.

Bear's nostrils flared. He pawed the ground and tossed his head, as if telling Grace he wasn't pleased with the other human entering his domain.

"Bear doesn't like strangers."

Caveman didn't get the hint. Instead he stood in the stall with the brush in his hand, not moving or getting any closer to the horse.

Grace opened her mouth to ask Caveman to leave, but he started speaking soft, nonsensical words in a deep, calming tone.

Bear tossed his head several times, not easily won over, but he didn't paw the ground or snort his dissent. Soon the animal lowered his head and let Caveman reach out to scratch behind his ears.

"I'll be damned," Grace whispered.

Caveman covered Bear's ears. "Shh. Don't let that foul-mouthed biologist scare you," he whispered.

The horse nuzzled the man's chest and leaned into the hand scratching his ear.

"So, not only are you a Delta Force soldier, you're a horse whisperer?" Grace snorted.

"I told you. I'm from Montana."

"And one of those odd jobs just happened to be on a ranch?"

He grinned. "Yes and no. I grew up on a ranch. I worked there during the summers for spending money."

"A cowboy. My mother warned me about getting involved with a cowboy."

"From what you said, your father was one."

"Exactly why she warned me." Though her mother was still crazy in love with her father, even after over thirty years of marriage.

"Why cowboys?" Caveman asked.

She met his gaze head-on. "They tend to like their horses better than their wives."

"Horses don't talk back as much, or make you fold laundry."

Grace chuckled. "I've had my share of sassy horses."

"Okay, so they don't make you clean the house."

"And I've cleaned my share of stalls." She crossed her arms over her chest and raised her eyebrows. "Care to try again?"

"I can sell a horse that's giving me a hard time, thus getting money for my trouble. Getting rid of a woman costs a heck of a lot more than ditching a horse."

"Okay, you got me on that one," Grace said. "But a horse won't be warming your bed and giving you children."

"Most of my married friends don't have sex more now that they're married. In fact, the kids suck the life out of their wives' sex drive."

"But your buddies have someone to come home to. People who care about them."

"Sometimes. Then there are the Dear John letters they get when in a hellhole fighting the enemy with their hands tied behind their backs by politicians. Meanwhile the wife back home has been having an affair with the banker next door."

Grace's brows rose. "Cynical much?"

Caveman shrugged. "I've seen some of the toughest soldiers commit suicide because they can't go home to salvage the relationship."

Caveman had worked himself up a rung on Grace's perception ladder with his horse trick. But she wasn't ready to fall for the big guy, yet. And despite her mother's warning not to fall for a cowboy, she had a soft spot in her heart for them, since her father had been one.

Hell, a man who had a way with animals, who'd been raised a cowboy, was a war hero and looked as good as Caveman could easily find his way beneath her defenses. If she wasn't careful, he might be the next victim of her curse.

Grace held out her hand. "I can take care of Bear."

He handed her the brush. "I'll haul the water."

"Not necessary. As soon as he's done eating, I'll let him out in the pasture. There's a trough in the paddock." She rounded the horse to the other side and went to work brushing his coat.

Caveman's presence raised the temperature of every blood cell in Grace's body. Fully aware of his every move, she knew when he left the stall. She let out a sigh and relaxed a little as she worked her way toward the horse's hindquarters.

The stall door squealed softly, announcing Caveman's return. He'd retrieved a currycomb and went to work on Bear's tangled mane and tail. Soon the horse was fully groomed, full of grain and ready to be turned loose in the pasture.

Yeah, the soldier had gone up another rung. Not every man would take the time to groom a horse. Not every man knew how to do it right.

She'd have to talk to Caveman's boss and ask him to send someone else. How would she approach the request? *Please send someone who isn't quite as drool-worthy. Maybe someone who is happily married, has a beer belly, belches in public and is not at all interesting.*

Grace hooked Bear's halter and led him through the barn and out to the gate.

Caveman moved ahead of her and had the gate open before she got there.

She let go of Bear's halter and the horse ran into the pasture, straight for the water trough.

Grace backed up, trying to get out of the way of the gate. Her foot caught on the uneven ground and she tipped backward.

Caveman caught her in his arms and hauled her up against his chest. "Are you all right?"

No, she wasn't. Cinched tightly to the man's chest, she could barely breathe, much less think. She tried to tell herself that the malfunctioning of her involuntary reflexes had nothing to do with how close Caveman was to her. Neither were his arms, which were hooked beneath her breasts, causing all kinds of problems with her pulse and blood pressure. "I'm fine. Seriously, you can let go of me."

For a long moment, he stared down at her, his arms unmoving. "Anyone ever tell you that your eyes sparkle in the moonlight?"

And there went any measure of resistance. "No." Whether her one-word answer was in response to his question or in response to her rising desire, she refused to pick it apart.

"They do," he said. "And your lips clearly were made to be kissed."

Her heart hammering against her ribs, Grace watched as Caveman lowered his head, his mouth coming so close to hers she could feel the warmth of his breath on her skin. She tipped her head upward, her eyelids, sweeping low, her pulse racing. Dear Lord, he was going to kiss her. And she was going to let him!

A BREATH AWAY from touching his mouth to hers, Caveman came to his senses. What was he thinking? This woman had nearly died that day. He was responsible for her safety, not for making a pass at her. As much as he wanted to kiss her, he shouldn't. It would compromise his ability to remain objective. Then why had he mentioned how her eyes sparkled and how her lips were meant to be kissed?

Because, man! He wanted to kiss her. With a deep sigh, he untangled his arms from around her.

Grace opened her eyes and blinked. Even in the moonlight, Caveman could see the color rise in her cheeks. She stepped out of his reach, careful not to trip again, straightened her blouse and nodded. "Thanks for catching me. In the future, I'll do my best not to fall."

As she headed back to the house, he followed closely behind her, using his body as a shield. Should the shooter decide to follow her to her home, he wouldn't have a clear target. He'd have to go through Caveman first.

Once inside the house, Grace gathered a blanket and pillow, handed them to him and pointed to the couch. "You can stay on the couch."

The couch beat his truck and the front porch, but it might still be too close.

Grace disappeared into the only bathroom in the house.

Caveman could hear the sound of the shower and his imagination went wild, picturing the beautiful biologist stripping out of her clothes, stepping into the shower and water running in rivulets down her naked body.

He left the blanket on the couch and slipped out onto the front porch. Yeah, sleeping on the hard, wood planks with a solid wood door locked between them would be the right thing to do. Knowing she'd be in the bed down the hall made his groin tight and guaranteed he wouldn't sleep any better than the night before when he'd caught a few hours cramped in the front seat of his truck.

Tomorrow, he'd speak with Kevin about assigning another one of the team members to watch over Grace. Apparently, he'd been too long without a woman. What else would make him so attracted to Grace when he'd only known her a few hours?

The door behind him opened and Grace stuck her head through the screen door. "The shower's all yours."

She wore a baggy T-shirt that hung halfway down her thighs. If she had on shorts, the shirt covered them. And when she turned to the side, her shirt stretched over her chest.

Caveman sucked in a breath and his jeans got even tighter.

She wasn't wearing a bra beneath the shirt. The beaded tips of her nipples made tiny tents against the fabric.

What had she said? Oh, yes. The shower was all his. He really should have told her he didn't need one and that he would sleep outside. But no, that might require more explanation than he was prepared to give. And it might scare her to think the man who was supposed to protect her wanted to jump her bones. "I'll be there in a minute."

"Okay." She started to turn, paused and then faced him. "Thank you for rescuing me today."

"You're welcome." *Now, go straight to your bedroom and lock your door.* Caveman clenched his fists to keep from reaching out and dragging her into his arms. "Have a good night," he said, his voice huskier than usual.

Again, she started to turn, changed her mind and stepped through the door, closed the distance between them. When she stood in front of him, she raised up on her toes and brushed her lips across his cheek. Before Caveman could react, Grace turned and ran back into the house.

He groaned and adjusted the tightness of his jeans. Yeah, he wouldn't get much sleep. When he could move comfortably again, he walked out to his truck, grabbed his duffel bag from the backseat and returned to the house, locking the front door behind him. He made another pass through the house, checking all of the doors and windows with the exception of Grace's bedroom.

When he was certain the house was locked down, he entered the bathroom, shucked his clothes and turned on the cold water. After several minutes beneath the icy spray, he was back in control, his head on straight and his resolve strengthened.

Grace Saunders was off-limits. Period. End of subject.

He lay on the couch, his gun close by, and stared at the ceiling for the next few hours. Finally, in the wee hours of the morning he fell asleep and dreamed of making love to a beautiful, sandy-blond-haired biologist who loved wolves. Even in his dream, he knew he was treading the fine line of professionalism, but he couldn't resist. The crow of a rooster jolted him away as the gray light of predawn edged through the window.

He had breakfast on the table by the time Grace emerged from her bedroom.

"You're kind of handy to have around." She yawned and stretched. "Not only do you rescue damsels in distress, you can scramble eggs? You'll make someone a great wife."

"Don't get used to it. I cooked out of self-defense." He handed her one of the two places of fluffy yellow eggs. "I was starving."

She smiled and padded barefoot to the table. "What's the plan for today?"

"I thought we'd stop by the tavern and see if Kevin and his computer guy have come up with any potential murder suspects."

"You think they might have more than the sheriff and his deputies have come up with?"

"Hack, Kevin's computer guy, is a pretty talented techie. He's been following up on the Vanders family and their connections in the community. He might have found someone who was as trigger-happy as the Vanders."

Grace chewed on a bite of toast and swallowed. "What's wrong with people? In the past, all we had to complain about was the weather and taxes. Now people are shooting at each other. Last night all I could think about was Mr. Khalig's family. Did he leave a wife and children behind? People who loved him and looked forward to his return?"

Her face was sad, making Caveman want to wrap his arms around her and make everything okay. But he couldn't. No amount of hugging would bring back a dead man. Hugging was a bad idea, anyway. He'd promised himself that he'd steer clear of temptation.

Caveman looked down to keep from staring at Grace's sad eyes. He poked his fork at his eggs. "Not everyone is bad or crazy."

"You're right." She chuckled. "I was lucky enough one of the good guys was there when I needed someone." She ate the rest of her eggs and toast with a gusto most women didn't demonstrate.

Caveman finished his breakfast, as well. When he reached for her plate, she held up her hand. "I'll take care of the dishes since you cooked." She took his plate to the sink, and filled it with water and soapsuds.

Having grown up on a ranch where his mother worked outside as much as his father did, Caveman couldn't stand by and not help. He grabbed a dry dish towel and stepped up beside Grace. "You wash, I'll dry. We'll get it done in no time."

She smiled, and it seemed like the sun chose that moment to shine through the window.

Caveman forced himself to focus on the dish in his hand, not the sun in Grace's hair.

When they were done, and the dishes were stacked neatly in the cabinet, Grace disappeared into her bedroom and came out wearing boots and a jacket, her hair brushed neatly and pulled back into a ponytail.

Caveman liked her hair hanging down around her shoulders, the long straight strands like silver-gold silk swaying back and forth with each step. Lord help him, he was waxing poetic in his head. His buddies back in his unit would have a field day if they knew. "Come on. We need to stop by the sheriff's office and give him your official statement and see what else they can tell us about the shootings."

"I hope they were able to retrieve Mr. Khalig's body."

Caveman stepped out on the porch and searched the tree line and shadows for movement before he allowed Grace out of the house. "I spoke briefly with Kevin on the phone. They did. He's with the coroner in Jackson. They'll provide a report as soon as they can."

Grace locked the front door and followed Caveman to the truck.

Within ten minutes, they were inside the sheriff's office.

Grace gave her statement. The sheriff recorded the session and made notes. When she was done, he stared across the table at her. "I'd like to think you'll be okay. Since you didn't see who it was, you can't identify the shooter. For your sake, I hope he lays low and leaves you alone."

"I wish I *had* seen him. I'd rather know and be hunted than not know. As it is, it could have been anyone." She pushed to her feet.

The sheriff did too and held out his hand.

She ignored the hand and hugged the older man. "Thank you, for all you do. Give your wife my love."

Caveman felt a stab of envy for the hug the sheriff was getting from the pretty biologist.

Sheriff Scott hugged her back and patted her back. "You be careful out there. Can't have our favorite wolf lady getting hurt."

Caveman gave his brief statement of how he'd found Grace and thanked the sheriff.

"Where to?"

"Operations Center," Caveman said, a little more brusquely than he intended. That jolt of envy for a friendly hug Grace had given the sheriff had set Caveman off balance. He barely knew Grace. Perhaps the hit he'd taken to his leg and all the morphine he'd had during the operation and recovery had scrambled his wits. He needed to get his head on straight. Soon. He wasn't going to be around long enough to get to know the woman, nor was he in the market for a long-term relationship. He had a unit to get back to.

But the sway of Grace's hips, and the way she smiled with her lips and her eyes, seemed to replay in his head like a movie track stuck in replay mode.

By the time they had debriefed Kevin and Hack, the computer guru, they'd missed lunch and the evening crowd had begun to gather at the tavern below.

"Want to grab something to eat before we head back to my house?" Grace's lips twisted into a wry grin. "I don't cook often, and I'm certain it was a fluke you actually found something in the refrigerator for breakfast."

"Sure," Caveman said. "Then we can stop at the store for some groceries, if it's still open when we're done."

"I'm game."

For the second time in the past two days, Caveman and Grace entered the tavern and asked for a seat in the dining area.

"If you ever want to find out what's going on, you need to

people-watch in the tavern or go to the grocery store. Mrs. Penders knows all of the gossip."

"Then we're definitely going to the store next."

"Hi, Grace, good to see you again. Who's this?"

Grace smiled at a pretty, young waitress with bleach-blond hair. "Lisa Lambert, this is Max Decker. You can call him Caveman. He's a…friend of mine."

Lisa grinned. "Caveman? Is that a statement on how you are with the ladies?" She winked. "Nice to meet you." She held out a hand.

Caveman shook it, and gave Lisa a smile. "Nice to meet you, Lisa."

"You know, if it's all the same to you," Grace said. "I'd like to get the food to go and eat it at home."

"We can do that," Lisa said. She took their order and hurried to the back. She returned a few minutes later with two glasses of water and a smile. "The cook said it will take him ten minutes."

"Great." After Lisa left, Caveman leaned toward Grace. "See anyone here that might be your killer?"

She glanced around the room. "I see a bunch of people I've known all my life. I find it hard to believe any of them could be a killer. I grew up with some of them, went to church on Sunday with others and say hello to others at community functions."

"Anyone who might have a beef with the pipeline inspector?"

Grace studied the people. "Some of the men worked on the pipeline. Maybe the ones who were laid off are angry because Mr. Khalig still had his job? I don't know. I work with wolves, not pipeline workers."

"What about the property owners the pipelines cross?" Caveman asked.

"Maybe. I'm not sure who they are, though. The pipelines cross the entire state. Mr. Khalig was on federal land when he was shot."

A few minutes later, Lisa returned with a bag filled with two covered plates.

Handing her several bills, Caveman told her to keep the tip. He had turned to leave when he heard a commotion behind him.

"I don't care what you say!" a slurred male voice yelled over the sound of other patrons talking.

Caveman spun toward the bar to see a man leaning with his back to the bar. "The BLM isn't a law unto themselves. You have no right to confiscate a man's herd or have him arrested for trespassing on the land his cattle have grazed on since his great-great-grandfather settled this area."

"If the man doesn't pay the grazing fees for his animals, and he doesn't remove them from federal property, he forfeits them to the government," another man said, his voice lower. "It's in the contract he signed."

A pause in general conversation allowed Caveman to hear the man's quiet response. "Who are the two arguing?"

"The man at the bar is Ernie Martin," Grace said. "He poured all his money into raising Angora goats, counting on the subsidies the government gave ranchers for raising them. The subsidies were cut from the federal budget, and now he's facing bankruptcy."

"And the other guy?" Caveman prompted.

"Daryl Bradley. He's a local Bureau of Land Management representative. They sent him in to feed information to the agency on how it's going out here. They had a man who wouldn't pay his grazing fees try to shoot the sheriff. It's been pretty volatile out here. *You* should know. I heard you had a hand in rescuing the school bus full of kids just the other day."

He nodded. "Vanders was the man who tried to shoot the sheriff. And it was his sons who kidnapped the kids. That could have turned out a whole lot worse than it did."

Grace nodded. "It was bad enough old Mr. Green died. He was a good man."

Caveman nodded. "Thankfully, all of the kids survived."

Grace shook her head. "I never would have thought members

of our little community could be that desperate they could kill a kind old man and kidnap a bunch of innocent kids."

"It ain't right," Ernie shouted. "How's a man supposed to make a living when the government is out to squeeze every ounce of blood from his livelihood? The land doesn't cost the government anything to maintain. *We* fix the fences. *We* provide the water and feed for the cattle. And the BLM collects the money. For what? To fund some pork belly program nobody wants or needs."

"The BLM hasn't raised the fees in years," Daryl said. "We haven't even kept up with inflation. It was time."

"That's taxation without representation. Our forefathers dumped tea in a harbor to protest the government raising taxes without them having a say in it." Ernie slammed his mug on the bar, sloshing beer over the top. "It's time we take back our country, the land our grandfathers fought to protect, and boot the likes of you out."

Daryl stood, pushing back his chair so hard it tipped over and crashed to the floor. "Is that a threat?"

"Call it whatever you want," Ernie shouted. "It's time we took matters into our own hands and set things straight in the US."

A tall, slender man rose from his chair and ambled over to the fray. "Oh, pipe down, Ernie. You're just mad because they cut the government subsidies for Angora goats."

Grace leaned close to Caveman. "That's Ryan Parker. Owns the Circle C Ranch."

"Yeah, you're right, I'm mad." Ernie poked a finger toward Ryan. "I sold my cattle to invest in those damned goats. It's like they timed it perfectly to close me down. I've already had to sell half of my land. It won't be long before I sell the other half, just to pay my mortgage and taxes." He puffed out his chest. "The government has to understand the decisions they make affect real people."

"That's why we go to the voting booths and elect the representatives who will take our message to Washington." Ryan waved toward the door. "Go home, Ernie."

"And what good will voting do?" Ernie shouted. "You're not in much better shape. What has our government done for you? You had to sell most of your breeding stock to make ends meet. How are you going to recover from that? Not only that, you didn't have a choice on that pipeline cutting through your property. What if it breaks? What if it leaks? Your remaining livestock could be poisoned, the land ruined for grazing."

"Or we could all die in the next volcanic eruption. We can't predict the future." Ryan crossed his arms over his chest. "No one made you sell all of your livestock to invest the money in goats. Any ranch owner worth his salt knows not to put all his eggs in one basket."

"So now you're saying I'm not worth my salt?" Ernie marched across the floor and stood toe-to-toe with Ryan.

Caveman tensed and extended a hand to Grace. "Might be getting bad in here. Are you ready to go?"

Her gaze was riveted on the two men shouting at each other. "Think we should do anything to stop them?"

"My job is to protect *you*, not break up a barroom fight."

"I didn't go to war to fight for your right to collect subsidies from our government." Ryan glared down at Ernie. "You made a bad financial decision. Live with it."

"Why, you—" Ernie swung his fist.

Ryan Parker caught it in his palm and shoved it back at him. "Don't ever take a swing at me again. I won't let it go next time."

Ernie spat on Ryan's cowboy boots. "You're one of them."

"And if you mean I'm a patriot who loves my country and fought to keep it free for dumbasses like you, then yes. I'm one of them. What have you done for your country lately, Ernie?"

Ernie rubbed his fist. If his glare was a knife it would have skewered Ryan through the heart. "I might not have joined the military, but I'm willing to fight for my rights."

"And what rights are those? The right to raise goats at the

taxpayer's expense?" Ryan shook his head. "Get a real life, Ernie. One that you've earned, not one that you've gambled on and lost."

Ernie's face turned a mottled shade of red. He reached into his pocket, his eyes narrowing into slits.

Grace started toward the man before Caveman realized what she was doing.

He leaped forward and grabbed her arm, pulling her back behind him.

"But Ernie's going to do something stupid," Grace said. "Ryan's one of the good guys."

"I'll handle it," Caveman said between clenched teeth. "Stay out of it," he ordered and strode toward the angry man.

"You'll see." Ernie eased his hand out of his pocket, something metal and shiny cupped in his palm. Based on the size and shape, it had to be a knife. "You and every other governmental tyrant will see. Just you wait, Parker." Ernie's brows drew together and he took a step toward Ryan. "You'll see. We'll have a free America again. And it won't be because you went to fight in a foreign country. We'll bring the fight back home where it belongs."

"What do you mean?" Ryan stood his ground.

Caveman also wanted to know what the belligerent Ernie meant by bringing the fight home, but he wasn't willing to wait for the angry drunk to explain.

Ernie started forward, cocked his arm, preparing to thrust his hand at Ryan.

Caveman popped Ernie's wrist with his fist in a short, fast impact that caused the man to drop the knife. "Sorry. Didn't mean to bump into you," he said and kicked the knife beneath a table, out of Ernie's reach.

Clenching his empty hand into a fist, Ernie glared at Caveman and then turned his attention back to Ryan. "It won't be long. And you'll see."

Two other men stepped between Ernie and Ryan. "You've said enough," one of the men muttered.

"That's fine." Ernie snorted. "I'm done here." He turned toward the door and pushed his way through the crowd that had gathered around him and Ryan. "Move. Get out of my way."

As the tavern returned to its normal dull roar of voices, Caveman made his way back to where he'd left Grace. "What was Ernie talking about, *bringing the fight back home*?"

Grace's brow formed a V over her nose. "I'm not sure. We've heard rumblings about a militia group forming in the area. But that's the first I've heard anyone actually talk about bringing the fight here." She glanced around as if looking at the crowd with fresh eyes.

"Who were the guys who stopped Ernie?" Caveman looked for the men, but didn't see them. They'd disappeared into the crowd and Ryan had stepped up to the bar to pay his bill.

"That was Quincy Kemp and Wayne Batson. Quincy was the one who spoke to Ernie. He's not the nicest or most reputable individual in Grizzly Pass. But he does make good sausage. All of the hunters go to him to have their antlers mounted and the meat turned into steaks, sausage or jerky."

"He's a butcher *and* a taxidermist?" Caveman asked.

"Yes. He has a shop in town, but he lives off the grid. His home is up in the hills. He uses wind and solar power and hunts for his food."

"Pretty good shot?"

"I'd say he'd have to be to feed himself and his family." Her lips pulled up on the corner. "As for Wayne Batson, he nearly went bankrupt when ranching got too expensive. He sank a lot of money into making his place a sportsman's paradise, building high fences around his ten-thousand-acre ranch and stocking it with exotic deer, elk, wolves and wildcats. He also has one of the most sophisticated outdoor rifle ranges in the state. Men come to train on his range and hunt on his land."

"Maybe we should ask the sheriff to check their alibis."

"Wayne and Quincy are highly skilled hunters." Grace smiled. "But, if we were looking for the best hunters in the area as our potential shooter, you'd have to question half the people in this county alone. You know how it is. Most men in these parts grew up with a guns in their hands. They're all avid hunters and are good with a rifle and scope. We even have a man from here who became the state champion rifle marksman."

"You're right. It was the same in Montana. I guess I've been in other parts of this country too long, where most people wouldn't know how to load a gun, much less shoot one."

"Most of them don't need one to survive." She gathered her purse. "We should go. I need to log my notes into the project database and notify my boss of the loss of Loki."

Normally, Caveman would have held the door for Grace, but he wanted to go out first and scan the parking lot for danger before he allowed her to leave the relative security of the tavern.

He stopped in the doorway and looked around.

Three men stood near a truck talking in hushed voices, their faces intense. One of them was Ernie Martin. The other men had their backs to Caveman, but based on the one's greasy brown hair and slouchy blue jeans, he appeared to be Quincy Kemp, the local meat processor and taxidermist. The other had the swaggering stance of the man Grace had called Wayne Batson.

"What's going on," Grace asked, her breath warming Caveman's shoulder, sending a thrill of awareness through him.

"Ernie, Wayne and Quincy are having a conversation."

"I'm not afraid of them," she said.

He looked around for any other threats. The sun had set and the gray of dusk provided enough light to make their way to their truck, but not enough to see into the shadows. "Stay close to me. When we get to the truck, get in and stay down. Don't provide any kind of silhouette."

"I'm still not quite convinced the shooter is actually after me anymore. He has to know by now that I couldn't identify him. Otherwise someone would have been knocking at his door."

"That doesn't mean he won't take pleasure in keeping you guessing. A man who'd hang a dead wolf's collar on your door might go to the trouble of continuing to scare you." Caveman handed her up into the passenger seat. "Even if you're not scared of him, I might be. For you, of course." He winked, his hand on the door. "Again, stay down until we're back at your house."

She rolled her eyes, but complied, doubling over in her seat, bringing her head below the dash, out of sight of any passerby, or shooter aiming at the truck.

Caveman climbed into the truck, started the engine and pulled out of the Blue Moose parking lot onto the road headed toward Grace's house.

Chapter Eight

"I feel silly bending over this long." Grace lay over, her face near the sack of food, the smells making her mouth water. "Are we there yet? My stomach is rumbling."

"Rather silly than sorry," he said.

"Easy for you to say. You're not the one scrunched over your seat." She straightened for a moment and worked the kink out of her neck. "Seriously, this is nuts. I went all day without anyone making a move. Nobody is going to shoot at me at night."

A sharp tink sounded and a hole appeared in the passenger seat window a few inches away from Grace's head. "What the hell?" She reached out her hand to touch the round hole. Splinters of glass flaked off at her touch.

"Get down!" Caveman yelled and swerved into the middle of the road.

Someone was shooting at them! Caveman jerked, his hand, twisting the steering wheel to the right. He cursed and held on, straightening the truck before he plowed into a ditch and flipped the vehicle.

Caveman steadied the vehicle, slammed his foot on the accelerator and sped forward. When he glanced at the matching holes in the window, his heart stopped for a second. Those were bullet holes. Had Grace been leaning a few inches forward in her seat, those bullets would have hit her in the head.

His gut clenched.

Grace lay doubled over, her head between her knees to keep from being seen by the enemy. "Should we go straight to the sheriff's office?" she asked from her bent position.

"Probably, but I'm not sure what that will accomplish since the sheriff will have gone home by now," Caveman said.

"Should we go to my house? We could call the sheriff from there." The shooter already knew where she lived and had been there the day before.

"Is there anywhere else we could go?" Caveman asked.

Grace shook her head. "We could drive up to the park at Yellowstone and see if they can fit us into one of the cabins."

"And if they can't?" Caveman glanced across the console at her.

"We could drive on into Jackson Hole. There's bound to be a hotel there."

"That's a lot of driving late at night."

"Then we go to my place," she decided. "I don't like leaving my horse for too long, anyway. If this guy shoots wolves, he doesn't have a sense of compassion in dealing with animals. He could decide to hurt my horse."

"Almost there," Caveman pulled into her driveway and shone the headlights at her small cottage. Nothing seemed amiss. Then he drove around the side of the house and shone the headlights at the small barn. The lights reflected off the horse's eyes, but everything appeared normal.

He parked at the rear of the house.

"I know," Grace said. "I'm to stay put while you check it out." She sighed. "I'm sorry about your window."

"Don't worry about it. I'm glad you weren't hit." He pushed open the door to his truck. The overhead light illuminated Grace's pale face and worried eyes.

He reached over and touched a hand to her cheek, wanting to take her into his arms, as if by doing so he could protect her from whoever was shooting at her. "If you had any doubts the shooter is after you, I hope you're convinced now."

"I am," she said, quietly. "Completely." She covered his hand with hers and leaned into his palm. "But why? I still don't have a clue who it is. It's not like I'm a threat to him."

"Doesn't matter at this point. What does matter is that we get you inside that house safely before the gunman has the chance to get here from his previous location."

"Caveman?"

"Yeah."

"Thanks for being here for me."

Caveman pressed his lips together. "Don't thank me until the gunman is caught." She was still in danger and he could be the best bodyguard around, but a skilled sniper could take someone out from up to four hundred yards away.

He wasn't sure what they'd do next. He didn't see any other option but to stay inside the house, avoid all the windows and pray whoever was shooting wouldn't get lucky and hit Grace. Though he'd only known her a very short time, he wouldn't want anything to happen to the dedicated biologist.

Chapter Nine

Grace felt strange running for the door of her house. This was Grizzly Pass, Wyoming, not some village in a war-torn nation. People didn't shoot at you for no reason.

Unless you witnessed a murder, and the killer was crazier than a rabid skunk, and fired on you when you were driving home from town.

Ducking low, Grace ran up the porch steps.

Caveman was right behind her, using his body as a shield to protect hers, again. Was he insane?

When her hand shook too much to insert the key in the lock, Caveman took the key from her and opened the door. With his palm on the small of her back, he hurried her through and closed the door behind them.

She rounded on him, realizing too late that she hadn't given him much room to get in the door and close it. She stood toe-to-toe with the man, feeling the heat radiating off his body. "Why do you keep doing that?"

He raised his hands to cup her elbows. "Doing what?"

"Using your body to shield mine? You don't have to take a bullet for me." She touched his arm. "You hardly know me."

He gave her a half smile. "Let's just say, what I know, I like and admire." His lips twitched and his eyes twinkled. "You're the first woman I've met who likes beer. What's not to love about you?"

Her heart warmed at his playful words. If she wasn't such a deadly jinx, she'd be tempted to flirt with the man. "Well, don't do it, again. I don't think I could live with myself if something happened to you because of me." She set her purse on the hall table and would have walked away, but Caveman took her hand and laced his fingers with hers.

"Sweetheart, I'm here to protect you. I'm not going to leave you exposed to a sniper's sights."

"I'm not your sweetheart, and you should wear a bulletproof vest if you're going to be around me." She stared up into his eyes, her own stinging. Her chest ached with an overwhelming fear for his life. "I don't want to be the cause of another death."

"You have to stop beating yourself up." He raised her hand to his lips, pressed a kiss to her knuckles and sent sparks shooting through her veins. "Khalig didn't die because of you."

"I know." She stared at where his lips had been. She wished he would claim her mouth instead of wasting kisses on her fingers. But, no, that wouldn't work. Grace shook her head. "I can't do this to you."

"Do what?"

"Nothing." She pulled her hand free and turned away.

Caveman caught her arm and pulled her around to face him. "Do what to me?" He cupped her cheek in his palm. "Drive me crazy? Too late. For some reason, I'm insanely attracted to you. But every time I think I'm about to kiss you, you pull away, or my head gets screwed on straight. Well, I'm tired of doing the right thing. I swear your eyes are saying yes, but the next thing I know, you're running. Is it something I said? Is it my cologne? I'll change it."

Grace rested her hand on his chest as tears welled in her eyes. "Don't say nice things. Don't try to kiss me."

"Why not?" He brushed his thumb across her lips. "You're beautiful. And I might be reading too much into your body language, but I think you want to kiss me, too."

Yes, she did. But now, she couldn't. "I can't do this to you."

He stepped closer, bringing his body nearer to hers, the warmth crushing her ability to resist. "Can't do what to me? Talk to me, Grace. You're not making sense."

"I can't curse you."

He leaned his head back, his brows forming a V in the center of his forehead. "Curse me? I don't understand."

"I'm cursed. If you kiss me, I'll jinx you. I don't want something terrible to happen to you." She curled her fingers into his shirt, knowing she should push him away, but she couldn't. Now that they were so close, her brain stopped thinking and her body took over. She wanted, more than anything, for him to kiss her.

"Let me get this straight. You think that by kissing me, you'll jinx me?" He stared down at her for a long moment. Finally, he said, "What in the Sam-dog-hell are you talking about?"

Her brows lifted and her lips twitched. "Sam-dog-hell?" She gave a shaky laugh.

"Don't change the subject." He brushed his thumb across her lips again, his glance shifting to his thumb's path. "I was just about to kiss you."

"I didn't change the subject. And you can't kiss me." She was saying one thing while she allowed him to tip her chin up, her lips coming to within a breath of his. "Kissing me is a really bad idea," she whispered.

"Damn it, Grace, if kissing you is a bad idea, then color me bad. I have to do it." He bent to claim her lips. "Curses be damned," he muttered into her mouth, sliding his tongue between her teeth, claiming her tongue with a warm, wet caress that curled Grace's toes.

She pressed her body against his, longing to be closer, their clothes just one more barrier to overcome so that she could be skin-to-skin with this big soldier who'd take a bullet for a relative stranger. What had she done to deserve him?

Nothing. So how could she stand there kissing him, knowing it would put him in mortal danger? Grace pushed against his chest, though the effort was only halfhearted and less than convincing.

His arms tightened and then loosened. "If you really want me to let go, just say the word." He stared down into her eyes. "Otherwise, I'm going to continue kissing you."

She fell into his gaze, her heart hammering against her ribs. Slowly, her hands slid up his chest to lock behind his head, pulling him down for that promised kiss. "If you die, I'll never forgive myself."

He chuckled. "I'll take my chances." Then he kissed her until her insides tingled and she forgot the need to breathe. When he raised his head, she lowered her hands to the buttons on his shirt, working them loose as fast as her fingers could push them through the holes. Her goal was to get to the skin beneath, before her brain kicked in and reminded her why she shouldn't be kissing him and whatever else might come next.

As she reached for the rivet on his blue jeans, he captured her hands in his. "Are you sure about this? You know I want it, but I don't want you to do something you'll regret later."

She caught her lower lip between her teeth and stared down at the button on his jeans, wishing he hadn't stopped her, praying her brain wouldn't kick in. "You're a soldier, right?" she said.

"Yes. So?"

"You've lived through some pretty serious battles, I assume?"

"Again, yes."

"You can take care of yourself, right?"

"I can."

"Then kiss me and tell me you'll be all right."

"Grace, no one is guaranteed to live to old age." He threaded his hands through her hair. "We have to live every day like it could be our last."

"Yeah, but I don't want your life to be cut short because of me."

"Let *me* make that choice. The only decision you need to make is whether you want to make love here, against the wall or take it to the bedroom?"

Her pulse raced, and her breathing grew ragged. "Here. Now." She ripped open the button on his jeans and dragged the zipper down.

Caveman grabbed the hem of her shirt, pulled it up over her head and dropped it on the hall table. Then he bent to kiss her neck, just below her ear. He nibbled at her earlobe and trailed his lips down the length of her neck. Continuing lower, he tongued the swell of her right breast, while pushing the strap over her shoulder and down her arm.

Past anything resembling patience, Grace reached behind her and unclipped her bra. Her breasts freed, she shrugged out of the garment and it fell to the floor.

Caveman cupped both orbs in his hands and plumped them, thumbing the nipples until they hardened into tight little beads. He bent to take one into his mouth, sucking it deep, then flicking it with the tip of tongue.

Grace moaned and arched her back, wanting so much more. They still had too many clothes on. She shoved her hands into the back of his jeans, cupped his bottom and pulled him close. His shaft sprang free of his open fly and pushed into her belly.

"I want to feel your skin against mine," he said, his words warm on her wet breast.

"What's holding you back?" she managed to get out between ragged gasps.

"These." He flipped the button of her jeans through the hole and dragged the denim down her legs. Dropping to his haunches, he pulled off her cowboy boots and helped her step free. As he rose, he skimmed his knuckles along her inner thigh, all the way up to the triangle of silk covering her sex.

His gaze met hers as he hooked the elastic waistband of her panties and he dragged them over her hips and down her thighs.

Her body on fire, Grace couldn't take it anymore. She pushed his jeans down his legs and waited for him to toe off his boots, kicking them to the side. He shucked his pants, pulling his wallet from the back pocket before he slung them against the wall. Then they were both naked in the hallway of her home.

A cool waft of air almost brought her back to her senses.

Before it could, Caveman retrieved a condom from his wallet, tossed the wallet on the hallway table and handed her the packet. "We might need that."

"I'm glad *someone* is thinking," she said. She sure wasn't. Grace tore open the foil, rolled the condom over his engorged shaft all the way to the base. Sweet heaven, he was hard, long and so big, her breath caught and held.

Caveman tipped her chin and brushed a light kiss over her lips, then scooped her up by the backs of her thighs and wrapped her legs around his waist. Pinning her wrists to the wall above her head, he pressed his shaft to her damp entrance. "Slow and easy, or hard and fast?"

Her eyes widened. No man had ever asked her how she liked it. Not even her husband. She assumed it was up to the guy to establish the pace.

She only took a moment to decide. With her body on fire, her channel slick and ready, there was only one choice. "Hard and fast."

He eased into her, let her adjust to his thickness and then pulled out. Dropping his grip on her wrists, Caveman held her hips, his fingers digging into the flesh. Soon, he was pumping in and out of her, moving faster and faster, their movements making thumping sounds against the wall.

Grace held on to his shoulders, her head tipped back, her breath lodged in her chest as wave after wave of sensations ebbed through her, consuming her in a massive firestorm of desire. When she thought it couldn't get any better, he hit the sweet spot and sent her catapulting over the edge. She held on, riding him to the end.

One last thrust and he drove deep inside, pressing her firmly against the wall, his staff throbbing inside her. He leaned his forehead against hers, his breaths short and fast, like a marathon runner's.

A minute passed, and then two.

Grace didn't care, she teetered on the brink of a euphoric high. He could do it all again, and she'd be perfectly happy.

Caveman tightened his hold around her and carried her into the master bedroom, where he laid her on the bed. In the process, he lost their connection.

Grace ached inside, the emptiness leaving her cold. But not for long.

He slipped onto the mattress behind her and pulled her back to his front. His still-hard shaft nudged her between her legs and pressed against her entrance, sliding easily inside. Slipping his arms around her, he held her close, driving the chill from the air and her body.

She could be content to lie with him forever. After making love against the wall and being completely pleased, she could imagine how much more satisfying making love in the comfort of a bed might be.

If he stayed with her through the night, she vowed to find out before morning.

Pushing all the niggling thoughts of her curse to the back of her mind, she snuggled closer, giving him time to recuperate before she tested his ability to perform more than once in a night.

A CURSE. CAVEMAN had wanted to laugh off Grace's mention of it, but she'd been very adamant to the point she'd held him at arm's length. Until she couldn't fight the attraction another minute. He felt a twinge of guilt for teasing her into abandoning her cause and making love to him.

"So why is it you think I will be cursed?" he said, nuzzling the back of her ear.

She stiffened in his arms.

Caveman could have kicked himself for bringing it up after the most amazing sex he'd had in a very long time. "Never mind. I'm not very superstitious, anyway."

For a long time, she lay silent in his arms.

He began to think she'd gone to sleep.

"My high school sweetheart died in a head-on collision the night after I lost my virginity to him," she said. "He was eighteen."

Caveman kissed the curve of her shoulder. "Could have happened to anyone."

"That's what I thought." She inhaled deeply and let it out. "My husband died on our honeymoon. The day after we got there. We went parasailing. The cable holding his chute to the boat broke. He had no way to control the parachute. It slammed him into a cliff and he crashed to the rocks below. He was only twenty-four."

"Just because two of the guys you cared about died doesn't mean you are cursed."

She snorted softly. "A couple years ago, I decided to get back into the dating scene. I met a nice man. We dated three times. After our third date, I didn't hear from him for a few days. I called his cell phone number. A woman answered. I asked where he was. She broke down and cried, saying he'd died in a farming accident."

"Grace, you can't blame yourself for their deaths. Sometimes your number is just up. Those cases were all unrelated and coincidental."

"No, they were related. I cared about all three of them. The common denominator was me." She eased away from him, turned and faced him, her head lying on the pillow, her hand falling to his chest. "I haven't had a date since. I keep on friendly but distant terms with the men in my life." Her gaze shifted from his eyes to where her hand lay on his chest. "Until you." She looked up again. "Now...dear Lord, I've cursed you."

He kissed her forehead and pulled her into his arms. "You

aren't cursed and nothing's going to happen to me just because we made love tonight."

Grace rested her cheek against his chest, her head moving back and forth. "I shouldn't have risked it. You've been good to me, rescuing me when I was thrown from my horse. This is no way to repay you."

"I didn't ask for payment. I made love to you because I find you intelligent, sexy and brave."

"Not brave," she said, burying her face against his chest. "I ran when Mr. Khalig was killed."

"You had no choice."

"I did. I chose to run."

"You chose to live." He pressed a kiss to her forehead. "Sleep. Tomorrow is another day."

"Tomorrow's another day," she echoed. Her hand slid down his chest to touch him there. "But there's still tonight."

And just like that, he was ready. He jumped out of the bed, ran to where he'd left his wallet in the hallway and returned with protection for round two.

Later, while Grace slept, he slipped from the bed and used the phone in the hallway to call Kevin before midnight. He filled him in on the bullets fired at Grace in his truck. "We will make a full report to the sheriff in the morning. Did the coroner get a positive ID on the body?"

"Yes. It was RJ Khalig."

Caveman's chest tightened. "I should have gotten there sooner."

"How could you have?" Kevin asked. "You didn't know where 'there' was."

His head told him the same, but the man was his assignment and he'd let him down. "Anything on his cause of death?"

"He definitely had a gunshot wound to the chest. The coroner is still trying to determine whether or not it was enough to kill him, and whether he was alive or dead when he fell over the cliff."

Caveman walked into Grace's living room and nudged the curtain aside to look out at the street in front of her house. "My bet is that he was dead. Whoever shot him went back to finish the job." Moonlight shone down on the grass, the driveway and the street. Nothing moved. No vehicles passed.

"We'll know when the coroner's report is complete. In the meantime, how's Ms. Saunders?"

His pulse leaped and his groin tightened. Ms. Saunders was amazing. "Holding her own, but scared."

"She has every right to be." Kevin said something, but the sound was muffled. "I need to go. My wife is getting jealous of my job."

"Sorry to call so late."

"Don't be. I'm here for you. It's like I told you in the beginning, there's a lot more going on than meets the eye. I have a feeling this area is a powder keg waiting for someone to light the fuse."

As much as he would like to disagree with his new boss, he couldn't. In his gut, he knew the man was right.

"Stop by the loft in the morning," Kevin said. "Maybe Hack will have something on the men who were arguing in the tavern earlier."

"Will do." Caveman ended the call.

A sound drew his attention from the scene through the front window to the woman standing in the doorway to the living room. She stood in the meager light from the moon edging its way around the curtains. Her sandy-blond hair tumbled around her shoulders, her lips were swollen from his kisses and she'd loosely wrapped the sheet from the bed around her naked body.

"For someone who wasn't sure she wanted to make love, you're sending all the wrong signals." He chuckled and stalked toward her, his eyes narrowing as he got closer.

"I woke up, and you were gone."

"Not far. I couldn't leave, knowing there was a beautiful woman keeping the sheets warm."

"The sheets are cold." She lifted her arms to wrap around his neck. As she did, the sheet drifted down past her hips and floated to pool at her ankles.

"Mmm. Perhaps I need to warm them again." He bent, scooped her up into his arms and carried her back to the bedroom. "I'm out of condoms," he said, as he laid her out on the bed and climbed in beside her.

"We'll make do." She touched his cheek. "I just hope that since you're not going to be around for longer than this assignment lasts, you will be immune to the curse."

He turned his face into her hand and kissed her palm. "You're not cursed. And what if I stick around longer?" Now that he was in Wyoming, and the trouble Kevin had mentioned was turning out to be very real and imminent, he didn't see a pressing need for him to return to his unit, just to be sidelined until his leg was 100 percent and he could pass a fitness test. He could stay in Grizzly Pass and get to know Grace a little better, make love to her again...and again.

"Seriously." She brushed her lips across his. "Promise me that you won't fall in love with me. Not that you are or anything. But just to be safe, please...promise me."

His heart twisted. Promise not to love her? Hell, he'd only just met her. How could he fall in love with her so quickly? He kissed her palm again. "Don't you think it's a little early to think about love?" He pressed his lips to the tip of her nose. "Lust, I can understand—"

She touched a finger to his lips. "Please. Just promise."

Caveman opened his mouth to comply, but the words lodged in his throat. "I—" The words she wanted to hear refused to leave his lips. He couldn't even think them. Not love Grace? His twisting heart seemed to open into a gaping void at the thought of leaving Grizzly Pass and never talking to her again. He looked around the room, searching for the right words, knowing there weren't any. His gaze paused at the window. Light shone around the edges of the curtain, a bright white light getting lighter by the moment. He shot a glance at the clock on the nightstand. Was it already morning?

The green numbers on the digital clock read 12:36.

His pulse leaped, he grabbed Grace and rolled to the far side of the bed and off, taking her with him. Just as they landed hard on the floor, a loud crashing sound filled the air, the bed slid toward them, and the mattress upended and slammed them against the wall. Drywall crumbled, sending the ceiling and loose insulation cascading down around them, filling the air with dust so thick Caveman wouldn't have been able to see his hand in front of his face. If he could get his hand free to raise to his face. He and Grace were trapped between the mattress and the wall, unable to move.

Chapter Ten

Grace struggled to turn her head to the side, pulled her face out of a pillow and gasped for air. Something heavy lay on top of her and the mattress held her tightly against the wall. "Caveman?"

He coughed, making his body wiggle against hers, explaining the weight lying across her. "Grace? Are you all right?"

"I think so," she said. "But it's hard to breathe."

An engine sounded really close and the smell of exhaust warred with the dust filling her lungs. "What happened?" she whispered, barely able to draw in enough air to activate her vocal cords.

"I think someone crashed into your house."

"Dear God. How?" She tried to draw in a deep breath, but with everything smashing her to the floor and wall, she couldn't. The darkness surrounding her was nothing compared to the dizzying fog of losing consciousness. If they didn't get out of there soon, she'd suffocate.

"I…can't…get up." Caveman twisted his shoulders, his hands pressing down on her, searching for something else to brace against and finding nothing.

"Just push against me," she said.

"I'm sorry." He braced a hand on her chest and shoved himself backward, sliding down her body, inch by inch. As he moved past her chest, she was able to get a little more air to her lungs. She dragged it in, uncaring that it was filled with dust. The oxygen cleared her brain.

"I'm out," Caveman said.

She heard the sound of boards being kicked to the side. Then she heard the engine revving and the metal clank of gears shifting; the pressure eased off the mattress and her.

She lay for a moment, letting air fill her lungs. Then she struggled to push the heavy mattress off her.

Suddenly the bed shifted and fell away from her.

Caveman leaned down, extending a hand.

Grace took it and let him draw her to her feet and into his arms.

He held her for a long time, smoothing his hand over her hair. Finally, he pushed her to arm's length and swept his gaze over the length of her. "Are you all right? No broken bones, concussion, abrasions?"

She shook her head and stared around at the disaster that was her bedroom. "Maybe a bruised tailbone, but nothing compared to what it could have been if you hadn't thought so quickly." The front wall was caved in, the ceiling joists lay on the floor, electrical wires sparked dangerously close.

"Where's your breaker box?" Caveman asked.

"In the kitchen."

He scooped her up into his arms and waded through the splintered two-by-fours and broken sheets of drywall until he reached the intact hallway. There, he set her on her feet, grabbed her hand and led the way to the kitchen.

Grace took him to the breaker box in the pantry.

He flipped the master switch, shutting off all electricity to the house. "Gas?"

"Propane tank out back."

Caveman hurried to the front hallway and returned a minute

later wearing his jeans. He handed her the clothes she'd shed earlier, her boots and her purse. "Put these on and stand out on the porch while I shut off the gas to the house."

Grace dressed on the back porch, shivering in the cold.

Caveman returned and put his arm around her.

"What happened?" she asked, trembling uncontrollably.

"Someone drove my truck into the house."

"Oh, no. Did it ruin your truck?"

Caveman chuckled. "You were almost killed and you're worried about my truck? Sweetheart, you have to get your priorities straight."

"You were in the same place I was. Which means you were almost killed, as well." She leaned into him, slipping her arm around his waist. "If you hadn't noticed the lights headed our way…"

"Sorry about the rough landing, but at least we're alive."

"The driver?" she asked.

"Took off. I'm sure he's long gone by now." With his arm still around her, he led her down the back porch stairs and away from the damaged house. "We can't stay here tonight."

"We could go to my folks' place. I have a key." Grace laughed, the sound more like a sob. "If you want to dig it out. It's somewhere in my jewelry box on my dresser…"

"Beneath all the rubble." Caveman shook his head. "Hopefully Kevin can help us out."

"I can't believe someone drove your truck into my house." She turned back. "I can't leave it like this. What if it rains?"

Caveman stared up at the clear night sky. "It's not supposed to rain for a couple days. We can come back in the morning and see what we can salvage." He steered her toward the front of the house where his truck stood, the front end smashed in, one of the tires flat. "We'll have to take your vehicle, unless you want to wait while I attempt to change that flat."

"We'll take my SUV." Grace fished in her purse, pulling out

her keys. She handed them to Caveman. "I'd drive, but I'm not feeling very steady right now."

"Don't worry. I'll get us there."

Sitting in the passenger seat of her SUV didn't make her feel any better. Nothing about what had happened in the last thirty-six hours felt right.

Except making love to Caveman. And he wasn't much more than a stranger. A stranger who'd saved her life three times now. That had to make up for the fact that they'd known each other such a short amount of time.

"I think it's time to wake the sheriff." Caveman turned the key in the ignition.

It clicked once, but the engine didn't turn over.

Caveman's hand froze on the key, his brows descending. "Grace, get out."

"But we can't take your truck. It's damaged."

"Just get out. Now!" He reached across the seat, pulled the handle on her door and shoved her through. "Run!"

The pure desperation in his tone shook Grace out of the stunned state she'd been in since her world had come crashing down around her. Her feet grew wings and she ran faster than she had since the high school track team. She didn't know where she was going, as long as it was away from the vehicle.

Twenty feet from her old but trusted SUV, the world exploded around her for the second time that night. She flew forward, landing hard on the ground, the air forced from her lungs, her ears ringing.

She lay for a moment, trying to remember how to breathe.

"Caveman," she said and pushed up to her knees. "Caveman!" she shouted, but couldn't hear an answering response due to the loud ringing in her ears. She ran back to the burning hulk that had been her SUV. He'd been so adamant about getting her out of the vehicle he hadn't had time to get himself out.

Grace reached for the door handle of the burning vehicle. She couldn't leave him in there, she had to get him out. The heat made her skin hurt. Right before her hand touched the metal handle, a voice shouted.

"Grace!"

The sound came to her through her throbbing ears and over the roar of the fire. She turned toward it.

Caveman rounded the edge of the blaze and ran toward her. He pulled her away from the flames and held her close.

Several minutes passed, neither one of them in a hurry to move away.

A siren sounded in the distance and then another. Soon the yard was filled with emergency vehicles. The sheriff's deputy was first on the scene, followed by all of the vehicles belonging to the Grizzly Pass Volunteer Fire Department.

The Emergency Medical Technicians checked Grace and Caveman. Other than a few scrapes and bruises they'd live to see another day.

Soon the blaze was out.

Grace checked on her horse in the pasture on the other side of the barn. The fire had been in the front yard. The barn had sustained no damage, but her horse galloped around the paddock, frightened by the sirens and the smoke.

Caveman helped her catch the horse and soothe him. When she finally released him, he ran to the farthest point away from the smoke.

Grace made certain he had sufficient water before she returned to the front of the house. She and Caveman gave a detailed description of the bullets fired on their way home, and what had happened to her house and finally her vehicle. Caveman borrowed a cell phone from the deputy and placed a call to Kevin. The DHS agent offered to let them sleep in the loft above the tavern until they could come up with another arrangement.

The sheriff appeared shortly after they'd finished their account. He wore jeans and a denim jacket and looked like he'd just gotten out of bed.

Grace and Caveman recounted their story again for the sheriff's benefit.

"Grace, the man who killed Mr. Khalig is definitely after you. Do you know where you're going from here?"

"The Blue Moose Tavern."

The sheriff frowned. "They're closed."

"We'll be staying in the apartment above the tavern tonight," Caveman said.

"Come. You can ride with me," the sheriff said.

"Please." Grace didn't care who she rode with as long as there was a shower and a clean bed wherever they landed. Grace climbed into the back of the sheriff's vehicle. Caveman slid in next to her and pulled her into the crook of his arm. He was covered in dust and soot, but she didn't care. She was equally dirty, but alive. She nestled against him, but when she closed her eyes, images of the fire burned through her eyelids. Her pulse quickened and her heart thudded against her ribs.

"It's okay. We're going to be okay," Caveman said in that same tone he'd used on her horse. It worked on humans just as well.

Grace felt the tension ease. "I thought you were still in my SUV."

"I got out right after you." He smoothed his hand over her hair. "What's important is that we're both okay."

"I have my men watching the roads leading into and out of town," the sheriff said. "If someone is still out and about, they'll bring him in for questioning."

"Whoever did this will be long gone, if he's smart," Caveman said.

The sheriff glanced at them in his rearview mirror. "Whoever it was is getting more serious about these attacks."

"The question is why?" Grace said. "I couldn't see him from the distance when he killed Mr. Khalig. He should know by now."

"No search warrants have been issued," the sheriff said. "I

haven't called anyone in for questioning. He's in the clear. As far as we know, it could have been anyone."

"What good does it do to kill me?" Grace shivered. "I'm nobody. Just a biologist."

Caveman tightened his arm around her. "Who happened to be in the wrong place at the wrong time and witnessed a murder."

"And escaped before the shooter could kill you, too." Sheriff Scott glanced back at her in the rearview mirror. "You're the one who got away."

Another tremor shook Grace's body. "I can't keep running."

"You can't get out in the open and give him something to shoot at." Caveman held her close. "I won't let you."

"I won't stand by and let him get away with destroying my home, my car and my life."

Caveman frowned. "What do you propose to do?"

She shook her head. "I don't know, but I'll think of something." Snuggling closer, she laid her cheek on his chest. "After a shower and some sleep."

THE LOFT ABOVE the Blue Moose Tavern was a fully furnished apartment with a single bedroom, bathroom and a living room with a foldout couch. The living area had been transformed into an operations center with a bay of computers and a large folding table covered with contour maps.

Kevin and Hack, his computer guru, waited in front of the tavern when the sheriff dropped off Caveman and Grace. The two DHS employees led the tired pair up the stairs. After a quick debriefing, Kevin offered Grace clothes his wife had sent and sweats and a T-shirt for Caveman. "We'll help you sift through the debris at your house tomorrow. For tonight, we hope this will do." Kevin's wife had also sent along a toiletries kit with a tube of toothpaste, shampoo, soap and toothbrushes still in their packages.

Grace gathered the kit, the clothes and a fresh towel. "This is one of those times when I'll gladly claim the 'ladies first' clause." She disappeared into the bathroom leaving the men to discuss the events of the day.

"I don't like it," Caveman said as soon as Grace was out of earshot.

"I don't blame you," Kevin agreed.

"There have been too many near misses today and we have yet to identify who's doing it."

"Do you think maybe there's more than one person involved?" Kevin asked.

"I don't know. But what I do know is that whoever it is knows something about weapons and explosives. He wired Grace's ignition with a damn detonator." Anger bubbled up inside him, spilling over. Caveman stalked away from Hack and Kevin, his fists clenched. He needed to fight back, but he didn't have a clue who he was fighting against. He spun and strode back to where Kevin stood. "If I hadn't gone with my gut when the vehicle didn't start, Grace wouldn't be in this apartment now. If I hadn't been there when she came barreling out of the mountains and was thrown by her horse, she'd be dead."

Kevin nodded. "We're still trying to trace the crates we found in the abandoned mine. Someone did a good job transporting them so that no one could identify their origin. We did a count, though, and based on the empty boxes, there were one hundred AR-15s in those crates. You don't hide one hundred AR-15s just anywhere. Someone has an armory around here and they're stockpiling weapons and ammunition."

"And the infrared satellite images we had from a week ago indicated fifteen individuals who helped unload those weapons. The Vanders family would account for at least four of those heat signatures, which leaves eleven."

"Hell, that's half the people in this county," Caveman said.

"I know this town is small, but there are a lot of outlying homes and ranches comprising the entire community of Grizzly Pass." Kevin scrubbed his hand down his face. The shadows under his eyes made him appear much older. "People are preparing for something. It's our jobs to stop them before they hurt others."

Caveman paced the room again, thinking. "This Free America group. Who are the members?"

"We don't know for certain," Hack said. "LeRoy Vanders and his sons admit to being members. They're talking about who else."

"What about the loudmouth last night in the tavern? Ernie Martin," Caveman shot out.

Kevin nodded. "He's one we're watching."

"I've tapped into his home internet account and his cell phone." Hack pulled out his chair and sat at the bank of computers, bringing up a screen. "His computer is clean, and I'm not finding any significant connections on the cell numbers he calls. If he's communicating with the group, he's doing it in person or on a burner phone I can't trace." He tapped several keys, booting the computer to life.

"You don't have to stay and work through the night," Caveman said. "I'm with Grace. All I want right now is a shower and some sleep."

"Do you want one of us to stand guard while you get some rest?" Kevin asked.

"No." Caveman wanted to be alone. With Grace. "The sheriff will have a deputy swing by every half hour until daylight. We should be all right."

Kevin straightened. "Then we'll leave you to get some rest. The sofa folds out into a queen-size bed. You can find sheets and blankets in the chest at the end of the bed. Help yourselves to anything in the refrigerator. I had it stocked with drinks and snacks."

"Thanks." Caveman could hear the shower going in the other room.

Hack powered the computer off and followed Kevin to the door.

"If you need me, give me a call. I can be here in five minutes." Kevin held out his hand. "Bet you weren't counting on so much activity in Wyoming. Were you?"

Caveman shook the man's hand. "No, I thought this would be a mini vacation and I'd be on my way back to my unit."

"And now?"

"I'm beginning to understand your concerns." And he couldn't leave, knowing Grace was in trouble.

"So you'll stay a little longer?"

"As long as you need me and my unit doesn't."

Kevin nodded. "Glad to hear it. We need good soldiers like you."

"I'll do what I can."

"I'm only five minutes away, as well," Hack said. He held up his cell phone. "Call, if you need me."

"Roger." Caveman closed the door behind the two men and twisted the dead bolt lock. Not that a dead bolt would have stopped a truck from crashing through Grace's bedroom wall. He hurried to the back of the apartment, stripping off his dirty clothes and kicking off his boots. The shower was still going when he stepped through the bathroom door.

He pushed the curtain aside and slipped into the tub.

"I wondered how long it would take you to get rid of those two." Grace turned around, her body clean and glistening beneath the spray. "I was beginning to prune." She slid a handful of suds over his chest, making mud out of the dirt, soot and dust.

Caveman didn't care. She could smear mud all over his body if she wanted as long as her hands were doing the smearing. She poured shampoo into her palm and lathered his hair.

With his hands free to explore, he lathered up and smoothed his fingers over her shoulders and down to her breasts, where he tweaked the nipples into tight buds. Moving lower, he cupped her sex and parted her folds, strumming the nubbin of flesh between.

She moaned and widened her stance. "No protection," she

said, her voice catching in her throat as he flicked her there again.

"This isn't about me."

Grace moaned again, her hand sliding over his shoulders, washing away all of the grime, dirty bubbles carrying it down the drain. "Not all about me." She wrapped her hands around his shaft and stroked the length of him.

It was his turn to groan.

Touching and testing the sweet spots, they felt their way to an orgasm that left Caveman satisfied and frustrated at the same time. First thing in the morning, he'd hit the local drug store for reinforcements. This woman's appetite rivaled his own, and he didn't want to be caught unprepared.

By the time they'd explored every inch of each other's body, the water had cooled to the point of discomfort.

Caveman turned off the shower, grabbed a towel and gently dried Grace. She returned the favor and sighed, her face sad.

"Why so sad?" he asked. "Didn't you like that?"

"Too much." She took his hand and led him to the bed. "I'm going to miss it when you're gone."

"Who said I'm going anywhere?"

"You know what I mean." She lay down on the bed and scooted over, making room for him. "You said it yourself. You're only going to be here for a short time."

"What if I decide to stay?" He might not have a job to go back to in the army. If the Medical Review Board didn't clear him, he'd be discharged, or given a desk job. He'd rather move back to Montana or Wyoming than take a desk job.

Grace's brows descended. "You can't stay. Look what nearly happened tonight. You were almost killed."

"But I wasn't. And neither were you."

She snuggled closer, her eyes drooping. "I'm too tired to argue about it. Just keep your promise, and don't do something stupid like fall in love with me." Her voice trailed off and her breathing grew steadier.

Caveman brushed a strand of hair away from her cheek and bent to kiss her. "I never made that promise. And it might be too late." Never in a million years, would Max "Caveman" Decker have guessed he would fall in love with a woman after knowing her for less than a week. But the thought of leaving and going back to his unit didn't hold the same appeal. In fact, even the mention of leaving made him feel like someone had a hand on his heart, squeezing the life out of him.

Maybe it was too soon for love, but only time would tell. Caveman wasn't so sure he'd have the time to find out, if Khalig's killer had his way with Grace. Tonight would have been the end of her had Caveman left when he'd originally wanted. Now, he couldn't leave. Not as long as Grace was in danger.

Chapter Eleven

Grace slept until after ten the following morning. When she woke, she stretched her arm across the bed, expecting to feel a naked body next to hers. When she didn't, she opened her eyes.

Caveman was gone.

For a moment, panic ripped through her. After all that had happened, she'd begun to rely on him to rescue her. Then she reminded herself he wouldn't have left without saying good-bye. Not after last night.

They'd shared more than a near-death experience, they'd connected on a level even more intimate.

Male voices sounded through the paneling of the bedroom door.

Grace bolted to a sitting position, dragging the sheet up over her bare breasts. She'd forgotten that the living area was being used as the command center for the DHS representatives. They'd probably been there for at least an hour, while she'd slept in.

Her cheeks heated. She wondered if Caveman had risen before they arrived to spare her the embarrassment of the team finding them in bed together.

She rose, grabbed the clothes Kevin's wife had provided and

slipped into the bathroom. Five minutes later, she was dressed, had her hair pulled back into a neat ponytail and had brushed her teeth. She was ready to face the world. Or at least Kevin's team. She opened the door to the bedroom and stepped out.

The group of men standing around the array of computer monitors turned as one.

Heat rose into Grace's cheeks. Did they know she and Caveman had slept naked in the next room? Did she care? She squared her shoulders and forced a smile to her face.

In addition to Kevin, Caveman and Hack, three more men were in attendance. All there to witness Grace emerging from the back bedroom. Yeah, not what a woman wanted that early in the morning. "Good morning."

"Grace." Kevin stepped forward. "I trust you slept well?"

She nodded, her gaze going to the three men she didn't recognize.

Kevin turned to them. "Grace, have you met the other members of my task force?"

"No, I have not."

He turned to a big man with red hair and blue eyes. "This is Jon Caspar, US Navy SEAL. They call him Ghost."

Ghost shook her hand. "I've seen you around. Nice to meet you."

Kevin moved to the next man, who was not quite as tall as Ghost, but had black hair and ice-blue eyes. "Trace Walsh, aka Hawkeye, is an Army Ranger."

Grace shook hands with Hawkeye. "Pleasure to meet you."

He grinned. "The pleasure's all mine."

Caveman grunted behind her. If she wasn't mistaken, it was a grunt of anger, maybe jealousy? Her heart swelled.

The last man Kevin introduced had really short auburn hair and hazel eyes. Almost as tall as Ghost, he looked like he could chew nails and spit them out. "This is Rex Trainor."

"My friends call me T-Rex." The man stuck out a hand. "I'm with the US Marine Corps."

When T-Rex shook her hand, he nearly crushed the bones.

Introductions complete, Grace glanced at the computer monitors. "Am I missing something?"

Kevin shook his head. "Not at all. We were just going through some of the most likely suspects who live in the area."

"Like?" She stepped up beside Caveman and looked over Hack's shoulder at pictures of people on the different monitors. Some of them were mug shots, others were driver's license pictures or photos from yearbooks. She recognized most of them, having lived in the area for the majority of her life. Small-town life was like that.

"Quincy Kemp and Ernie Martin," Caveman said.

"Mathis Herrington, Wayne Batson," Kevin added.

"And, of course, Tim Cramer and the Vanders family, who have already been detained." Hack tapped the keys on the computer keyboard. "We've been trying to find the connection between all of them."

Grace yawned and stretched, her muscles sore from everything that had happened over the past couple of days. "Has anyone thought to ask Mrs. Penders at the grocery store?"

Four of the five men frowned.

Ghost grinned. "That's where my girl, Charlie McClain, goes when she wants to know what's going on. Mrs. Penders seems to have her finger on the pulse of everything going on in town."

"I'll go question her." Caveman turned toward the door. "Mrs. Penders is her name?"

Grace held up her hand. "You can't just barge in and interrogate the woman. She likes to gossip, not answer a barrage of very pointed questions. Since my house was destroyed last night, she'll be eager to hear all of the details straight from the horse's mouth. Give a little, get a lot." She glanced down at the clothes Kevin's wife had loaned her. "Kevin, tell your wife thank you for the loaner. I'll get them back as soon as I dig my wardrobe out from under the rubble."

"She said to keep them as long as you need them," Kevin said. "And we plan to help with the cleanup."

"Thanks, but I'd rather you found the killer." She drew in a deep breath and let it out. "I don't know how much longer I can play this game with him, before he scores." *With my death.* "Now, if you will excuse me, I'm going across the street to talk to Mrs. Penders and buy a few supplies I might need in the cleanup process."

"I'm going with you," Caveman said.

Grace shook her head. "You can't. Mrs. Penders will be more likely to talk if I'm alone."

"You can't waltz around town like anyone else." Caveman gripped her arms. "You have a killer after you. One who is a crack shot with a rifle and scope."

Placing a hand on his chest, Grace smiled up at him. "Then I'll zigzag, or whatever it is you trained combatants do to run through enemy territory."

The other men chuckled. Not Caveman.

His face hardened. "It's not a joke."

Her smile fading, Grace nodded. "I know. It's not every day you have someone drive a truck into your bedroom, or have someone shooting at you. I'll be careful and look for trouble before I cross the street."

"I'm walking you across the street."

Her first instinct was to argue, but one glance at Caveman's face and she knew she would lose that argument. And frankly, she liked having him around. "Okay." She walked to the door and followed Caveman down the steps to the street.

He looped his arm around her shoulders, pulling her close to his body. They probably appeared to be lovers who couldn't get enough of each other. After last night, the look fit Grace. She wondered if Caveman felt the same, or if he truly only thought of her as a temporary distraction until he returned to his unit.

At the corner of the grocery store, Grace stopped and placed a hand on Caveman's chest. "This is where I get off. I'll see you as soon as I get all of the information I can out of Mrs. Penders."

"I'll be right here. All you have to do is yell if you need me."

"Thank you." Then, before she could talk herself out of it, she leaned up on her toes and pressed her lips to his. It was meant to be a quick show of appreciation. However, she was more than gratified when Caveman took the kiss to the next level.

He cinched his arm around her waist, crushing her to his body, his lips claiming hers in a kiss that stole her breath away and made her knees turn to gelatin. Had Caveman not been holding her, she would have melted to the ground. When he set her away from him, she swayed.

She raised a hand to her lips. "Wow."

He chuckled, the warm, deep resonance of the sound heating her from the inside out. "I don't like you standing out in the open for long." He turned her toward the grocery store entrance, gave her bottom a pat and sent her on her way. "Hurry back. I have more where that came from."

She ran her tongue across her bottom lip, tasting him.

"On second thought, forget going inside. We can drive out to the local lake and make out in the backseat of my pickup."

She laughed. "You're not making this easy."

He held up his hands. "What am I supposed to make easy?"

"Letting go of you when you leave Grizzly Pass."

"Maybe that's my plan."

Her smile faded. "You have to, eventually."

"Let's not talk about that now. In fact, take your time inside. Don't come out until you see me walk by the windows. I want to look around town."

She snorted. "That won't take long."

"Exactly. So take all the time you need. Just don't come outside until I'm here to protect you."

She nodded. Grace wanted to run for the door, zip in, suck information out of Mrs. Pender's brain in record time and return for another of those soul-defining kisses.

She'd warned him not to fall in love with her, but maybe she'd been warning the wrong person. Grace needed to take her own advice. Perhaps the curse was on anyone *she* fell in love with, not who fell in love with her.

With no time to contemplate her thoughts, she stepped into the store and greeted the female store owner with a smile. "Good morning, Mrs. Penders."

"Grace, honey, I was shocked to hear someone bulldozed your house last night. What can I do to help?"

OUTSIDE, LEANING ON a light post, Caveman studied the people who entered and exited the small store. The only one of its kind in town, it had the corner on the market. If people wanted more than what the Penderses offered, they had to drive thirty minutes to an hour to the nearest big town. Too far for a loaf of bread or a gallon of milk.

After a few minutes, he pushed away from the light post and walked to the end of the block—still within a reasonable distance to listen for a scream or see someone entering the store who might appear to be there for nefarious reasons rather than to buy a can of soup or a loaf of bread.

From his vantage point at the street corner, he could see to the end of Main Street. A storefront on the opposite side had a stuffed bear outside on the sidewalk. Not the teddy bear of the fake fur, cotton-filled variety. No, this was an eleven-foot tall grizzly, professionally mounted by a skillful taxidermist. He stood on his hind legs, his front legs outstretched, the wicked claws appearing to be ready to swipe at passersby. And the mouth was open, every razor-sharp tooth on display. Yes, Quincy Kemp was very good at making the carcasses appear alive.

With a quick glance toward the grocery store to make certain Grace hadn't ended her information-gathering mission early, he turned toward the meat processing and taxidermist shop.

The door stood open; the scents of cedar, pepper and the

musk of animal hides filled his senses, bringing back memories of a similar place in Caveman's hometown. In states where hunting was the major pastime of residents and tourists, every town seemed to have one of these kinds of stores.

A man emerged from a back room, wiping his hands on a towel. "What can I do for you?"

Caveman recognized him as Quincy Kemp. "I heard you made jerky."

"You heard right," Quincy said with one of the best poker faces Caveman had encountered.

"Do you happen to have buffalo or venison jerky?"

The man nodded and pulled a plastic butter tub from beneath the counter, opened it and selected a strip of jerky. "Try before you buy. I don't do refunds. This is buffalo."

Caveman popped the piece of jerky in his mouth and then chewed and chewed. The explosion of flavors made his mouth water.

Quincy crossed his arms over his chest, lifted his chin and looked down his nose at Caveman. "Well?"

"Good. I'd like to purchase a pound of the buffalo jerky."

While Quincy weighed several strips of the flavored, dried meat, Caveman wandered around the store. Besides a glass case of jerky and a refrigerated case of raw meat labeled Beef, Venison, Buffalo, Elk and Red Deer, there were numerous animals mounted on the wall.

"Did you do all of these?" Caveman waved at the lifelike animals staring down at him from shelves and nooks along the wall.

Quincy slipped the strips of jerky into a plastic bag and sealed it before answering. "Yeah. That'll be fifteen bucks."

Caveman fished his wallet out of his pocket, which reminded him he needed to hit the store for a refill of condoms. He placed a twenty on the counter. "What kinds of animals have you done?"

"What you see."

Caveman had noticed the bear, bobcat, rattle snake, elk, moose and coyote. "What about mountain lion?"

"I've done a couple."

"Bobcat?"

He shrugged. "Four."

"Is there an open season on bobcat and mountain lion?"

The man's eyes narrowed. "Do you have a point?"

"Just wondering. I might like to buy a hunting license while I'm here."

Quincy slapped the change on the counter and pushed the plastic bag of jerky toward Caveman. "Hunting season isn't open until the fall. If that's all you want, I don't have time to talk. I have work to do."

Caveman lifted the bag of jerky and grinned. "Thanks."

Quincy didn't wait for Caveman to leave the store before he returned to the back room.

Caveman would like to have followed the man to the back to see what job he was all fired up about. The man looked like someone who could chew nails. Not that he scared Caveman, but he wouldn't take kindly to being followed.

But then, Caveman could claim he wanted to see Quincy's work in case he wanted the man to stuff his next trophy kill. Not that Caveman ever killed just for the trophy. He hunted back in Montana, but always ate what he bagged.

Easing behind the counter, Caveman worked his way to the door leading to the back of the building. Quincy had left it open, presumably to hear for customers entering the shop.

Through the door was a workroom filled with hides and tools of the taxidermist trade. A short corridor led to a workshop in the back. The meat packaging plant was probably at the end of the hallway.

Quincy was nowhere to be seen.

Caveman studied the hides, curious about what the taxidermist did.

"Hey!" Quincy emerged from a door in the back. "What are you doing back here?"

Startled by the man's abrupt appearance, Caveman snapped around, his legs bent in a ready stance, his fists clenched in a defensive reflex. "I had a question for you."

"Well, take it out to the front. Nobody comes back here, but me."

"Sorry." Caveman held up his hands in surrender. "I didn't touch anything."

"Doesn't matter. You don't belong back here." Quincy marched toward him.

Caveman backed through the door, pretending to be afraid, but ready to take on the man if he pushed him too far. "I wanted to know if you could stuff a wolf I hit on my way into town. I threw him in the back of my truck, hating to waste a good-looking hide. I think he'd look really great in my man cave back home in North Carolina."

"Man, you need to get rid of the carcass. It's illegal to keep a wolf, dead or alive, in the state of Wyoming."

"So you wouldn't stuff him? What if I sneak him in here at night? Could you?"

"Hell, no. I don't plan on spending the next five years in jail. Been there, done that. I'm never going back. I'd die before I let them take me back."

"Okay. I totally understand. No worries. I'll find someone else to do it."

"You won't."

"Won't what?"

"Find another taxidermist. No one will touch a wolf, unless the government commissions it."

"Well, there goes my idea for a centerpiece in my living room." Caveman raised a hand in a half wave. "I guess that's all I needed to know. I must say, I'm disappointed."

Quincy's mouth formed into a tightly pressed line and his eyes narrowed.

Caveman waved the bag of jerky again. "Thanks again for the jerky and all the information on taxidermist rules in Wyoming." He left the shop and strolled down the street toward the tavern, his gaze on the grocery store where he'd left Grace.

When he was far enough away from Quincy's shop, Caveman crossed the street and waited outside the grocery store, chewing on the buffalo jerky he'd purchased from Quincy, wondering what the man might be hiding in the back of his building. Perhaps he'd bring it up to Kevin and let the boss decide who he could send in to check. At this point, from what Caveman could tell of his role with Task Force Safe Haven, his primary purpose was to protect Grace from a killer. Kevin and the others could do the sleuthing to find out if what was happening in Grizzly Pass was a terrorist plot to take over the government.

"MARK RUTHERFORD SHOULD be available to help you fix the damage to your house. He's a good handyman and carpenter. And Lord knows he could use the work," Mrs. Penders said. "What with his daddy having to pay the additional grazing fees when he just forked out a wad of cash to install a new pump in his well. I'm sure Mark would appreciate the extra income."

"I'll check with him as soon as I assess the damage. I just can't understand why someone would deliberately crash into my house."

"Are you sure it wasn't an accident?"

"No, it was deliberate. He broke into the truck and drove it into my bedroom wall as if he knew I was in bed." Grace glanced around the store. "I'll need some trash bags and cleaning supplies."

"Sweetie, let me help you."

"Oh, I can't take you away from the register."

"There's no one in the store right now. I want to help." Mrs. Penders locked the register and led the way down the aisle of cleaning supplies, plucking off a couple bottles of disinfectant spray and cleaner. "I don't know what's going on in town, what with the Vanderses going crazy and kidnapping a busload of little ones. And now someone's murdered Mr. Khalig. He came into the store the other day for a bag of butterscotch candies." She smiled sadly. "Such a nice man. I imagine his wife will be devastated."

"Who would want to kill Mr. Khalig?"

Mrs. Penders rounded the end of the cleaning supplies aisle and started up the one with paper products and boxes of trash bags. She grabbed one of the boxes, read the front and put it back, selecting one with a larger number of bags. "Mr. Khalig worked as an inspector for the pipeline. If he doesn't approve what's going on, the pipeline shuts down. He could have reported some safety issues. Some people think he's the reason they got laid off."

"Did he ever say anything about any safety issues?" Grace asked, taking some of the cleaning supplies from Mrs. Penders. They walked back to front of the store and set the items on the counter.

"I could use some paper plates and disposable cutlery. I have a feeling my electricity will be off and on as they work on my house."

Mrs. Penders turned and led the way to the plastic forks and spoons. "Mr. Khalig wasn't allowed to discuss his work on account of confidentiality. But I could tell he wasn't happy with what he was finding. He started out warm and friendly. The longer he was here, the quieter and more secretive he became. And he kept looking over his shoulder, like someone was watching him." Mrs. Penders sighed. "And somebody had to have been, in order to shoot him from a distance. Poor, poor man. How awful."

"How do you know all of this?"

Mrs. Penders carried the boxes of spoons and forks to the counter and gave Grace a smile. "I just do. As for who, there are quite a few people I can think of. All of them worked for the pipeline and lost their jobs. The sheriff should start there. I mean look at what happened with Tim Cramer. He lost his job with the pipeline, his wife filed for divorce and now he's in jail. He was so desperate he helped with that kidnapping."

"He couldn't have been the one to kill Mr. Khalig. He was in jail when it happened."

"True. But there are others on the verge of bankruptcy, losing their homes and destroying their families." Mrs. Penders clucked her tongue. "Such a shame. I wish that pipeline had never crossed this state."

"Most of those who worked for the pipeline would have moved out of state to find jobs by now."

"Yes, but they wouldn't be as desperate." Mrs. Penders unlocked the register. "It's as if someone is sabotaging this area and the people in it."

"Who would do that, and why?" As Mrs. Penders rang up Grace's purchases, Grace put them into a bag. "We don't have anything here anyone would want."

"Maybe they want the pipeline to fail, but then maybe not, if they shot the inspector who could have shut down the whole thing." Mrs. Penders took Grace's money and handed her the change. "Then there are the folks who are tired of everything to do with the government. They would prefer to have the entire state of Wyoming secede from the United States. Bunch of crazies, if you ask me. Even scarier, they're a bunch of armed nut jobs."

"Do you know any of them?"

"Nobody comes out and says they're part of the group Free America. But I have my suspicions."

"Who?"

The older woman glanced around to make sure no one else was in the store. "I think Ernie Martin, Quincy Kemp, Don Sweeney and Mathis Herrington belong to that group. I'm sure there are a lot more who aren't as vocal. Some not from this county, but a county over."

"If they aren't telling you, how do you know?"

The older woman lifted her chin. "I have ears. Sometimes they run into each other in the store while I'm stocking shelves. I can hear them talking. In fact, I'm pretty sure they're having some meeting tomorrow night."

Butterflies erupted in Grace's belly. "Where?"

Mrs. Penders shrugged. "I don't know. Ernie and Quincy were in here buying lighter fluid and briquettes earlier today for a barbeque. They said something about getting together at the range."

"Range?" Grace's mind exploded with possibilities. "As in front range? Good Lord, that could be almost anywhere." Or maybe... "Or do they mean like a gun range?"

A mother carrying a baby in a car seat walked into the store.

The store owner smiled at the woman. "Good morning, Bayleigh, how's Lucas?"

The young mother smiled. "He's finally sleeping through the night."

"That's wonderful. Are you here for that formula you ordered?"

"I am," Bayleigh answered.

Mrs. Penders raised her finger. "One minute. I'll get it from the back."

"Please, take your time," Bayleigh said. "I have other shopping to do."

Grace gathered her bags. She couldn't take up any more of Mrs. Penders's time. "Thank you for everything, Mrs. P."

"Let me know if you need anything. Remember to check with Mark Rutherford. He's got time on his hands and probably can start right away on the repairs."

"I'll do that." Grace paused at the entrance, a frown pulling at her brows. A meeting at the range. When she spotted Caveman waiting outside, she pushed through the door and hurried toward the man who made her heart beat faster. "We need to talk to the team."

Chapter Twelve

Caveman paced the length of the operations center.

"How do you propose we get an invite to that meeting tomorrow evening?" Kevin asked. "We're not even sure what Mrs. Penders meant by 'the range.'"

"I'd bet my last dollar it's Wayne Batson's gun range," Ghost said.

Hack nodded. "He has the fences and security system in place to hold off an initial attack. And his computer system has a helluva firewall. I've yet to hack into it."

"Sounds like someone with something to hide," Caveman said.

"Why don't we just walk in?" Grace asked.

All five men turned toward her.

"Walk in?" Kevin asked. "What do you mean?"

"By now, everyone in town will know I've been the target of a shooter and someone who likes crashing trucks into my house. What if I ask Wayne to give me some time on his range, maybe even shooting lessons?"

"No way," Caveman said. "Putting you on a rifle range with a bunch of loaded weapons is a recipe for getting shot. What if the shooter is Wayne or one of his buddies?"

"So, I take my bodyguard and announce it to the world I'm going to the range. The sheriff knows, everyone in town knows. If someone shoots me at the range, they'll have to shoot Caveman, too. They might get away with an accident killing one person, but they won't get away with killing two."

Anger tinged with a healthy dose of fear bubbled up inside Caveman. "So who shall we offer up as the one?" He shook his head. "It's too dangerous."

Grace turned toward Kevin. "At the very least, we go in, find the weaknesses of Batson's security system, leave and come back at night when we can slip in under the cover of darkness."

Caveman couldn't believe what she was saying. If one of Batson's friends was the shooter, he'd have no trouble lining up his sights and taking her down. "There is no 'we' in slipping back into Batson's property." He poked a finger at her. "*You're* not going anywhere."

"But I'm the one with the big target on my back."

Crossing his arms over his chest, he refused to back down. "Exactly. Now you're beginning to understand."

Her frown deepened and her cheeks reddened. "Don't patronize me, Max Decker. I'm the one who has to keep looking over her shoulder. I'm the one whose house is now a wreck. I have the biggest stake in finding the killer. I deserve to go."

"But you don't deserve to die." His face firmed and his eyes narrowed. "You're not going."

Her chin lifted. "Then I'll go without you. I need practice with my .40-caliber pistol, and I don't need your permission." She started for the door. "Gentlemen, I have a house to sift through and arrangements to make to get me onto Batson's rifle range." She sailed past Caveman and almost made it to the door when he grabbed her arm and yanked her back.

"We need to talk," he said. He couldn't let her walk out the door unprotected and waltz into the enemy's camp. If Batson was truly the enemy. "Let's at least talk this through before we go off half-cocked."

"I'm done talking." She glared at the hand on her arm. "Let go of me."

"Grace." Kevin stepped over to where they stood by the door. "We need to make a plan. We also need to understand who we're dealing with. What motivation does Wayne Batson have to host a Free America meeting on his range?"

"Maybe he's training recruits for the takeover of the government," Ghost offered. "The message Charlie picked up off that social media site was clear. They're planning a takeover of something."

"Why would Batson lead the charge?" Kevin asked. "He has to have a reason."

Grace pressed her fingers to the bridge of her nose. "I don't know. Wayne Batson seems to be the only person in the county who has pulled himself up out of hard times. When he was faced with bankruptcy, he found investors and turned his ranch into a sportsman's paradise. Why destroy a good thing by plotting against the government?"

"Having been in a bad situation, maybe he harbors animosity toward the government for some reason," Hawkeye said. "You never know what will push a man over the edge and make him think he has to take control of the world."

"Are you saying we might be barking up the wrong tree?" Grace asked. "That Batson might not be our guy? His ranch with the rifle range might not be the meeting place?"

Kevin shook his head. "No. I think you're on to something."

"Then what's your plan?" She planted her fists on her hips. "If I take Caveman with me to practice my shooting skills, we can at least get inside and look around."

Caveman turned toward Kevin. "What do you have in the way of communications equipment? We had the radio headsets we used when we stormed the Lucky Lou Mine in the rescue attempt to save the kidnapped kids. Could we have something like that? And do you have any kind of webcam we can hide in a pen?"

Kevin grinned. "You must have me mistaken with the CIA."

Hack spun in his chair and opened his mouth to say something.

Before he could, Kevin held up his hand. "As a matter of fact, I invested some of the project funding in just what you're talking about. We have a webcam button we can attach to your shirt. Hack will get you two wired up."

Grace smiled. "Thank you."

Caveman wasn't happy about the situation, but he could either shut up and go, or send someone else with Grace. The woman was going whether or not he wanted her to. And because he found himself just a little bit protective of her, he didn't trust anyone else to take care of her as well as he would. Not that the others weren't fully capable. They just didn't have the connection he had with her.

Hack went to a footlocker in the corner, unlocked the combination lock and pulled out radio headsets and a small case with a little white button. "Doesn't look like much, but it sends a pretty clear picture to our computer." He handed it to Grace. "The idea is to replace a button on a shirt, so it will take a little bit of sewing skills." He handed her a small sewing kit like the ones found in hotel rooms.

"I can handle that." She glanced at Caveman. "Since your shirt has the buttons and you'll know better what to look for, you should have the camera on you. I can sew this onto your shirt."

"I'm pretty handy with a needle and thread, if you'd rather I did it," he offered.

"No use taking off your shirt. Let me call Batson and see if we can even get onto the range this afternoon."

Hack looked up the Lonesome Pine Ranch and passed her the contact number.

Grace pulled her cell phone from her purse, entered the number and waited.

Part of Caveman wished no one would answer or, if they did, they wouldn't allow her to book time on the gun range.

"This is Grace Saunders. I've had some troubles lately with someone following me."

Caveman snorted softly. Grace had conveniently left off the fact that someone was not only following her, but trying to kill her.

"Thank you. Yes, I'm okay," Grace said. "The sheriff suggested I call and see if I could get some time on the range to practice with my pistol. The sooner the better. I was hoping to get out there this afternoon. It will be two of us. Me and my... boyfriend." She paused, nodding at whatever the person on the other end of the call was telling her. "That would be great. Four o'clock works perfectly. Yes, we'll bring our own guns. I'll see you at four. Thank you." She clicked the end call button and looked across at Caveman. "We're on for four o'clock. I might have to dig my pistol out from under the rubble of my bedroom."

"I have one you could use," Kevin offered.

"If I can't find mine, I'll take you up on the offer," Grace said. "In the meantime, I'd like to get something going on the cleanup effort at my house. I don't want to wait until it rains and ruins even more of my belongings."

For the next few hours, Grace was on the phone with an insurance adjuster and a handyman.

Caveman took her out to her house to meet with the adjuster. Once the man left with a page full of notes, Caveman started sorting through broken boards and crumbled drywall to get to Grace's nightstand where she kept her pistol. He helped her locate the boxes of bullets she'd need at the range.

They cleared enough debris to allow her to get into her drawers and closets to pack several suitcases. Without a way to lock her home, she couldn't stay in the house until the wall was back up.

Grace called Mark Rutherford, the handyman Mrs. Penders had recommended. He showed up, surveyed the damage and gave her an estimate on how much it would cost to fix it. He'd only take a week to clear the debris and rebuild the wall. He'd need the better part of the next week to do the finishing work on the inside and outside.

Throughout the day, he watched Grace handle the disaster of her house with calm and patience, talking to the handyman and the adjuster with a smile and a handshake. The sheriff came out to survey the damage in the daylight and take pictures of the house and the truck. When she told him she'd be going out to Wayne Batson's range for target practice, he nodded.

"It's a good idea to be proficient and have confidence in the handling of your own weapon."

She didn't tell him why she'd chosen Batson's range or that there might be a meeting of the Free America group there the next night.

Caveman was tempted, but he figured she didn't want the sheriff to try to talk her out of it.

His gut clenched all day. He was torn between calling the whole thing off and going through with the plan. If they could get in and out without being shot and killed, they could bring back enough information for the task force team to enter the secure ranch compound. The team could find out what the rebel group was planning and maybe determine who might have killed Mr. Khalig.

After the sheriff left, Caveman brought a mug of hot cocoa out to the porch for Grace and insisted she sit for a few minutes. She chose the porch swing and sat far enough over for Caveman to join her. "How did you make hot cocoa?"

Caveman grinned. "I found a camp stove in a closet."

For a few minutes, they shared the silence, sipping cocoa and staring at the caved-in portion of her home.

"Why would a rebel group like Free America want to kill a pipeline inspector? They don't work for the government. They contract out to the big oil companies." Grace sighed. "I hope we're not wasting our time going out to the Lonesome Pine Ranch, chasing a wild goose."

"If you're concerned, why don't you stay in town and let me

go alone? The activities of the Free America group are a concern of Task Force Safe Haven. Kevin's responsibility as an agent with the Department of Homeland Security is to keep our homeland safe. If this group is planning to take a government facility that would be considered an act of terror. We have to investigate. This is the first real information we've received on when and where they will meet. We have to check it out. But you don't."

"If they have anything to do with Mr. Khalig's death and the subsequent threats to my life, I sure as hell have to go. I refuse to continue playing the victim. It's time I fought back."

Caveman took her empty cup and set it on the end table beside the swing and put his next to it. Then he took Grace's hands in his. "I want you to promise you won't do anything that will make Batson or his employees think we're spying on him. If he is part of this rebel group, he might want to keep it under wraps. In which case, he might go to all lengths to keep that secret."

"I promise I will do my best not to draw unnecessary attention. We'll get in there, and get out with the data your team needs to do what they have to do to protect our nation."

"Then we'd better get going. Your appointment is for four o'clock." He stood, pulled her to her feet and into his arms.

She rested her hands on his chest. "Are you going to kiss me?"

He chuckled. "I'm thinking about it."

Her hands slipped up around his neck. "Stop thinking, and start kissing."

"Do you still think your curse will be the death of me?"

"Not if we don't fall in love."

If her curse was real, he was doomed. In the short amount of time he'd been with Grace, she'd found her way into his mind, body and soul. He knew there would be no going back. Convincing her that she wouldn't kill him with a crazy curse would be the first challenge. Figuring out where they'd go from Grizzly Pass would be the second.

She laced her fingers at the back of his head and pulled his head down to hers. "Now, are you going to kiss me?"

"Damn right, I am." His lips crashed down on hers, his tongue pushing past her teeth to caress hers. This was what he'd wanted all day.

Grace didn't hold back. Her tongue twisted and thrust, her body pressing tightly to his.

When he had to breathe again, Caveman rested his cheek against her temple. "I worry about you," he whispered.

"You don't have to. I can make my own decisions and live with the consequences of my actions."

His chest tightened as if someone was squeezing him really hard. "If you're fortunate enough to live."

GRACE CLENCHED HER hands in her lap, as she stared at the road ahead, with every intention of staying alive. As far as she was concerned, she was going to get in some target practice with her handgun. Then she'd leave. If they just happened to find out more about a certain antigovernment organization, so be it. She'd keep those little gems of information to herself until she was off the Lonesome Pine Ranch and back where it was safe.

She had no problem letting the trained soldiers handle the major spying mission, although she would love to be a fly on the wall and listen in on the Free America meeting. After all, it was her country, too. She didn't appreciate terrorists trying to take over the land of the free and the home of the brave.

But she wasn't trained in combat tactics and would slow them down. She'd help them more by gathering information that would help them infiltrate after dark.

She'd sewn the webcam button onto Caveman's shirt and watched as he tucked the radio communication device in his ear. She put one in hers as well, but she wasn't as confident using it. She turned her head away from Caveman. "Can you hear me?"

"Loud and clear," he said.

"We can hear you, too," Hack said from his desk in the operations center.

Grace grinned. "I feel like I fell into a spy movie."

"Yeah, well, this isn't make-believe. Stick to the script and keep a low profile."

"Got it." Grace's heartbeat sped as Caveman pulled up to the gate of the Lonesome Pine Ranch and punched the button on the control panel.

"Grace Saunders and Max Decker here for range practice," he said into the speaker.

"Welcome. Please drive through." The giant wrought-iron gate swung open.

Caveman pulled through the gate.

Grace glanced over her shoulder as the big gate closed. Her breath caught in her throat. For a moment, she felt like an animal caught in a trap. Forcing a calm she didn't feel, she smiled over at Caveman. "Ready for some target practice?"

"You bet." He laid his hand over the console.

Grace placed hers in his for a brief squeeze before he returned his grip to the steering wheel.

Signs for the gun range directed them to turn before they reached the big house perched on top of a hill. The road ended in a small parking area. Wayne Batson waited for them, a holster buckled around his hips. In his cowboy boots, jeans and leather vest, he looked like a man straight out of the Old West.

A shiver rippled across Grace's skin. What if this man was the one who'd been shooting at her? Would he take the opportunity now to kill her? Maybe she'd been a little too naive to think a killer wouldn't shoot her in broad daylight even when the sheriff knew where she was going.

Instead of an old-fashioned revolver in the holster, Wayne had a sleek, dark-gray pistol, probably a 9-millimeter by the size and shape.

Grace pasted a smile on her face and climbed out of the truck.

"Good afternoon, Mr. Batson. Thank you for letting me come out for some target practice on such short notice."

"My pleasure," he said. "I hear you're having a little trouble and want to make sure you can defend yourself."

She nodded. "I've had this gun since I graduated from college, but I don't get nearly enough practice with it."

"No use having one if you don't know how to use it properly," Batson said.

"I told her the same." Caveman stepped up to Batson and held out his hand. "Max Decker. You must be Wayne Batson, the owner of Lonesome Pine Ranch?"

Batson nodded and shook his hand. "It's been in the family for over a century. I hope to keep it in the family for another century." He glanced from Caveman to Grace. "Show me what you have in the way of firepower."

Grace pulled out the case with her .40-caliber H&K pistol. It was small, light and fit her hand perfectly.

Caveman brought out a 9-millimeter Glock.

Batson assigned them lanes on the range and handed them paper targets. Once the targets were stapled in place, they stood back at the firing position.

Batson joined Grace in her lane. "How often do you fire this weapon?"

"At least once a year."

"That's not nearly enough to feel comfortable holding and aiming." He demonstrated the proper technique for holding a pistol and then had her show him the same.

"How's it been here at the Lonesome Pine since you turned it into a big game hunting ranch?" Grace asked.

"Business is good," he answered, his tone clipped.

Grace lined up her sites with the target. "Lot of people from out of state?" She squeezed the trigger, remembering not to anticipate the sound and slight movement of the gun. The pungent scent of gunpowder reminded her of her father and the first time he'd taken her out to shoot. As his only daughter, he wanted her to be safe and know how to defend herself should she have to. Her heart squeezed hard in her chest. Her father would be horrified to know she'd been the target of a killer. He'd be on the first plane back to Wyoming from their retirement home in Florida.

Grace refused to call them and tell them she was in trouble. They'd fly back in an instant and place themselves in the line of fire. She'd be damned if she let some low-life killer touch her family. Now if only she could stay alive so they didn't come back to a funeral.

She studied Wayne Batson out of the corner of her eye.

He was tall, muscular and lean. The man would have been incredibly handsome, but for the slight sneer on his lip that pushed him past handsome to annoyingly arrogant.

She fired several rounds, adjusting her aim, working for a tighter grouping.

Batson holstered his gun and turned toward Caveman. "Do you have any questions?"

Caveman gave him a friendly smile. "I have one. Do you have many locals come out to fire on your range, or is it mainly the out-of-towners?"

Grace ejected her magazine and made slow work of loading bullets, wanting to hear every word of the conversation between Batson and Caveman.

"I get locals who need a place to practice with real targets at specific distances. They come to improve their skills for hunting season, just like my out-of-towners. The only difference is that the locals can come more often."

"How do you keep the game contained inside the perimeter?" Caveman asked, while reloading his magazine.

"You might have noticed on your drive in, we have high fences surrounding all ten thousand acres. It's one of the largest fully contained game ranches in the state. We offer guided hunts of all kinds."

"A client could select the preferred prey?"

Batson nodded. "My clients can be very specific."

"You've stocked the ranch with animals, and they can choose what they want to hunt?" Caveman asked.

"Yes."

Caveman smacked the magazine into the grip of his pistol and stared across at Batson. "The fences keep all of them in?"

"Only the best materials were used," Batson said. "We have high-tech monitoring to detect breeches so that we can get to the exact location and fix them quickly."

"That had to cost," Grace said.

"My clients pay."

"Then why bother with a range like this if your big game hunts are paying the bills?"

"I've learned diversification is important. When all we had were cattle and horses, we had some hard times. I almost lost the ranch to the government for back taxes. I promised myself I'd never get in that situation again. I will not let the government take my family home, like they're trying to take the Vanderses'."

"You sound pretty adamant," Grace said.

Batson's jaw tightened. "I am."

Grace fit her magazine in the grip of her handgun and slammed it home. She stared down the barrel at the target and squeezed the trigger. Five rounds fired made five little holes on the silhouette target where the heart would be on a man. All her father's lessons came back with a little practice.

"Nice," Caveman commented. He brought his weapon up, aiming it downrange. "One other question for you, Mr. Batson."

"Shoot."

Caveman fired five rounds, hitting the silhouette target in the head, the holes the bullets made in such a tight grouping they appeared to be one big hole. He turned toward Batson with a friendly smile. "What do you prefer, handgun or rifle?"

Grace had been ejecting her magazine from her pistol. When she heard Caveman's unexpected question, she fumbled the magazine and it fell to the dirt.

Batson's eyes narrowed. For a moment, Grace didn't think the game ranch owner would answer the question.

"It depends on several things—how close I plan to get to the target, how accurate I want to be and how intelligent my quarry is." He touched a hand to his ear where he had a very small Bluetooth earpiece. "What is it, Laura?" He listened for a moment and then spoke. "Fine, let them in." His gaze returned to Grace. "Pardon me. It seems the sheriff wants to see me."

"The timing couldn't be better," Caveman said. "It's starting to get dark and we need to head back to town."

"Good." Batson nodded. "I don't usually leave guests on the range without supervision."

"Then we'll head out." Grace left the magazine out of her pistol, pulled back the bolt and inspected the chamber to make sure it was empty. Then she laid the weapon in its case. "Thank you for allowing us to come out on such short notice."

They shook hands with Batson and stowed the gun cases in the backseat of Caveman's truck.

The sheriff's vehicle was pulling up as they drove away. Grace slowed and started to lower her window.

"Just wave and keep driving," Caveman advised.

"Won't the sheriff think that strange?"

"I'm not concerned about what the sheriff thinks." Caveman waved her forward. "I want to use the time he keeps Batson occupied to leave slowly and capture as much information as I can about the security system used around the perimeter."

Grace slowed, nodded and pulled past the sheriff as she headed down the road toward the gate.

Caveman studied the fences and the gate, making comments aloud about the cameras located at the top of the gate pillar, aimed at the road.

Once they were through the gate, Grace crept along the highway, moving slowly enough Caveman could study the fencing. "I didn't notice it before, but stop for a minute."

Grace glanced in the rearview mirror. Nobody was behind

her so she pulled to the side of the road and stopped. "Why are we stopping?"

"I want to test a theory." He opened his door, reached toward the ground and came up with a rock the size of a golf ball. Then he tossed it toward the fence wire. When the rock hit the fence, a shower of sparks shot out.

Grace gasped. "It's electric."

"Pretty expensive fencing for a game ranch."

"That'll keep the game in," Grace said.

Caveman's eyes narrowed to slits. "And uninvited guests out."

Wayne Batson had more than a game ranch on his huge spread: he had a locked-down compound capable of keeping out nosy people. As Grace drove back to town, a chill spread over her body. Her friendly community of Grizzly Pass had a darker side she never knew existed.

Chapter Thirteen

It was late by the time Caveman finished debriefing the team. He learned Kevin had sent the sheriff out to the Lonesome Pine Ranch to run interference for them so that they could leave unimpeded.

"While you two were on the inside, we had a drone flying over," Kevin said. "Between the information you two collected and the footage from the drone, we'll have our hands full tonight, determining the best way we can get in before the meeting tomorrow."

"Could we grab a bite to eat before we start?" Caveman asked.

"We can do better than that," Kevin said. He held out a key. "I got you two a suite at Mama Jo's Bed-and-Breakfast a couple blocks away. You can eat, catch some sleep and come back in the morning to see what we found."

"You don't need us?" Grace asked.

"With four of us looking at the monitors, it will be crowded enough. And you two have already done enough. Get some food and rest. Tomorrow will be another day. We'll brief you on the plan then."

Hack chuckled. "We hope to *have* one by then. I anticipate pulling an all-nighter."

Caveman would have liked to have stayed and looked over the drone images, but he was hungry, and he bet Grace was, too.

They called down to the tavern and ordered carryout. A few minutes later they left the team, collected their food and drove to the quaint Victorian house just off Main Street. They had all of the second floor, which consisted of two bedrooms, a shared bathroom and a sitting room, complete with a television and a small dining table.

"I'm going to hit the shower before I eat," Grace said. "I feel dusty from being out on the range this afternoon."

"Want company?" Caveman asked.

"What do you think?" She smiled, dragged her shirt up over her head and dropped it on the floor. Turning, she walked into the bathroom, half closed the door and then dangled her bra through the opening.

Caveman was already halfway out of his clothes, tripping over his boots as he kicked them off.

The next minute, he was in the shower with Grace, lathering her body, rinsing, kissing and repeating the process until they had the bathroom steaming. They made love under the warm spray and stayed until the water chilled. By the time they'd dried, the night had settled in on Grizzly Pass. Traffic slowed on Main Street and folks went home to their families.

Caveman and Grace ate their dinner and then moved to the king-size bed where they made love again. Nearing midnight, they lay in each other's arms, sated, but not sleepy.

"We should go back to the operations center and see if they've discovered anything new," Grace said.

Caveman sighed and brushed his lips across hers. "I know you're right. But I can't help it. I don't want our time together to end."

"Me, either." She sighed, too, and kissed him hard.

He would have stayed right where he was, with Grace's warm

body pressed against his, but they weren't done for the night. Caveman rolled out of the bed and extended his hand. "Ready?"

She shook her head, laid her hand in his and let him pull her to her feet. "I'll only be a minute." Grace grabbed her clothes and hurried into the bathroom.

"I'll call and let Kevin know we're coming," Caveman said. He made the call to learn Kevin, Hack, Ghost, T-Rex and Hawk-eye were still up and poring over the videos. They'd noted a few items of interest they wanted to show Caveman. "Good," he said. "We'll be there soon."

He dressed quickly, pulled on his boots and waited by the window. From their room, he had a good view of Main Street and the front of Quincy Kemp's meat packing shop. It was dark, like most of the businesses in town at that hour. He wondered what was in the back of Quincy's shop that the man hadn't wanted Caveman to see. Could he have the wolf carcass, preparing it to be stuffed? And, if he did, he would know who killed it. Or was he hiding the AR-15s in one of his freezers behind big slabs of meat?

Dressed in a black turtleneck shirt and black jeans, Grace stepped up beside him and looked through the window. "What are you looking at?"

"Quincy's place. I went there while you were with Mrs. Pend-ers. He didn't want me in the back of his building. He was pretty adamant about it. Which makes me think he has some-thing to hide."

"What are you thinking?" She pulled on her boots and straightened. "Want to go there first?"

"I can send another member of the team to investigate."

"Why? They have enough on their plates. Obviously, Kemp isn't in his shop now. Not with all of the lights out, and no one moving around. We could get in, do a little spying and leave with no one the wiser."

His lips quirked on the corners. "You realize you're talking about breaking and entering."

"We're not stealing anything," Grace argued.

"It's still illegal."

"You're right." She chewed on her bottom lip. "You can't afford to be caught. It might get you in trouble with the military."

He didn't like the calculating look in her eyes. "What are you thinking?"

"That I'm brilliant, and you don't have to commit a crime. You could keep watch outside while I go in and poke around. That way you aren't in on the crime. If I'm caught, I'll be the only one charged."

"Have you heard of aiding and abetting?" Caveman countered.

She shrugged. "You just have to deny everything. I'll tell them I snuck off, leaving you wondering where I'd gone. It will all be on me."

"I'm surprised you would even consider it." He reached for her hand. "I took you for a by-the-books kind of woman."

Her lips thinned into a tight line. "I was, until someone started shooting at me. Desperate times call for...you know."

"Desperate measures." Caveman didn't like Grace's plan at all, but his gut told him Quincy was hiding something in the back of his shop. "Look, you're not going anywhere without me."

She smiled up at him, her brows rising in challenge. "Then I guess you'll be breaking the law with me, because I'm going into Quincy's place to see what he was hiding from you."

He slipped his arm around her waist and kissed her. "You're a stubborn woman, Grace Saunders."

"I have to be in my line of business."

"I'll bet you do." He kissed her again and then turned to scan what he could see of the street and buildings around Quincy's shop. Other than the tavern, the town of Grizzly Pass had more or less rolled up its sidewalks.

Grace headed for the door. "If we're going to do this, we should get moving."

Caveman shrugged into his jacket and followed. "Stay close."

"I told you, I don't like you playing the role of my bullet shield." She pulled on a dark coat and swept her hair up into a ponytail.

"Humor me, will you?" He grabbed her hand and led her out of the bed-and-breakfast, hugging the shadows of the building to the corner where it connected to Main Street. The road was clear of people and vehicles as far as Caveman could tell, but he didn't know who might be watching from any of the buildings.

"Come on." He looped his arm over her shoulder and pulled her close. "We're just lovers on a late-night stroll."

"I like the sound of that," Grace whispered. "It would be even better if we weren't on someone's hot target list."

They crossed the street and walked past Quincy's place, turned down the next street and slipped into the back alley behind the meat packaging store.

Fortunately, the light over the back entrance was burned out, leaving the area completely in shadows.

Caveman slipped a knife from his pocket and pushed the blade in between the door and the jamb. With a few jiggles, he disengaged the lock, opened the door and hurried both of them inside.

Grace lifted her cell phone and shone the built-in flashlight around the room. The very back of the building was the meat packaging area with stainless-steel tables, sinks and refrigerators. The scents of blood, raw meat and disinfectants warred with each other.

Caveman checked the big walk-in freezers first. Finding nothing inside other than slabs of meat and big carcasses, he closed the doors. A quick survey of the rest of the room revealed nothing unusual or suspicious.

Quickly moving on, he led the way to a long corridor with a door on either side. This area separated the meat processing operations from the taxidermy workroom. He tried the handles. One was locked, the other wasn't. He pushed it open, only to find a variety of cleaning supplies: mops, aprons, bottles of disinfectant and various packaging supplies. The room was nothing more than a closet with shelves. Caveman checked the walls and floors for hidden doors.

"Anything?" Grace asked from the hall.

"Nothing." He left the supplies closet, locking it behind him.

Moving to the door across the way, Caveman used his knife to disengage the lock. Inside, he found an office with a desk, file cabinet and shelves. This room wasn't much bigger than the janitor's closet. Neither room was as wide as the shop front or the meat processing rear.

Caveman exited the office for a moment and walked into the taxidermy work area. It was as wide as the meat processing area, but square.

Grace gasped.

"What's wrong?"

She pointed to the hide of what appeared to be a black wolf. Tears welled in her eyes. "Loki." She shook her head, her fists bunching. "The bastard killed Loki."

Caveman pulled her against him and held her for a brief moment. "I'm sorry. But we have to keep moving."

"I know." She wiped a tear from her cheek and pushed away, turning her back to the wolf she'd raised from a pup.

Caveman's heart pinched at her sadness, but they had bigger, more immediate problems. "The office and supply room aren't as deep as the two work rooms. Where's the rest of the space?"

He hurried back into the office and checked the walls. In the back corner, on the far side of a large filing cabinet, was a wall with a pegboard attached. On the board, different tools hung neatly. Everywhere else in the office boxes were stacked on the floor, blocking access to the walls, except in front of the pegboard lined with tools.

Caveman pushed the pegboard and the entire wall moved just a little. He tapped on the wall, creating a hollow sound. Running his fingers along the outer edge of the pegboard he traced one end and then the other. Halfway down the right side, his finger encountered a hidden latch. He released it and the pegboard and wall swung toward him.

"I'll be damned," Grace muttered behind him.

He glanced back at the woman standing in the doorway of the office. "Could you keep an eye on the hallway while I go in to check it out?"

Grace nodded. "Okay, but don't be too long." She shot a nervous glance over her shoulder. "I have a bad feeling about this."

"I'll hurry." He ducked into the room, shining his cell phone flashlight at the far walls, looking for windows to the outside. When he didn't locate any, he flipped the light switch on the wall and studied the contents of the room, his stomach clenching into a vicious knot.

Racks filled with guns stood in short, neat rows. Shelves lined the walls loaded with boxes of ammunition.

"I think I found at least half of the AR-15s here in this room."

"Uh, Max..." Grace's voice sounded strained behind him, closer than if she'd been in the hallway. "We have a problem."

Caveman turned to face her.

She stood with her head tilted backward, a darkly clothed arm wrapped around her neck, her eyes wide and frightened.

In the split second it took Caveman to realize what had happened, he was already too late.

Two probes hit him in the chest and a charge of electricity ripped through his body. He clenched his teeth to keep from crying out. Then he fell, his muscles refusing to hold up his frame.

"Caveman!" Grace screamed.

Unable to control his fall, he hit his head against the corner of a low cabinet and blackness engulfed him in a shroud of darkness and pain.

GRACE FOUGHT AGAINST the hands holding her, desperate to get to Caveman.

The man with the Taser moved forward, his head and face

concealed in a ski mask, his hands in leather gloves. He yanked Caveman's wrists together behind his back and slipped a zip tie around them, cinching it tightly. Then he rolled Caveman onto his side, pulled the probes out of his chest and nodded. "He's down."

A jagged cut on Caveman's temple oozed blood onto the floor.

Grace wanted to go to him, but the man holding her was so much stronger than she was, and his arm around her throat squeezed just hard enough to limit her air intake. Gray fog crept in on the corners of her vision. *No.* She couldn't pass out. She had to find a way to extricate herself and Caveman from this dangerous situation.

"What do we do with them?" one of the men asked.

"Boss wants them." Even with the mask, the man was easy to recognize just by his low, gravelly voice.

"Quincy," Grace said. "Don't do this. You won't get away with it."

"Shut up." Quincy backhanded her, his knuckles slamming into her cheekbone.

Grace's head whipped back with the blow and pain knifed through her. She fought the dizzying spinning in her head that threatened to take her down. "What are you going to do with us?"

"That's not for me to decide," he said.

"So you do the dirty work of capturing us, committing a crime to do it, and your boss sits back and lets you take the rap?"

He backhanded her again, this time hitting her in the mouth, splitting her lip. "You should have stayed out of this. Now, you'll pay the price for meddling."

Her jaw ached and the coppery taste of blood invaded her mouth. Anger roiled inside, pushing aside the wobbly feeling of an oncoming faint.

Caveman lay on the floor, his body still, and Grace could do nothing. The man holding her was a lot bigger and stronger. And there were two of them to one of her. Outnumbered and over-powered, she didn't have a choice. But she had to do something.

"You know you won't get away with this. There's probably a sheriff's deputy driving by as we speak."

Quincy's lip curled back in a snarl. "No one knows you're back here, and no one can see inside this part of the building. Even if the police came in, I'd be legally in the right. You two trespassed on private property. Last I checked, breaking and entering was illegal. I could shoot you and claim self-defense. Now, enough talk." He shoved a rag in her mouth, then threw a pillowcase over her head and down her arms. "Take her out to the van."

The big man holding her scooped her off her feet, slung her over his shoulder where she landed hard on her belly, the breath knocked out of her lungs. She couldn't see anything through the fabric of the pillowcase, but she could tell the man was carrying her back the way they'd entered the shop. When they stepped out of the building, cool night air wrapped around her legs. The sound of a metal door sliding sideways gave her re-newed determination to break free. She kicked and struggled, bucking in the man's grip.

Finally, she was flung away from him, landing on what she was sure was the floorboard of a commercial van. She hit the surface hard, her head bouncing off the metal.

Then something was stuck up against her arm and a jolt of electricity sliced through her. Her body went limp and her strug-gles ceased. But she could still tell a little of what was going on. Someone tied her wrists behind her back with a zip tie. Another body was dumped onto the floor beside her.

It had to be Caveman.

With her wrists bound and a pillowcase wrapped loosely around her head, her body in a catatonic state, she could do lit-tle to free herself or her head so that she could see. She vowed that as soon as she regained control of her muscles, she'd work her way out of the case and zip tie.

Meanwhile, she was conscious. She listened, trying to gauge which direction they were headed and how far they were going. She could tell when they left the back alley and emerged on paved highway. She guessed they were headed south on Main Street. If only she could get up, throw open the door and scream. Alas, she could barely wiggle her toes by the time she was certain they'd driven out of the little town.

Would they take them out to a remote location, shoot them and leave their bodies to rot?

Grace's chest tightened. She couldn't let that happen. All of this was her fault. If she hadn't witnessed the killer shooting at Mr. Khalig, none of this would be happening to her and Caveman.

Caveman.

He was the innocent bystander in all of this. And because she'd allowed him to get past the walls she'd erected around her heart, he would die.

She squeezed her fist, anger fueling her. When her toes tingled, she wiggled them. Slowly, the feeling came back to her legs and arms. She was able to roll onto her side, but she couldn't lift her arms to pull off the pillowcase. Instead, she scooted along the floor, trying to maneuver her way out of the fabric covering her head.

They had been traveling ten minutes when she finally made it out of the pillowcase.

Lifting her head, she looked around the interior of an empty utility van with metal sides and floors. The two men who'd captured them sat in the front seat, staring out the window as they slowed for a stop.

Grace tried to see what they were seeing. It appeared to be a gate of some sort.

The van lurched forward and the tires crunched on what sounded like gravel.

With little light to see by, Grace searched the interior of the van for something sharp to break the zip tie holding her wrists tightly together behind her. No sharp edges stuck out, no tools lay on the metal floor.

And Caveman lay as still as death.

She inched her way over to him and laid her face close to his. For a long moment she held her breath, praying he was still alive. Then she felt the warmth of his breath against her cheek. Her heart swelled with joy. He was still alive.

Somehow, she had to get them both out of the van and away from their captors.

The gravel road ended, but the van continued to move forward on a much bumpier, hard-packed road.

Several times, Grace tried to sit up, only to be flung across the van floor. She was better off lying on her side, praying they'd stop before she was bounced to death.

Caveman groaned softly and his legs moved. "Grace?" he whispered.

"I'm here," she replied softly, so as not to draw attention from the men in the front seats.

"Where are we?"

"We're in the back of a van and have been on the road for over twenty minutes as far as I can guess. Other than that, I'm not sure where we are. Based on the road conditions, I'd bet we're way out in the boondocks."

"Have they said what they're going to do with us?"

"No." She glanced at the back of the driver's head. "Quincy said something about it wasn't up to them. The boss would decide."

"So he's not in charge."

The van came to a jerky stop.

Grace waited for them to start up again, but they didn't. The engine switched off and the two men climbed out. A moment later, the side door slid open and moonlight shone into the interior.

Grace blinked up at the men.

Quincy had taken off his ski mask, but the other man hadn't.

They grabbed Grace by her upper arms and dragged her out of the van and onto her feet.

"Hurt her, and I'll kill you," Caveman said, his voice little more than a feral growl.

Quincy snorted. "That would be really hard to do when you're all tied up, now wouldn't it?"

They grabbed Caveman by the arms and slid him out of the van, dumping him on the ground at their feet.

He rolled to his side, bunched his legs and pushed to his feet. "What now?"

"Now, the fun begins," another voice said from behind Quincy and his accomplice. A big man wearing a combat helmet, camouflage clothing and carrying a military-grade rifle stepped between their two captors. His face was blackened with paint and he sported a pair of what appeared to be night-vision goggles pushed up onto his helmet.

"What do you mean, 'now the fun begins'?"

"I told you. I provide all kinds of prey for my clients—elk, lion, moose, bear and…human."

Grace gasped, a heavy, sick feeling filling her belly. "You can't be serious."

"Oh, I'm serious, all right."

Grace squinted, trying to see past the paint. "Wayne?"

The man sneered. "Surprised?"

"Actually, I am." She shook her head. "Why would you risk losing everything you have by killing people? You won't get away with it for long?"

"I've been getting away with it for the past five years. I'll continue to get away with it as long as no one finds the bodies. *Your* bodies."

"You're insane."

"No, I'm tired of the government stealing what's mine. I'm tired of working my butt off for the pittance you make off cattle, only for the government to steal every cent I make by charging an insane amount of taxes."

"You've been selling human hunts for the past five years?" Grace shook her head. "How did no one know this?"

"The people who work for me know not to say anything. And the people we hunt don't live long enough to tell."

"Was Mr. Khalig one of your *hunts*?" Grace's stomach churned so hard she fought to keep from losing her dinner.

Wayne snorted. "Hell no. He was a paid gig. And an easy target."

"Paid gig?" What was wrong with the man? He acted like killing a man was no worse than being paid to perform on stage.

"*Highly* paid gig." Wayne shifted his rifle to his other hand. "But that's not why we're here tonight."

"Why are we here?" Caveman asked, his gaze direct, the shadows cast by the bright moon making him appear dangerous.

"You two are going to be a little training opportunity for my men. A little night ops search-and-destroy. You get a chance to run. They get to practice and test their night hunting skills with live animals."

"That's like shooting lions in a zoo. Where's the sport in that?"

"Oh, there will be sport. We're going to let you loose, give you a little bit of a head start, and then we're coming after you."

"Unarmed?" Caveman goaded. "How is that a training exercise?"

"I can't turn over a loaded weapon to a trained soldier. How would we explain so many people with gunshot wounds?" Wayne nodded to Quincy. "Release them."

Quincy frowned. "Now?"

"Now." Wayne fixed his stare on Caveman. "If you make a move toward me or my men, I'll put a bullet in Ms. Saunders." He nodded. "Take her and leave. You'll only have five minutes to get as far as you can, before we come after you." He glanced down at his watch.

"Three minutes on foot won't get us far," Caveman pointed out.

"You're lucky I'm giving you that." He looked again at his watch. "Four minutes thirty-five seconds."

"Aren't you going to cut the zip ties?" Grace's pulse hammered so loudly in her ears she could barely hear herself think.

"Not my problem." Wayne Batson raised his brows. "Four minutes fifteen seconds."

"Grace, come on." Caveman pushed her with his elbow and herded her away from Batson.

She hurried with Caveman toward the tree line. Her last glimpse of the three hunters was the image of Quincy and the other man dressed in the combat helmet, multi-pocketed vests and camouflage clothing. They were in the process of loading ammunition magazines into their vests.

And she thought getting away from the men would be hard enough. *Staying* away from Wayne Batson and his thugs, while their hands were tied behind their backs, would be a lot more of a challenge than she could imagine.

Chapter Fourteen

They jogged into the tree line. Caveman's leg hurt like hell, but he refused to slow them down. "We have to get as far away from them as possible and find a rock hill or cliff to put between us and them. Are you able to run for long?"

"I can hold my own," Grace said. "I'm used to hiking in the hills. When I'm not working, I train to run half marathons."

Caveman snorted. "I'll have a hard time keeping up with you. Why don't you lead the way?"

"Do you think we're on Batson's ranch?" she asked, jogging alongside Caveman while they were on a fairly wide path between trees.

"That's my bet. Not only do those fences keep people out, they keep his pets in."

"Any chance we can get out of these zip ties?" she asked.

"As soon as we reach that outcropping of rocks. We have to put something solid and impenetrable between us and them for cover as well as concealment against their night-vision goggles." He glanced across at her face in the moonlight. "Can you run faster?"

"I'm game," she said, though her breathing had become more labored.

Caveman increased his speed, glancing back often enough to make certain Grace kept up. He was aiming for the base of the mountain he'd glimpsed through gaps in the trees. It appeared to be right in front of them, but looks could be deceiving, especially at night.

The full moon helped them find their way, but it also made it all too easy for Batson and his gang to see them. The sooner they made it into the hills, the better.

He figured the five-minute head start had long since expired and still they hadn't reached the relative safety of the mountain.

A crash behind him brought Caveman to a halt.

Grace lay on the ground, struggling to get to her feet. "Don't wait on me. I'll catch up," she insisted.

"Like hell you will." He squatted next to her. "Grab a sturdy tree branch or a jagged rock."

She did, rolled over to hand it to him and then worked herself to a sitting position. "What are you going to do with it?"

"I'm going to try and use it as a saw." He nodded. "But we have to keep moving. Lean on me to get up."

She leaned her shoulder against him and pushed herself to stand.

"Ready?" he said.

"Go." Grace followed him, keeping closer this time.

While he ran, Caveman rubbed the small tree branch against the plastic of the zip tie. It wasn't much, but he hoped with enough friction, it would eventually cut through.

They emerged in a small opening in the forest, finding themselves at the base of a bluff.

Caveman glanced each direction, then turned north toward a large outcropping of boulders. If they could get behind them, they could stop long enough to break the zip ties. But they couldn't stay long. They had to go deep into the mountains and stay alive long enough for Kevin and the team to figure out they were in trouble.

A sinking feeling settled low in his belly. Though he'd given Kevin a heads-up that they'd be over to review drone footage, he hadn't given him a definitive time. All they could hope for was that Kevin would get worried when they didn't show up within thirty minutes of the call. Still, the team wouldn't know where they'd gone, or where to start looking.

Their best bet was to avoid the hunters long enough to make it back to one of the perimeter fences. Then they'd have to figure out how to get through it and fast enough they could make it to a road and catch a ride to town. Timing would be crucial since Batson had the fence wired to tell him exactly where the breech occurred.

Caveman kept his thoughts to himself. Grace had enough to worry about just staying a step ahead of Batson and his gang.

In order for them to reach the giant boulders for cover, they would have to cross a wide-open expanse, flooded by bright moonlight.

"I don't know how close they are. When we start out across the open area, run as fast as you can and zigzag to make it harder for someone to sight in on you." He gripped Grace's arms. "Are you okay?"

She nodded, breathing hard. "I'll be fine. Let's go." With a deep breath, she took off running across the rocky terrain, dodging back and forth, leaping over brush and smaller boulders.

Caveman was right behind her, hoping the hunters hadn't yet caught up to them.

A shot rang out, kicking up the dirt near Caveman's feet. He ran faster, changing directions erratically, hoping the gunmen couldn't get a bead on him and take him out.

Grace had just made it to the boulder when another shot rang out. She stumbled and fell against the huge rock, righted herself and slipped out of sight.

Caveman dodged once more to the right, then sprinted the remaining ten steps and dove behind the boulder.

Grace was on her knees, breathing hard, but rubbing the zip tie against a jagged stone jutting out of the hillside.

"We don't have time to break these. We have to keep moving," Caveman warned.

The zip tie snapped. "I'm ready." She grabbed a sharp rock and pointed to a flat one. "Put your hands here." She quickly positioned him, then put all of her weight behind the sharp rock and cut through his zip tie.

Caveman took her hand and ran for a ravine thirty feet from where they were standing. Together, they climbed the side of the hill, working their way over the rocks upward to a ridge. If they could drop over the other side, they'd have a chance of staying out of range of the rifles. He wasn't sure how much longer Grace would last. His sore leg ached and he worried it slowed him down too much. They didn't have weapons and they couldn't fight back. He had to keep them moving.

Grace slipped beside him and slid several feet down the hillside and stopped abruptly when her foot hit a tree root. "Damn." She doubled over, clutching at her leg. She pushed to her feet, but fell back as soon as she put weight on her foot.

Caveman slid down next to her, his gaze scanning the bottom of the ravine. "What's wrong?"

"I think I've sprained my ankle." She looked up at him. "Don't stop. You have to keep going. Get help."

He pressed his lips together. "Grace, I'm not leaving without you." He bent, draped her arm over his shoulder and lifted her. "Come on. We're not stopping here."

Together, they limped up the side of the steep hill, slipping and sliding on the loose gravel. When they reached the top of the ridge, Caveman studied the other side. There was a steep drop-off close to where they stood and a trail leading down the other side. If they were careful, they might make it down to the bottom before the others caught up to them. From there, he could see the fence in the distance. And, if he wasn't mistaken, the cutaway between a stand of trees had to be the highway. "See that?"

"The fence," Grace said through gritted teeth. "Think we can make it?"

"I don't think it, I know it." With his arm around her waist, he hurried down the trail toward the bottom of the hill, knowing this trail was the path of least resistance and it would make it far too easy for the hunters to spot them from a distance and catch up to them all too quickly. They only had to get close enough to sight in on them.

A good sniper would be able to pick them off at two-hundred meters. A great sniper would be able to take them out at four-hundred. If they could get down to the trees before the hunters topped the ridge, they might have a little more of a chance to make it to the fence. At that point, they'd have to figure out how to keep from getting electrocuted.

HOPPING ON ONE foot all the way down the side of a hill wasn't getting them where they needed to be fast enough. And every time she bumped her right foot, pain shot through her, bringing her close to tears. She refused to cry. Not when they needed every bit of their wits about them to escape the insanity that was Wayne Batson. "Leave me," she begged. "I don't want you to die because of me."

"Not up for discussion," he said, grunting as he took the brunt of her weight and hurried her along. "Save your breath and mine."

She knew any further argument would be ignored and took his advice to save him further aggravation. They rounded several hip-high boulders as they neared the bottom of the hill. A shot rang out and pinged off one of the boulders.

A sharp stinging sensation bit Grace's shoulder. "Ow!"

"Get down!" Caveman pulled her down behind the boulder.

He looked ahead to the next big rock. "Can you crawl to the next one?"

"Probably faster than I could walk it by myself."

"Then go, while I distract them."

"What do you mean 'distract them'?" she asked, hesitant to leave him, even for a moment.

He shed his jacket and hung it on a stick. "Ready? Go!" He ran the stick up over the top of the rock.

Grace crawled as fast as she could over rocks, gravel and brush, bruising her knees, but not caring. When she made it to the next rock, she rolled behind it and called out, "Made it!" She sneaked a peek around the edge in time to see Caveman make his dash to join her.

He hunkered low and ran, diving behind the rock as two more shots echoed off the canyon walls. "Are you all right?" he asked, his attention on the hill above them.

"A little worse for the wear, but alive." She pressed a hand to the stinging spot on her shoulder and winced. When she brought her hand back in front of her, she grimaced. It was covered in dark warm liquid she suspected was her blood. She hid her hand from Caveman. If she was badly wounded, she wouldn't have been able to move her arm. Now wasn't the time to faint at the sight of blood.

"Right now, they have the advantage with their night-vision goggles. They can see us, but we can't see them."

She snorted. "They have all the advantages. They have the guns. We're unarmed."

He glanced behind them. "We could try for the tree line, but it's a long way."

"And I move too slowly." She shook her head. "Leave me here. Go for help. It's the only way."

"I'm not leaving you."

"Then what do you suggest?"

He glanced around the moonlit area. "The fence is two football fields away. Even if we could make it there, we don't have a way to cut through."

"Then that's out," she said.

"We've run out of places to hide. This is the last large boulder between us and them."

"True."

"We only have one choice." He drew in a deep breath and let it out. "We wait until they come to us."

Grace nodded, knowing the odds were stacked against them, but unwilling to admit defeat. She wouldn't go down without a helluva fight. "Then we have to be prepared."

"You're willing to stick it out?"

She chuckled. Her ankle hurt like hell, she was bleeding and she didn't know if she'd live to see another sunrise. "Seems like our only recourse. So, Army Special Forces dude, what can we do to get ready to rumble?"

"Stay here."

She laughed out loud. "Like I could get up and dance a jig?"

"You know what I mean. Don't poke your head out. Stay behind the rock so that I don't have to worry about what's happening while I'm not here."

She frowned. "Not here? Where are you going?" Grace reached out and touched his arm. "You can't leave the safety of the boulder. They'll shoot you."

He took her hand in his and looked down into her eyes. "I'm not dying today. I'm going to debunk your curse."

"Sweetheart, I hope and pray you do." She wrapped her other arm around his neck and pulled him close. "I'd really like to spend a little more time with you. Two days is not nearly enough."

"I'm thinking a life time won't be enough." He kissed her hard, his tongue sweeping across hers. Then he pulled away. "Now, I have to see what I can come up with. I'll be back."

"I'm counting on it," Grace whispered.

The night stood still. Not even the crickets or coyotes sang in the dark.

Caveman got up on his haunches, breathed in and out, then dove toward a stand of trees nearby.

The crack of gunfire rang out.

Grace flinched and strained her eyes, searching for movement in the shadows. She could hear the crunch of leaves and the snapping of sticks. Caveman was moving.

Another shot pierced the silence. This one seemed closer, though it was hard to tell when the sound bounced off the hillsides.

With her breath lodged in her throat, Grace waited for Caveman's return. She gathered stones, rocks and anything she could use as a weapon, no matter how puny they seemed compared to a high-powered rifle. She even scraped up a pile of sand next to her.

Then Caveman came running toward her. Just as he was about to make it behind the boulder, gunfire sounded so close, Grace yelped.

Caveman fell behind the boulder, his arms loaded with sticks and what looked like half a tree. He lay still for a moment, his breathing ragged.

"Are you okay?" Grace crawled toward him, pushing aside the sticks and brush.

"I'm fine, just winded." He drew himself up to a sitting position. "They're getting closer." He handed her several long sticks. "They aren't much, but you can use them like spears. The hunters have to come around the boulder to get to us. That's when we surprise them with these."

"What if they swing wide?"

"Hey, I'm trying to be positive. Help me out." He kissed her cheek. "Seriously, we could do with the power of positive thinking. It's just about all we have left."

"Okay, I'm positive they can swing wide and stay out of

spear range, but I'm willing to try anything. I'm not ready to leave this world."

"Good, because we're going to play dead," Caveman said.

"What?"

"You heard me. We're going to play dead. It's risky, but we don't have any other way to lure them in." He grabbed some of the bigger rocks and stones, placing them in circle around them where the boulder would not provide protection. "We'll lie as flat as we can against the ground, thus we won't present much of a target. They will have to come closer to finish us off. That's when we hit them. Got it?"

"Got it."

"Now, before they get any closer, we need to assume the dead cockroach position with our spears at our side." He waited while she lay on her back, her hand on her the spear.

Grace's pulse thumped hard in her veins, her breath came in shaky gasps. In her mind, she told herself she was not ready to die. She wanted to live. To kiss Caveman and make love to him again in the comfort of a bed.

"Shh." Caveman pressed a finger to his lips and laid down beside her. "They're coming."

Grace lay as still as death, her breath caught in her throat, trying not to make even the sound of her breathing.

As she remained there counting what could possibly be the last beats of her heart, she heard another sound. A *thump, thump, thumping* sound that started out soft, but grew louder with each passing minute.

"What the hell?" Caveman started to sit up. The crack of a gunshot sounded so close, it could have been right beside them.

Caveman dropped back down on his back and groaned loudly.

"Are you okay?" Grace whispered.

"I'm fine. That was for effect."

The thumping grew louder. "What's that sound?"

"I hope it's what I think it is."

"What?"

"The cavalry arriving to save the day."

Another shot rang out, and another, each getting closer. One kicked up rocks near Grace's hand. Another pinged against the boulder, ricocheted off the surface and hit the ground so near to her head she swore she could feel the whoosh of air.

Grace finally recognized the thumping sound as that of helicopter rotors churning the air. A bright light pierced the night, shining down to the ground.

"Stay down," Caveman said. "That light will make their night-vision goggles useless. I'm going after them."

"But you're unarmed," she cried out. She rolled onto her stomach and watched as Caveman disappeared into the darkness surround the ray of light.

A burst of gunfire ripped through the air, followed by an answering burst from the helicopter above.

Grace rose to her knees, her heart in her throat. Where was Caveman?

Chapter Fifteen

The helicopter was taking on fire. Caveman didn't want to get in the way as they fired back. He watched as the beam of light played over the ground.

There. One of the men stood near a tree, aiming his weapon toward the chopper.

Caveman was torn between going after him and staying close to Grace. If he let the man shoot at the helicopter, he could kill the men inside and possibly bring the helicopter down. A burst of semiautomatic gunfire erupted from the aircraft. The man caught in the beam of light dropped to the ground and lay still.

More shots rang out.

Caveman wanted to go after the hunters, but the light from the helicopter was blinding him, as well. Then a shot hit the bulb on the light and it blinked out. The chopper swung around and lowered to the ground.

Giving his eyes a few moments to adjust to the moonlight, Caveman hunkered low to the ground near a tree a couple yards from where Grace lay. A movement alerted him to someone moving nearby. He recognized the man as Quincy Kemp.

When the meat packer walked within three feet of Caveman's position, he raised his rifle, aiming at Grace.

Caveman swung the limb he'd been holding as hard as he could. The limb caught the man's arm, tipping the rifle upward as it went off.

Caveman struck again, catching Quincy in the chin, knocking him backward so forcefully he fell, hitting his head against a rock. The man didn't move.

Grabbing the rifle from the ground, Caveman searched the darkness for the last man standing. His gut told him it was Wayne Batson.

Shouts sounded off in the field near the helicopter. The silhouettes of men disengaged from that of the aircraft, all running toward Caveman's position. Still, he couldn't see Wayne. Where had he gone? Had he run as soon as the helicopter showed up?

Then a movement near the giant boulder caught his attention. Wayne Batson stepped out of the shadows and pointed his rifle at Grace where she lay on the ground. "Come any closer and I kill the girl!"

Caveman froze, his heart slammed to a stop. *No. Not Grace!* He wanted to shout. But he was afraid any movement would push Batson over the edge and he'd pull the trigger. The man was crazy. You couldn't reason with crazy.

Batson reached down, bending over Grace's inert form. Then the ground beneath him erupted.

Grace jerked the spear she'd been holding up into the man's belly. She rolled to the side at the same time, sweeping her good leg out to catch Batson's.

Batson pitched forward, falling onto the makeshift spear. He screamed out loud, and pulled the trigger on his rifle. The shots hit the dirt. He toppled to the ground beside Grace, losing his hold on the weapon. Grace tried to get away, but the man grabbed a handful of her hair.

Caveman lunged forward, kicked the rifle out of Batson's reach and slammed his foot into the man's face.

Batson flew backward, letting go of Grace's hair, and lay motionless.

Caveman scooped Grace up off the ground and held her in his arms, crushing her against him. "Sweet Jesus, woman. I thought I'd lost you!"

She wrapped her arms around his neck and pulled him close for a kiss. "I wasn't going anywhere without you. I told myself, I had to get out of this so that I could kiss you."

"Please. Kiss me all you want, because that's what I want, too."

"Caveman? Grace?" Kevin Garner's voice called out. "Are you two okay?"

Caveman broke off the kiss long enough to say, "We're alive." And he went back to kissing her.

"Are there anymore bogies? We counted three."

Grace broke their kiss this time. "Three were all there was. By the way. Thanks. Your timing was impeccable." She grinned at Kevin as the DHS man stepped out of the tree line and approached them.

"The sheriff's on his way," Hack said, emerging from the tree line, dressed in a bulletproof vest and helmet. He was carrying a satellite phone and an AR-15. "Thank goodness we decided to run the drone tonight, or we might not have found you."

Grace laughed. "Thank God for drones and Hack." She turned to Caveman. "As much as I love when you hold me close, you can set me on my own feet. Or foot."

Caveman shook his head. "If it's all the same to you, I'd rather get you back to town and have a doctor look at your ankle and that shoulder. You're bleeding all over me."

"Take the chopper," Kevin said. "We'll stay here and wait for the sheriff."

Caveman glanced across at Kevin. "Thanks."

Kevin smiled. "If you still want to go back to your unit at the end of the week, I'll make it happen."

Grace shot a look up at him.

Caveman shook his head. "If it's all the same to you, I'd like to stay and see this operation through to the end." His gaze dropped to Grace. "I'm just getting to know the locals. I'd like to get to know them a little better. Maybe something will come of it."

Kevin clapped a hand on his shoulder. "Yeah. They have a way of growing on you. As you can see, we can use all the help we can get."

"Count me in," he said. "In the meantime, I'll see that Miss Saunders gets to a doctor."

"You do that. When you're both rested up, stop by the loft for a debriefing."

"You got it." Caveman carried Grace to the helicopter.

"Isn't your leg bothering you?" Grace asked.

"What leg? I don't feel a thing except the beat of my heart."

She snorted. "The Delta Force soldier is a closet poet?"

"Hey, don't knock it." He set her in the seat and buckled the seat belt around her, his fingers grazing her breasts. Then he handed her a headset, helping her to fit them over her ears.

He climbed in next to her, buckled his belt and positioned a headset over his ears.

"Where did Kevin get a helicopter?" Grace asked into her mic.

"I think it's the one they used in the hostage rescue." He leaned over the back of the seat toward the pilot. "How did you get here so quickly?"

"I was still in town, waiting for some replacement parts I got in today," the pilot said into the headset. "I was due to fly out tomorrow, but I think I'll be delayed yet again."

As the chopper rose from the ground, the gray light of pre-dawn crept up to the edge of the peaks.

Caveman stared down at the men on the ground, standing guard over the hunters who'd gambled their lives on an evil sport and lost.

"Think they'll live to testify?" Grace asked, her voice crackling over the radio headset.

"I hope so. I'd like to know who paid Batson to shoot Khalig."

"Me, too."

"Somehow, I don't think we'll get that answer from Batson."

"No, he wasn't looking so good," Grace said, her face pale, her brow furrowed. "If he dies, that will be the first man I've ever killed."

"And hopefully the last."

Her lips firmed. "I refuse to feel bad about it. The man was pure evil."

"Agreed." He squeezed her hand. "In the meantime, I have more work to do. We still don't know why Mr. Khalig had been killed and who had paid Wayne Batson to do the job."

Grace nodded. "True."

Caveman tipped her chin up and stared down into her eyes. "Do you still believe you're cursed?"

Grace shrugged. "I have to admit, you dodged death enough in the past couple of hours it makes me think you're the only man who could possibly break the curse."

"You're not cursed."

"Okay. Maybe I'm not." She laid her hand in his, silence stretching between them. "Caveman?"

"Yes, sweetheart?" Despite talking into a radio, he'd never felt closer to her.

"Do you believe in love at first sight?" she asked.

"I didn't." He squeezed her hand and raised it to his lips. "Not until I met you."

"Excuse me," another voice sounded in Caveman's ear.

He shot a glance toward the pilot and grimaced.

"I hate to break up your little lovefest, Caveman, but we're about to land. I suggest you save the rest of it until you get her alone."

"Thanks, I will."

The chopper landed, Caveman climbed out and lifted Grace

out, but refused to set her on her feet until they were clear of the rotors.

Grace insisted they watch until the helicopter lifted off. Then she turned to Caveman. "Let's get to the doctor and back to the room. I think there's a shower calling my name."

"I hear my name in there, too."

"Darn right, you do."

He lifted her into his arms and kissed her, glad he'd been stuck with this strange assignment out in the wilds of Wyoming. This woman seemed to be his perfect match with the potential to be the love of his life. He planned on exploring that theory. One kiss at a time.

* * * * *

Keep reading for an excerpt of
The Rancher's Christmas Promise
by Allison Leigh.
Find it in
A Christmas Family Miracle anthology,
out now!

PROLOGUE

"YOU'VE GOT TO be kidding me."

Ryder Wilson stared at the people on his porch. Even before they introduced themselves, he'd known the short, skinny woman was a cop thanks to the Braden Police Department badge she was wearing. But the two men with her? He'd never seen them before.

And after the load of crap they'd just spewed, he'd like to never see them again.

"We're not kidding, Mr. Wilson." That came from the serious-looking bald guy. The one who looked like he was a walking heart attack, considering the way he kept mopping the sweat off his face even though it was freezing outside. March had roared in like a lion this year, bringing with it a major snowstorm. Ryder hadn't lived there that long—it was only his second winter there—but people around town said they hadn't seen anything like it in Braden for more than a decade.

All he knew was that the snow was piled three feet high, making his life these days even more challenging. Making him wonder why he'd ever chosen Wyoming over New Mexico in the first place. Yeah, they got snow in Taos. But not like this.

"We believe that the infant girl who's been under our protection since she was abandoned three months ago is your daughter." The man tried to look past Ryder's shoulder. "Perhaps we could discuss this inside?"

Ryder had no desire to invite them in. But one of them *was* a cop. He hadn't crossed purposes with the law before and he wasn't real anxious to do so now. Didn't mean he had to like it, though.

His aunt hadn't raised him to be slob. She'd be horrified if she ever knew strangers were seeing the house in its current state.

He slapped his leather gloves together. He had chores waiting for him. But he supposed a few minutes wouldn't make much difference. "Don't think there's much to discuss," he warned as he stepped out of the doorway. He folded his arms across his chest, standing pretty much in their way so they had to crowd together in the small space where he dumped his boots. Back home, his aunt Adelaide would call the space a *vestibule*. Here, it wasn't so formal; he'd carved out his home from a converted barn. "I appreciate your concern for an abandoned baby, but whoever's making claims I fathered a child is out of their mind." Once burned, twice shy. Another thing his aunt was fond of saying.

The cop's brown eyes looked pained. "Ryder—may I call you Ryder?" She didn't wait for his permission, but plowed right on, anyway. "I'm sorry we have to be the bearer of bad news, but we believe your wife was the baby's mother, and—"

At the word *wife*, what had been Ryder's already-thin patience went by the wayside. "My *wife* ran out on me a year ago. Whatever she's done since is her prob—"

"Not anymore," the dark-haired guy said.

"What'd you say your name was?" Ryder met the other man's gaze head-on, knowing perfectly well he hadn't said his name. The pretty cop's role there was obviously official. Same with the sweaty bald guy—he had to be from social services. But the third intruder? The guy who was watching him as though he'd already formed an opinion—a bad one?

"Grant Cooper." The man's voice was flat. "Karen's my sister."

"There's your problem," Ryder responded just as flatly. "My so-called *wife's* name was Daisy. Daisy Miranda. You've got the wrong guy." He pointedly reached around them for the door to show them out. "So if you'll excuse me, I've got ice to break so my animals can get at their water."

"This is Karen." Only because she was a little slip of a thing, the cop succeeded in maneuvering between him and the door. She held a wallet-sized photo up in front of his face.

Ryder's nerves tightened even more than when he'd first opened the door to find these people on his front porch.

He didn't want to touch the photograph or examine it. He didn't need to. He recognized his own face just fine. In the picture, he'd been kissing the wedding ring he'd just put on Daisy's finger. The wedding had been a whirlwind sort of thing, like everything else about their relationship. Three months start to finish, from the moment they met outside the bar where she'd just quit her job until the day she'd walked out on him two weeks after their wedding. That's how long it had taken to meet, get hitched and get unhitched.

Though the unhitching part was still a work in progress. Not that he'd been holding on to hope that she'd return. But he'd had other things more important keeping him occupied than getting a formal divorce. Namely the Diamond-L ranch, which he'd purchased only a few months before meeting her. His only regret was that he hadn't kept his attention entirely on the ranch all along. It would have saved him some grief. "Where'd you get that?"

The cop asked her own question. "Can you confirm this is you and your wife in this picture?"

His jaw felt tight. "Yeah." Unfortunately. The Las Vegas wedding chapel had given them a cheap set of pictures. Ryder had tossed all of them in the fireplace, save the one the cop was holding now. He'd mailed that one to Daisy in response to a stupid postcard he'd gotten from her six months after she'd left him. A postcard on which she'd written only the words *I'm sorry*.

He still wasn't sure what she'd meant. Sorry for leaving him without a word or warning? Or sorry she'd ever married him in the first place?

"You wrote this?" The cop had turned the photo over, revealing his handwriting on the back. *So much for vows.*

Ryder was actually a little surprised that it was so legible, considering how drunk he'd been at the time he'd sent the photo. He nodded once.

The cop looked sympathetic. "I'm sorry to say that she died in a car accident over New Year's."

He waited as the words sank in. Expecting to feel something. Was he supposed to feel bad? Maybe he did. He wasn't sure. He'd known Daisy was a handful from the get-go. So when she took a powder the way she had, it shouldn't have been as much of a shock as it had been.

But one thing was certain. Everything that Daisy had told him had been a lie. From start to finish.

He might be an uncomplicated guy, but he understood the bottom line facing him now. "And you want to pawn off her baby on me." He looked the dark-haired guy in the face again. "Or do you just want money?" He lifted his arm, gesturing with the worn leather gloves. "Look around. All I've got is what you see. And it'll be a cold day in hell before I let a couple strangers making claims like yours get one finger on it."

Grant's eyes looked like flint. "As usual, my sister's taste in men was worse than—"

"Gentlemen." The other man mopped his forehead again, giving both Ryder and Grant wary looks even as he took a step between them. "Let's keep our cool. The baby is our focus."

Ryder ignored him. He pointed at Grant. "My wife never even told me she had a brother."

"My sister never told me she had a husband."

"The situation is complicated enough," the cop interrupted,

"without the two of you taking potshots at each other." Her expression was troubled, but her voice was calm. And Ryder couldn't miss the way she'd wrapped her hand familiarly around Grant's arm. "Ray is right. What's important here is the baby."

"Yes. The baby under our protection." Ray was obviously hoping to maintain control over the discussion. "There is no local record of the baby's birth. Our only way left to establish who the child's parents are is through you, Mr. Wilson. We've expended every other option."

"You don't even *know* the baby was hers?"

Ray looked pained. Grant looked like he wanted to punch something. Hell, maybe even Ryder. The cop just looked worried.

"The assumption is that your wife was the person to have left the baby at the home her former employer, Jaxon Swift, shared with his brother, Lincoln," she said.

"Now, that *does* sound like Daisy." Ryder knew he sounded bitter. "I only knew her a few months, but it was still long enough to learn she's good at running out on people."

Maybe he did feel a little bad about Daisy. He hadn't gotten around to divorcing his absent wife. Now, if what these people said were true, he wouldn't need to. Instead of being a man with a runaway wife, he was a man with a deceased one. There was probably something wrong with him for not feeling like his world had just been rocked. "But maybe you're wrong. She wasn't pregnant when she left me," he said bluntly. He couldn't let himself believe otherwise.

"Would you agree to a paternity test?"

"The court can compel you, Mr. Wilson," Ray added when Ryder didn't answer right away.

It was the wrong tack for Ray to take. Ryder had been down the whole paternity-accusation path before. He hadn't taken kindly to it then, and he wasn't inclined to now. "Daisy was my wife, loose as that term is in this case. A baby born to her during our marriage makes me the presumed father, whether there's a test or not. But you don't know that the baby was actually hers. You just admitted it. Which tells me the court probably isn't on your side as much as you're implying. Unless I say otherwise, and without you knowing who this baby's mother is, I'm just a guy in a picture."

"We should have brought Greer," Grant said impatiently to the cop. "She's used to guys like him."

But the cop wasn't listening to Grant. She was looking at Ryder with an earnest expression. "You aren't just a guy in a picture. You're our best hope for preventing the child we believe is Grant's niece from being adopted by strangers."

That's when Ryder saw that she'd reached out to clasp Grant's hand, their fingers entwined. So, she had a dog in this race.

He thought about pointing out that he was a stranger to them, too, no matter what sort of guy Grant had deemed Ryder to be. "And if I cooperated and the test confirms I'm *not* this baby's father, you still wouldn't have proof that Daisy is—" *dammit* "—*was* the baby's mother."

"If the test is positive, then we know she was," Ray said. "Without your cooperation, the proof of Karen's maternity is circumstantial. We admit that. But you were her husband. There's no putative father. If you even suspected she'd become pregnant during your marriage, your very existence is enough to establish legal paternity, DNA proof or not."

The cop looked even more earnest. "And the court can't proceed with an adoption set in motion by Layla's abandonment."

The name startled him. *"Layla!"*

The three stared at him with varying degrees of surprise and expectation.

"Layla was my mother's name." His voice sounded gruff, even to his own ears. Whatever it was that Daisy had done with her child, using that name was a sure way of making sure he'd get involved. After only a few months together, she'd learned enough about him to know that.

He exhaled roughly. Slapped his leather gloves together. Then he stepped out of the way so he wasn't blocking them from the rest of his home. "You'd better come inside and sit." He felt weary all of a sudden. As if everything he'd accomplished in his thirty-four years was for nothing. What was that song? "There Goes My Life."

"I expect this is gonna take a while to work out." He glanced at the disheveled room, with its leather couch and oversize, wall-mounted television. That's what happened when a man spent more time tending cows than he did anything else. He'd even tended some of them in this very room.

Fortunately, his aunt Adelaide would never need to know.

"You'll have to excuse the mess, though."

MILLS & BOON

Want to know more about your favourite series or discover a new one?

Experience the variety of romance that Mills & Boon has to offer at our website:

millsandboon.com.au

Shop all of our categories and discover the one that's right for you.

MODERN

DESIRE

MEDICAL

INTRIGUE

ROMANTIC
SUSPENSE

WESTERN

HISTORICAL

FOREVER
EBOOK ONLY

HEART
EBOOK ONLY

f @millsandboonaustralia 🐦 📷 @millsandboonaus

Subscribe and fall in love with a Mills & Boon series today!

You'll be among the first to read stories delivered to your door monthly and enjoy great savings.

WE
SIMPLY
LOVE
ROMANCE

MILLS & BOON